CatStronauts

SPACE STATION SITUATION

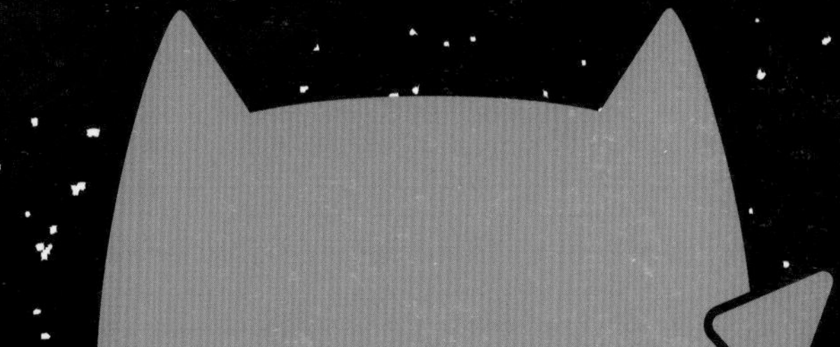

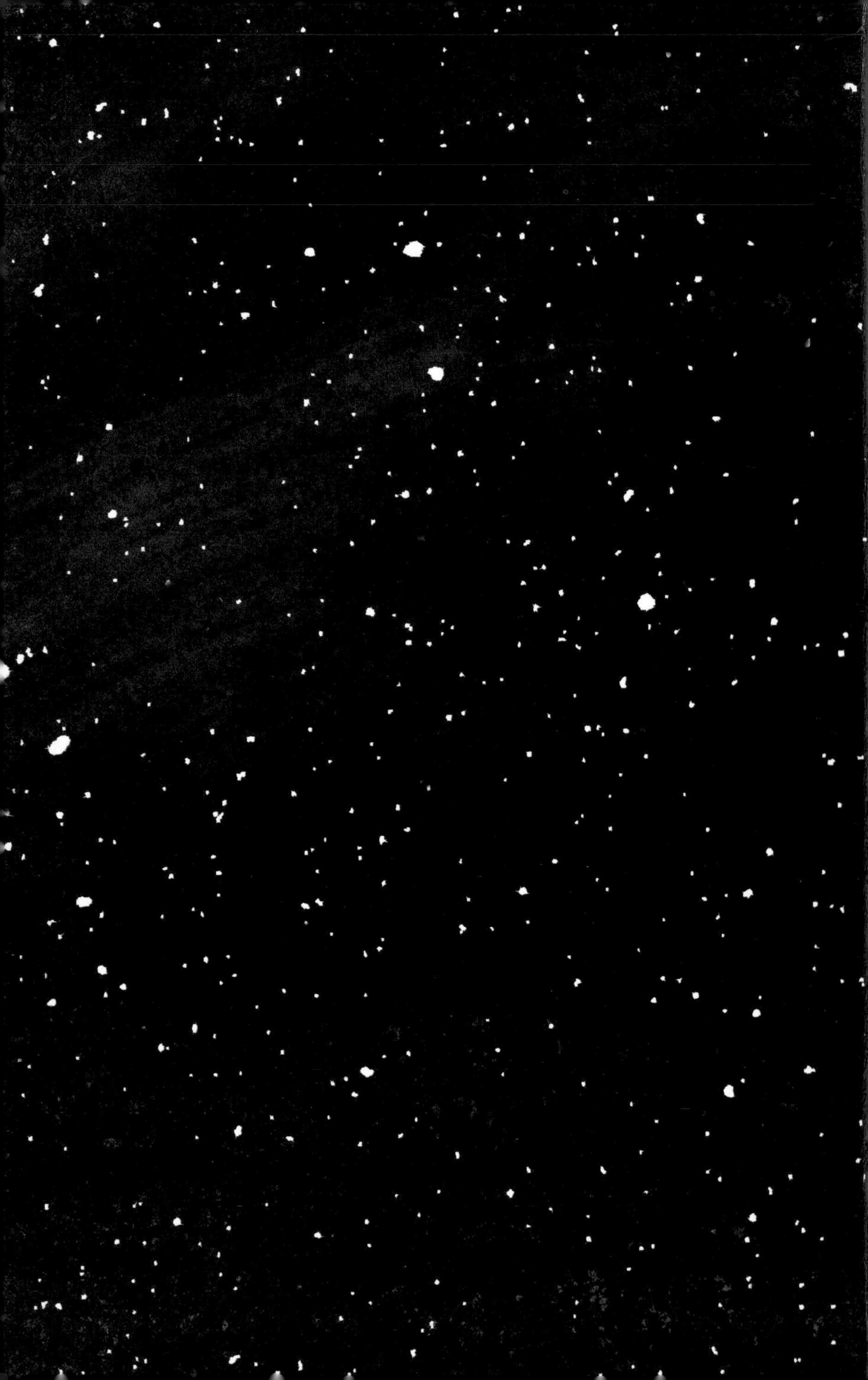

CatStronauts

SPACE STATION SITUATION

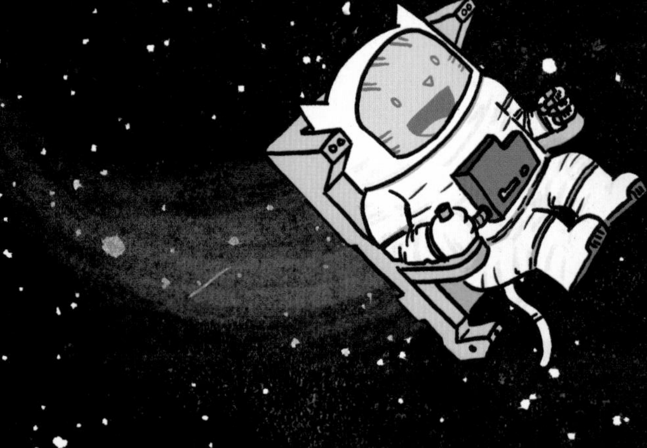

BY DREW BROCKINGTON

LB

Little, Brown and Company
New York Boston

Copyright © 2017 by Drew Brockington

Cover art copyright © 2017 by Drew Brockington.
Cover design by Angela Taldone.
Cover copyright © 2017 by Hachette Book Group, Inc.
Catstrofont software copyright © 2016 by Drew Brockington.

Little, Brown and Company
Hachette Book Group
1290 Avenue of the Americas, New York, NY 10104
Visit us at LBYR.com

First Edition: October 2017

Little, Brown and Company is a division of Hachette Book Group, Inc.
The Little, Brown name and logo are trademarks of Hachette Book Group, Inc.

The publisher is not responsible for websites (or their content) that are not owned by the publisher.

Library of Congress Cataloging-in-Publication Data
Names: Brockington, Drew, author, artist. | Title: CatStronauts : space station situation / by Drew Brockington. | Description: First edition. | New York ; Boston : Little, Brown, 2017. | Series: CatStronauts ; 3 | Summary: "The CatStronauts—elite cat astronauts—are aboard the International Space Station to repair the faulty Hubba Bubba Telescope, but have to contend with communications interference and a near disaster that leaves them down a member"— Provided by publisher. | Identifiers: LCCN 2017003433| ISBN 9780316307529 (hardcover) | ISBN 9780316307536 (trade pbk.) | ISBN 9780316307543 (ebk.) | Subjects: LCSH: Graphic novels. | CYAC: Graphic novels. | Astronauts—Fiction. | International Space Station—Fiction. | Outer space—Fiction. | Cats—Fiction. | Classification: LCC PZ7.7.B76 Cay 2017 | DDC 741.5/973—dc23 | LC record available at https://lccn.loc.gov/2017003433

ISBNs: 978-0-316-30752-9 (hardcover), 978-0-316-30753-6 (pbk.),
978-0-316-55894-5 (ebook), 978-0-316-55897-6 (ebook),
978-0-316-30754-3 (ebook)

Printed in China

1010

10 9 8 7 6 5 4 3 2 1

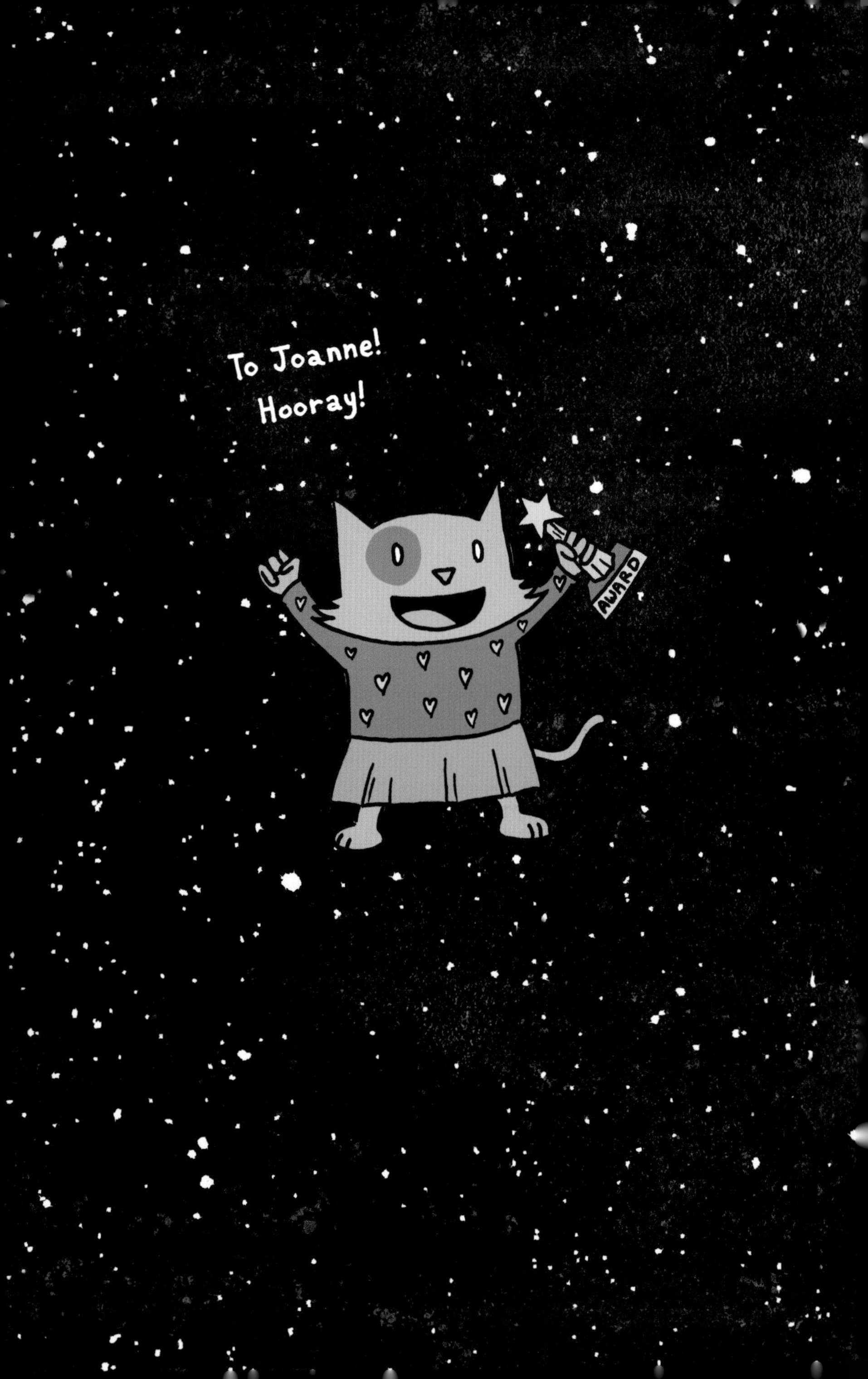
To Joanne!
Hooray!
AWARD

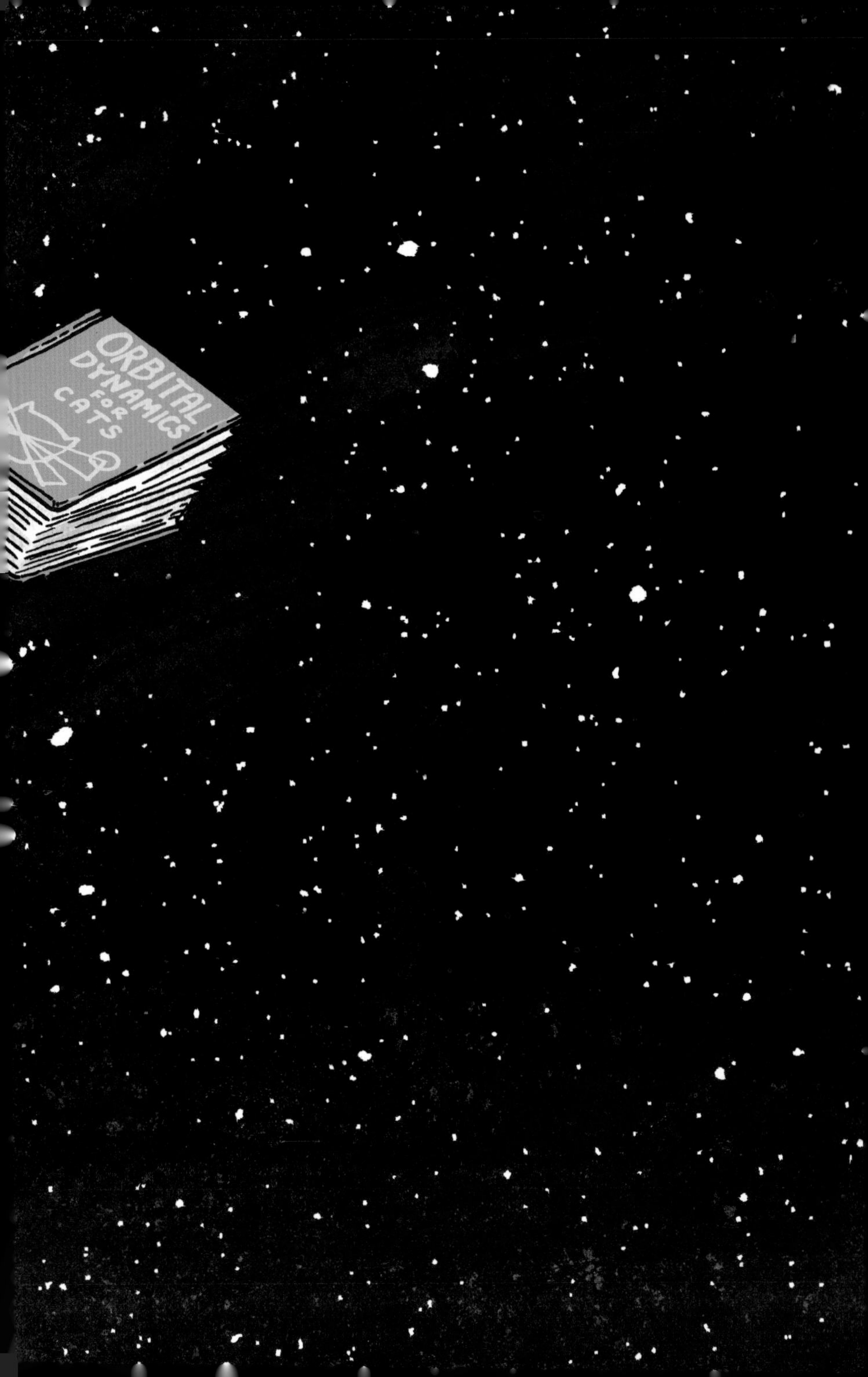
ORBITAL
DYNAMICS
FOR
CATS

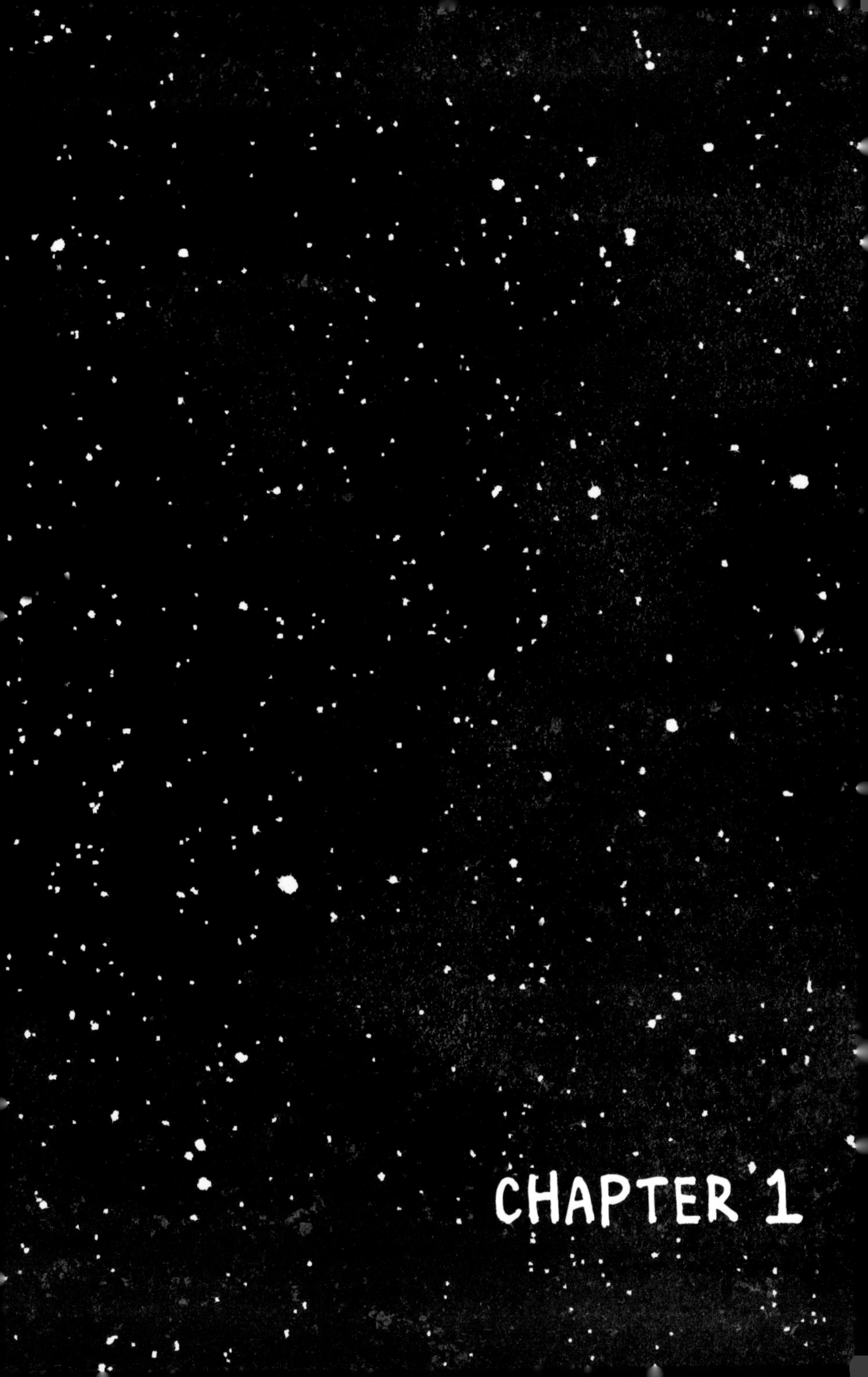

CHAPTER 1

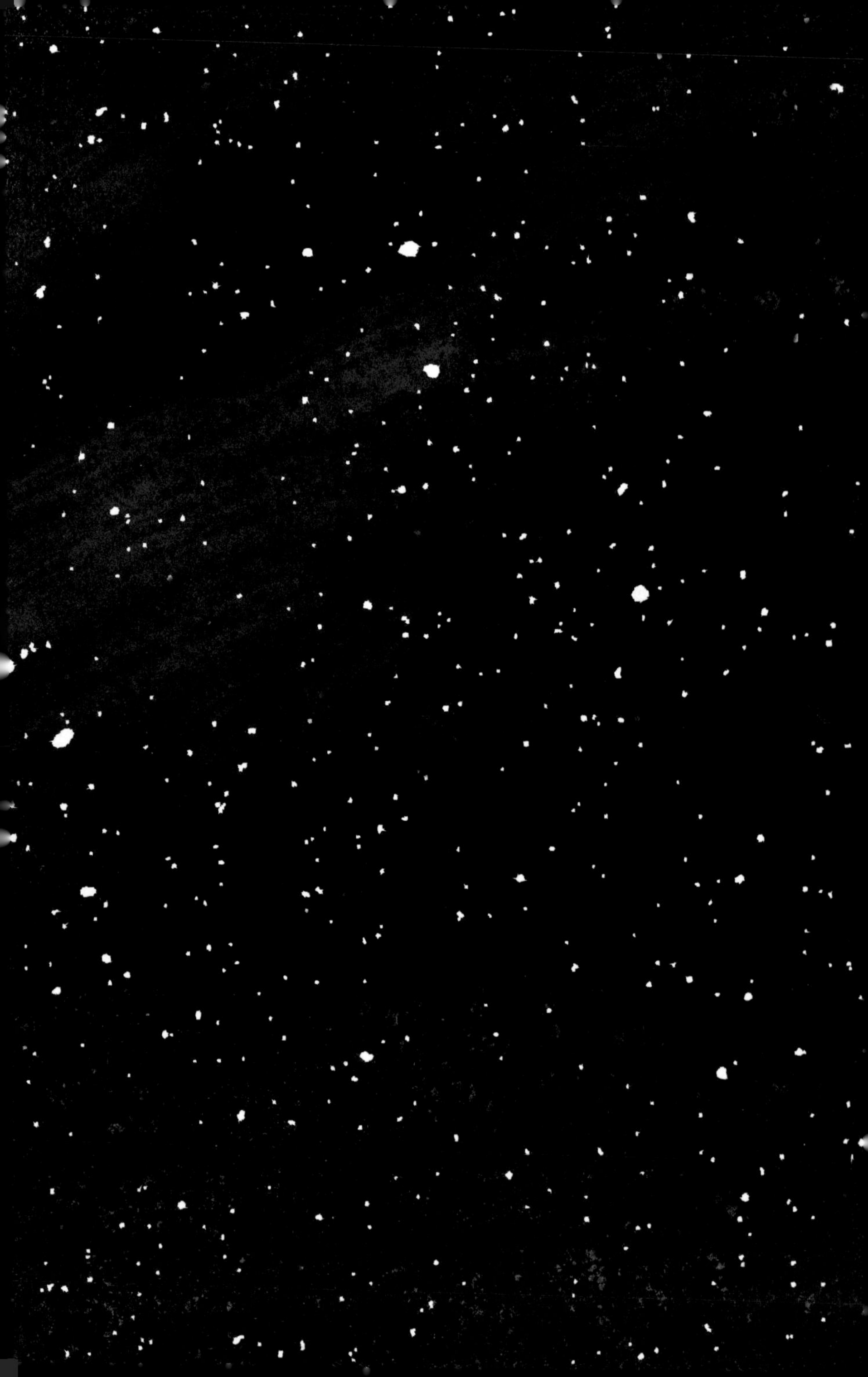

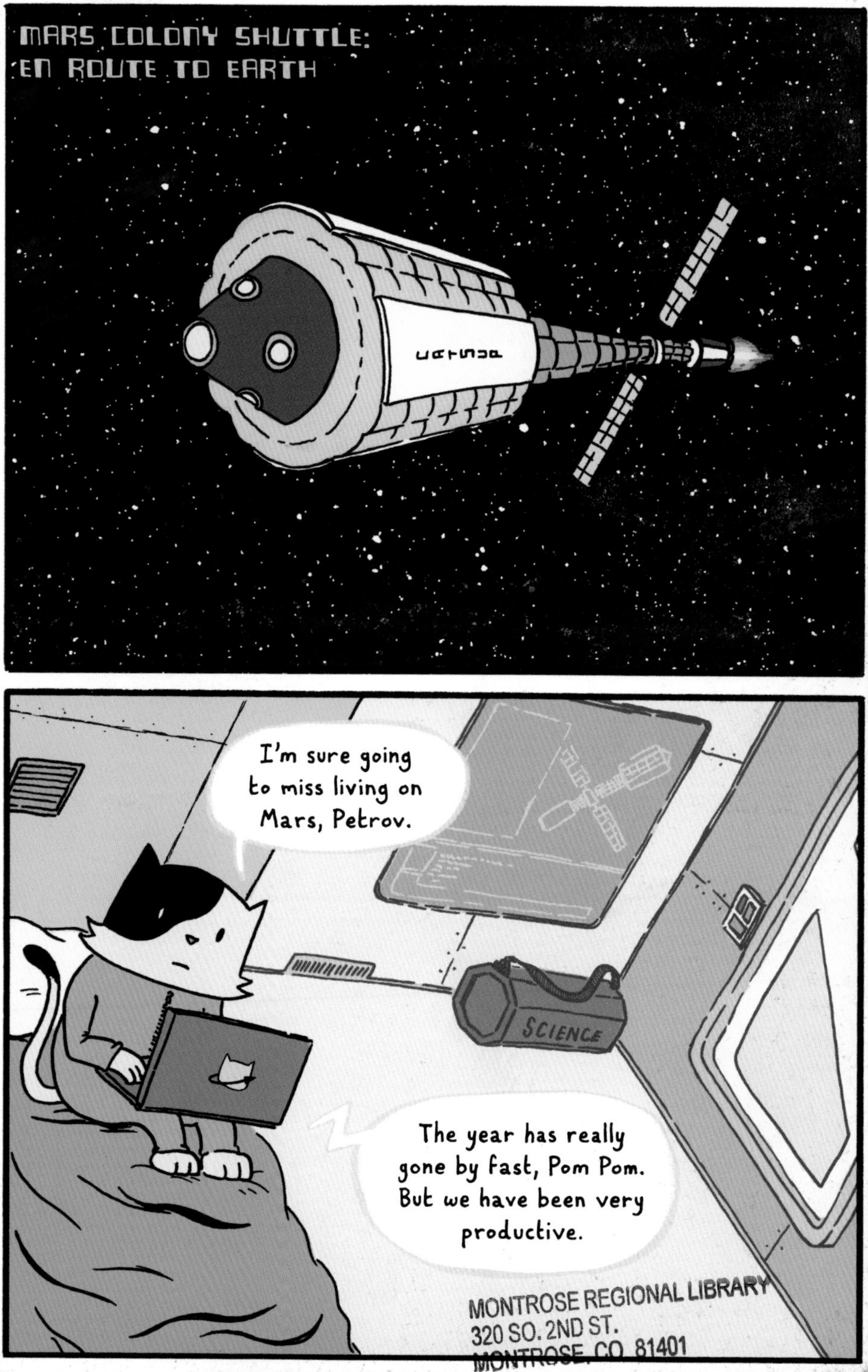
MARS COLONY SHUTTLE:
EN ROUTE TO EARTH
I'm sure going to miss living on Mars, Petrov.
SCIENCE
The year has really gone by fast, Pom Pom. But we have been very productive.

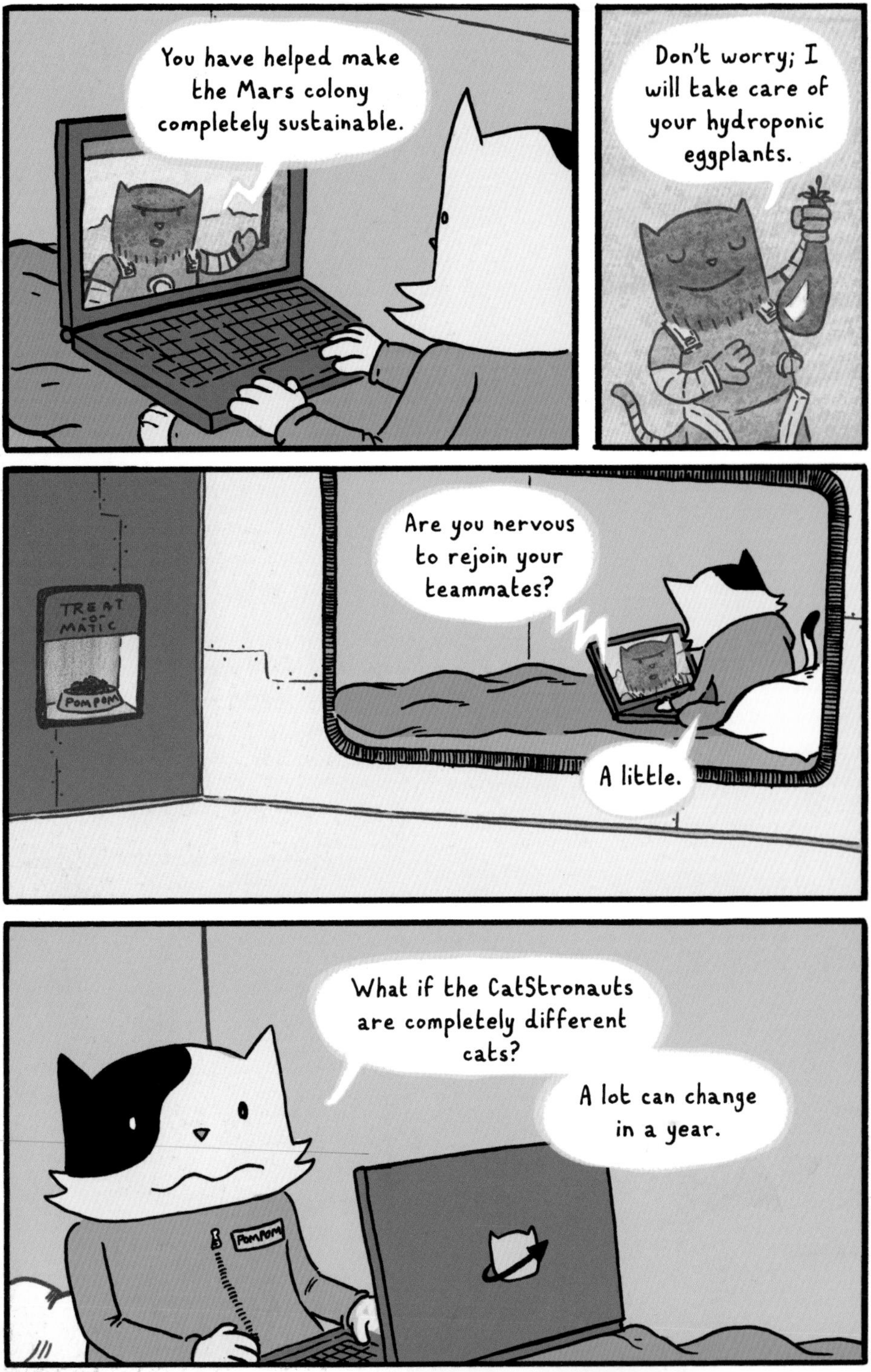
You have helped make the Mars colony completely sustainable.
Don't worry; I will take care of your hydroponic eggplants.
TREAT-O-MATIC
POMPOM
Are you nervous to rejoin your teammates?
A little.
What if the CatStronauts are completely different cats?
A lot can change in a year.
POMPOM

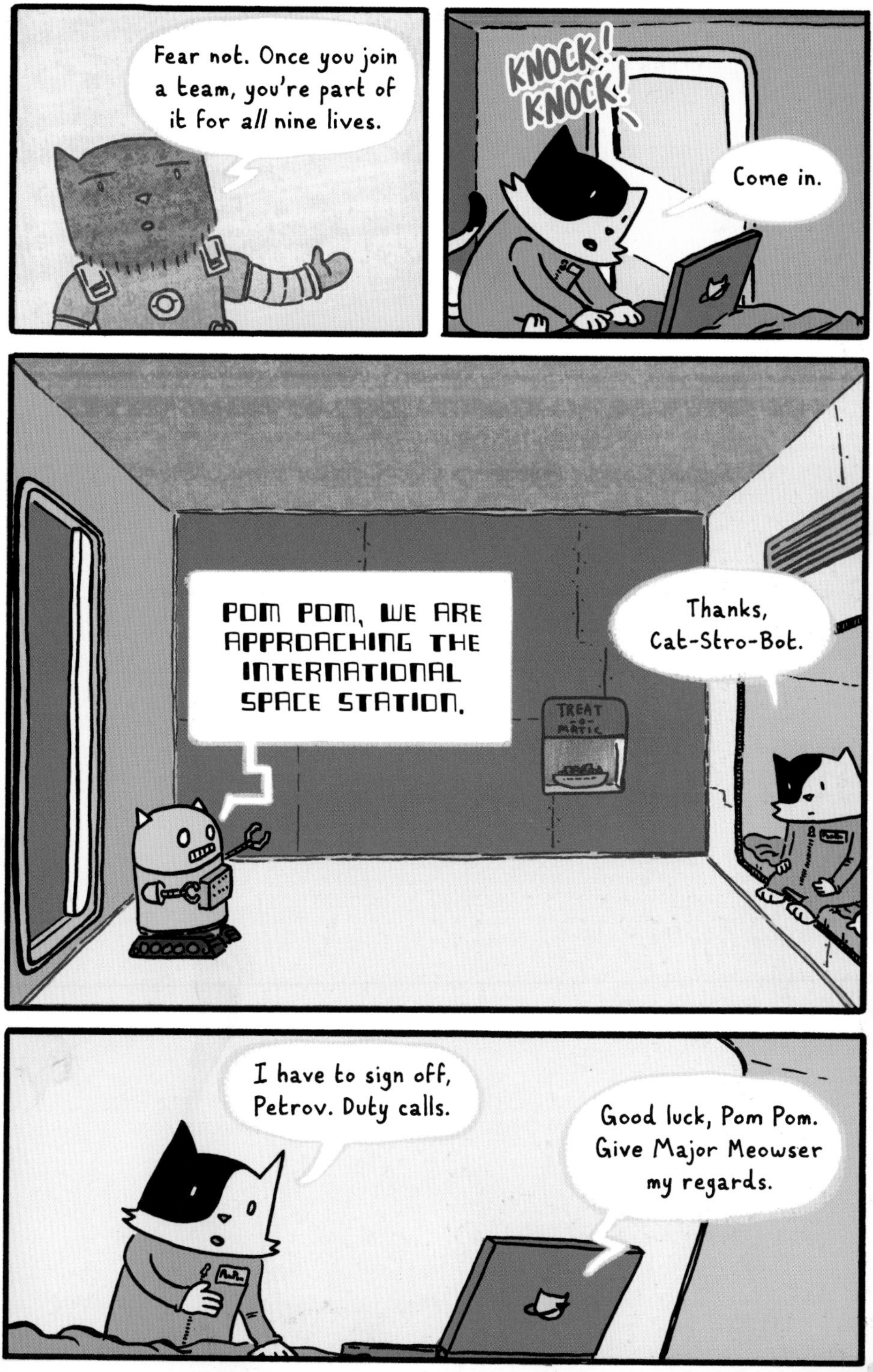
Fear not. Once you join a team, you're part of it for *all* nine lives.
KNOCK! KNOCK!
Come in.
POM POM, WE ARE APPROACHING THE INTERNATIONAL SPACE STATION.
TREAT -O- MATIC
Thanks, Cat-Stro-Bot.
I have to sign off, Petrov. Duty calls.
Good luck, Pom Pom. Give Major Meowser my regards.

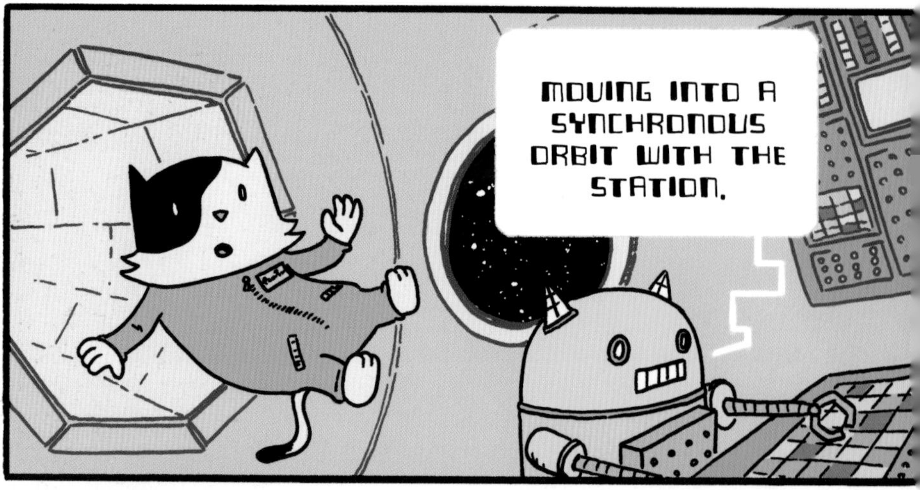
MOVING INTO A SYNCHRONOUS ORBIT WITH THE STATION.

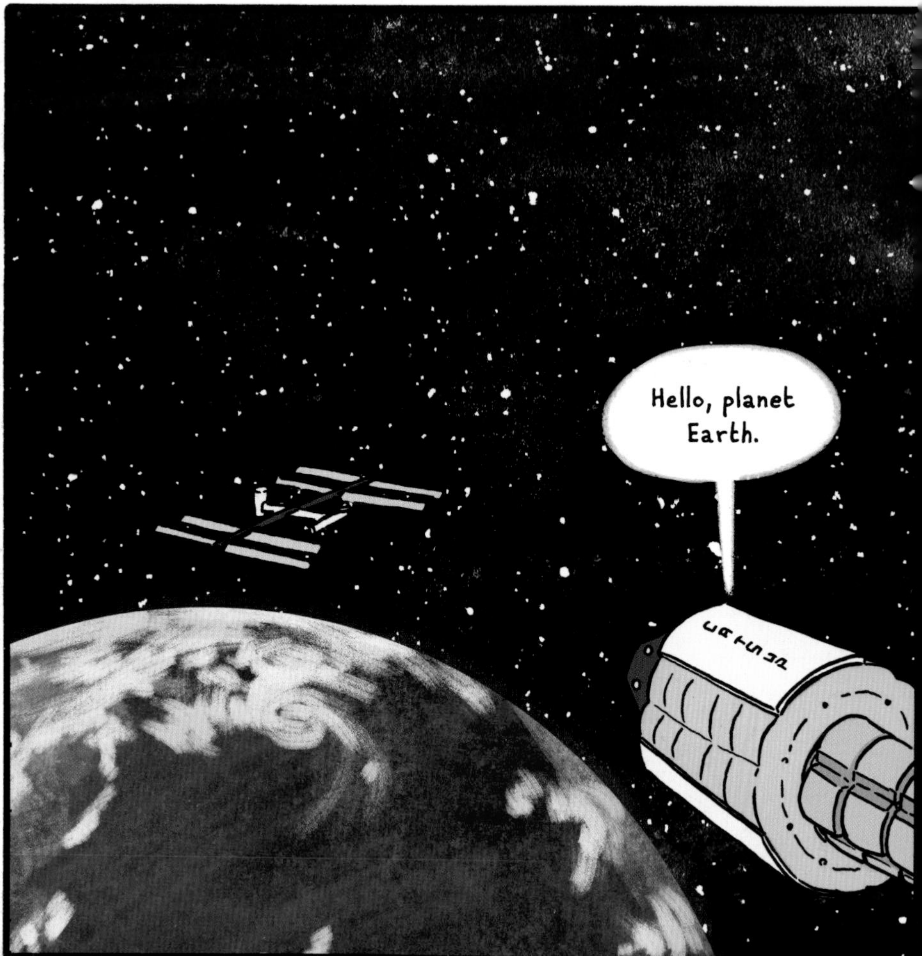
Hello, planet Earth.

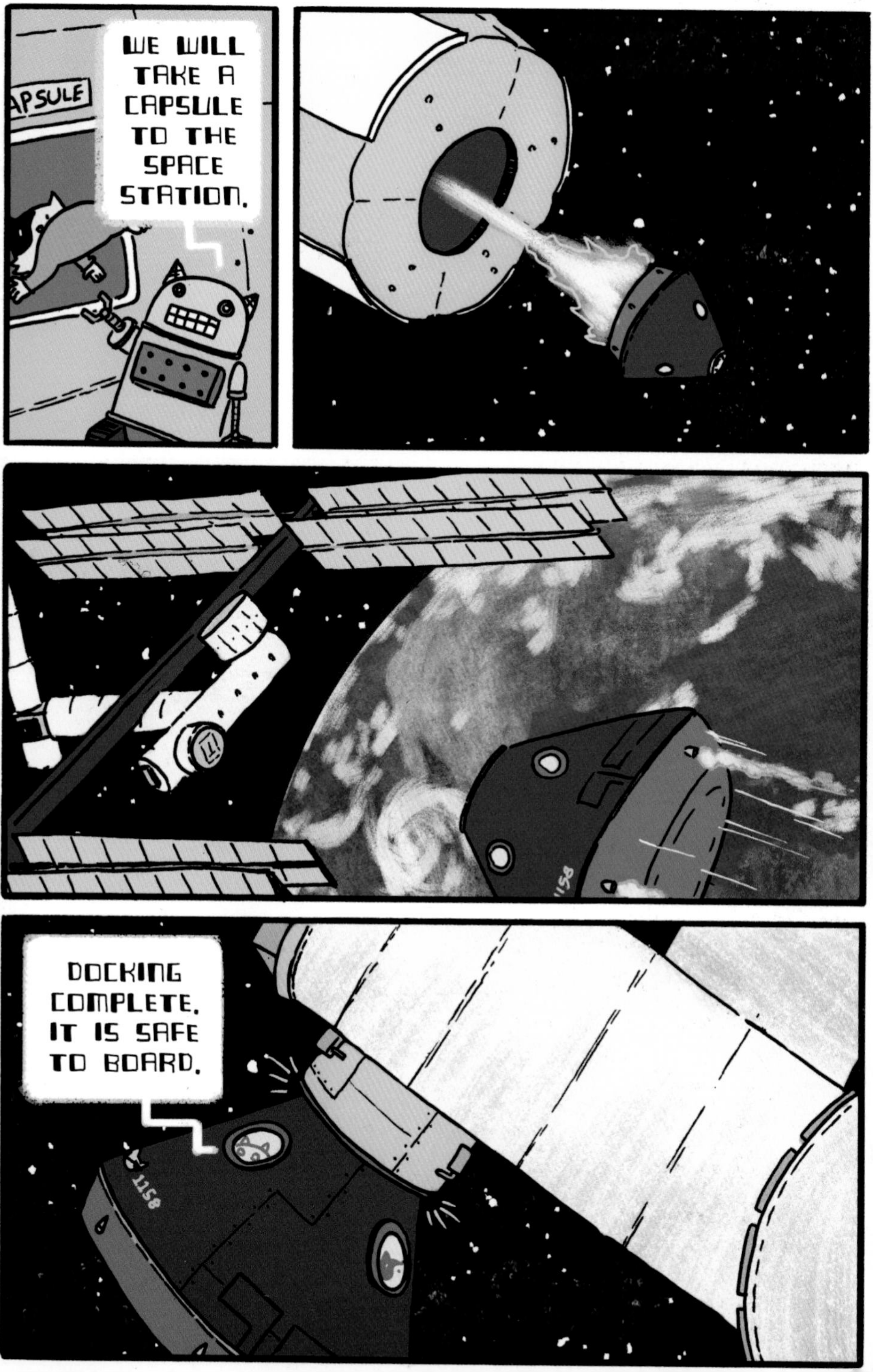
APSULE
WE WILL TAKE A CAPSULE TO THE SPACE STATION.
1158
DOCKING COMPLETE. IT IS SAFE TO BOARD.
1158

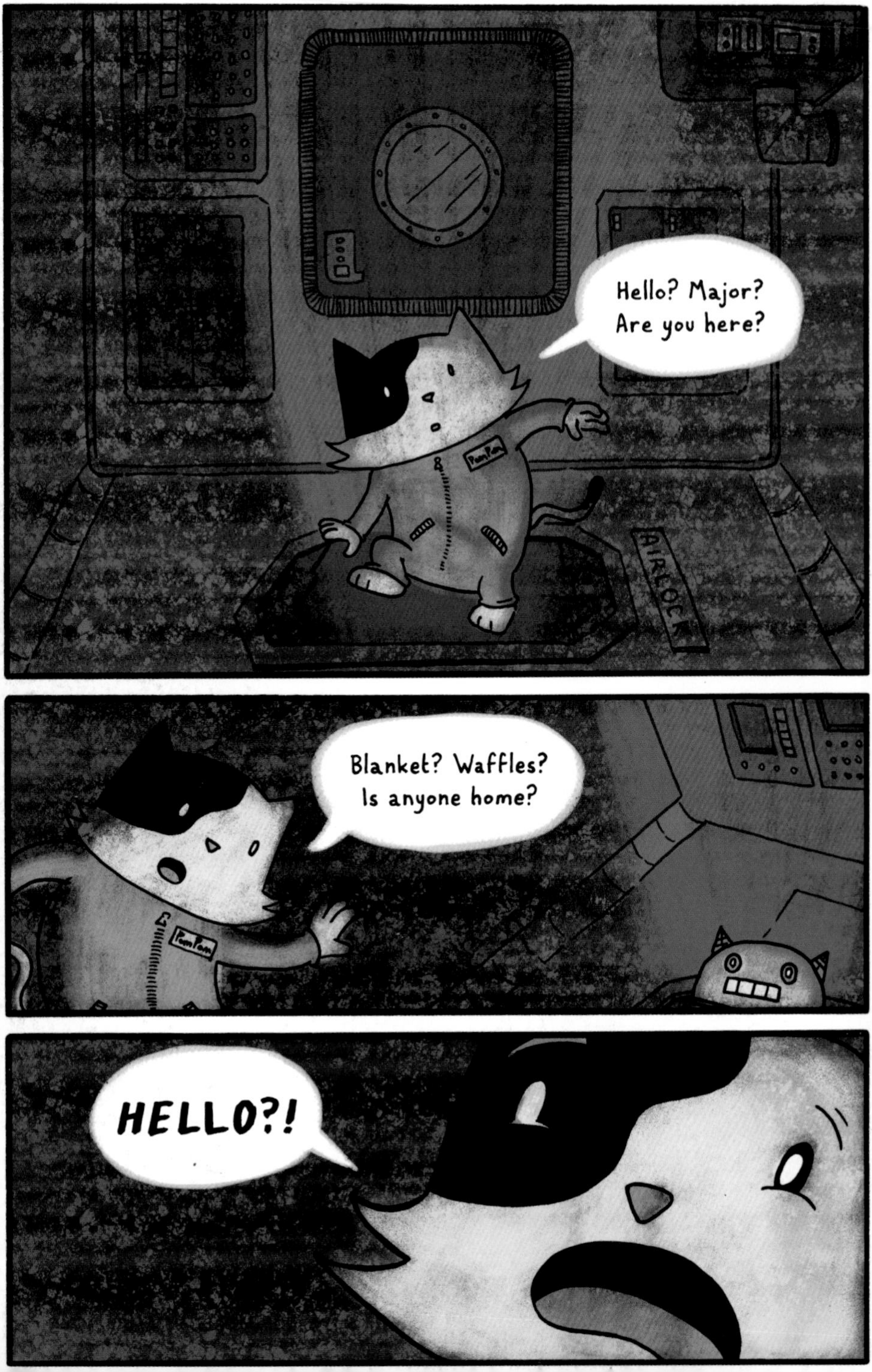
Hello? Major? Are you here?
AIRLOCK
Blanket? Waffles? Is anyone home?
HELLO?!

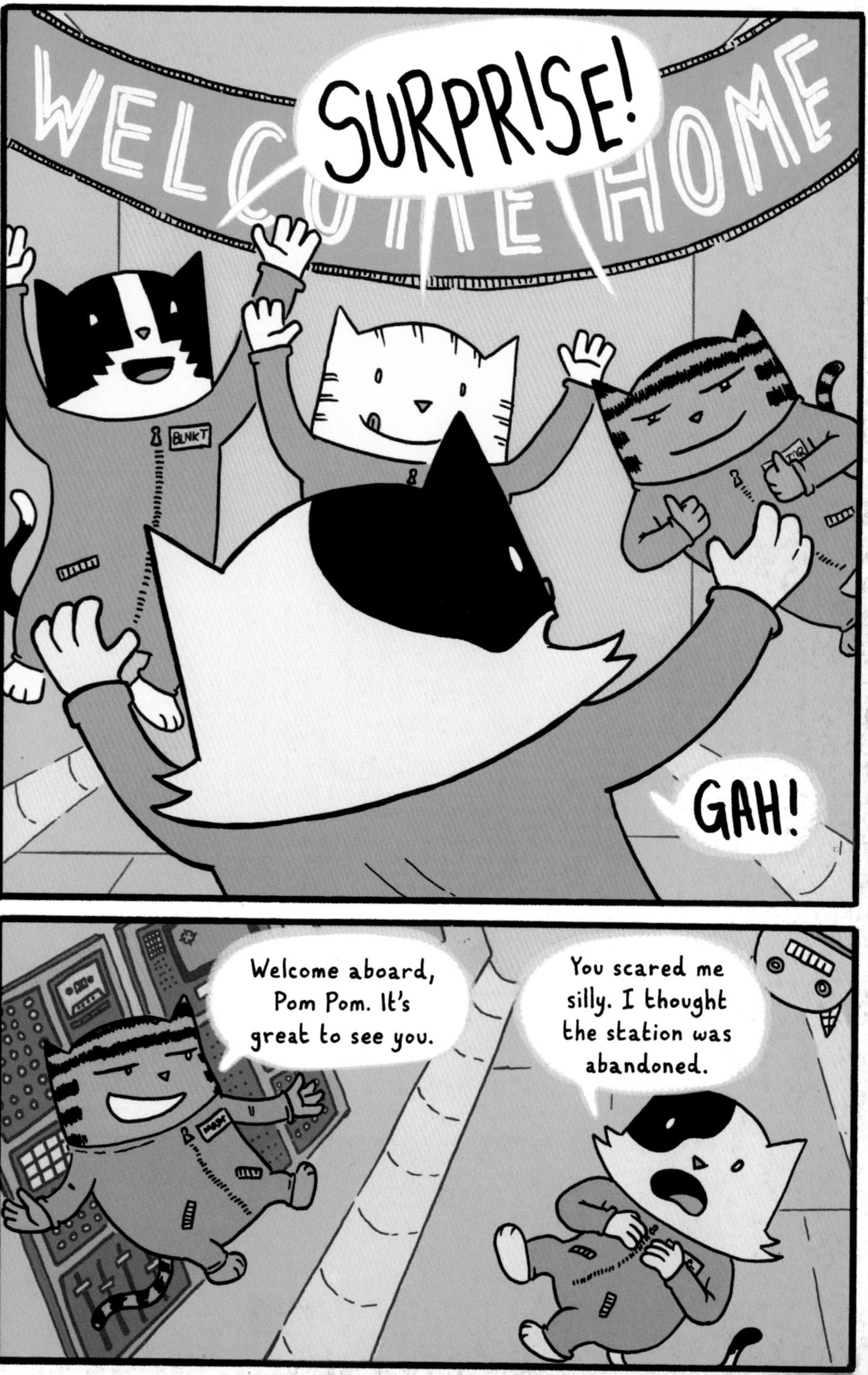
WELCOME HOME
SURPRISE!
BLNKT
GAH!
Welcome aboard, Pom Pom. It's great to see you.
You scared me silly. I thought the station was abandoned.

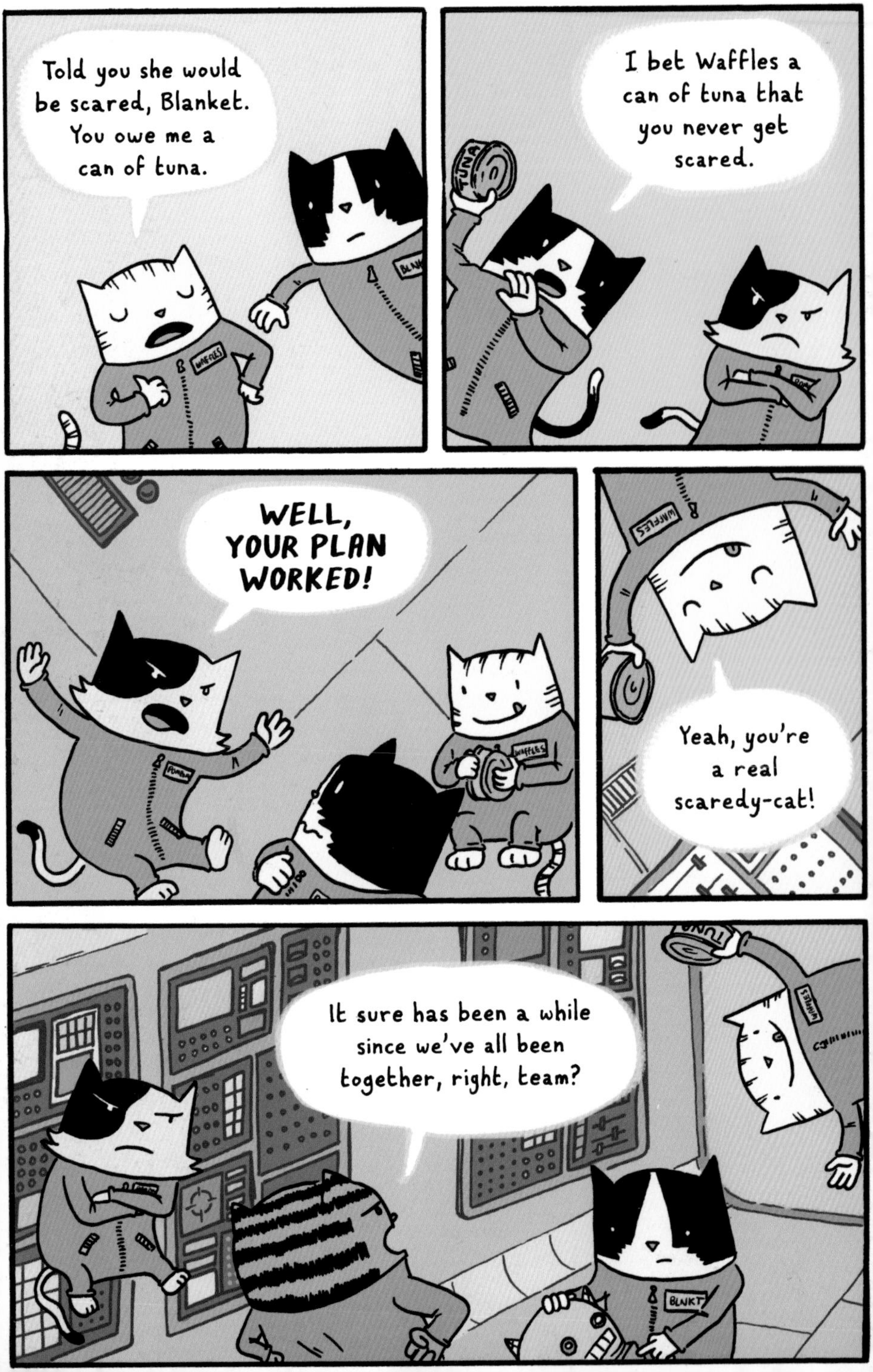

Told you she would be scared, Blanket. You owe me a can of tuna.
BLNKT
WAFFLES
I bet Waffles a can of tuna that you never get scared.
TUNA
WELL, YOUR PLAN WORKED!
WAFFLES
WAFFLES
Yeah, you're a real scaredy-cat!
It sure has been a while since we've all been together, right, team?
TUNA
BLNKT

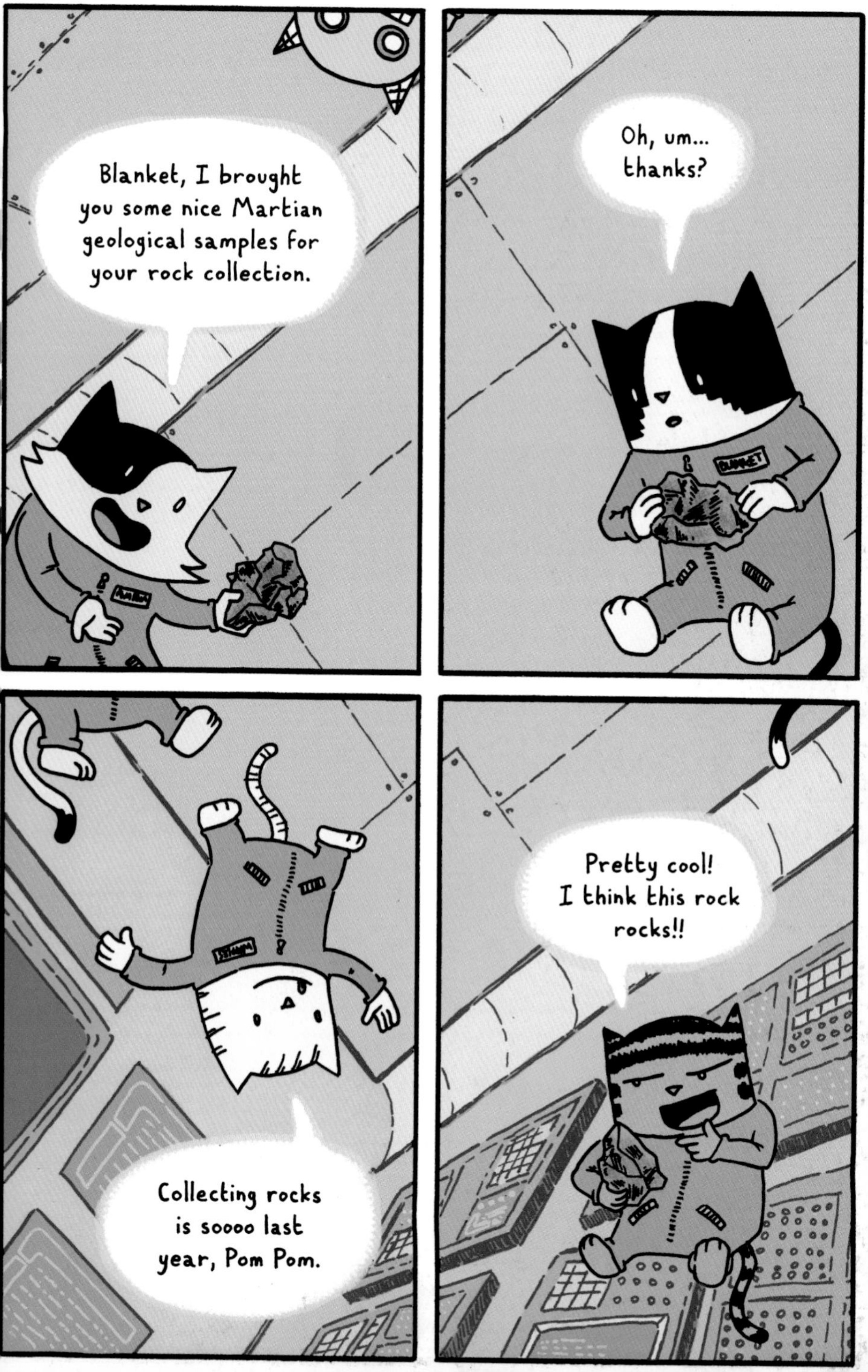
Blanket, I brought you some nice Martian geological samples for your rock collection.
Oh, um... thanks?
Collecting rocks is soooo last year, Pom Pom.
Pretty cool! I think this rock rocks!!

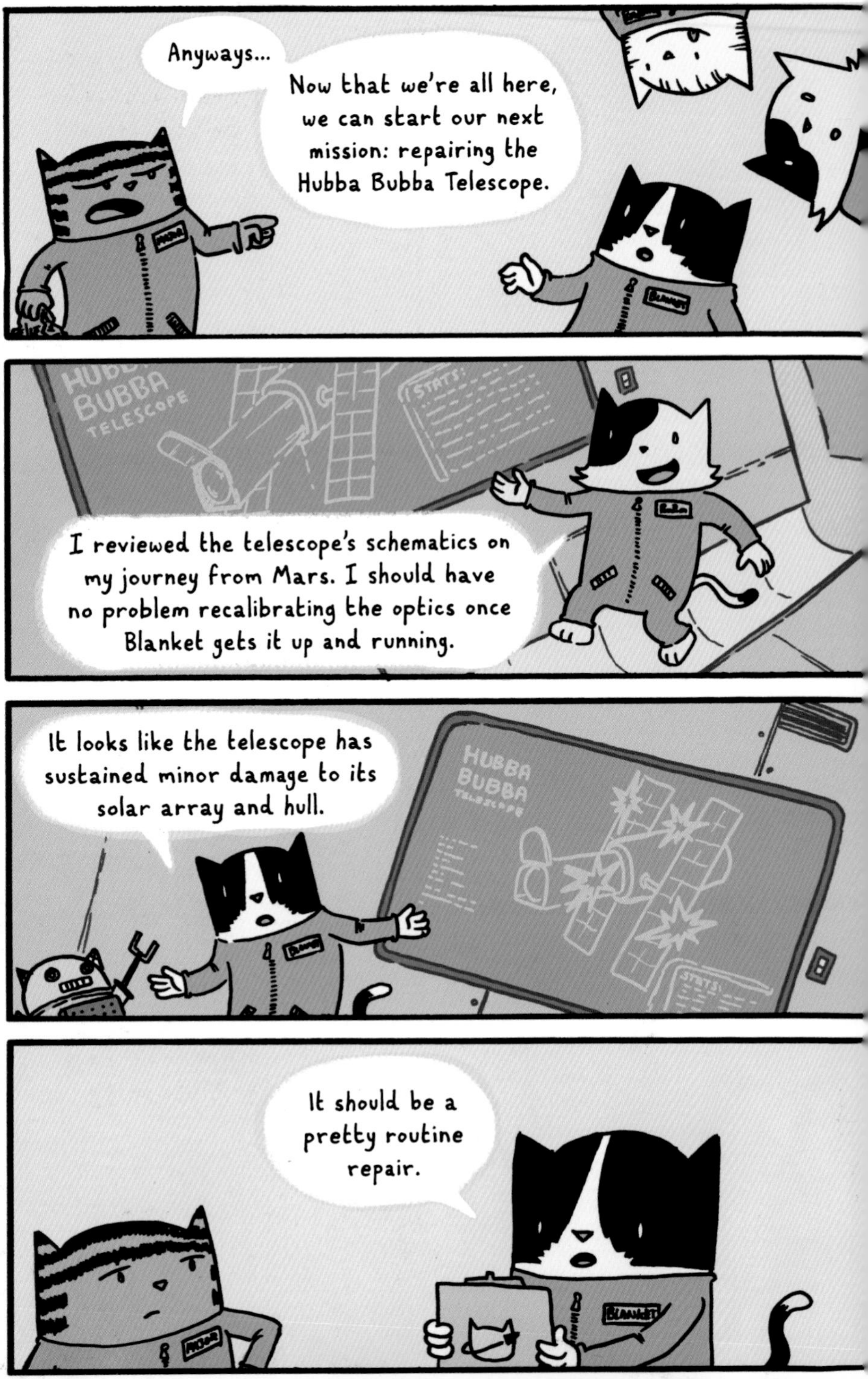
Anyways...
Now that we're all here, we can start our next mission: repairing the Hubba Bubba Telescope.
HUBBA BUBBA TELESCOPE
STATS:
I reviewed the telescope's schematics on my journey from Mars. I should have no problem recalibrating the optics once Blanket gets it up and running.
It looks like the telescope has sustained minor damage to its solar array and hull.
HUBBA BUBBA TELESCOPE
STATS:
It should be a pretty routine repair.
BLANKET

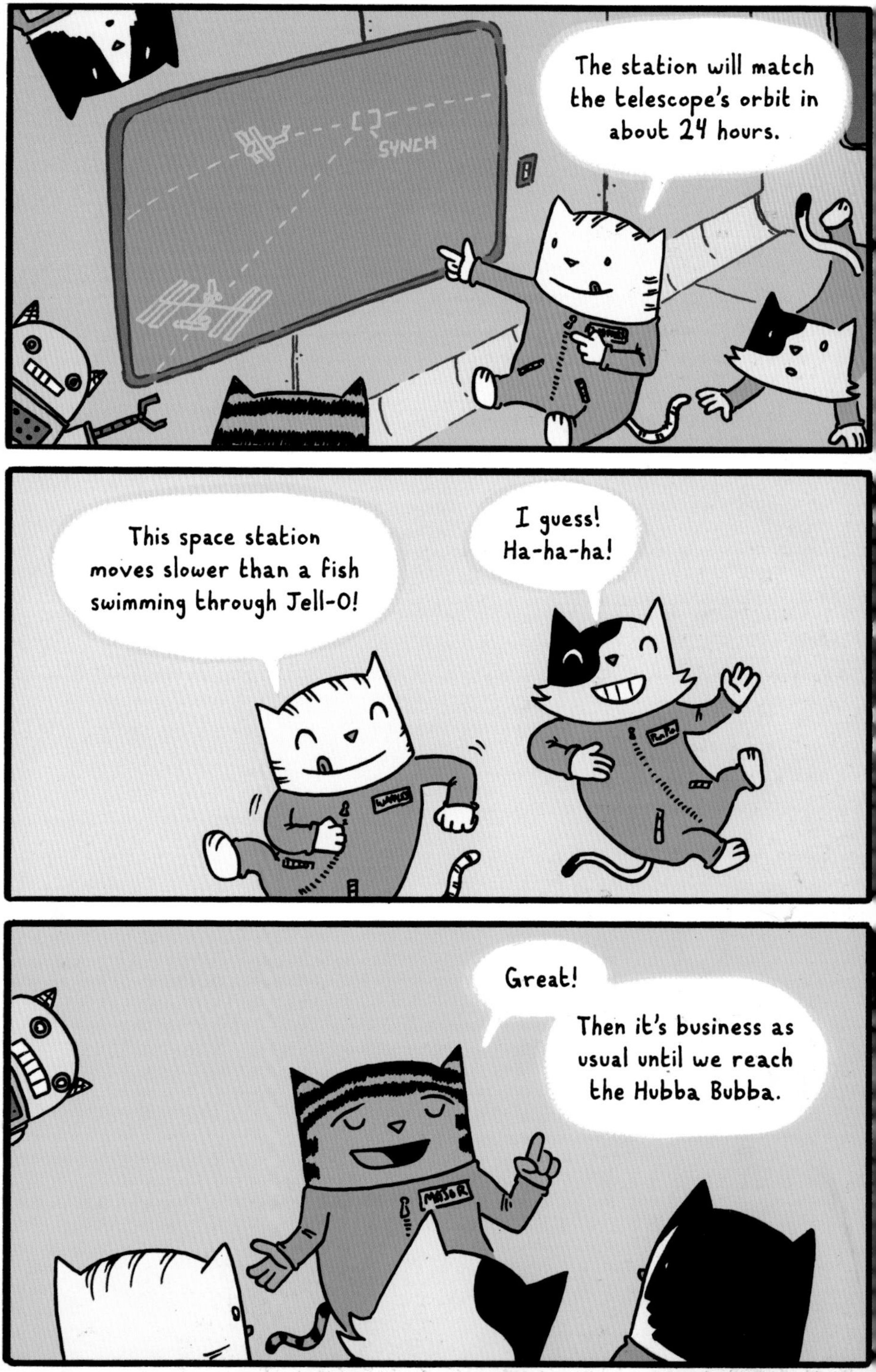
The station will match the telescope's orbit in about 24 hours.
SYNCH
This space station moves slower than a fish swimming through Jell-O!
I guess! Ha-ha-ha!
Great!
Then it's business as usual until we reach the Hubba Bubba.
MAJOR

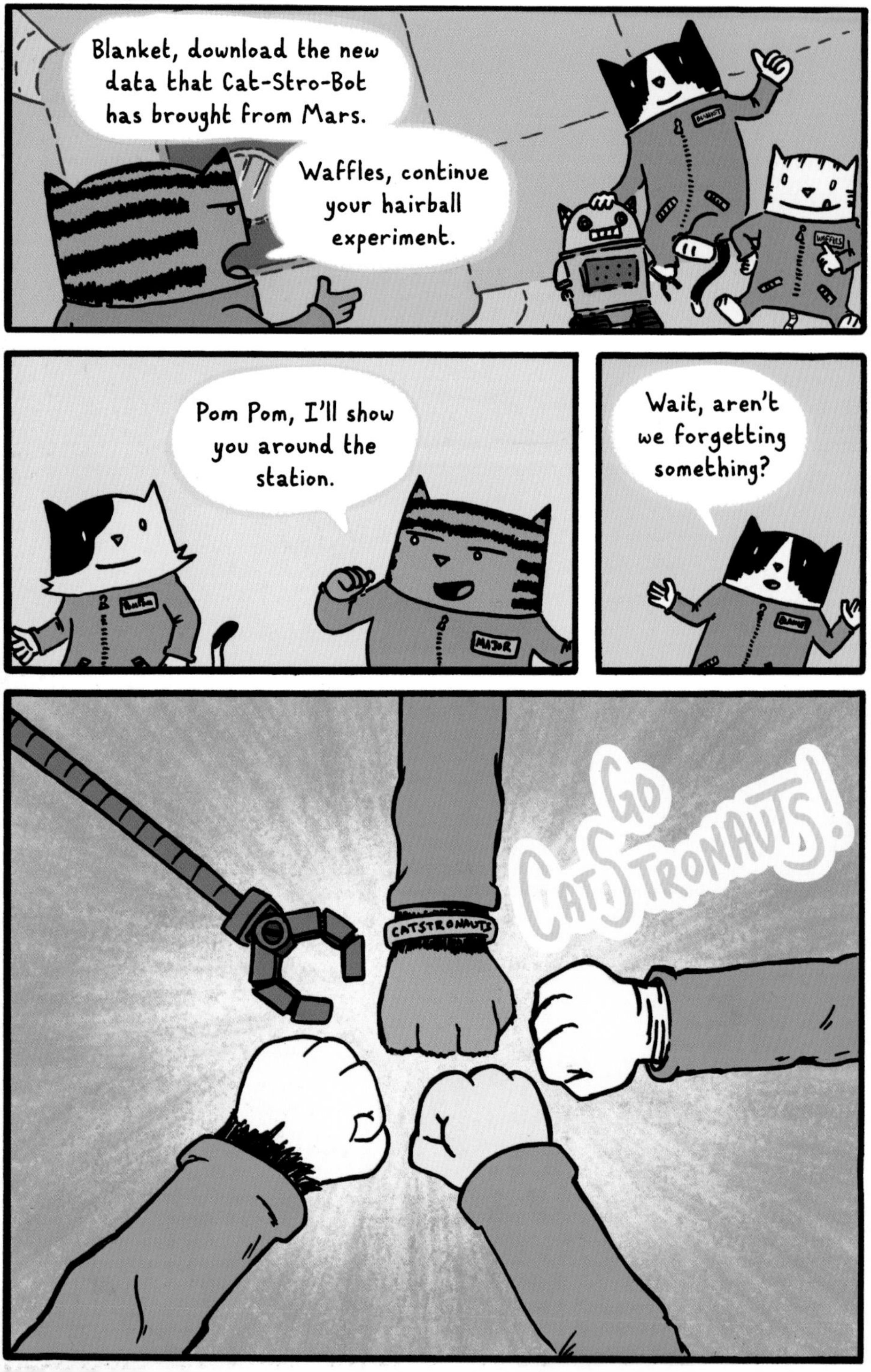
Blanket, download the new data that Cat-Stro-Bot has brought from Mars.
Waffles, continue your hairball experiment.
Pom Pom, I'll show you around the station.
Wait, aren't we forgetting something?
CATSTRONAUTS
GO CATSTRONAUTS!

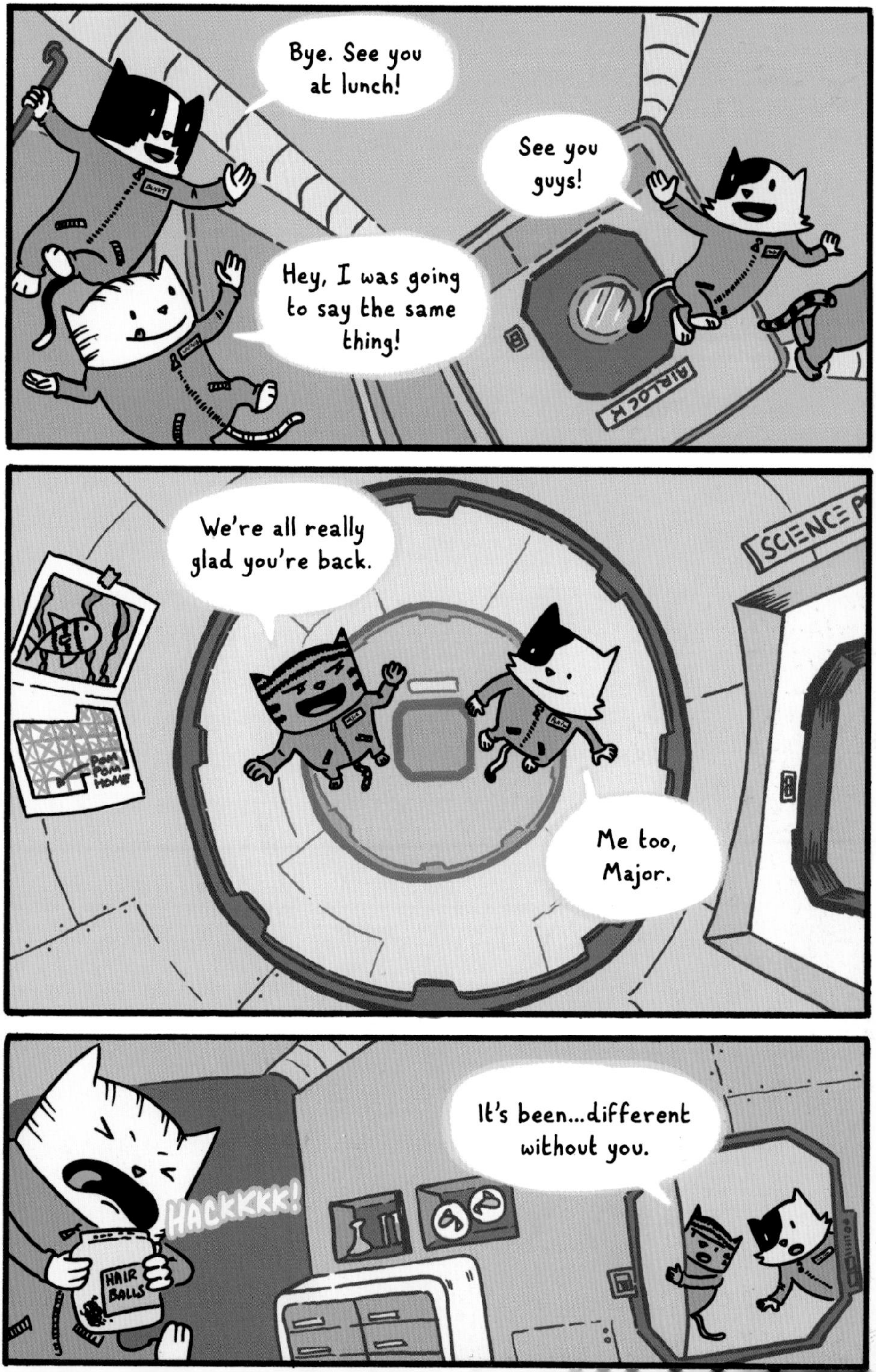
Bye. See you at lunch!
See you guys!
Hey, I was going to say the same thing!
AIRLOCK
We're all really glad you're back.
SCIENCE P
POM POM HOME
Me too, Major.
HACKKKK!
HAIR BALLS
It's been...different without you.

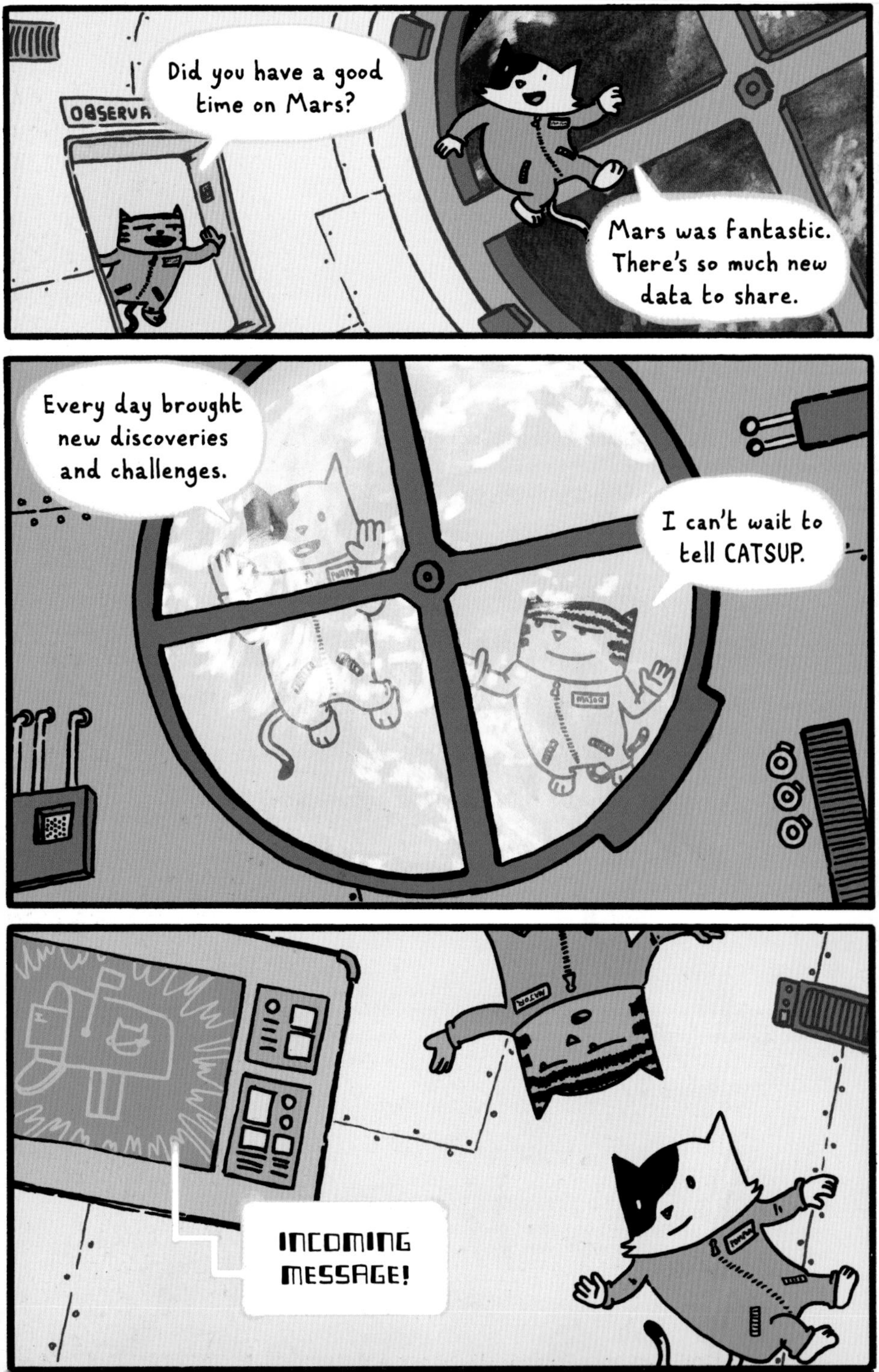
Did you have a good time on Mars?
Mars was fantastic. There's so much new data to share.
Every day brought new discoveries and challenges.
I can't wait to tell CATSUP.
INCOMING MESSAGE!

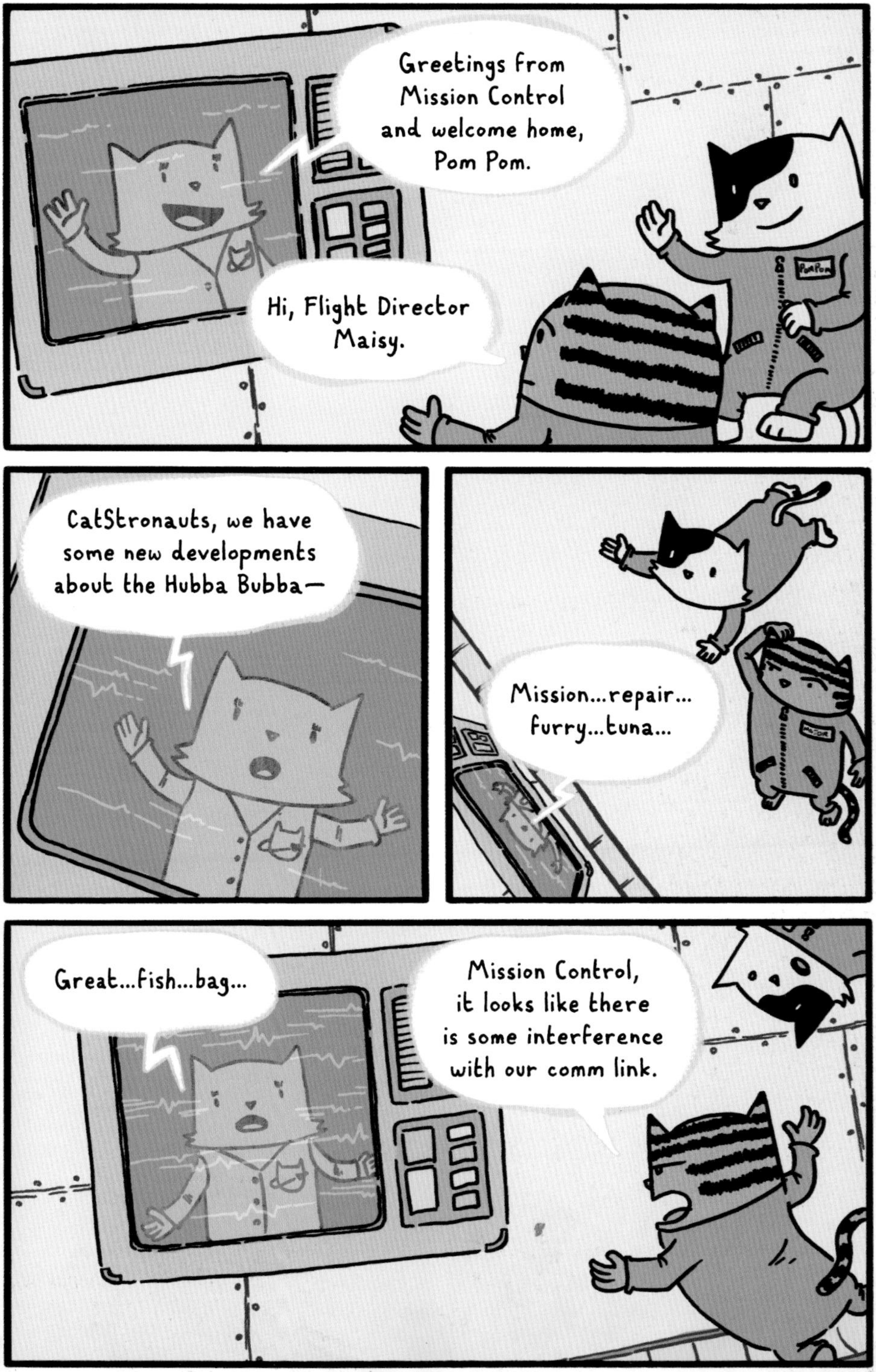

Greetings from Mission Control and welcome home, Pom Pom.
Hi, Flight Director Maisy.
CatStronauts, we have some new developments about the Hubba Bubba—
Mission...repair... furry...tuna...
Great...fish...bag...
Mission Control, it looks like there is some interference with our comm link.

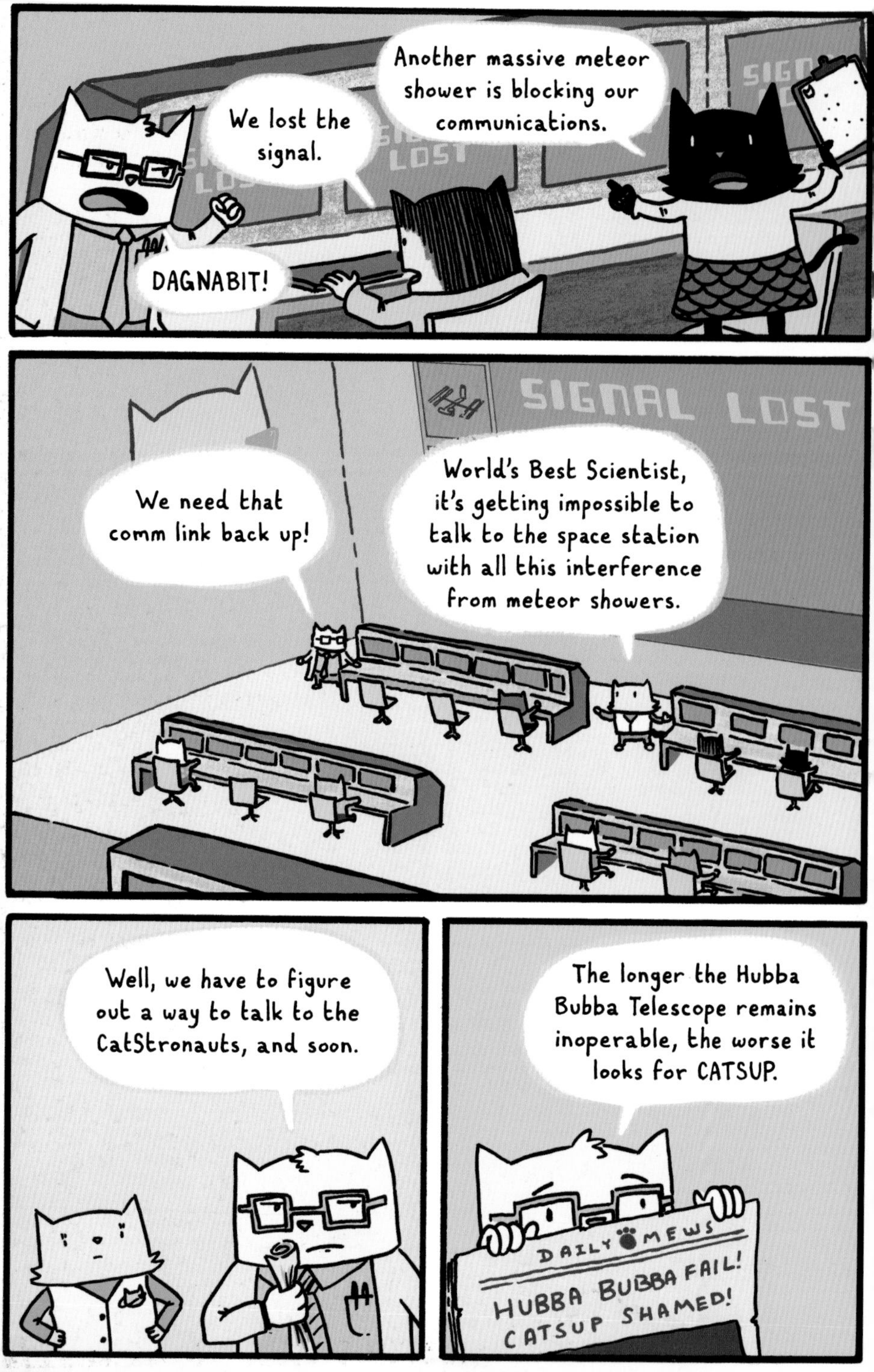

We lost the signal.
Another massive meteor shower is blocking our communications.
DAGNABIT!
SIGNAL LOST
We need that comm link back up!
World's Best Scientist, it's getting impossible to talk to the space station with all this interference from meteor showers.
Well, we have to figure out a way to talk to the CatStronauts, and soon.
The longer the Hubba Bubba Telescope remains inoperable, the worse it looks for CATSUP.
DAILY MEWS
HUBBA BUBBA FAIL! CATSUP SHAMED!

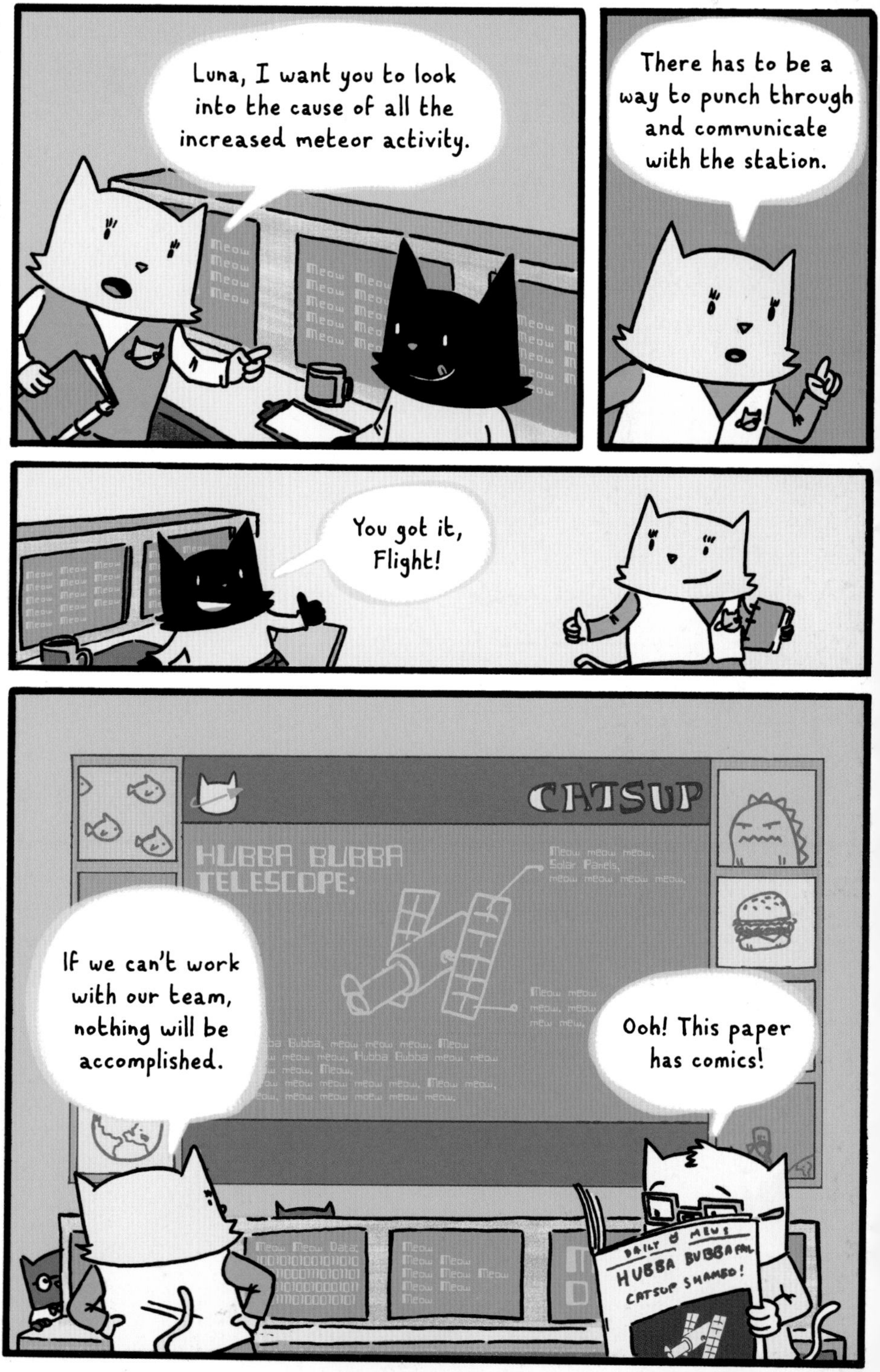
Luna, I want you to look into the cause of all the increased meteor activity.
There has to be a way to punch through and communicate with the station.
You got it, Flight!
CATSUP
HUBBA BUBBA TELESCOPE:
If we can't work with our team, nothing will be accomplished.
Ooh! This paper has comics!
DAILY MEWS
HUBBA BUBBA FAIL
CATSUP SHAMED!

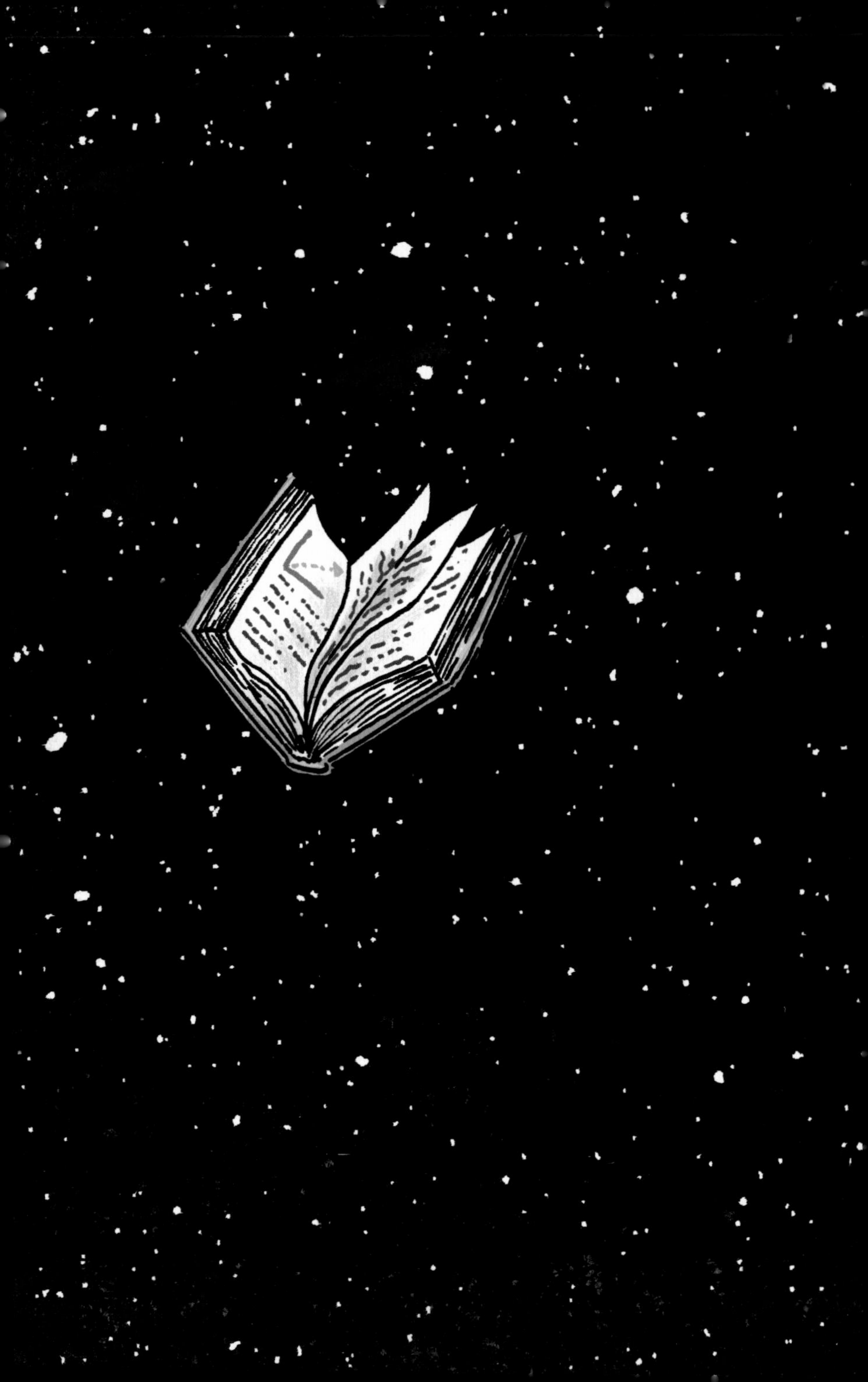

CHAPTER 2

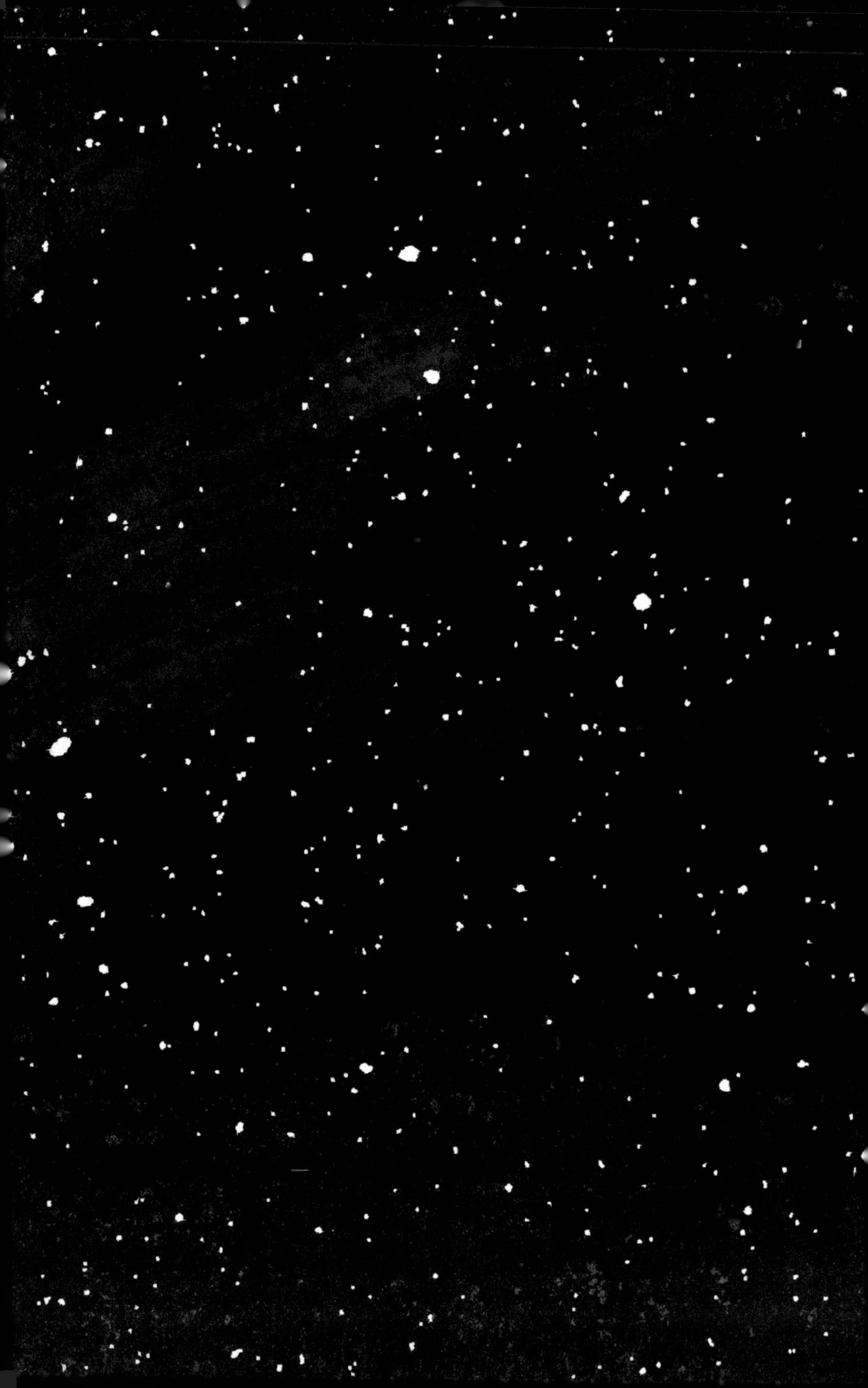

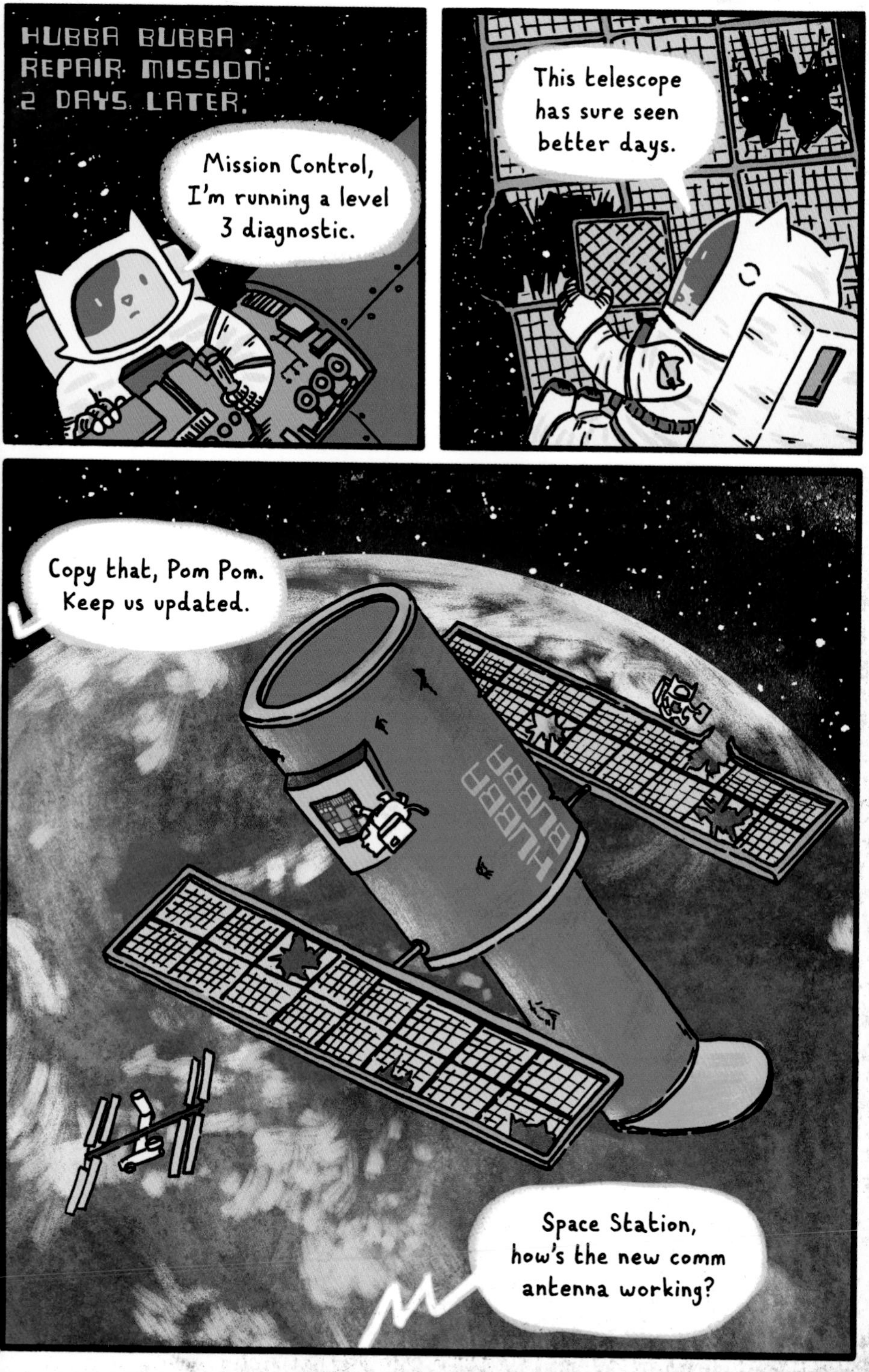
HUBBA BUBBA REPAIR MISSION: 2 DAYS LATER.
Mission Control, I'm running a level 3 diagnostic.
This telescope has sure seen better days.
Copy that, Pom Pom. Keep us updated.
HUBBA BUBBA
Space Station, how's the new comm antenna working?

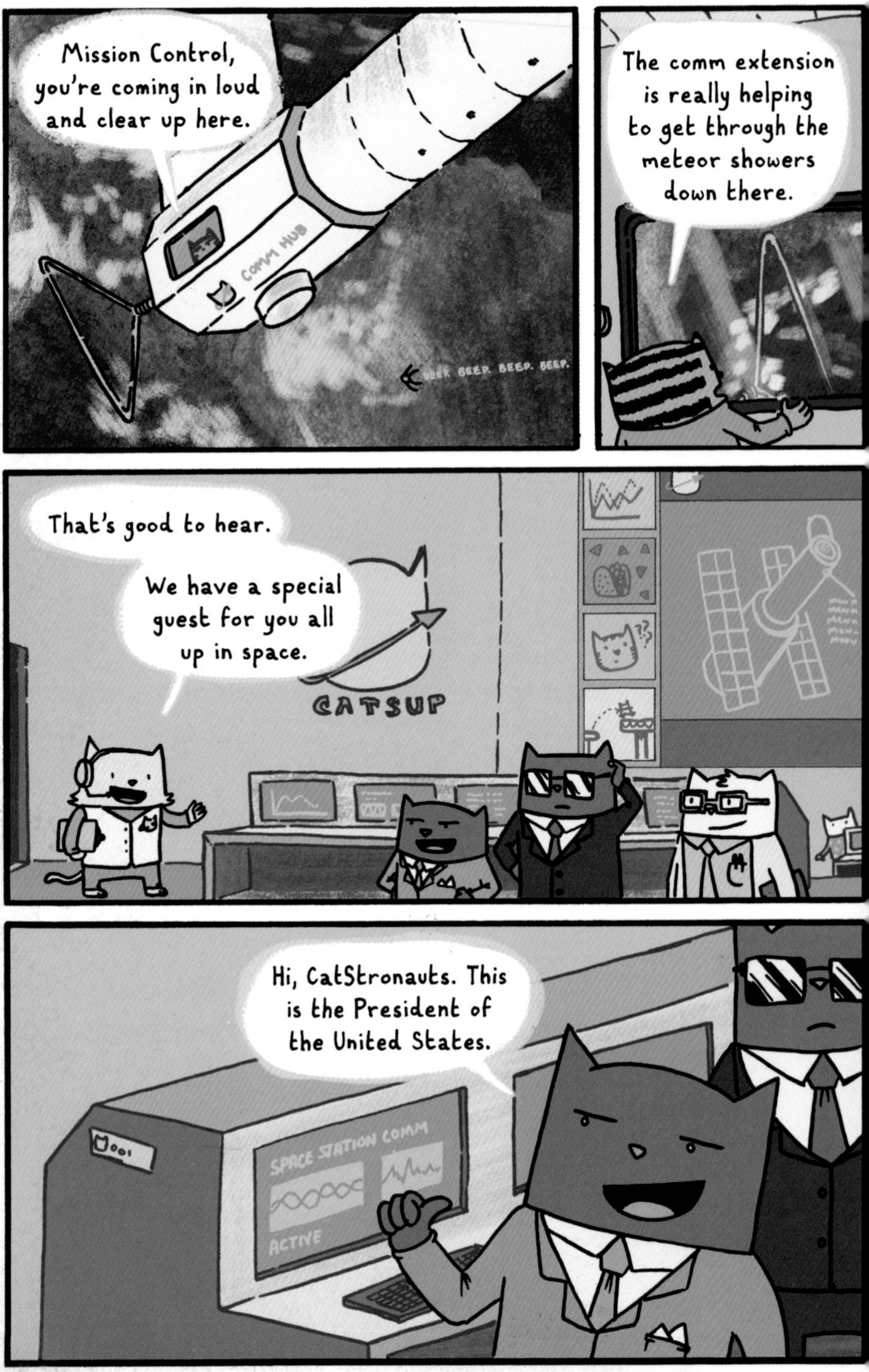
Mission Control, you're coming in loud and clear up here.
COMM HUB
BEEP. BEEP. BEEP. BEEP.
The comm extension is really helping to get through the meteor showers down there.
That's good to hear.
We have a special guest for you all up in space.
CATSUP
Hi, CatStronauts. This is the President of the United States.
001
SPACE STATION COMM
ACTIVE

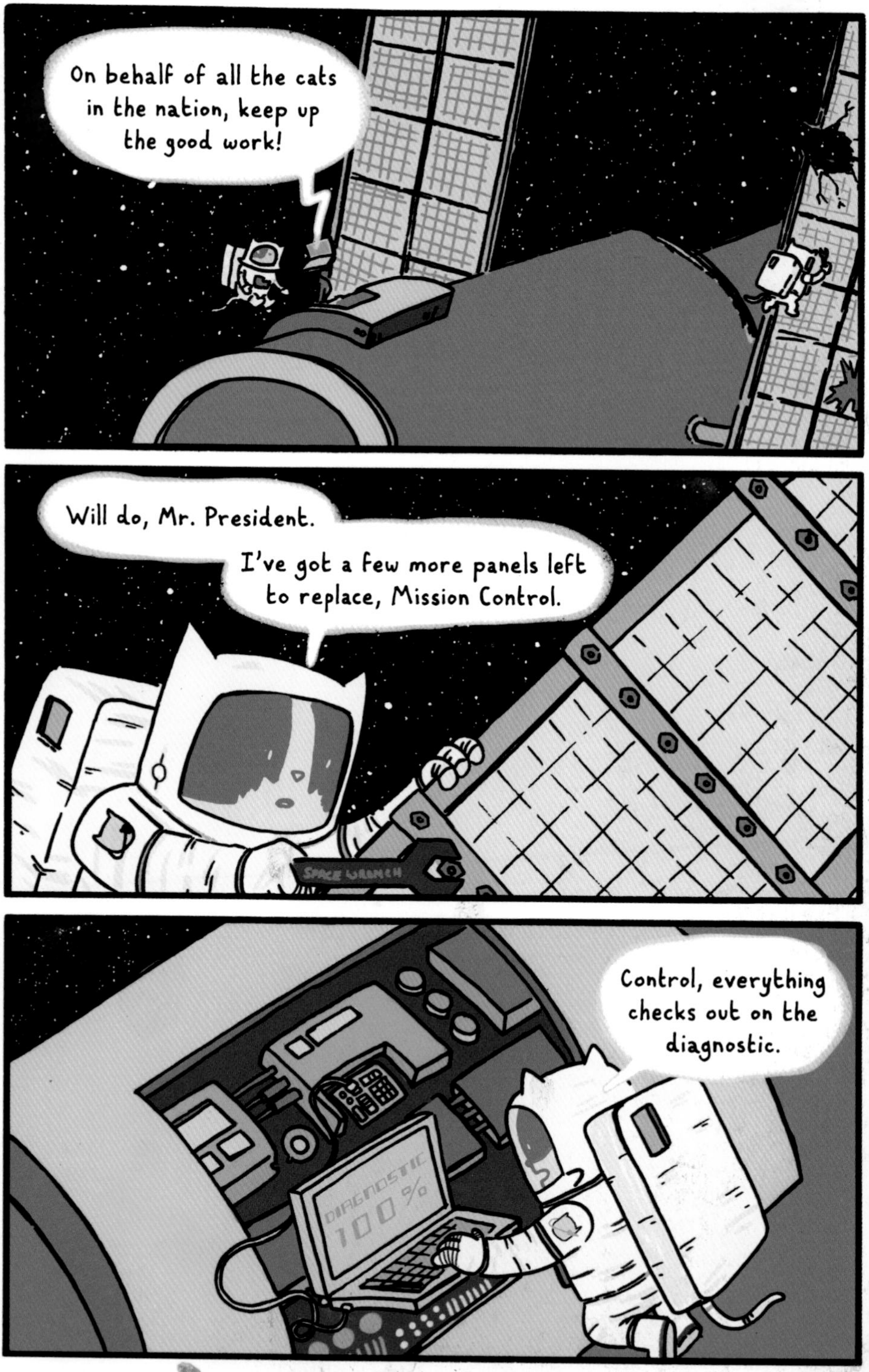
On behalf of all the cats in the nation, keep up the good work!
Will do, Mr. President.
I've got a few more panels left to replace, Mission Control.
SPACE WRENCH
Control, everything checks out on the diagnostic.
DIAGNOSTIC 100%

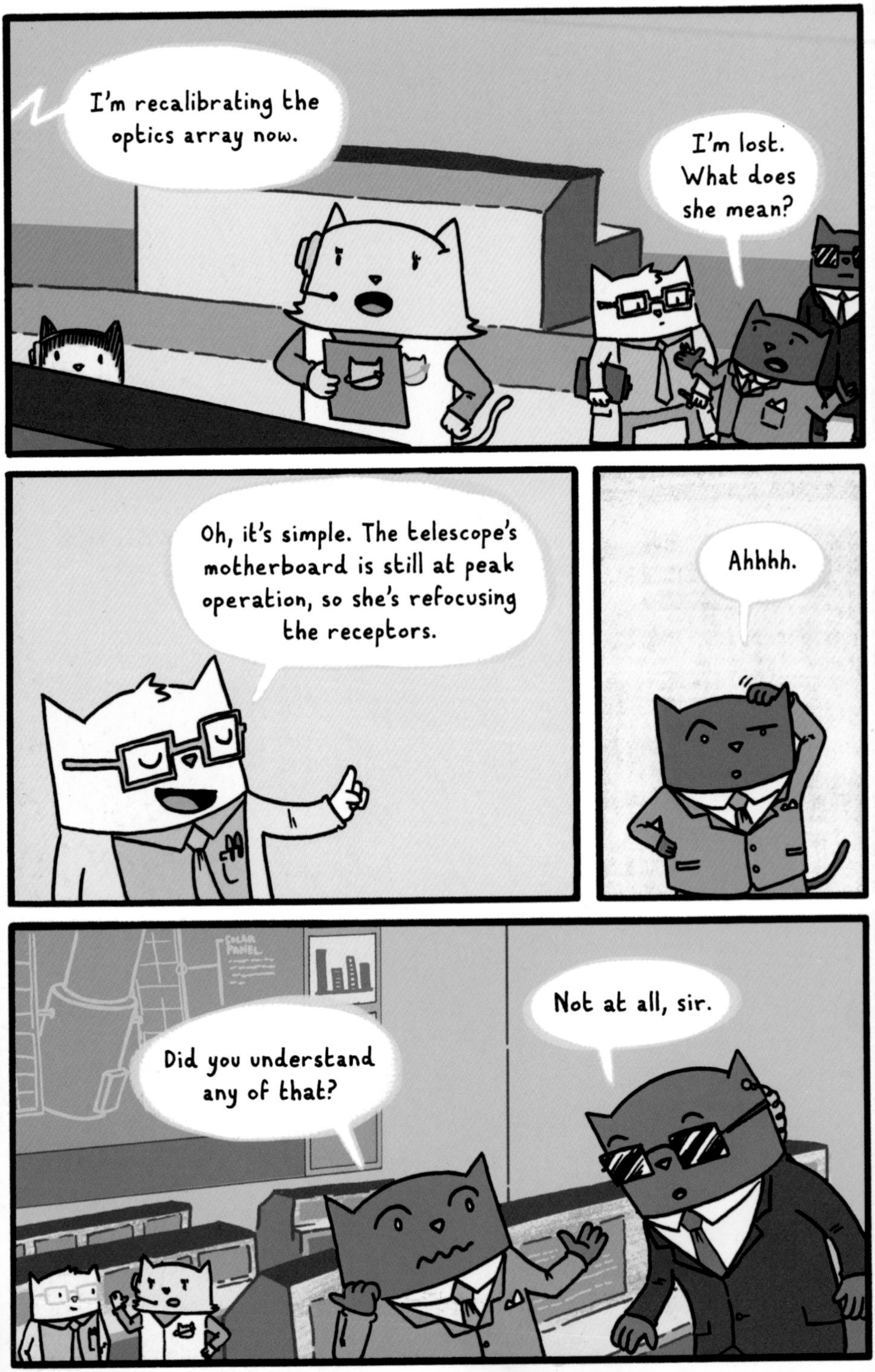
I'm recalibrating the optics array now.
I'm lost. What does she mean?
Oh, it's simple. The telescope's motherboard is still at peak operation, so she's refocusing the receptors.
Ahhhh.
Did you understand any of that?
Not at all, sir.

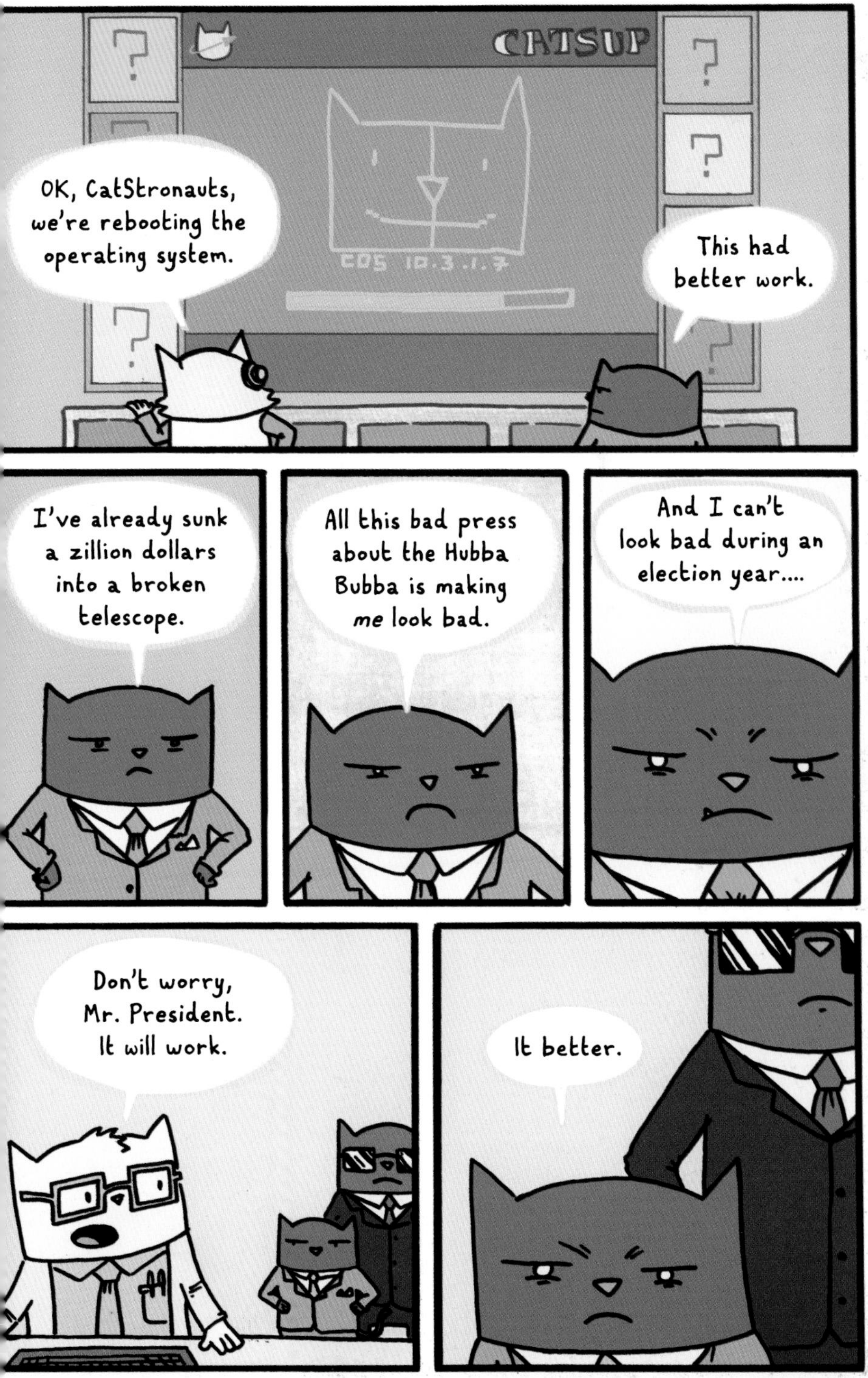
CATSUP
OK, CatStronauts, we're rebooting the operating system.
COS 10.3.1.7
This had better work.
I've already sunk a zillion dollars into a broken telescope.
All this bad press about the Hubba Bubba is making *me* look bad.
And I can't look bad during an election year....
Don't worry, Mr. President. It will work.
It better.

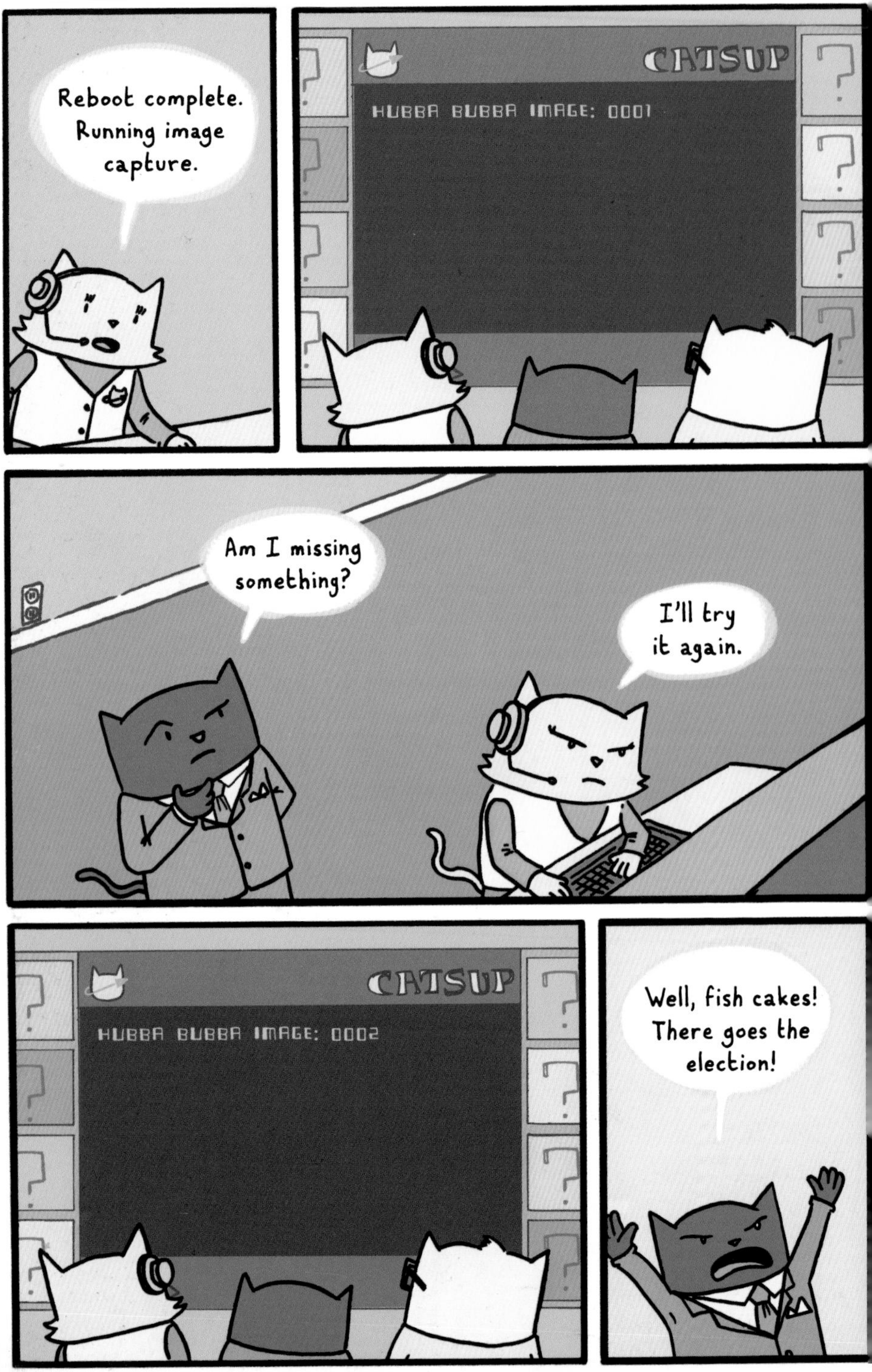
Reboot complete. Running image capture.
CATSUP
HUBBA BUBBA IMAGE: 0001
Am I missing something?
I'll try it again.
CATSUP
HUBBA BUBBA IMAGE: 0002
Well, fish cakes! There goes the election!

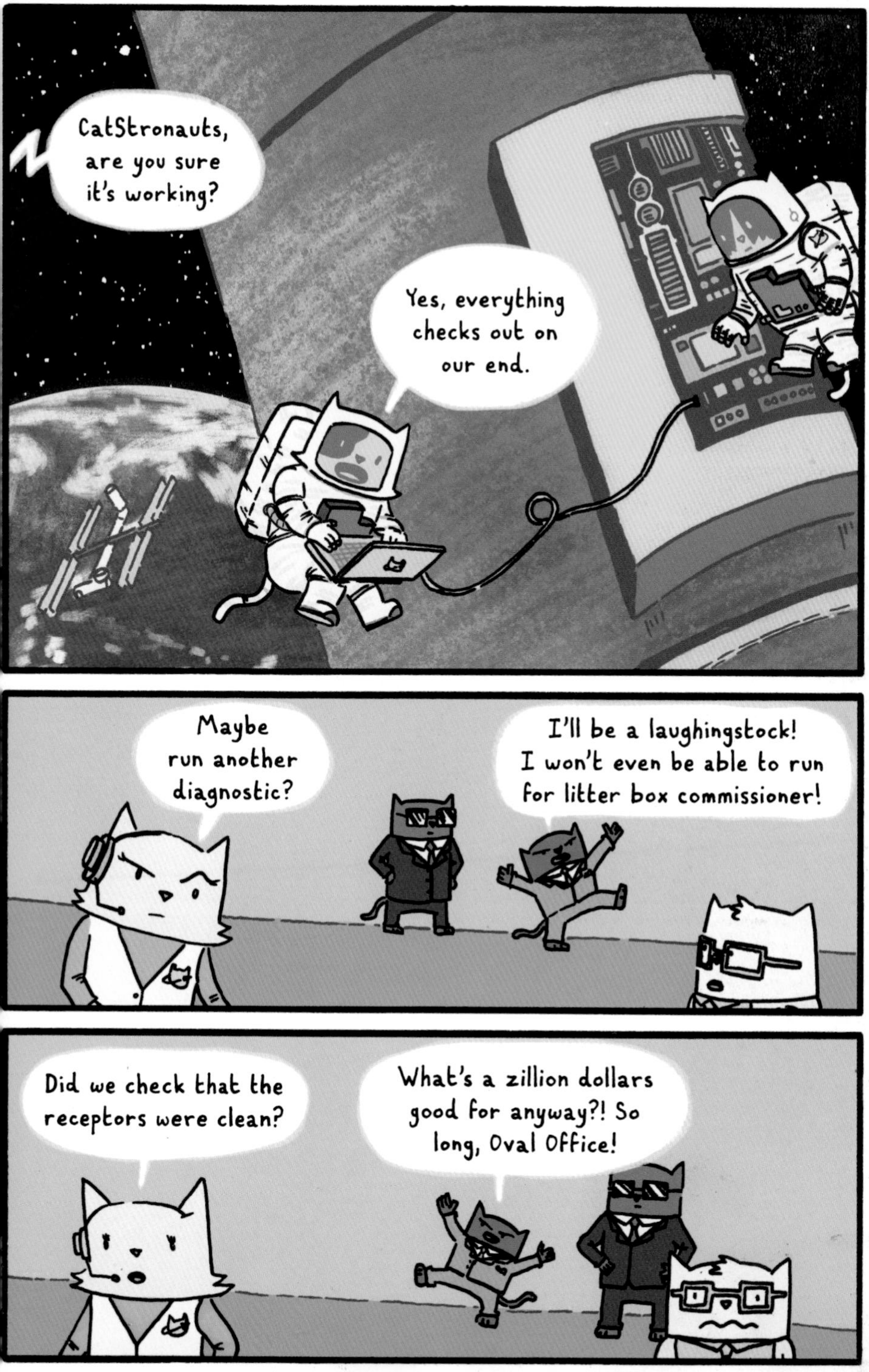
CatStronauts, are you sure it's working?
Yes, everything checks out on our end.
Maybe run another diagnostic?
I'll be a laughingstock! I won't even be able to run for litter box commissioner!
Did we check that the receptors were clean?
What's a zillion dollars good for anyway?! So long, Oval Office!

Flight, I'm picking up increased meteor activity heading toward the Hubba Bubba.

This is Major Meowser in the station, confirming Control's reports.

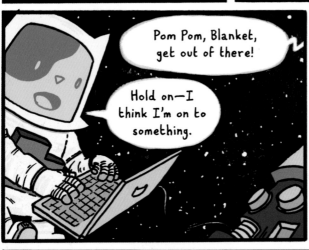

Pom Pom, Blanket, get out of there!

Hold on—I think I'm on to something.

That is a *direct order*, Pom Pom! Leave now!

OK. We're leaving.

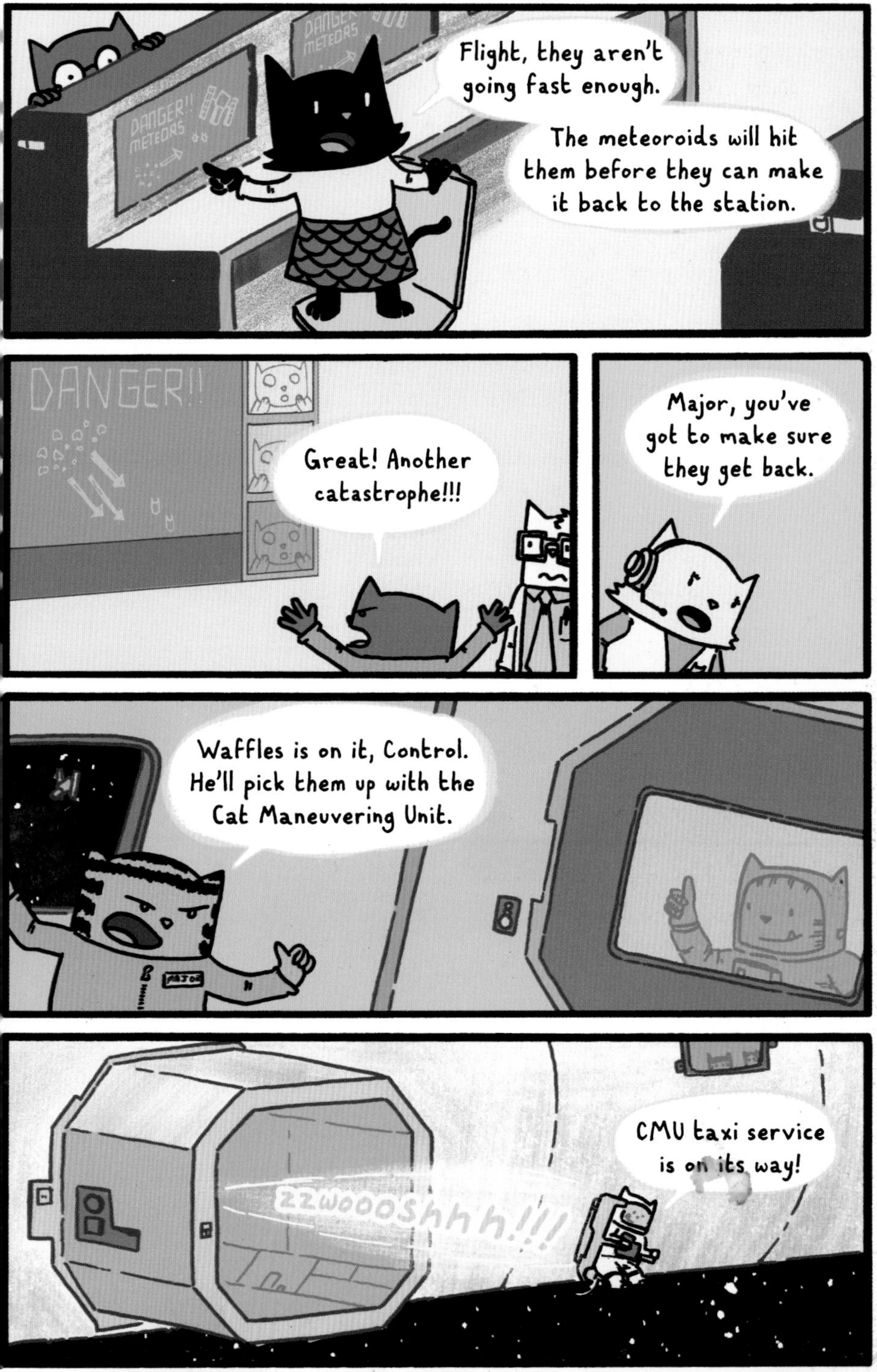
DANGER!! METEORS
Flight, they aren't going fast enough.
The meteoroids will hit them before they can make it back to the station.
DANGER!!
Great! Another catastrophe!!!
Major, you've got to make sure they get back.
Waffles is on it, Control. He'll pick them up with the Cat Maneuvering Unit.
ZZWOOOShhh!!!
CMU taxi service is on its way!

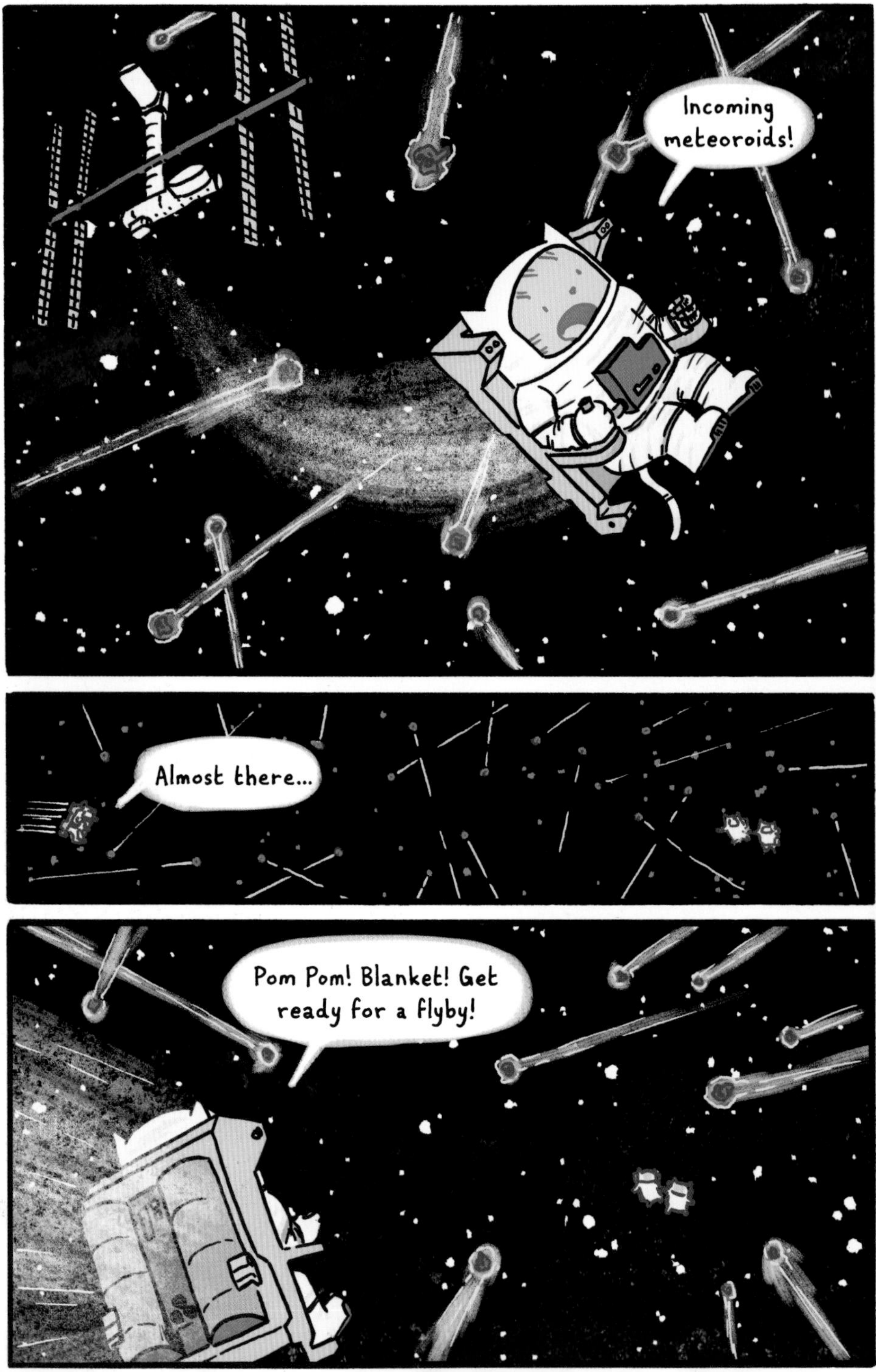
Incoming meteoroids!
Almost there...
Pom Pom! Blanket! Get ready for a flyby!

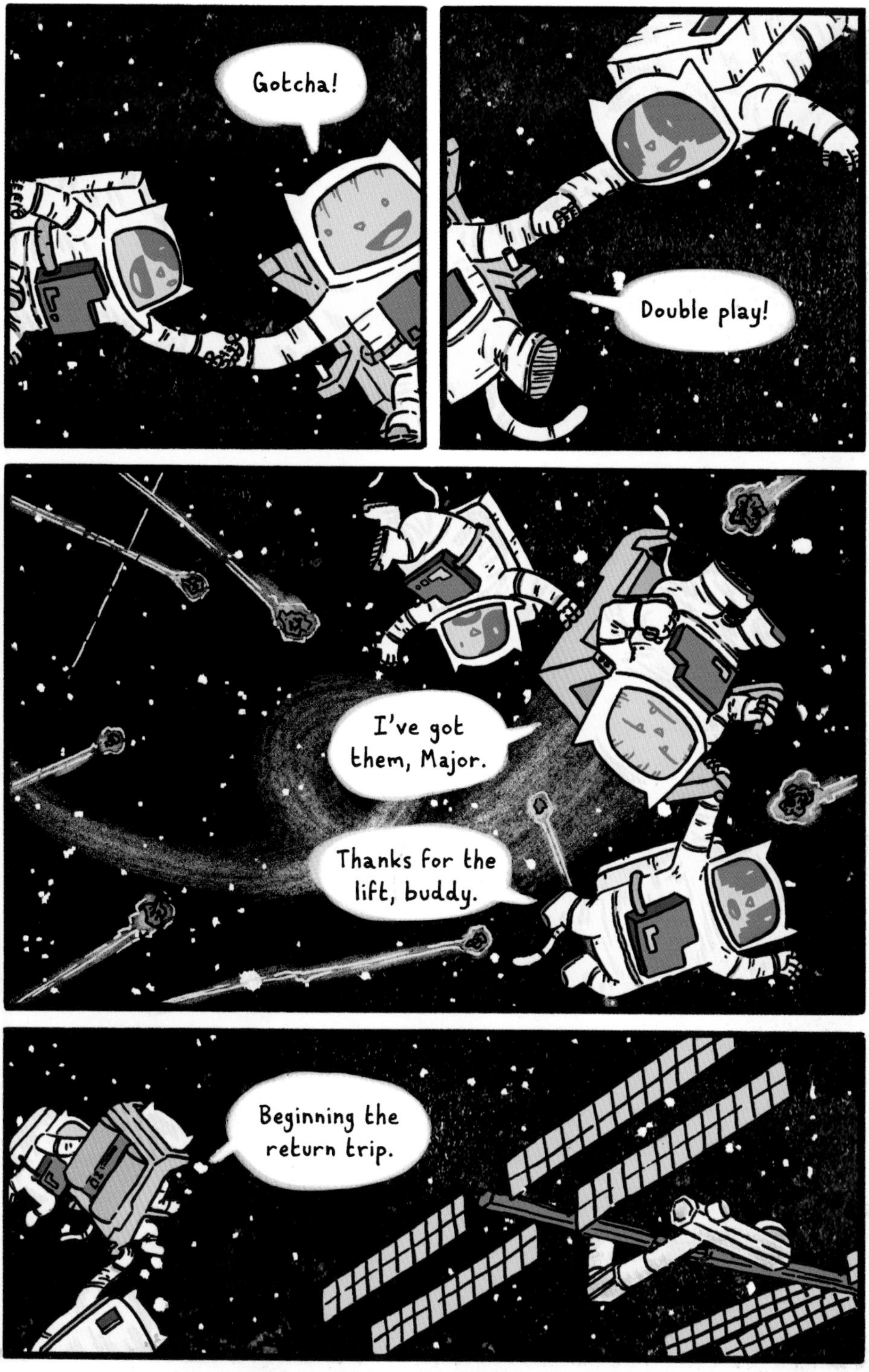
Gotcha!
Double play!
I've got them, Major.
Thanks for the lift, buddy.
Beginning the return trip.

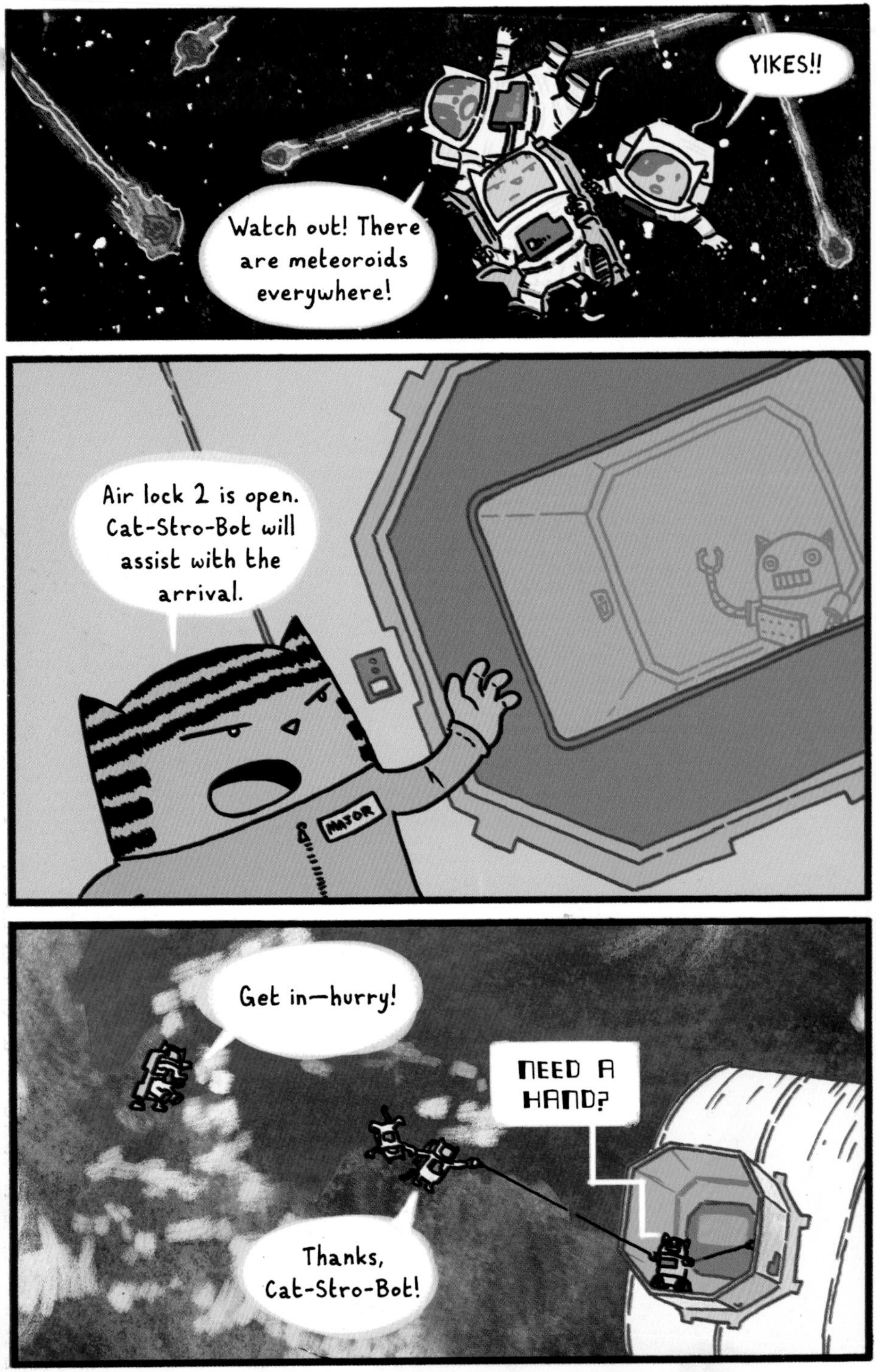
YIKES!!
Watch out! There are meteoroids everywhere!
Air lock 2 is open. Cat-Stro-Bot will assist with the arrival.
MAJOR
Get in—hurry!
NEED A HAND?
Thanks, Cat-Stro-Bot!

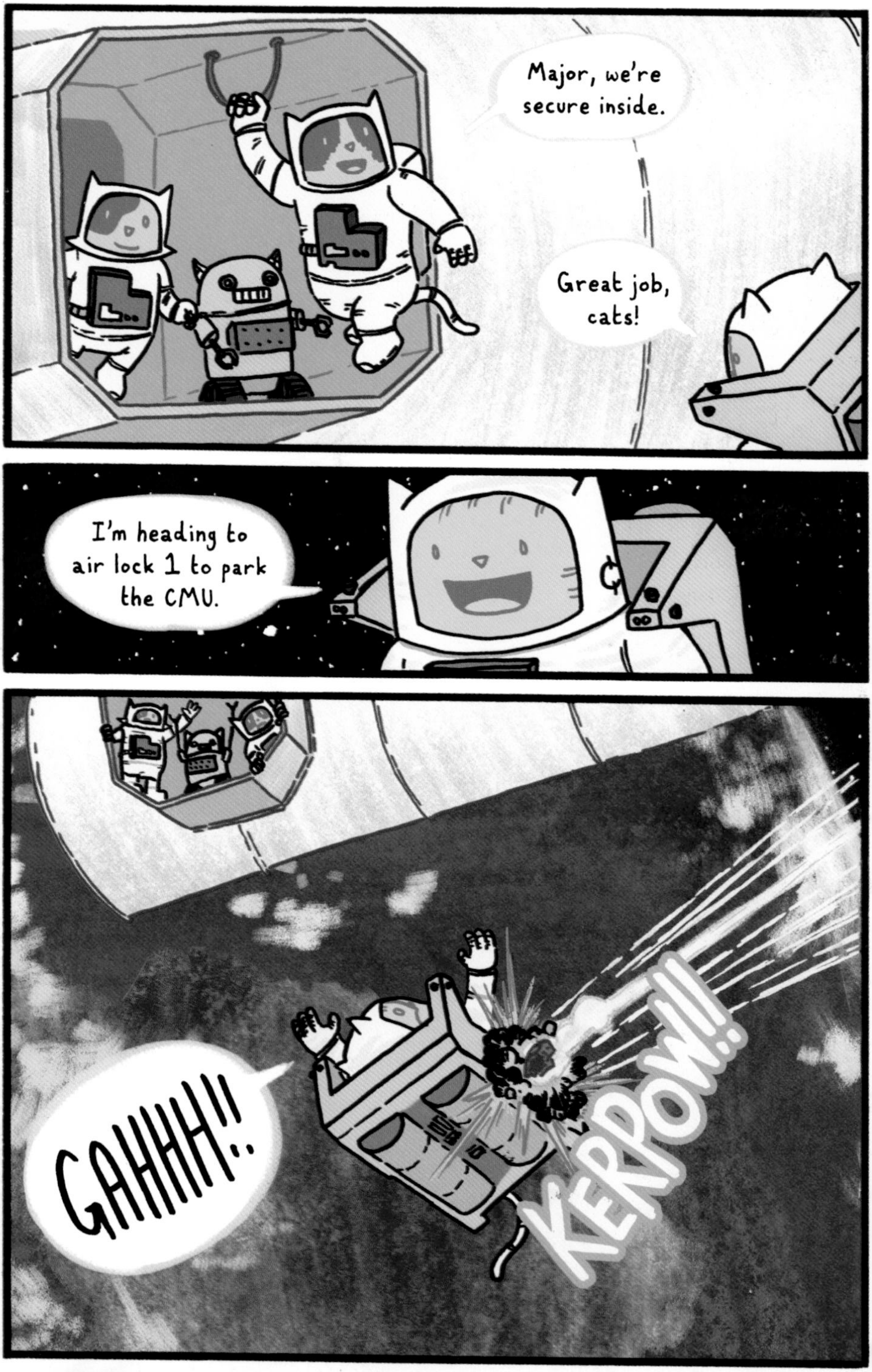
Major, we're secure inside.
Great job, cats!
I'm heading to air lock 1 to park the CMU.
GAHHH!!
KERPOW!!

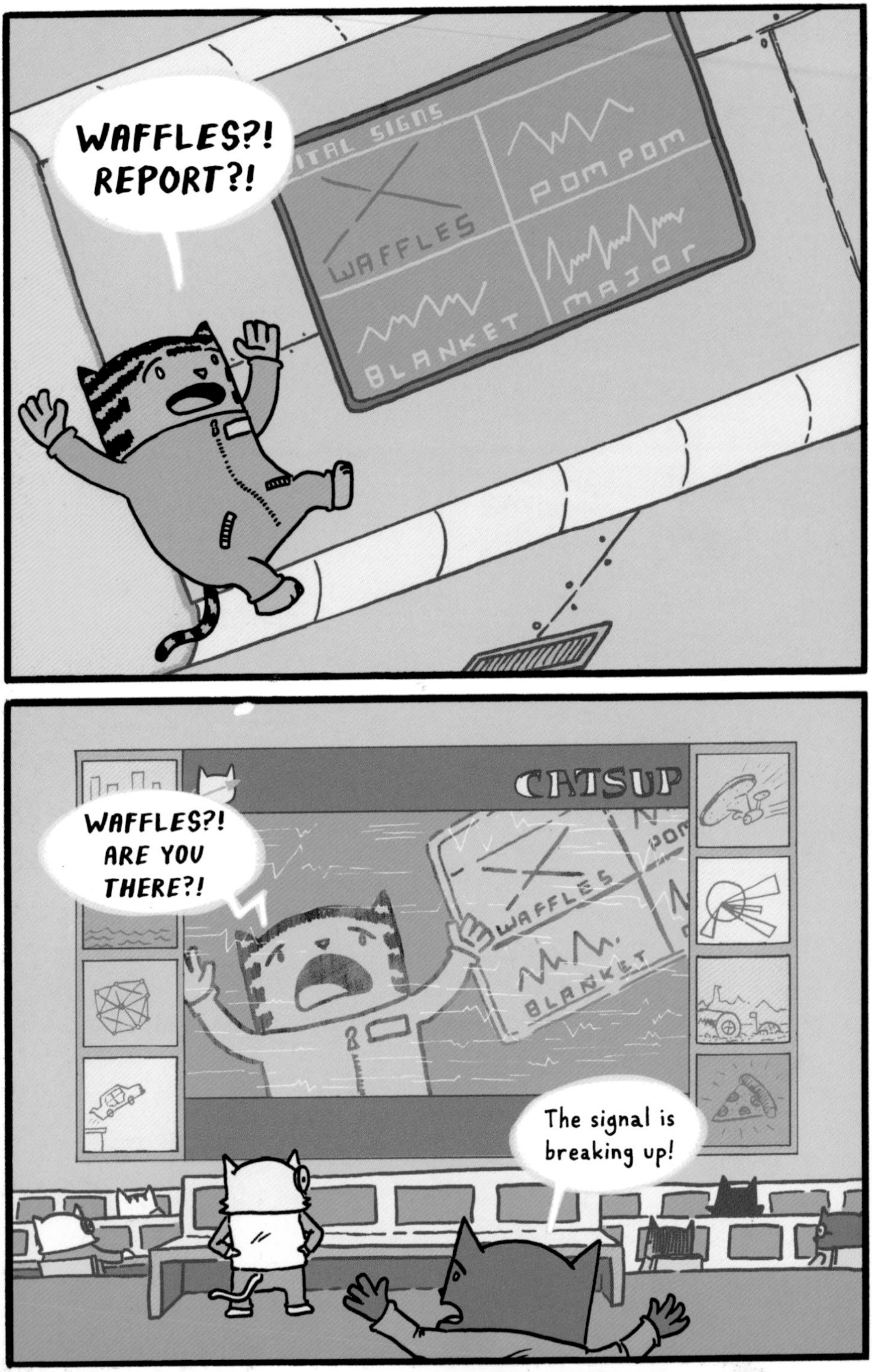
WAFFLES?! REPORT?!
ITAL SIGNS
WAFFLES
POM POM
BLANKET
MAJOR
CATSUP
WAFFLES?! ARE YOU THERE?!
WAFFLES
BLANKET
The signal is breaking up!

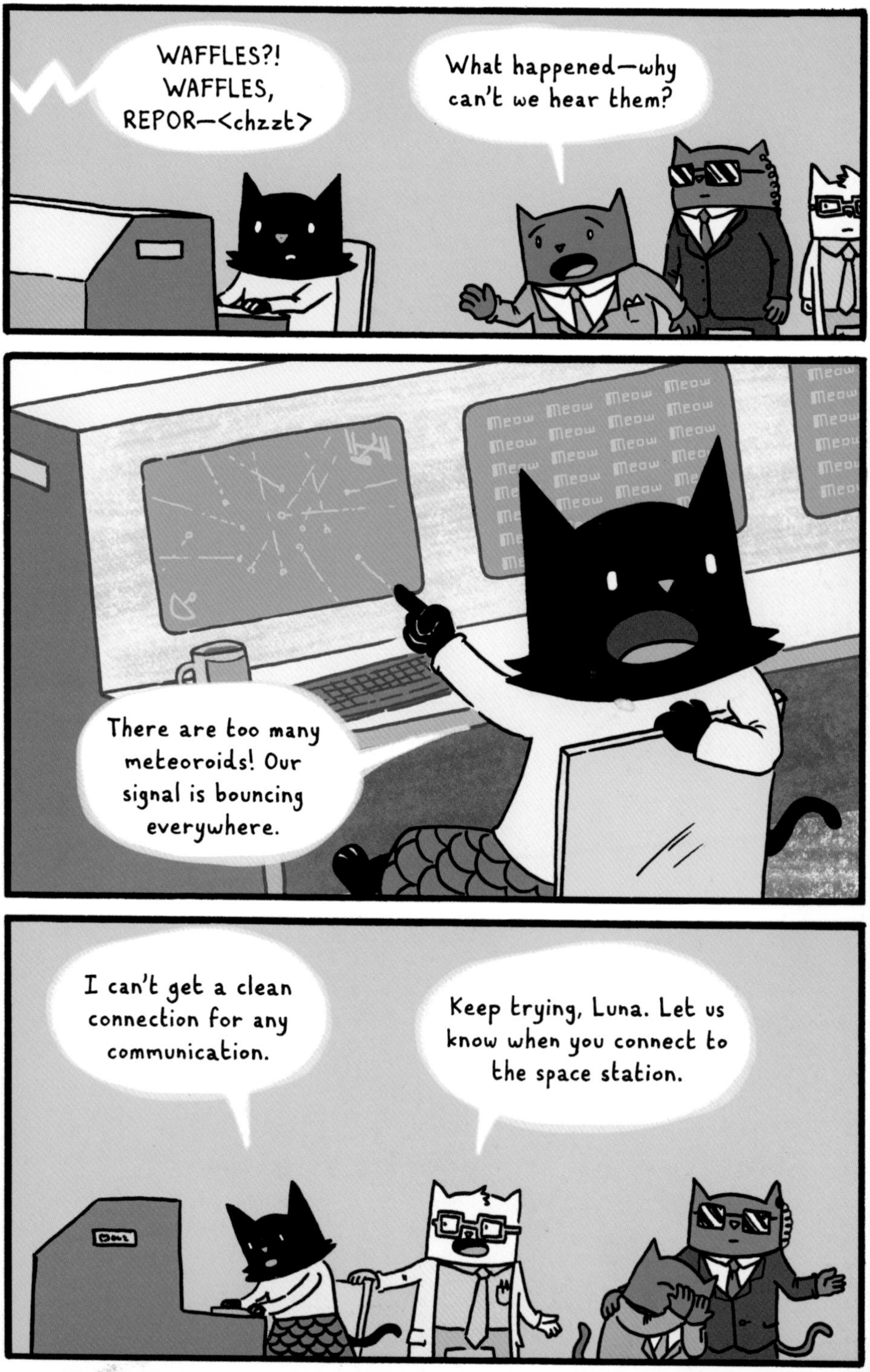
WAFFLES?! WAFFLES, REPOR—<chzzt>
What happened—why can't we hear them?
There are too many meteoroids! Our signal is bouncing everywhere.
I can't get a clean connection for any communication.
Keep trying, Luna. Let us know when you connect to the space station.

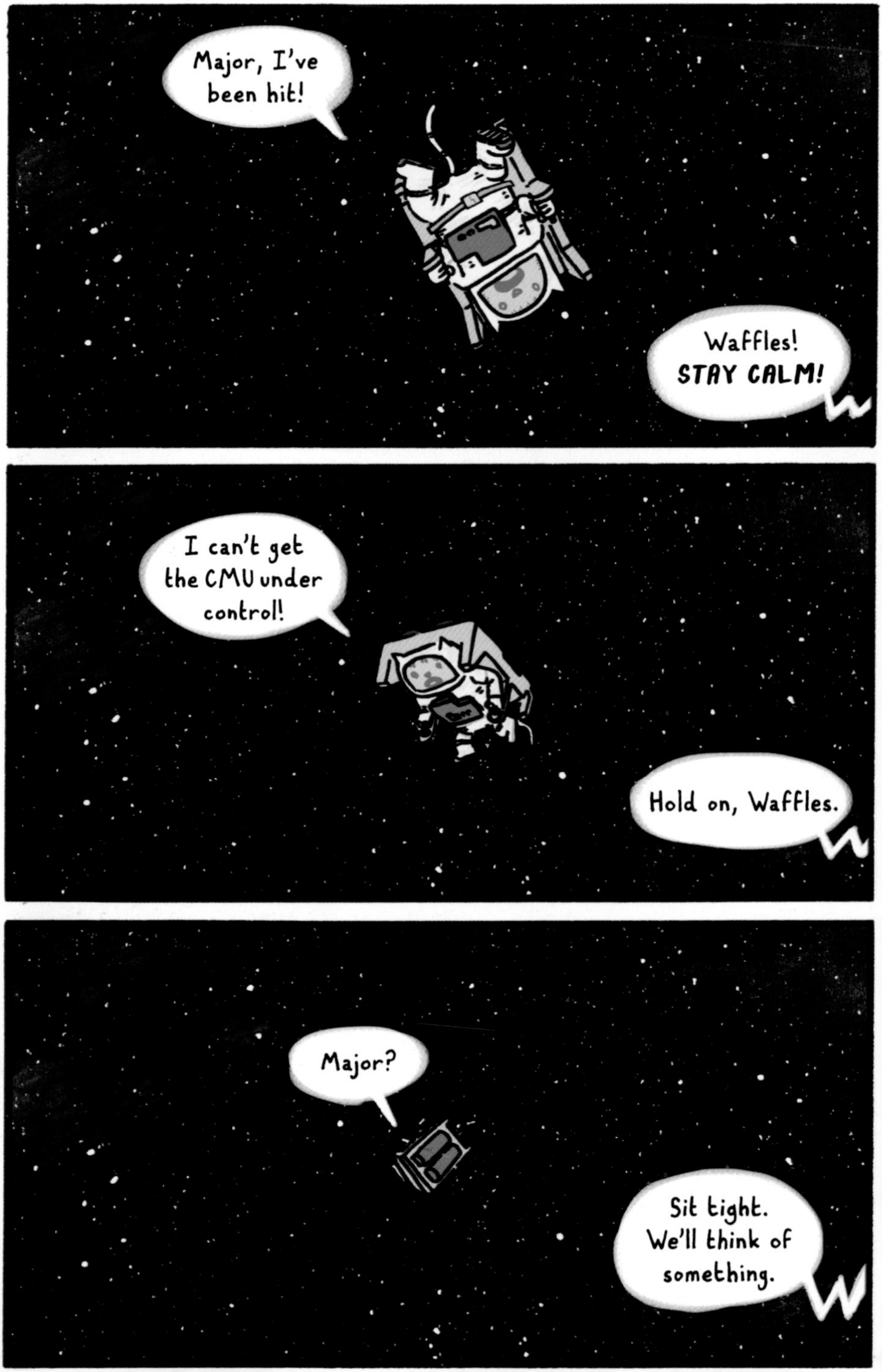
Major, I've been hit!
Waffles! STAY CALM!
I can't get the CMU under control!
Hold on, Waffles.
Major?
Sit tight. We'll think of something.

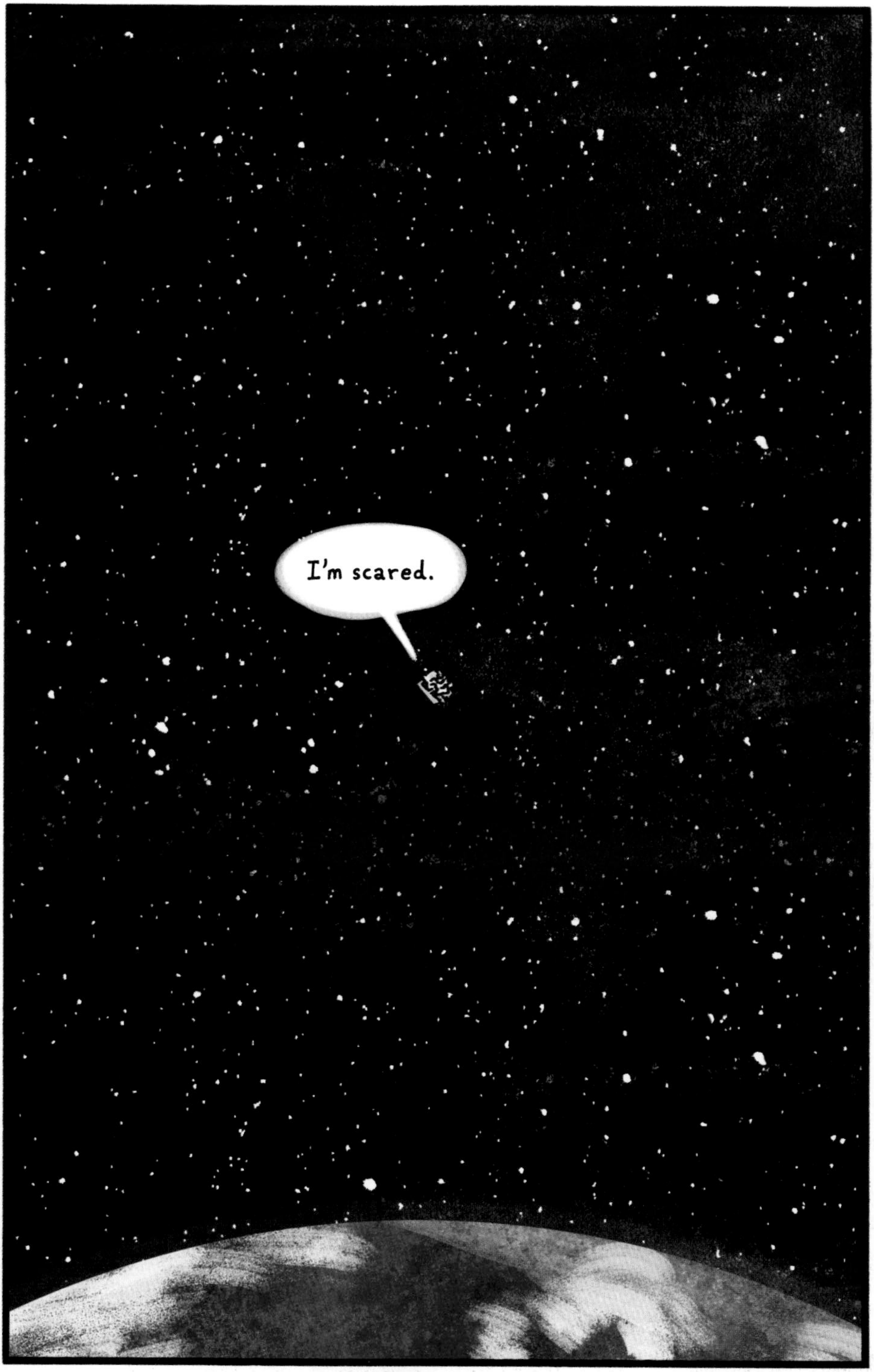
I'm scared.

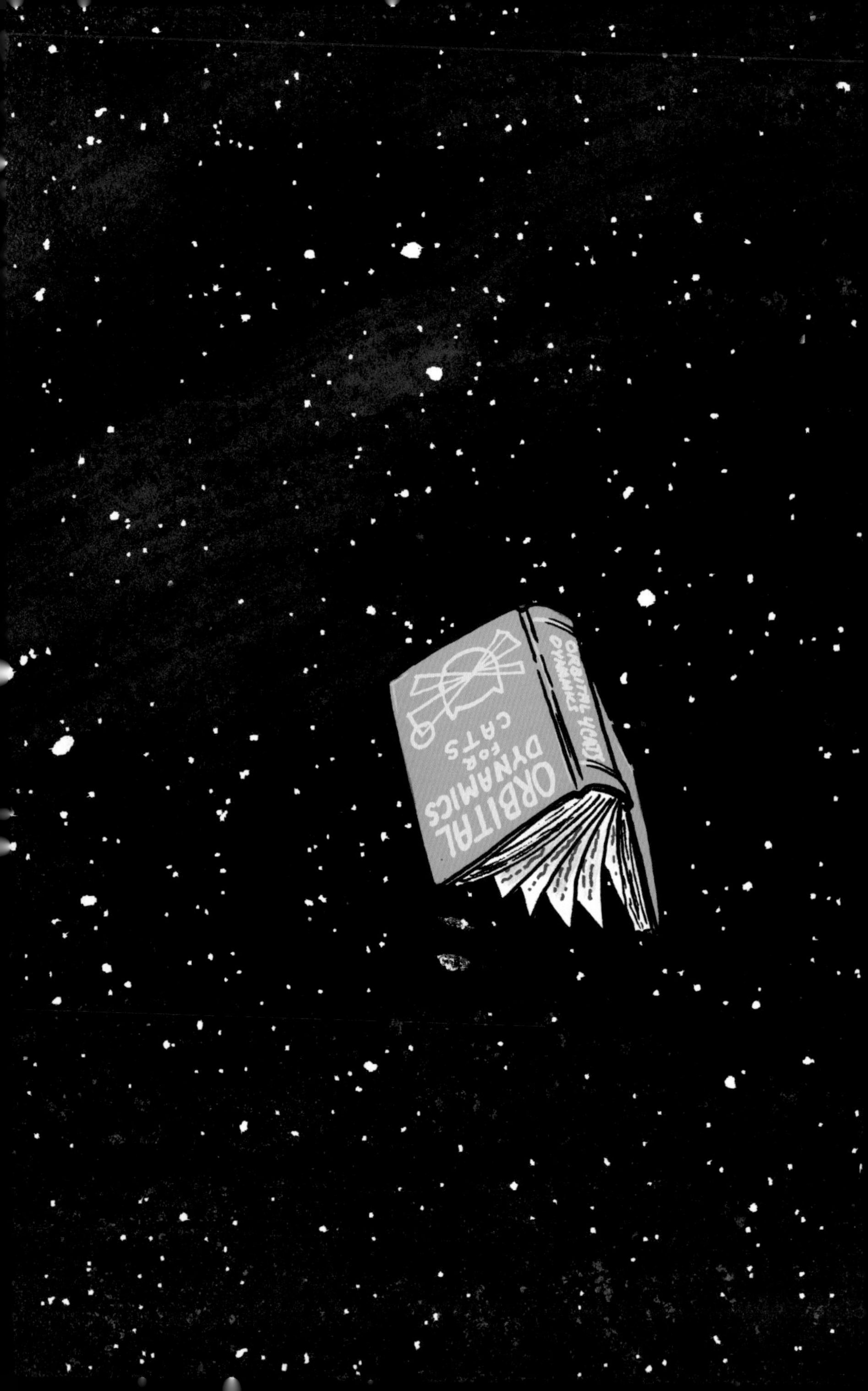
ORBITAL
DYNAMICS
FOR
CATS

CHAPTER 3

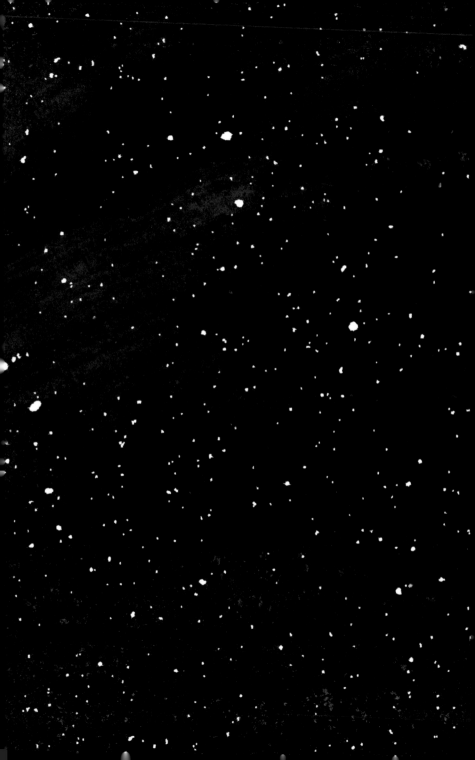

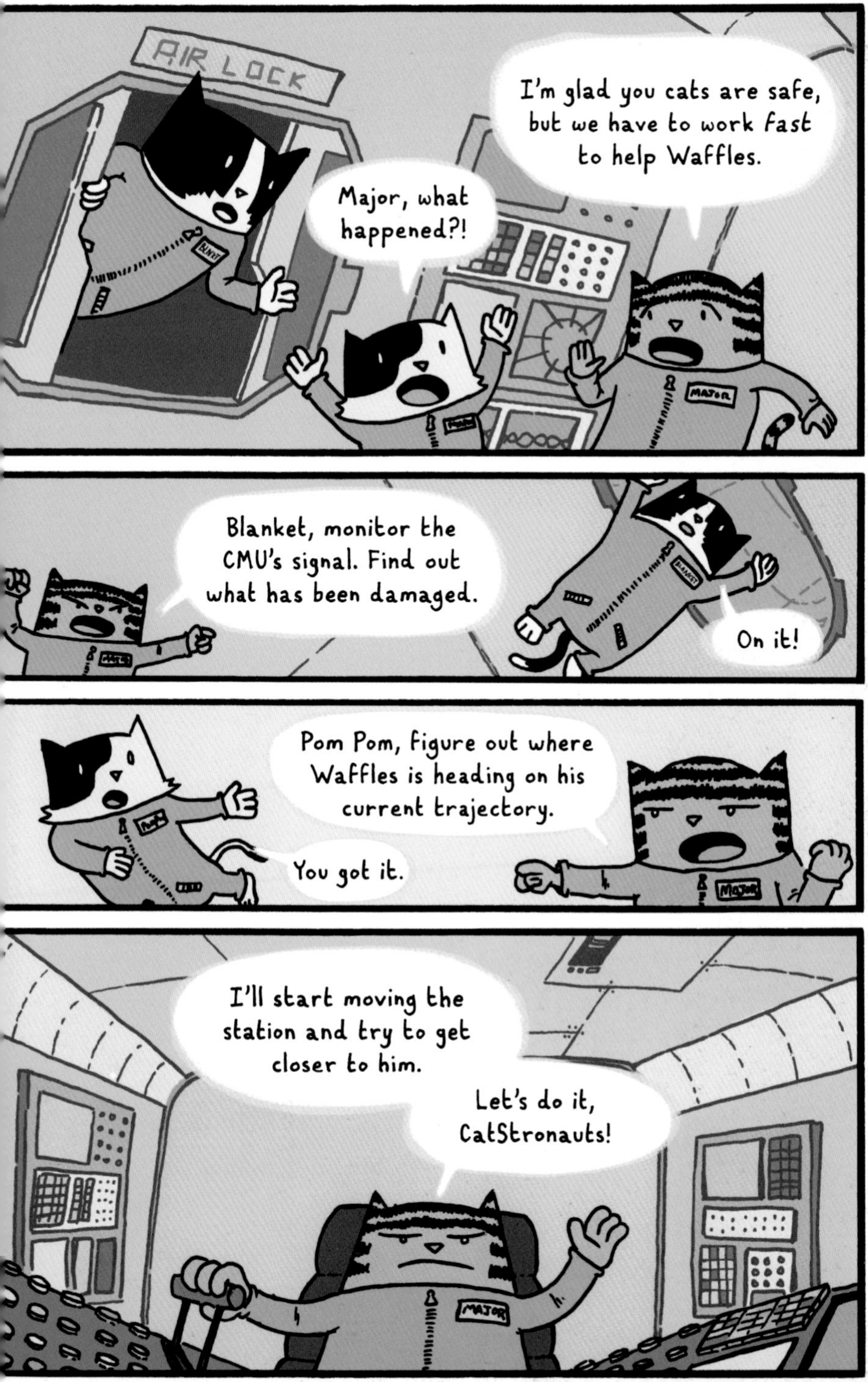
AIR LOCK
Major, what happened?!
I'm glad you cats are safe, but we have to work fast to help Waffles.
Blanket, monitor the CMU's signal. Find out what has been damaged.
On it!
Pom Pom, figure out where Waffles is heading on his current trajectory.
You got it.
I'll start moving the station and try to get closer to him.
Let's do it, CatStronauts!

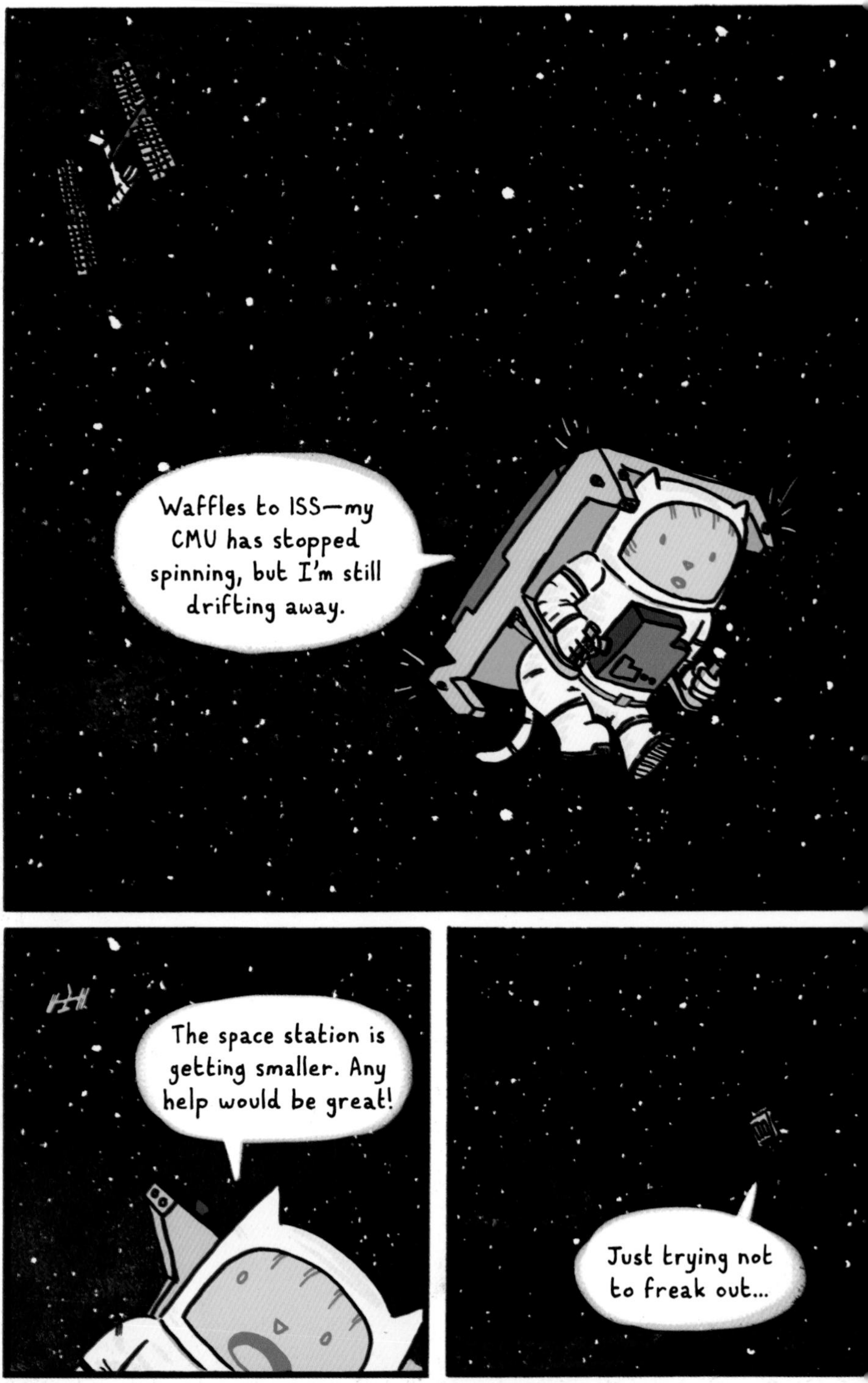
Waffles to ISS—my CMU has stopped spinning, but I'm still drifting away.
The space station is getting smaller. Any help would be great!
Just trying not to freak out...

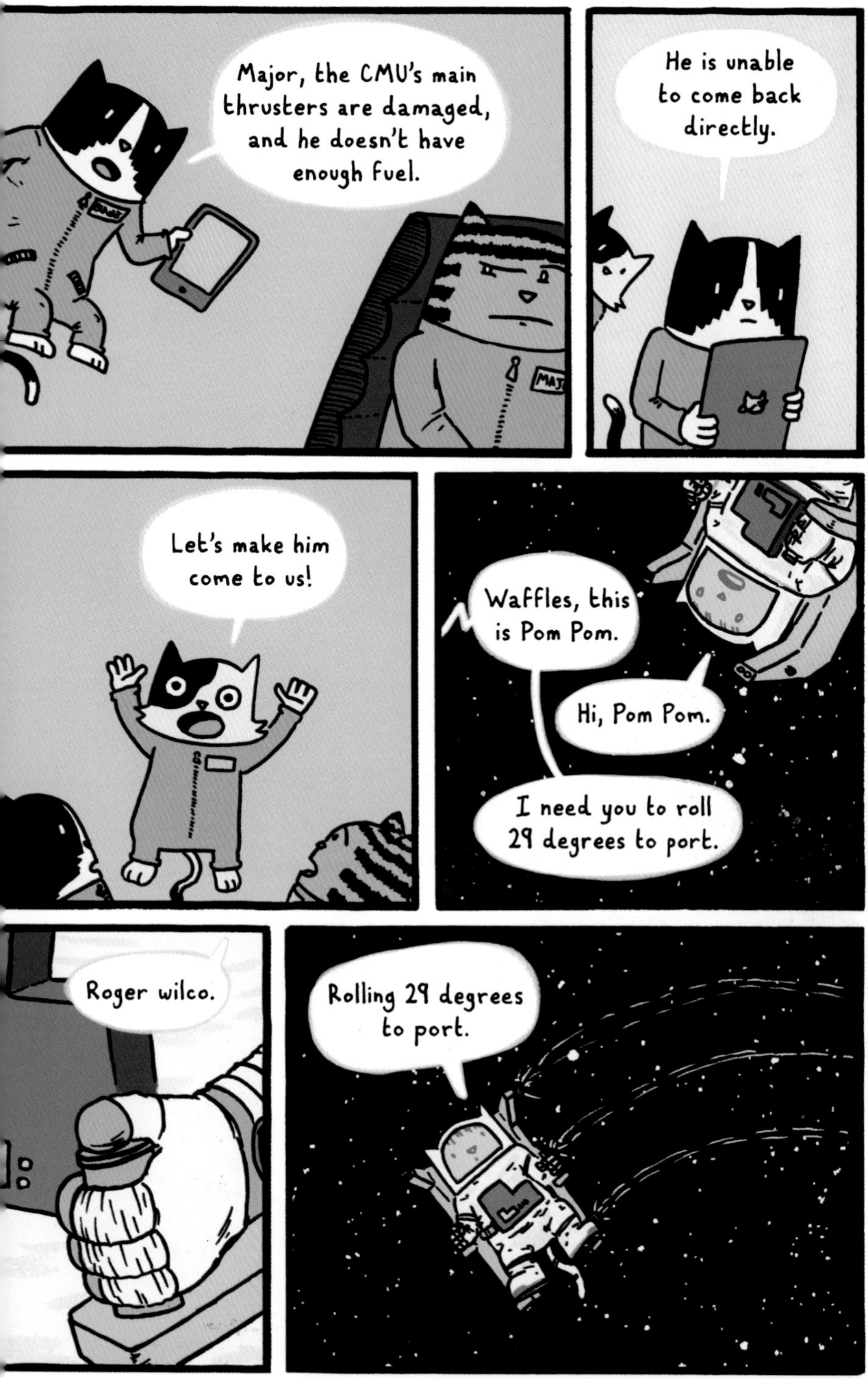
Major, the CMU's main thrusters are damaged, and he doesn't have enough fuel.
He is unable to come back directly.
Let's make him come to us!
Waffles, this is Pom Pom.
Hi, Pom Pom.
I need you to roll 29 degrees to port.
Roger wilco.
Rolling 29 degrees to port.

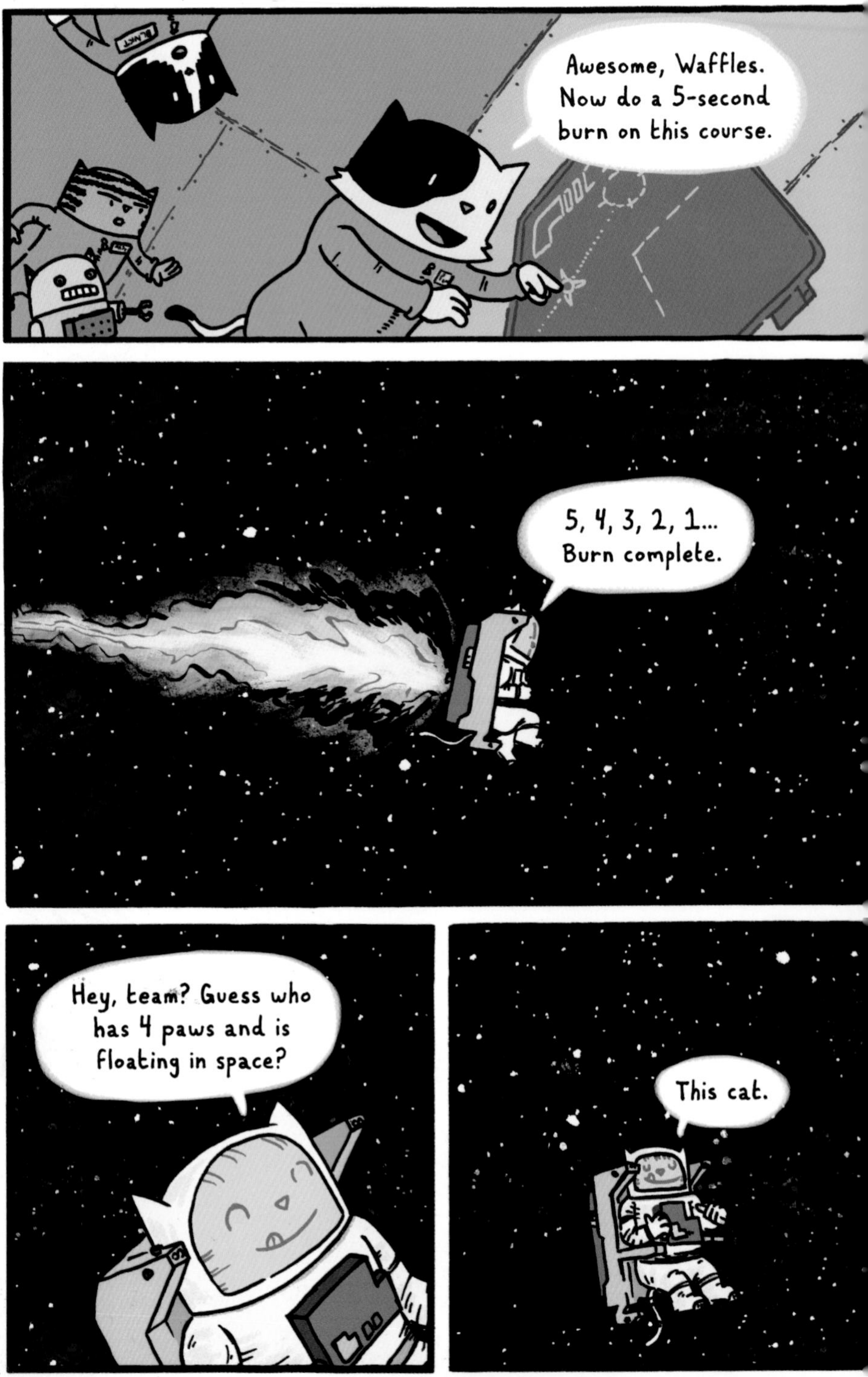
Awesome, Waffles. Now do a 5-second burn on this course.
5, 4, 3, 2, 1... Burn complete.
Hey, team? Guess who has 4 paws and is floating in space?
This cat.

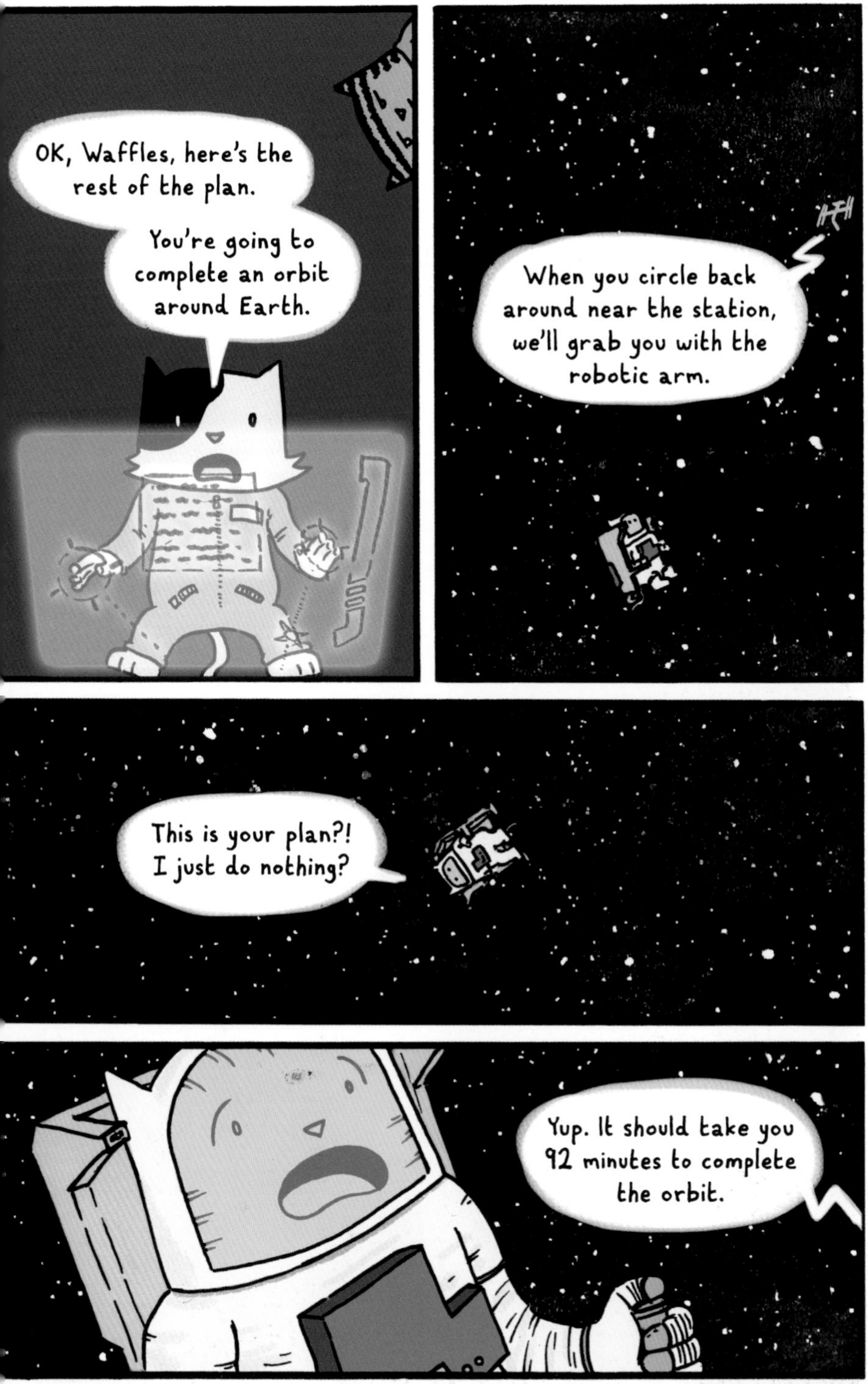
OK, Waffles, here's the rest of the plan.
You're going to complete an orbit around Earth.
When you circle back around near the station, we'll grab you with the robotic arm.
This is your plan?! I just do nothing?
Yup. It should take you 92 minutes to complete the orbit.

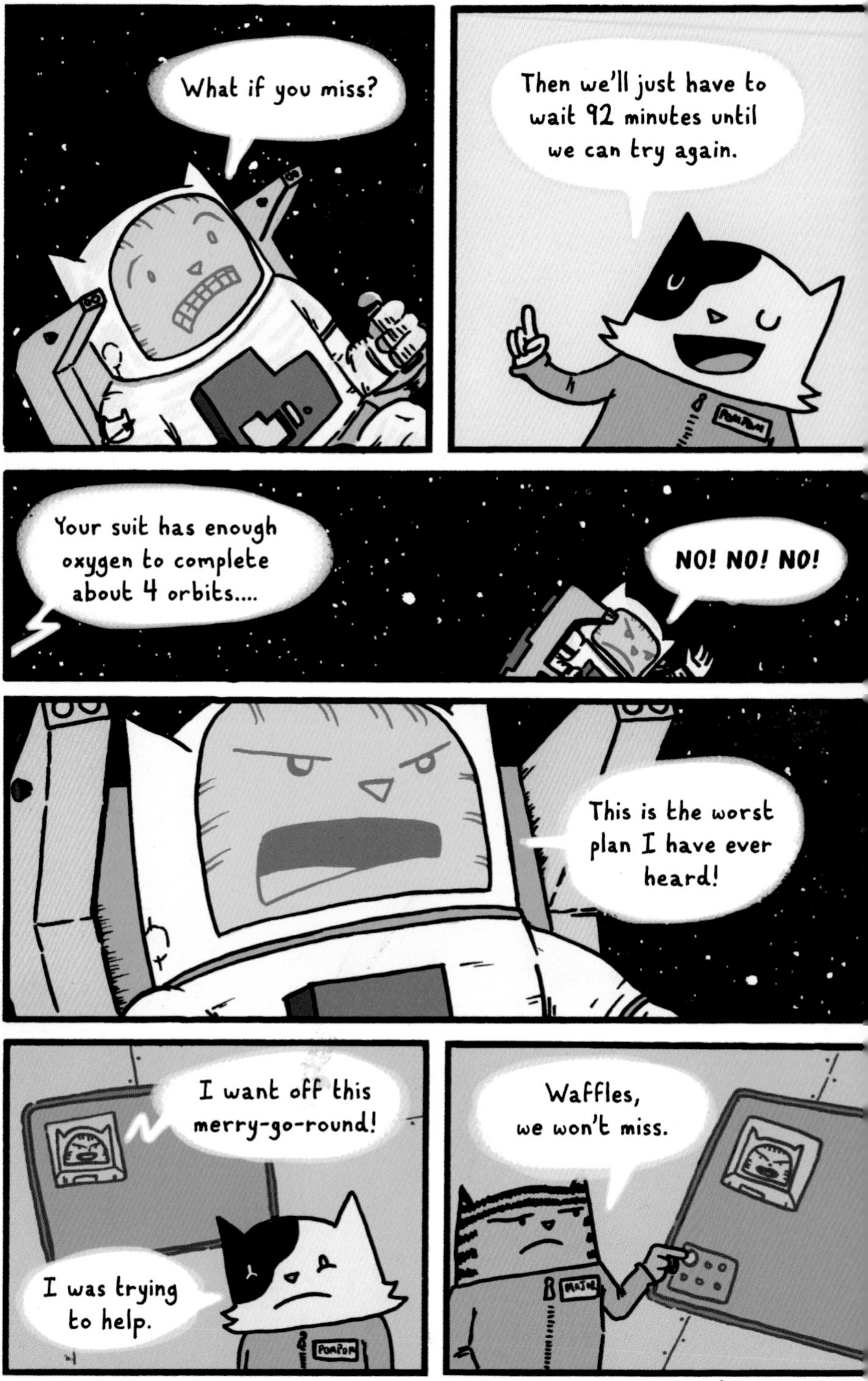
What if you miss?
Then we'll just have to wait 92 minutes until we can try again.
POMPOM
Your suit has enough oxygen to complete about 4 orbits....
NO! NO! NO!
This is the worst plan I have ever heard!
I want off this merry-go-round!
I was trying to help.
POMPOM
Waffles, we won't miss.
MAJOR

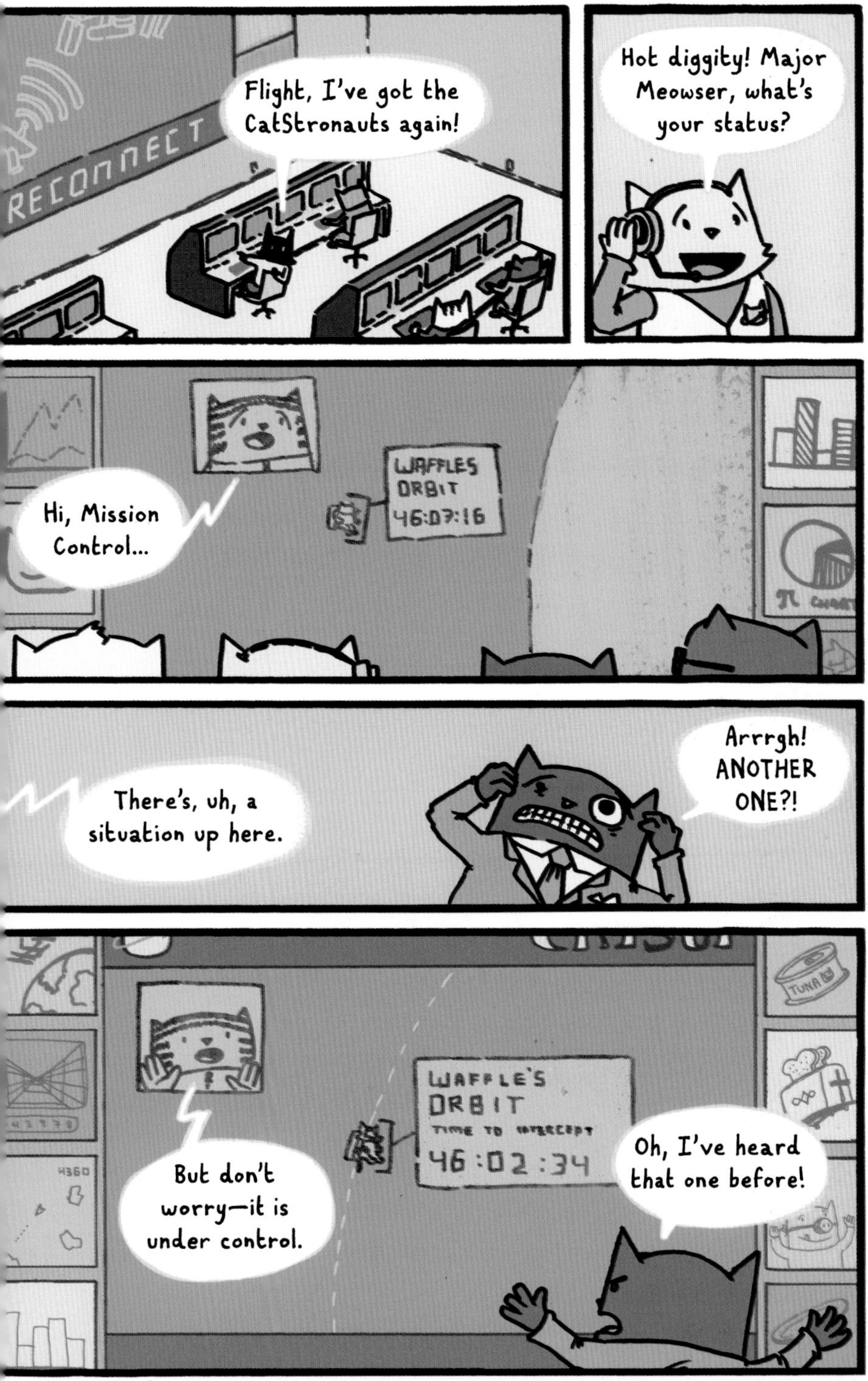
RECONNECT
Flight, I've got the CatStronauts again!
Hot diggity! Major Meowser, what's your status?
WAFFLES ORBIT 46:07:16
Hi, Mission Control...
There's, uh, a situation up here.
Arrrgh! ANOTHER ONE?!
WAFFLE'S ORBIT TIME TO INTERCEPT 46:02:34
TUNA
But don't worry—it is under control.
Oh, I've heard that one before!

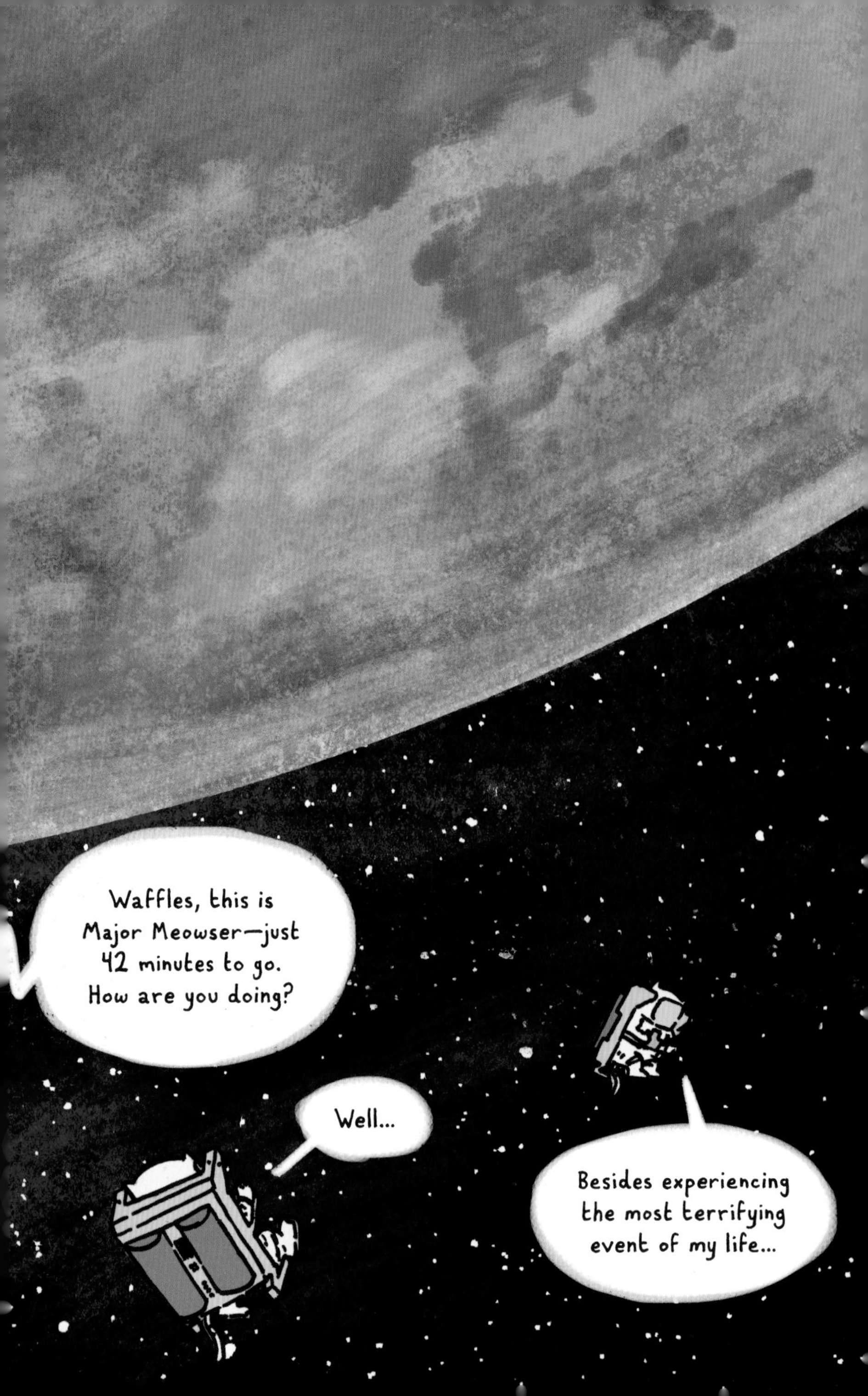
Waffles, this is Major Meowser—just 42 minutes to go. How are you doing?
Well...
Besides experiencing the most terrifying event of my life...

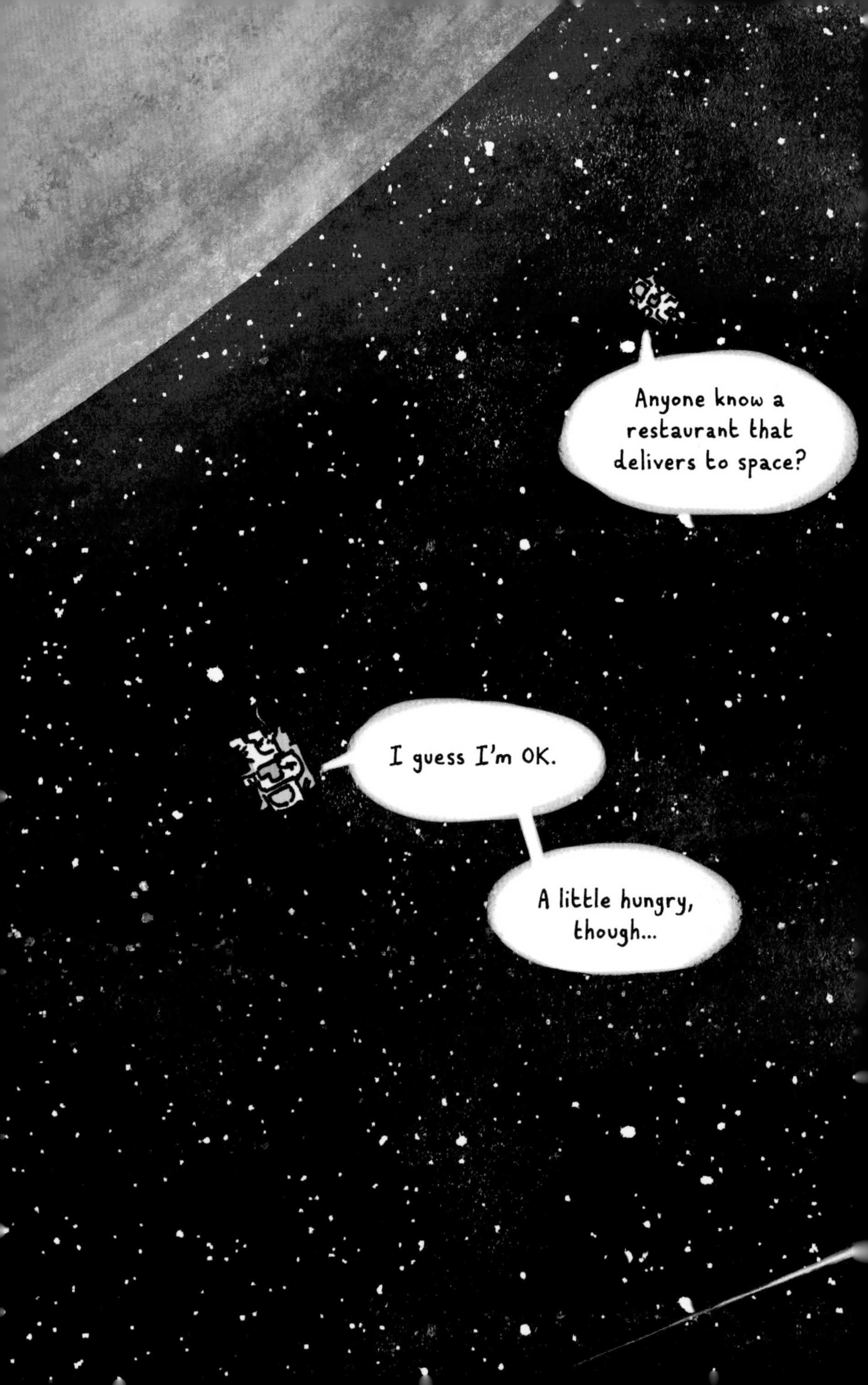
Anyone know a restaurant that delivers to space?
I guess I'm OK.
A little hungry, though...

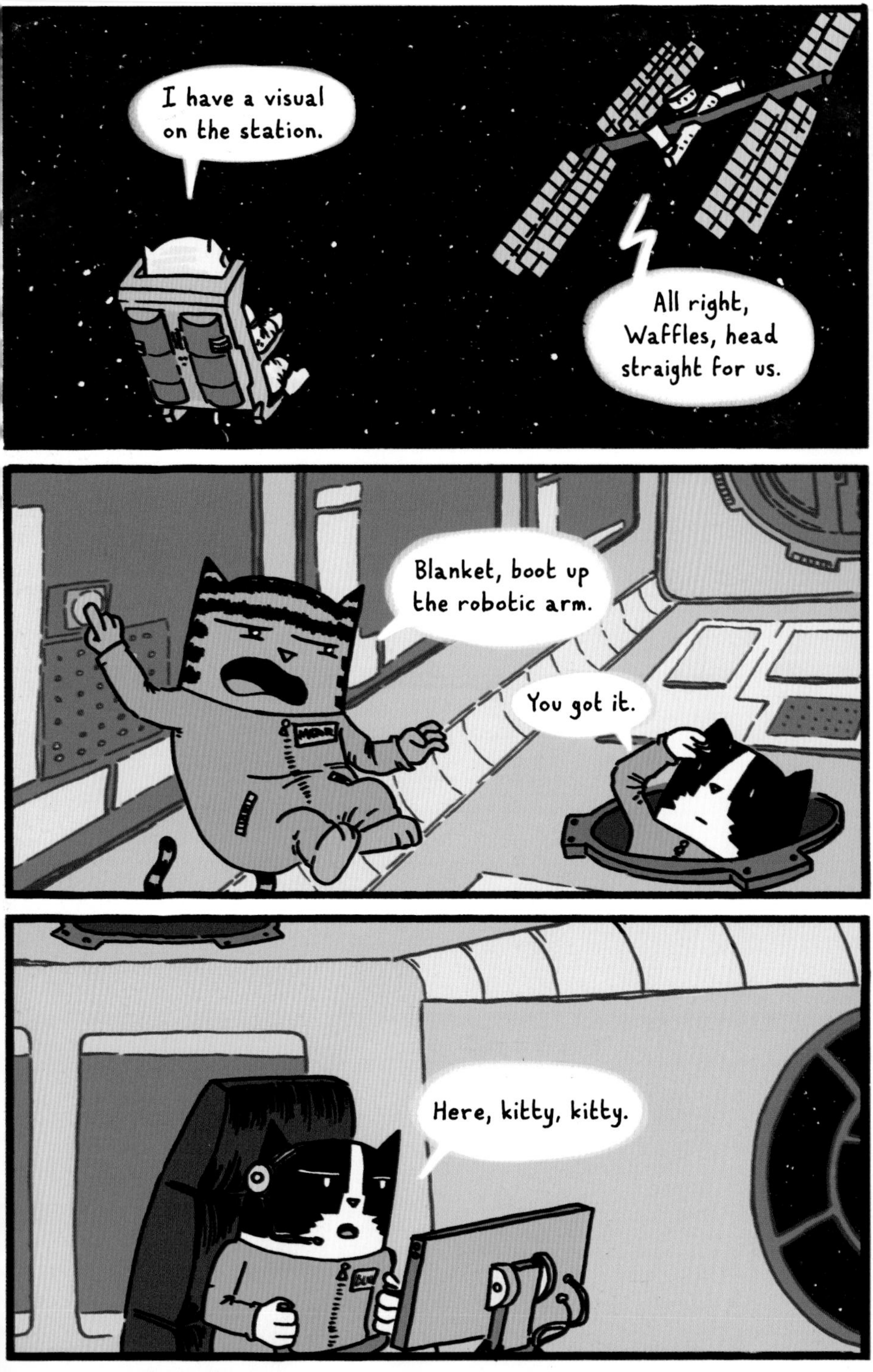
I have a visual on the station.
All right, Waffles, head straight for us.
Blanket, boot up the robotic arm.
You got it.
Here, kitty, kitty.

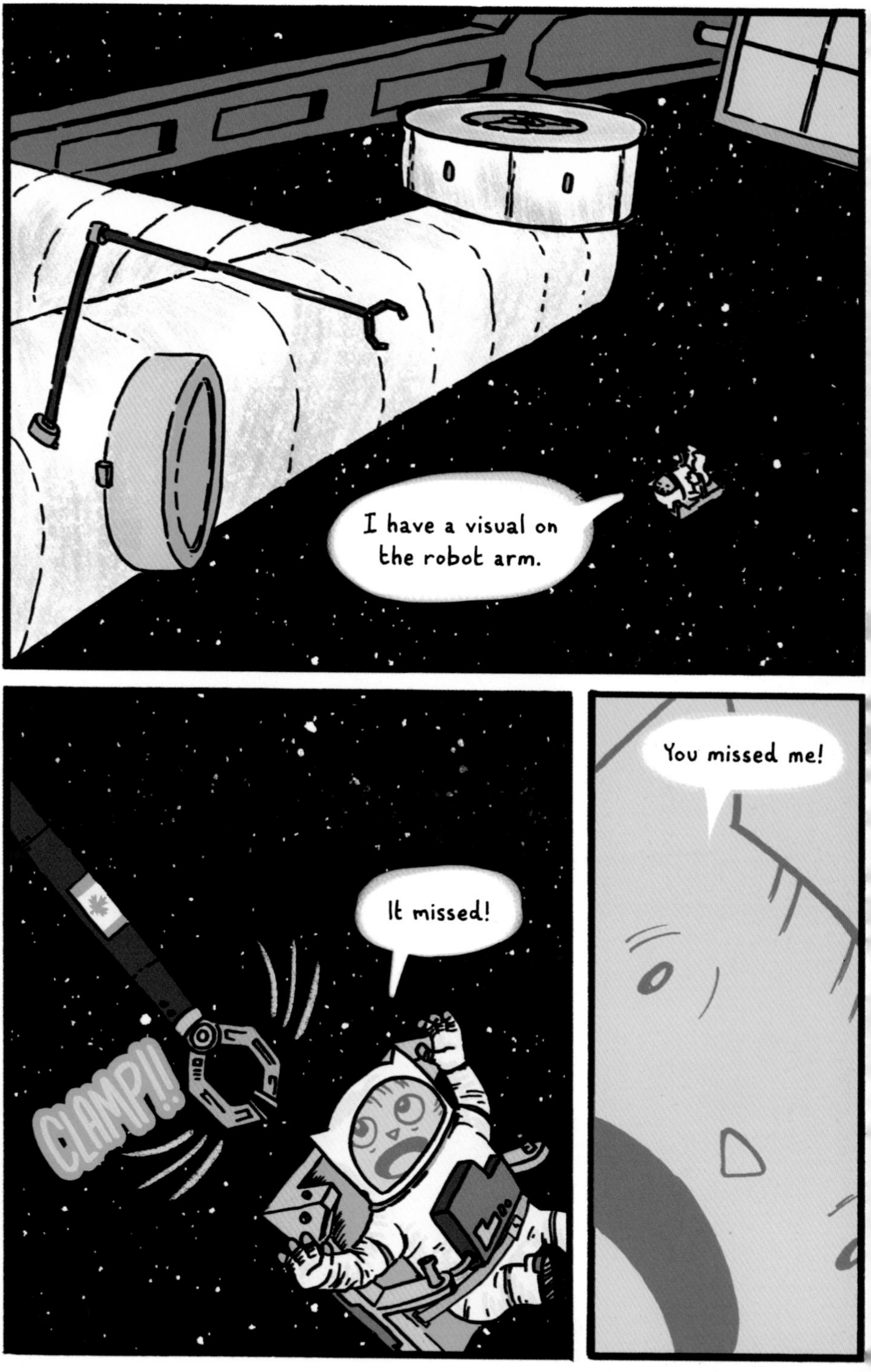
I have a visual on the robot arm.
It missed!
CLAMP!!
You missed me!

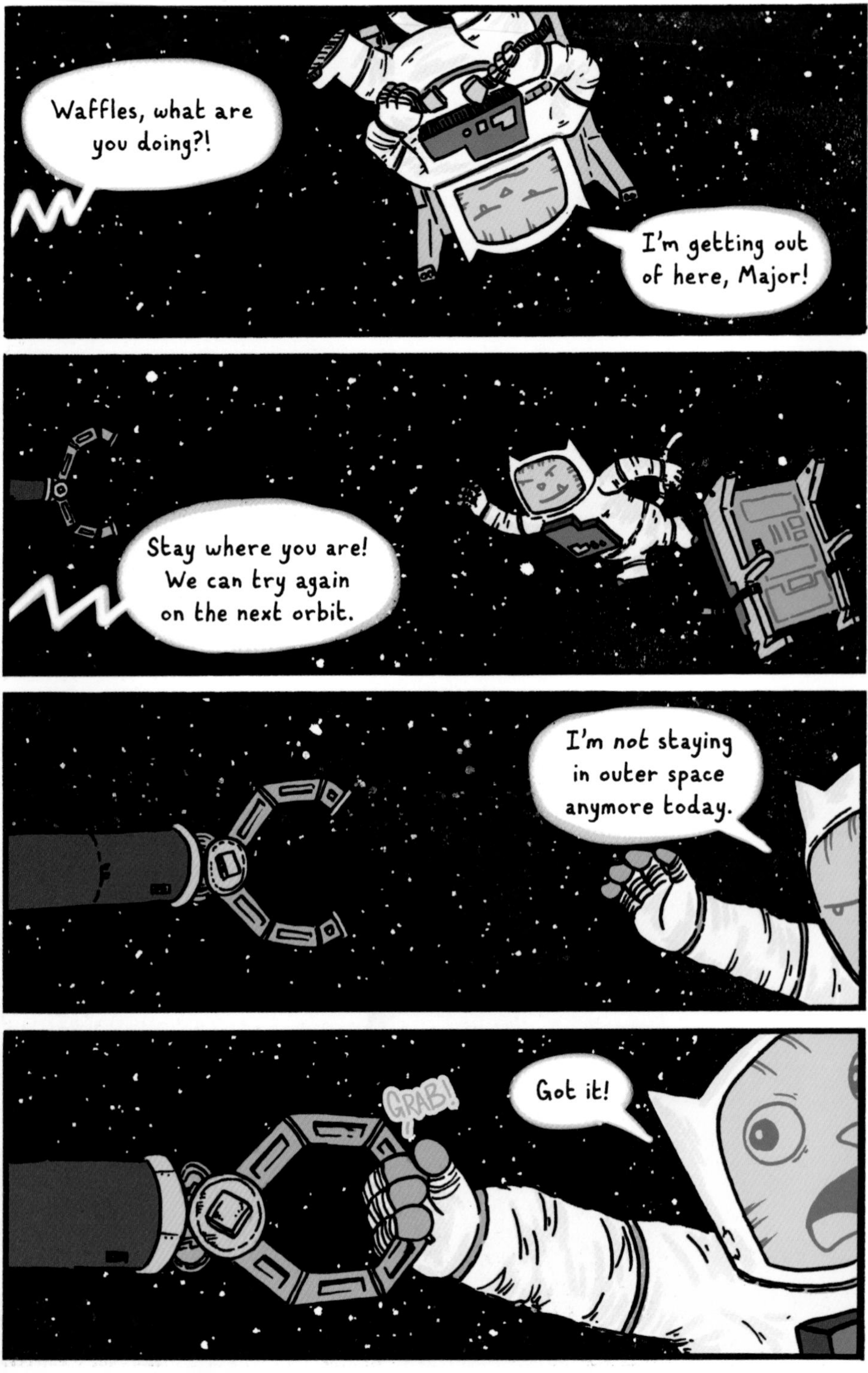
Waffles, what are you doing?!
I'm getting out of here, Major!
Stay where you are! We can try again on the next orbit.
I'm not staying in outer space anymore today.
GRAB!
Got it!

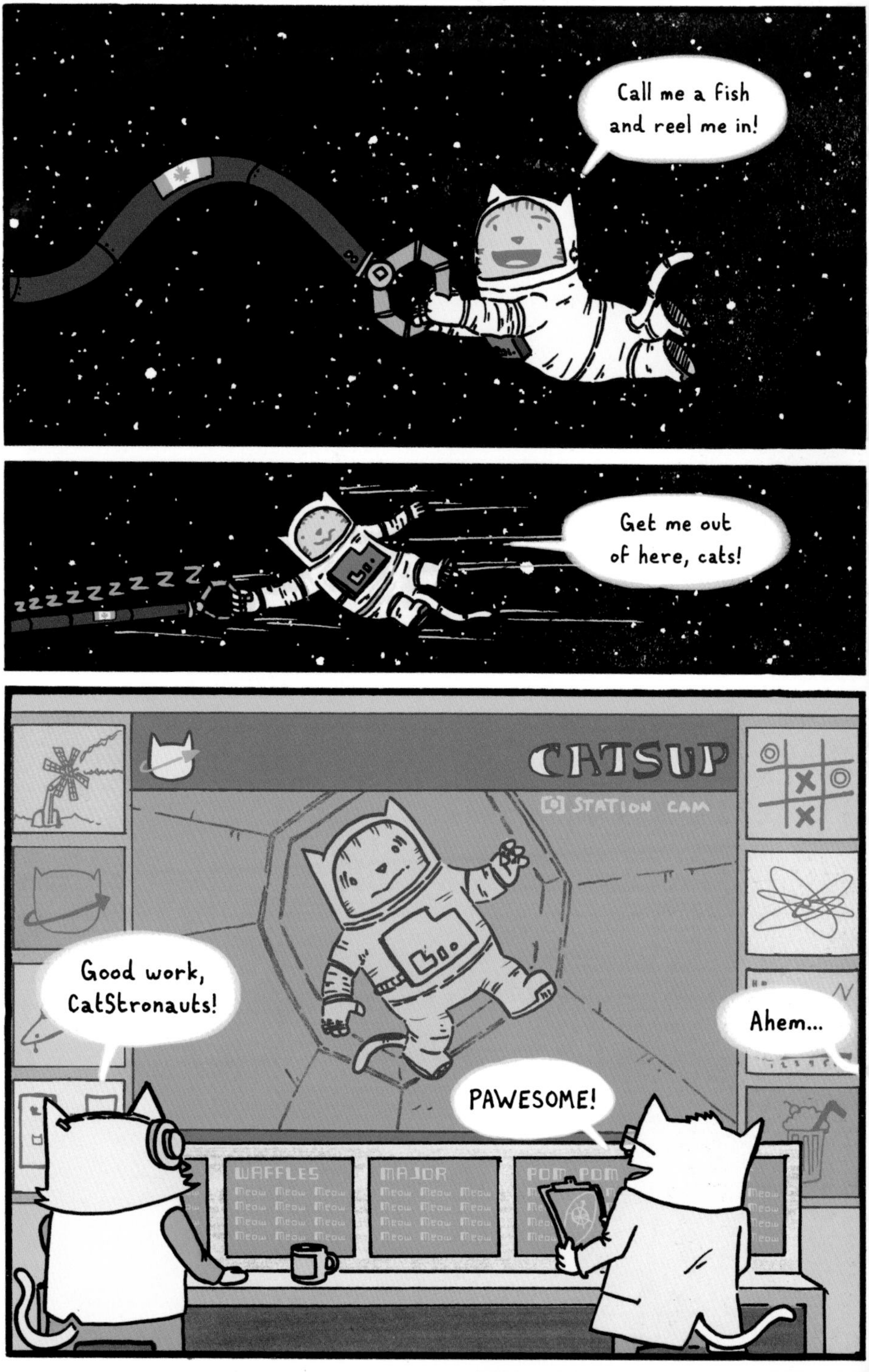
Call me a fish and reel me in!
Get me out of here, cats!
CATSUP
STATION CAM
Good work, CatStronauts!
PAWESOME!
Ahem...
WAFFLES
MAJOR
POM POM

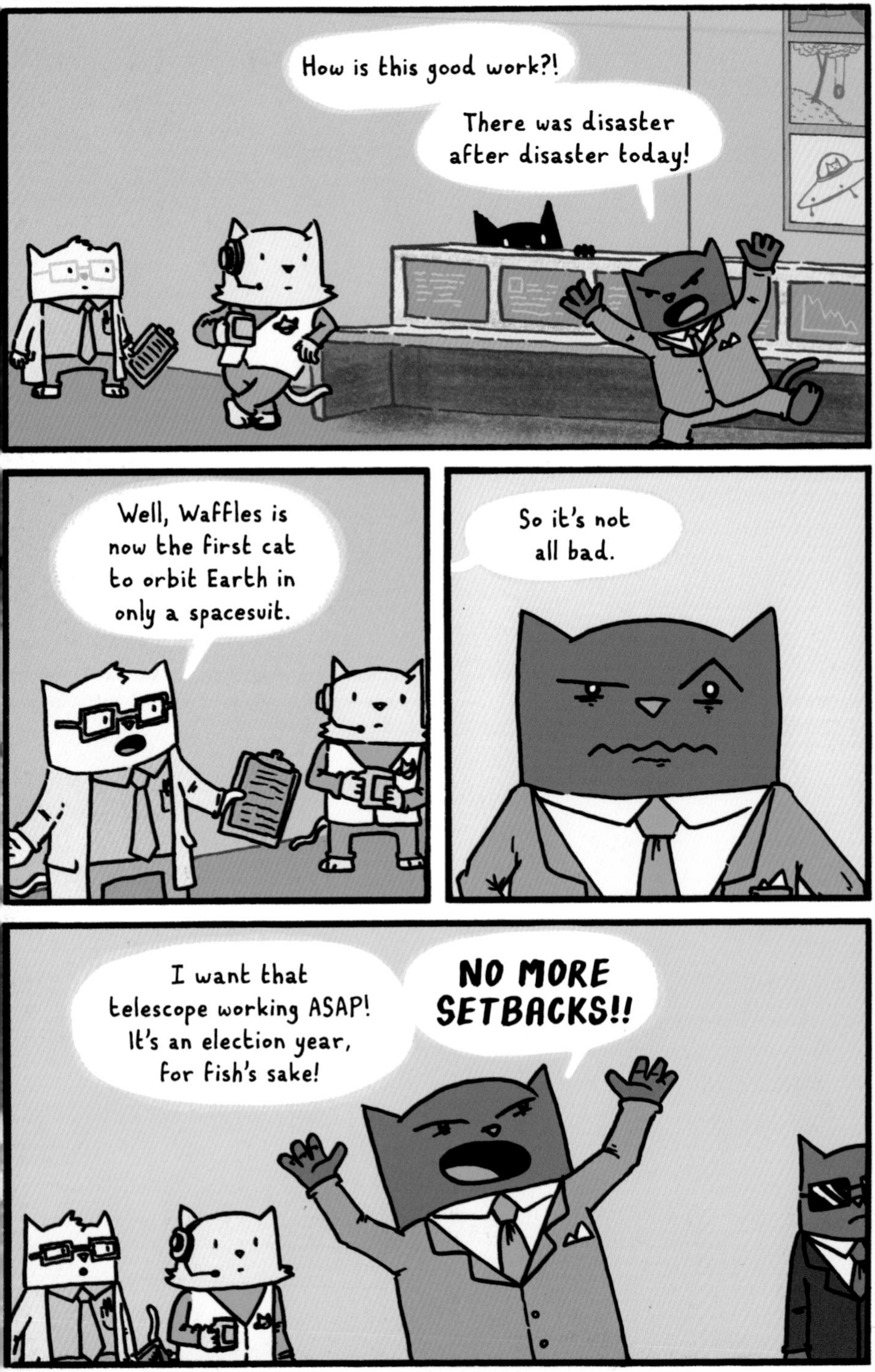

How is this good work?!
There was disaster after disaster today!
Well, Waffles is now the first cat to orbit Earth in only a spacesuit.
So it's not all bad.
I want that telescope working ASAP! It's an election year, for fish's sake!
NO MORE SETBACKS!!

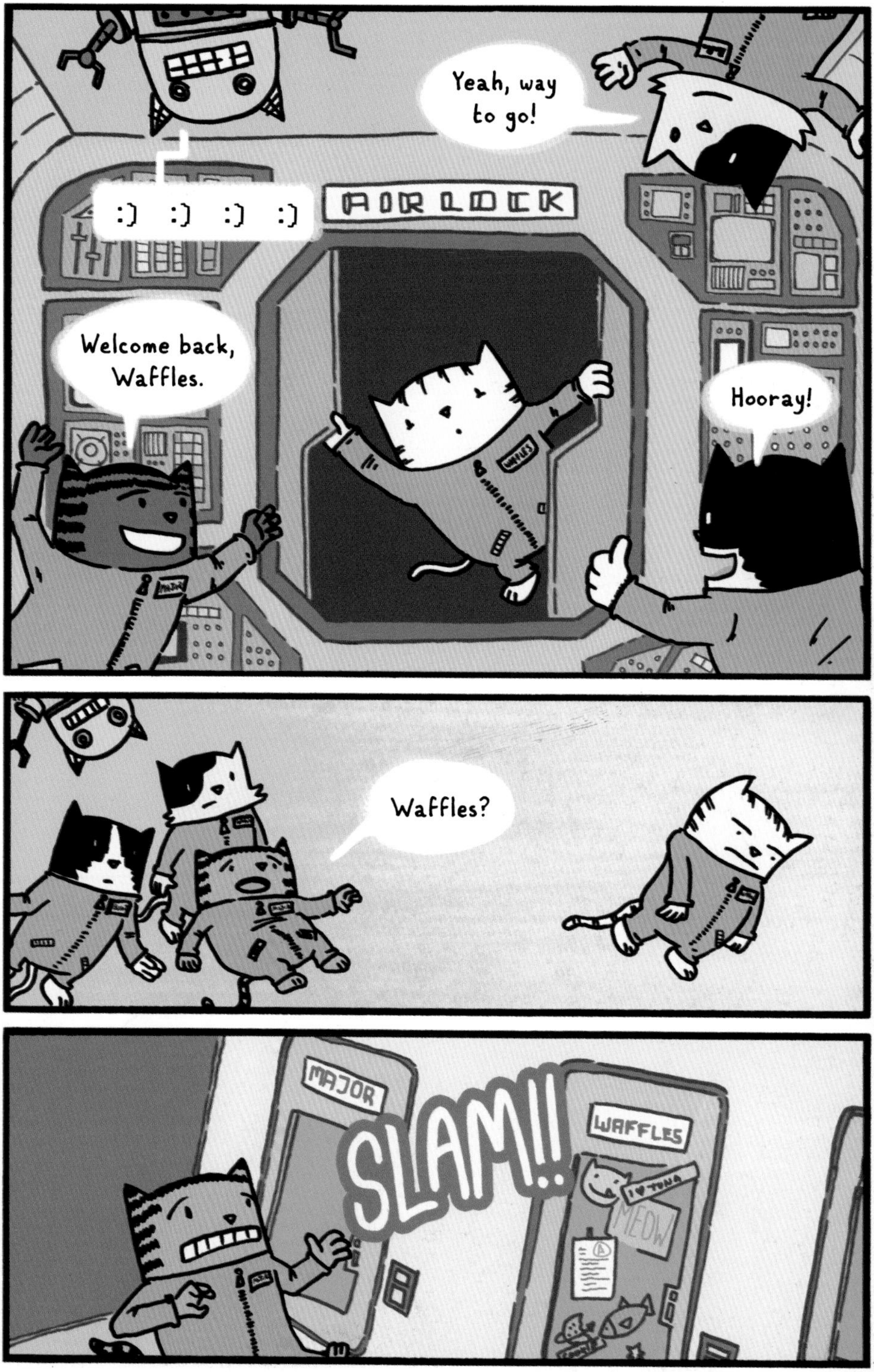
:) :) :) :)
Yeah, way to go!
AIRLOCK
Welcome back, Waffles.
Hooray!
Waffles?
MAJOR
SLAM!!
WAFFLES
I ♥ TUNA
MEOW

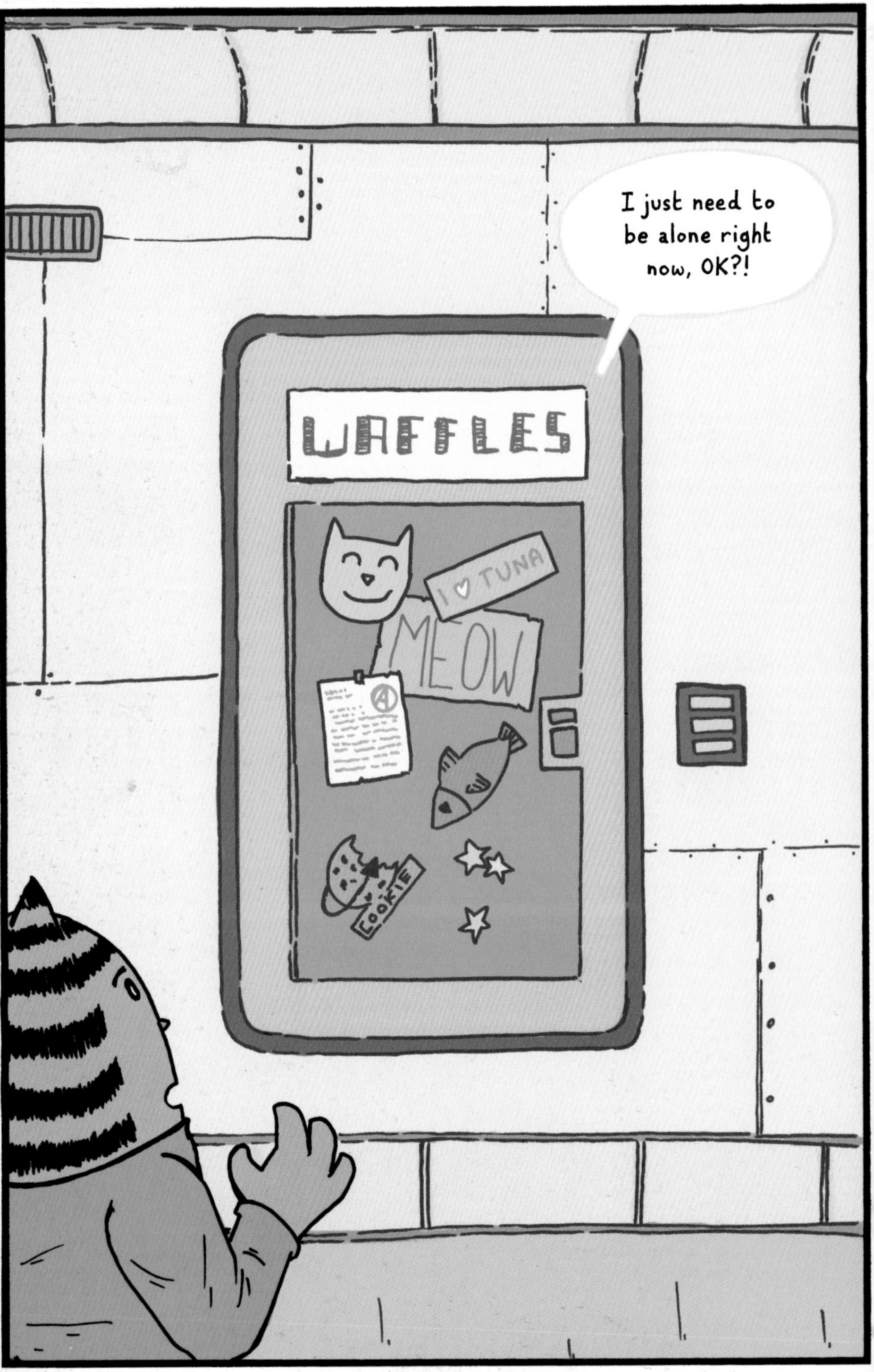
I just need to be alone right now, OK?!
WAFFLES
I ♡ TUNA
MEOW
COOKIE

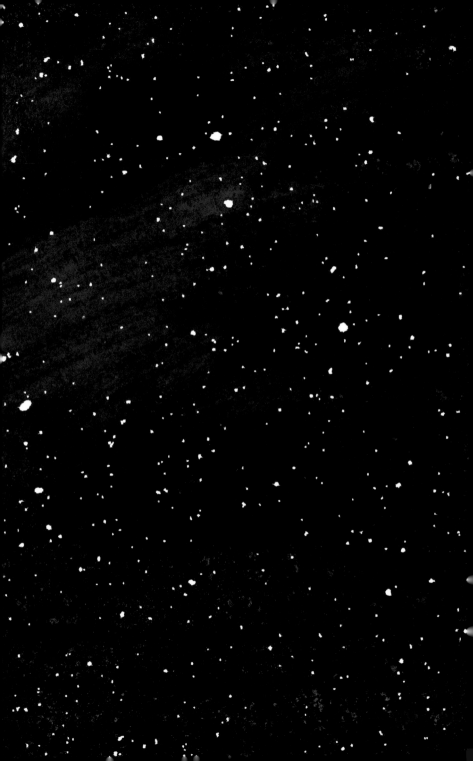

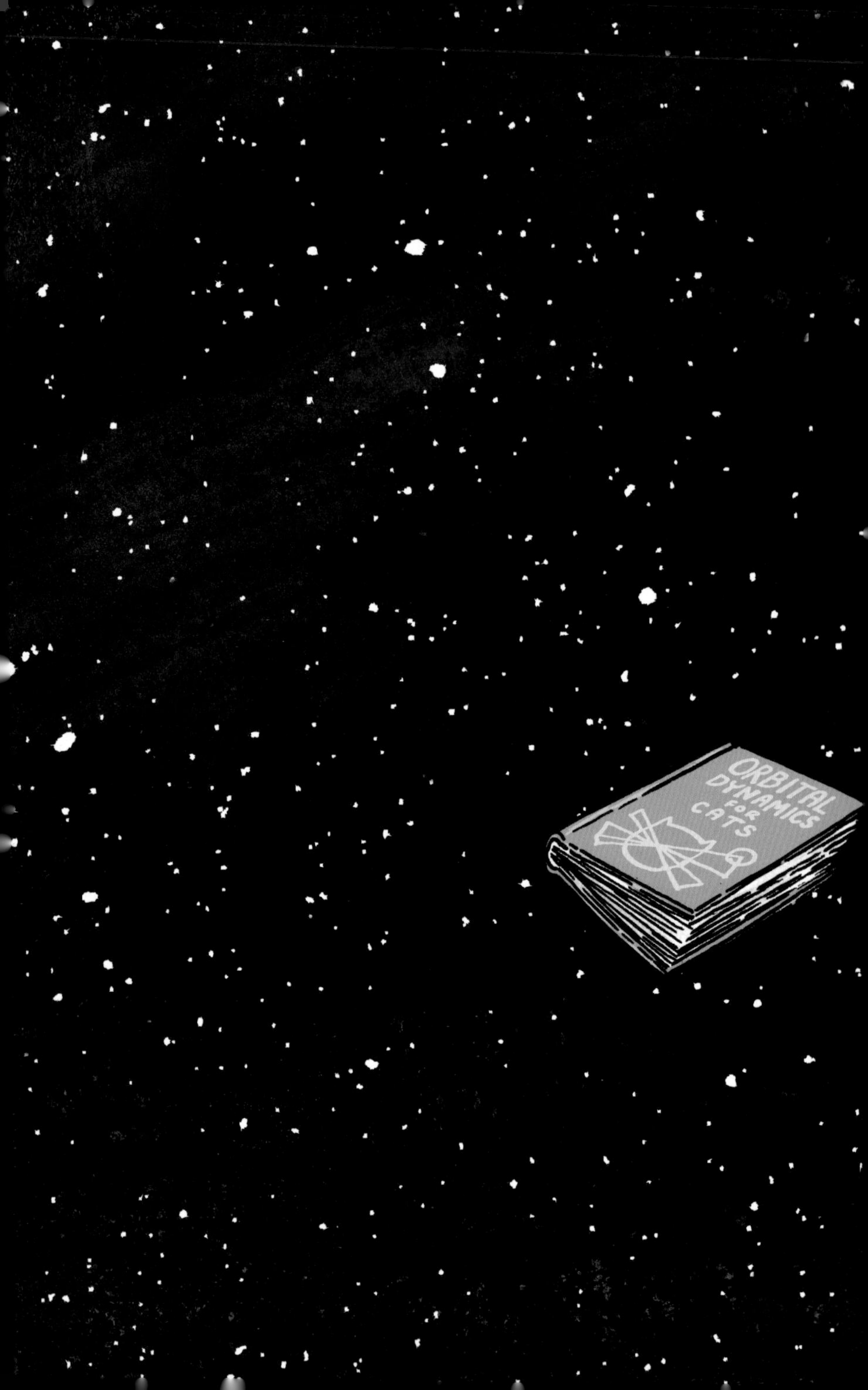
ORBITAL
DYNAMICS
FOR
CATS

CHAPTER 4

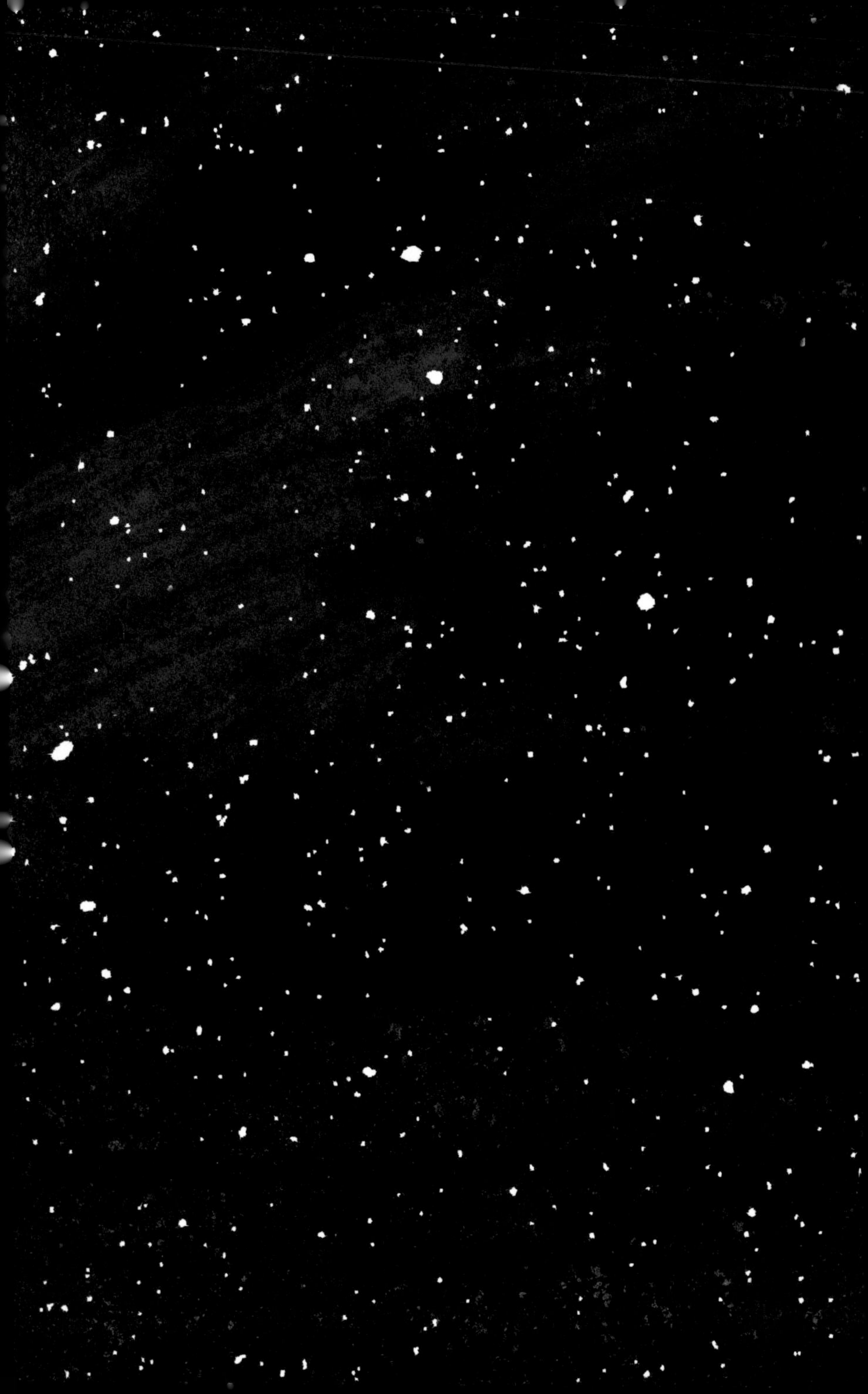

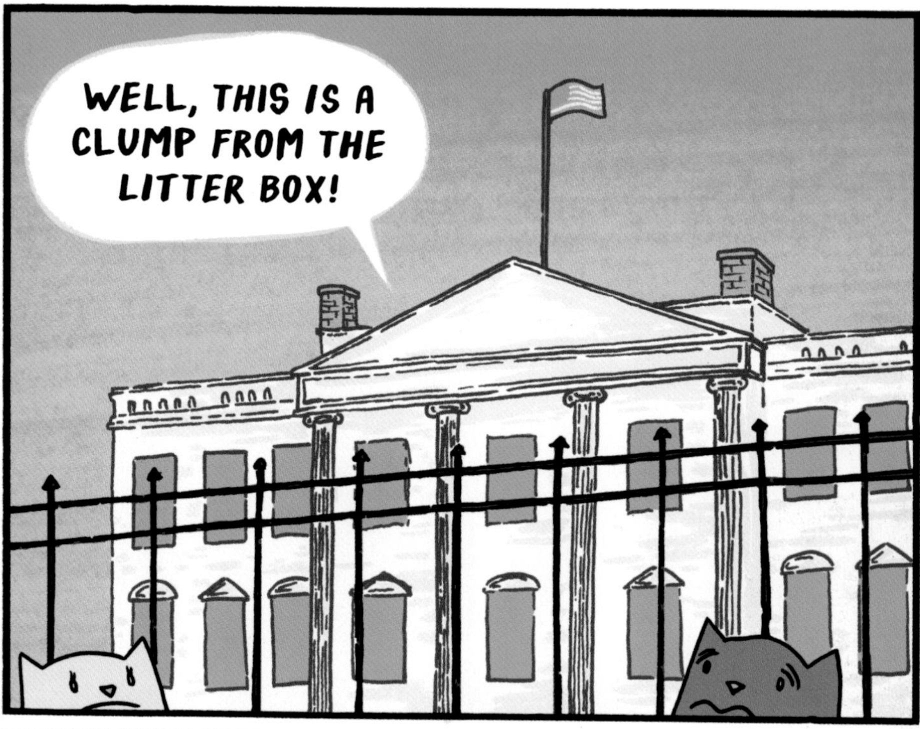
WELL, THIS IS A CLUMP FROM THE LITTER BOX!

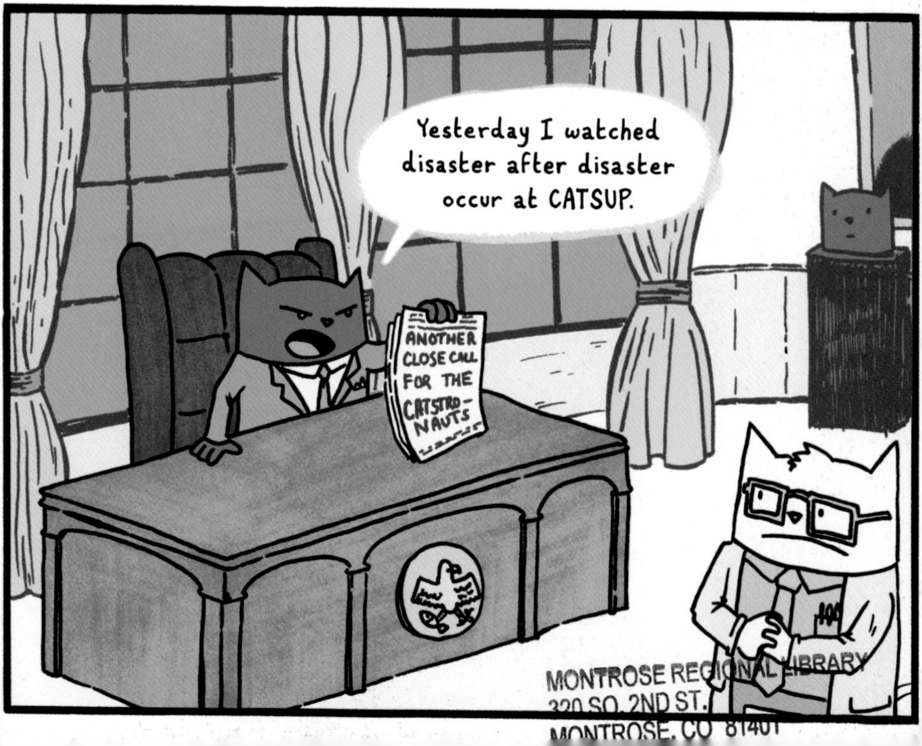
Yesterday I watched disaster after disaster occur at CATSUP.
ANOTHER CLOSE CALL FOR THE CATSTRONAUTS

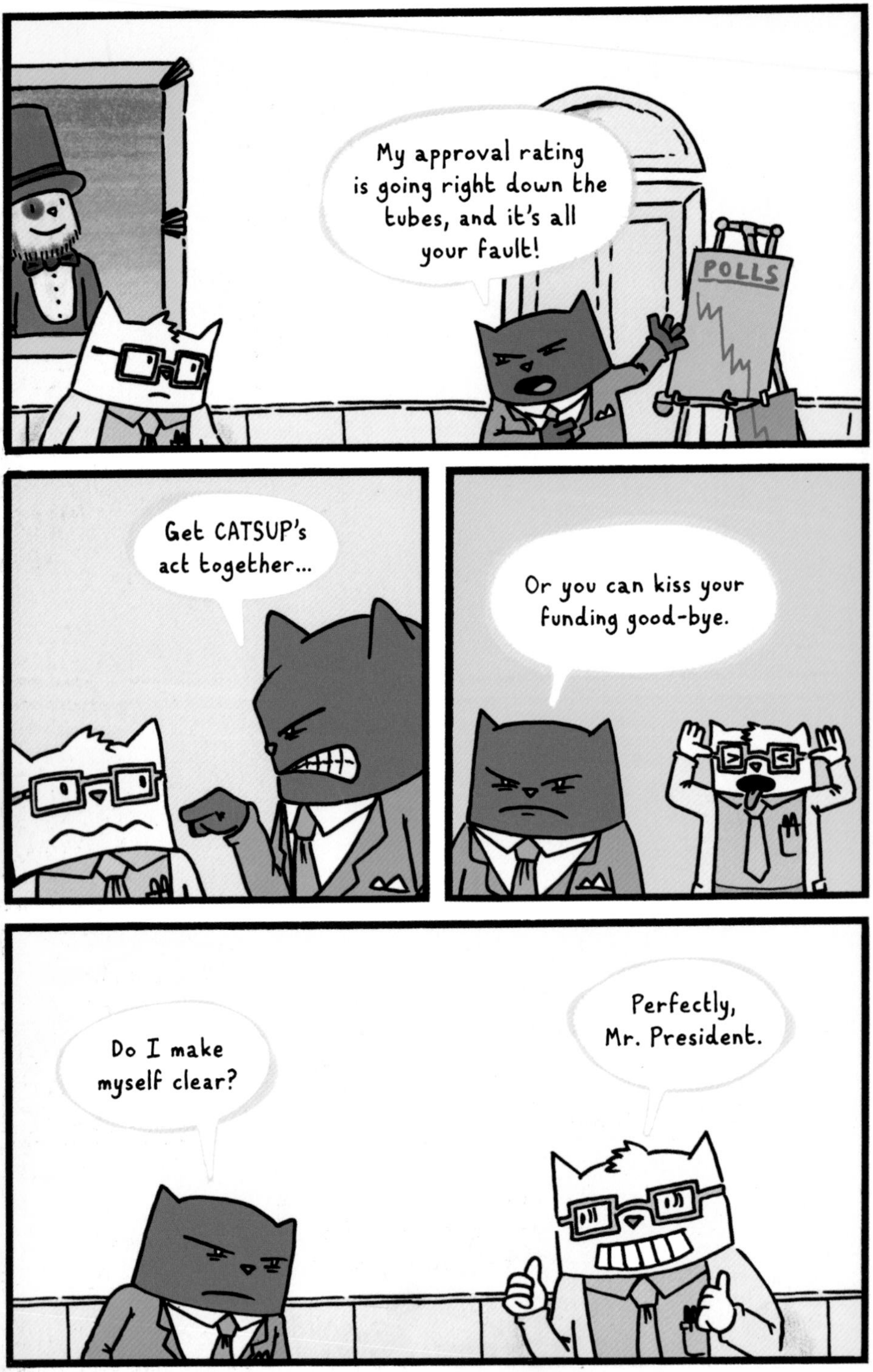
My approval rating is going right down the tubes, and it's all your fault!
POLLS
Get CATSUP's act together...
Or you can kiss your funding good-bye.
Do I make myself clear?
Perfectly, Mr. President.

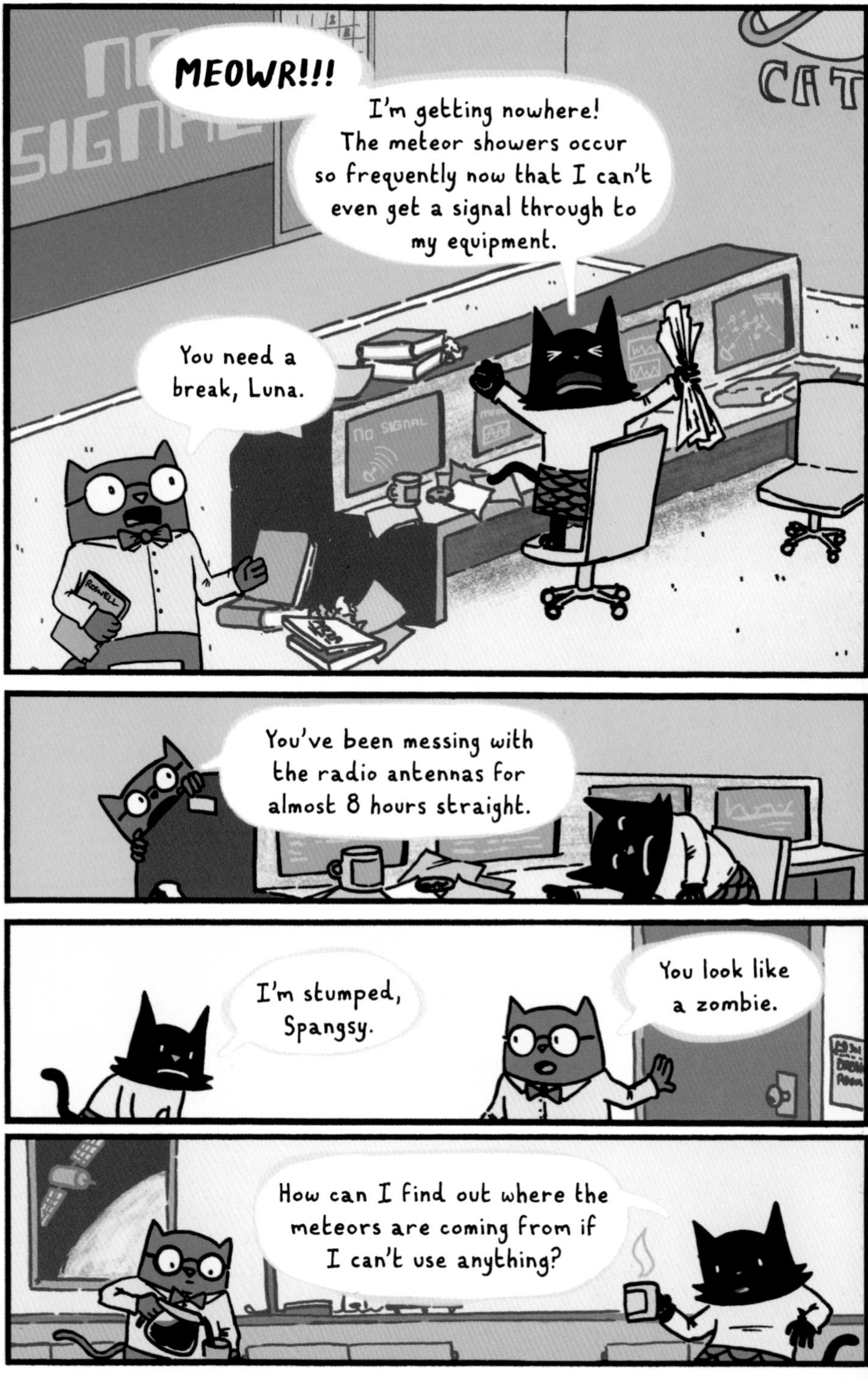
MEOWR!!!
I'm getting nowhere! The meteor showers occur so frequently now that I can't even get a signal through to my equipment.
You need a break, Luna.
NO SIGNAL
ROSWELL
You've been messing with the radio antennas for almost 8 hours straight.
I'm stumped, Spangsy.
You look like a zombie.
How can I find out where the meteors are coming from if I can't use anything?

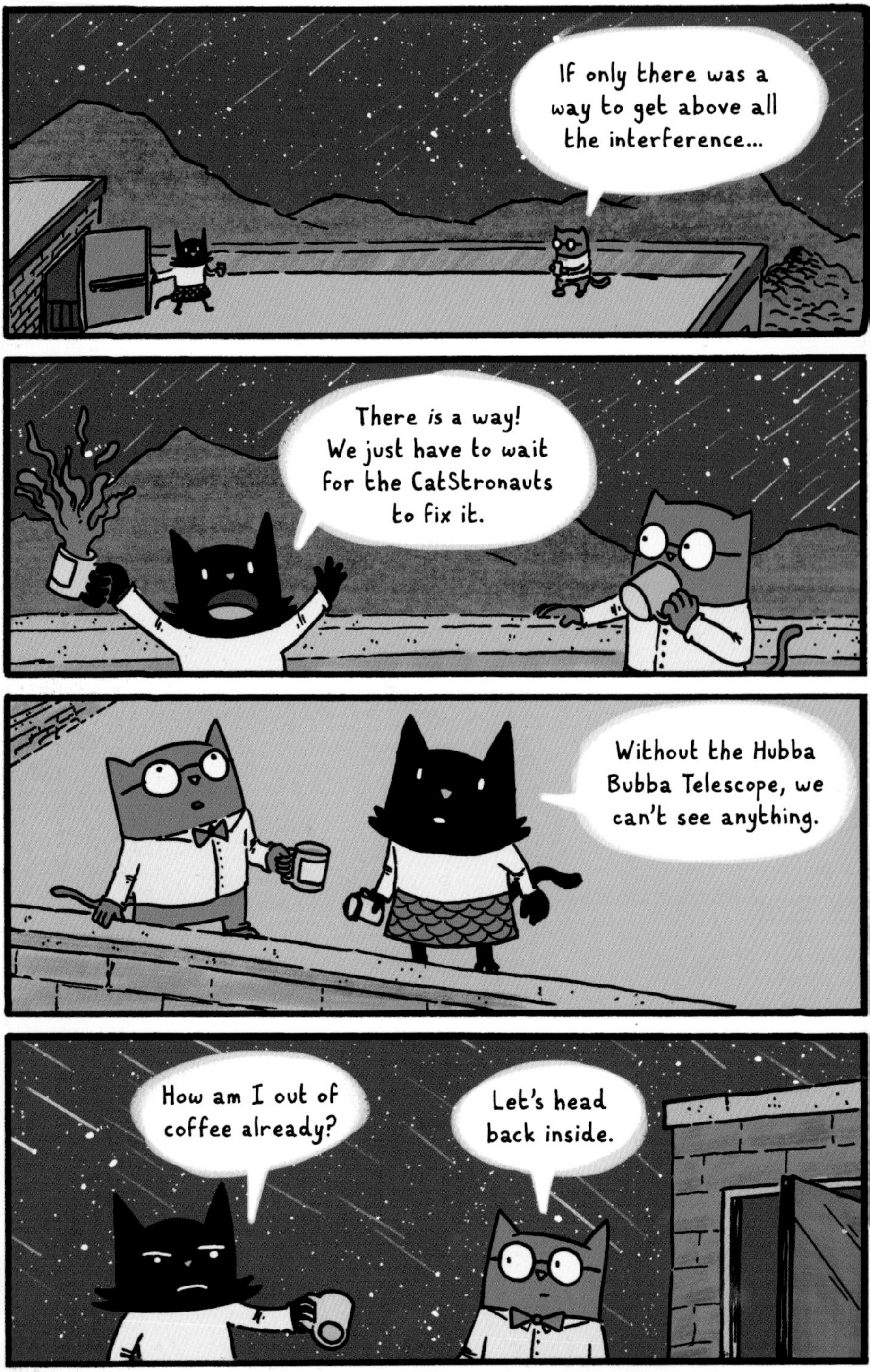
If only there was a way to get above all the interference...
There *is* a way! We just have to wait for the CatStronauts to fix it.
Without the Hubba Bubba Telescope, we can't see anything.
How am I out of coffee already?
Let's head back inside.

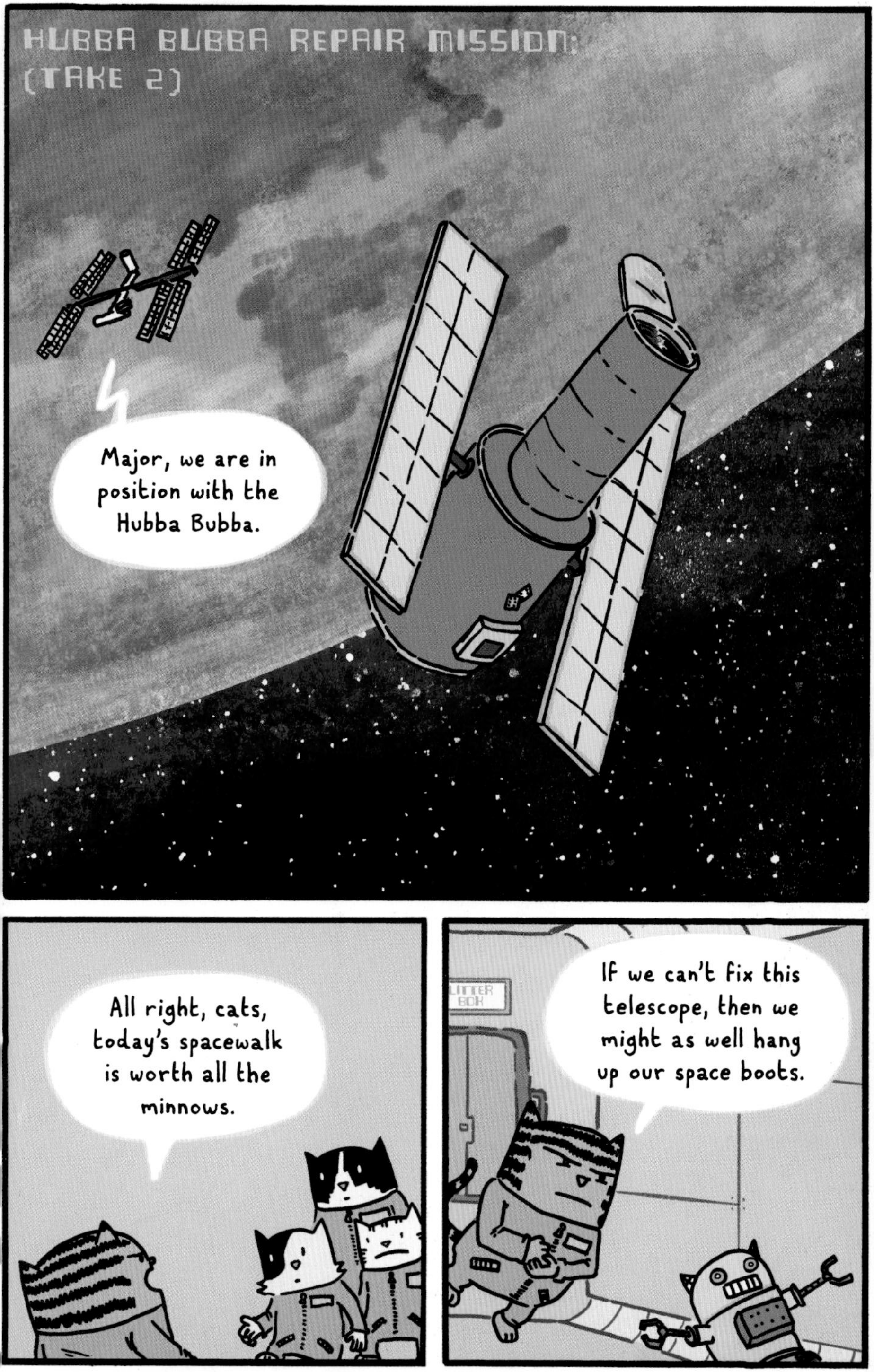
HUBBA BUBBA REPAIR MISSION:
(TAKE 2)
Major, we are in position with the Hubba Bubba.
All right, cats, today's spacewalk is worth all the minnows.
LITTER BOX
If we can't fix this telescope, then we might as well hang up our space boots.

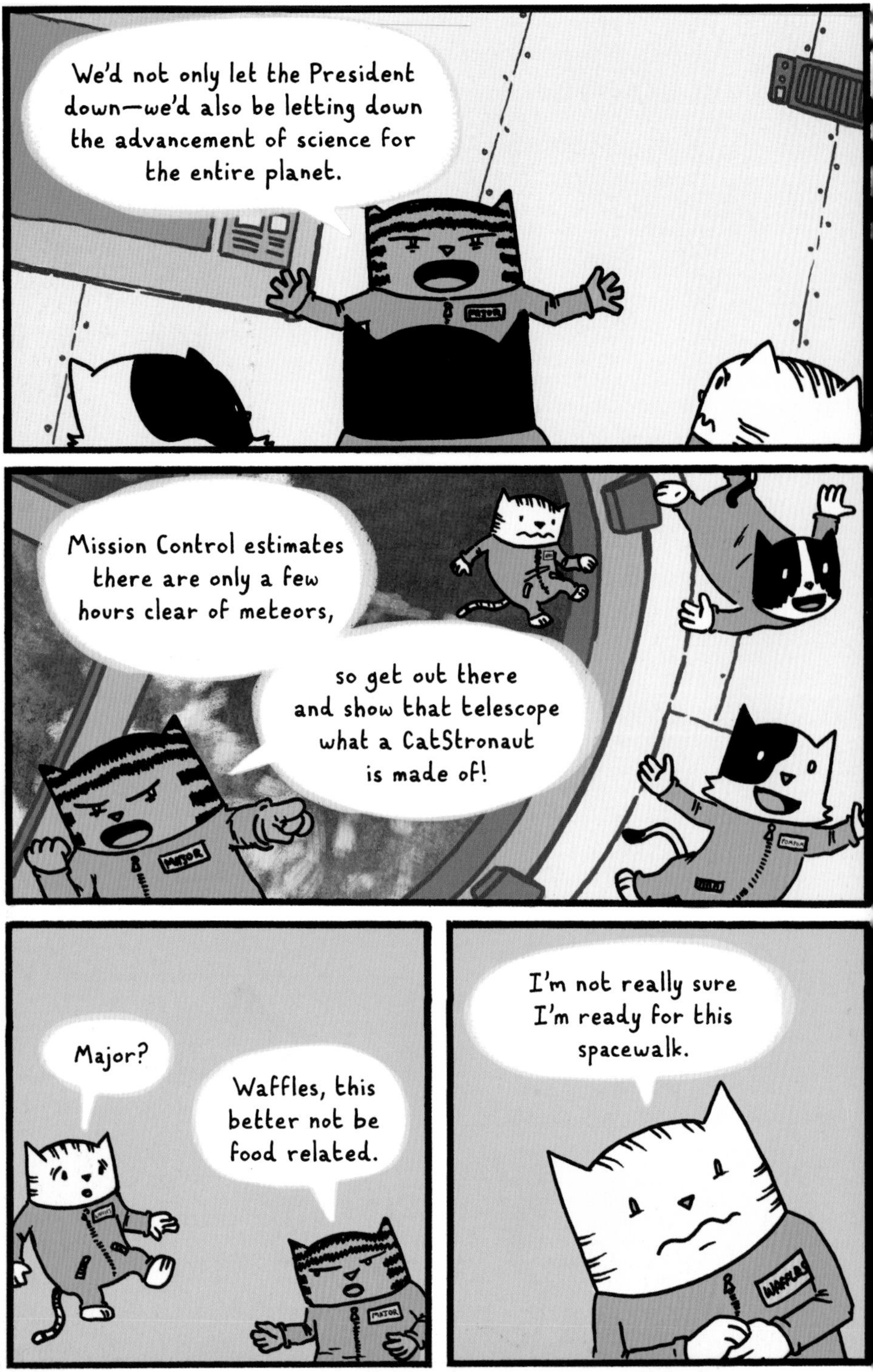
We'd not only let the President down—we'd also be letting down the advancement of science for the entire planet.
Mission Control estimates there are only a few hours clear of meteors,
so get out there and show that telescope what a CatStronaut is made of!
Major?
Waffles, this better not be food related.
I'm not really sure I'm ready for this spacewalk.

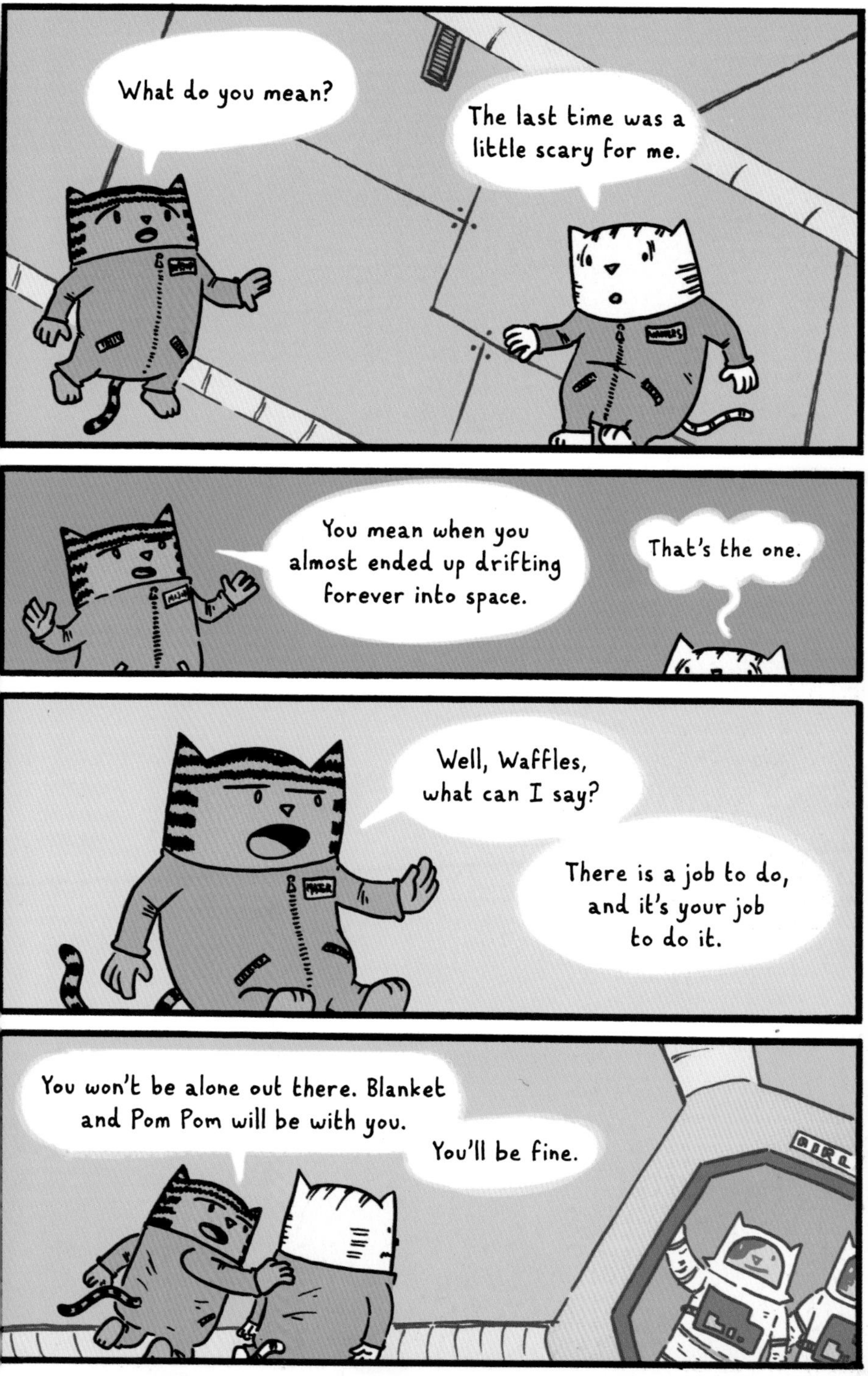
What do you mean?
The last time was a little scary for me.
You mean when you almost ended up drifting forever into space.
That's the one.
Well, Waffles, what can I say?
There is a job to do, and it's your job to do it.
You won't be alone out there. Blanket and Pom Pom will be with you.
You'll be fine.

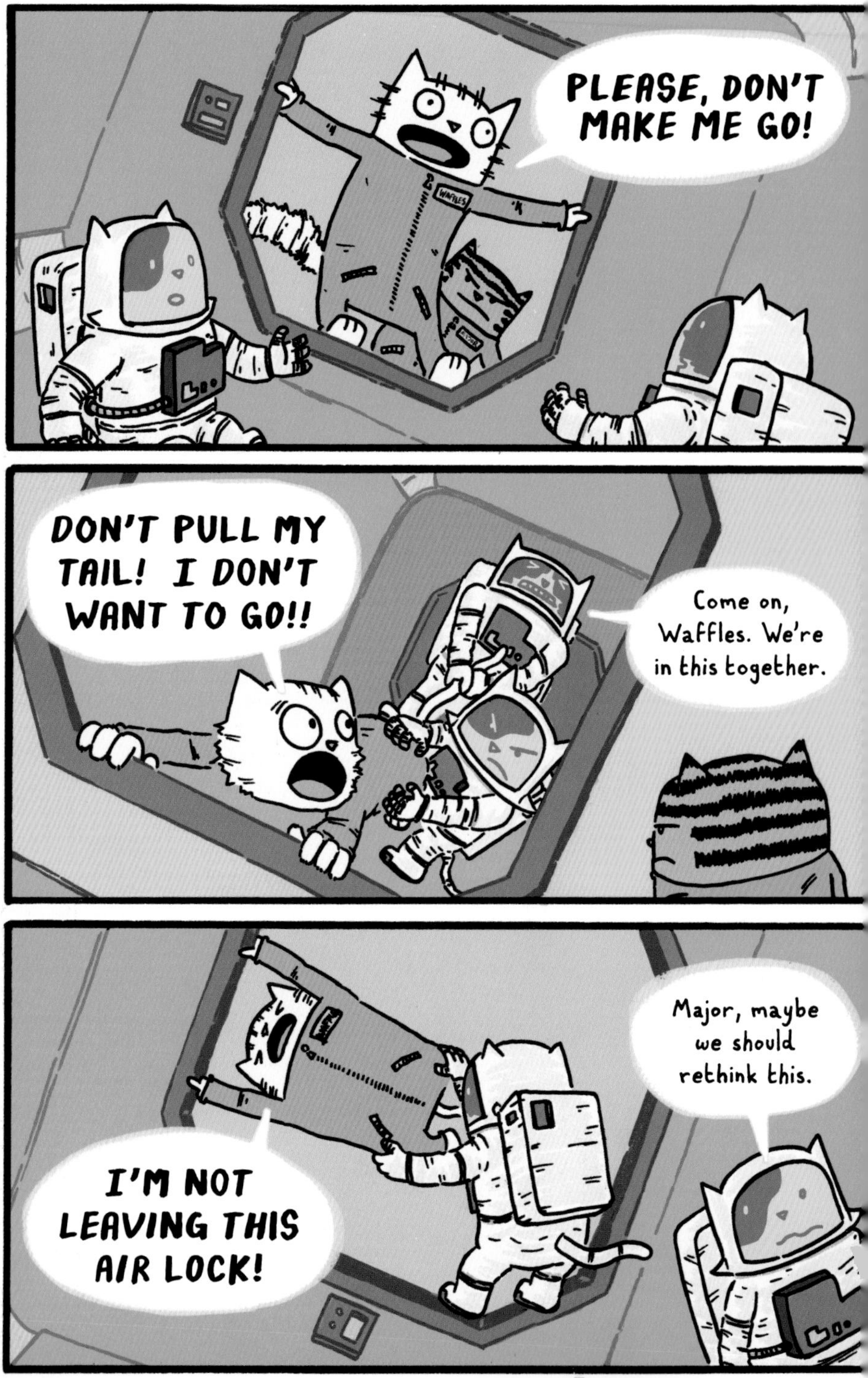
PLEASE, DON'T MAKE ME GO!
WAFFLES
DON'T PULL MY TAIL! I DON'T WANT TO GO!!
Come on, Waffles. We're in this together.
Major, maybe we should rethink this.
I'M NOT LEAVING THIS AIR LOCK!

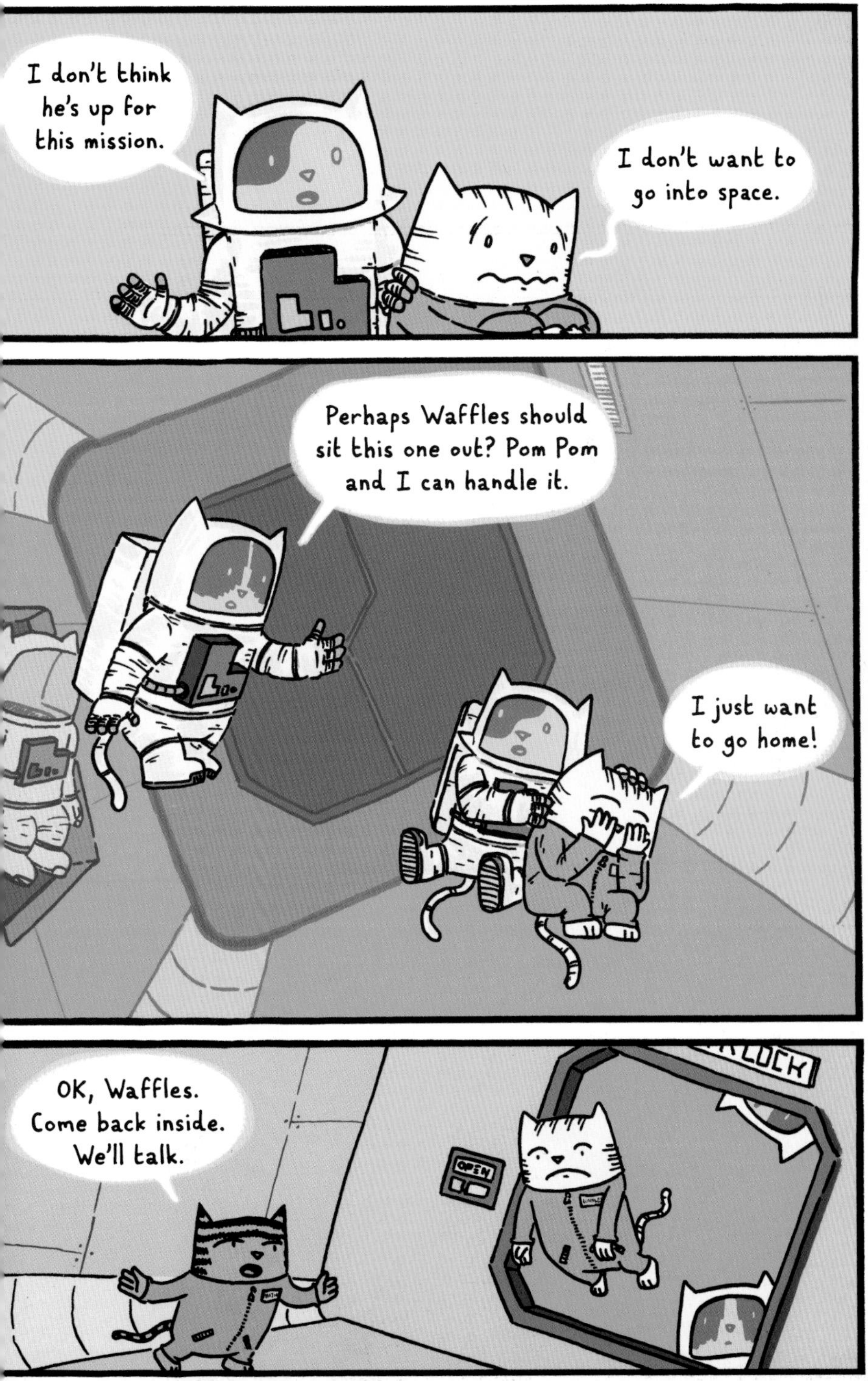

I don't think he's up for this mission.
I don't want to go into space.
Perhaps Waffles should sit this one out? Pom Pom and I can handle it.
I just want to go home!
OK, Waffles. Come back inside. We'll talk.

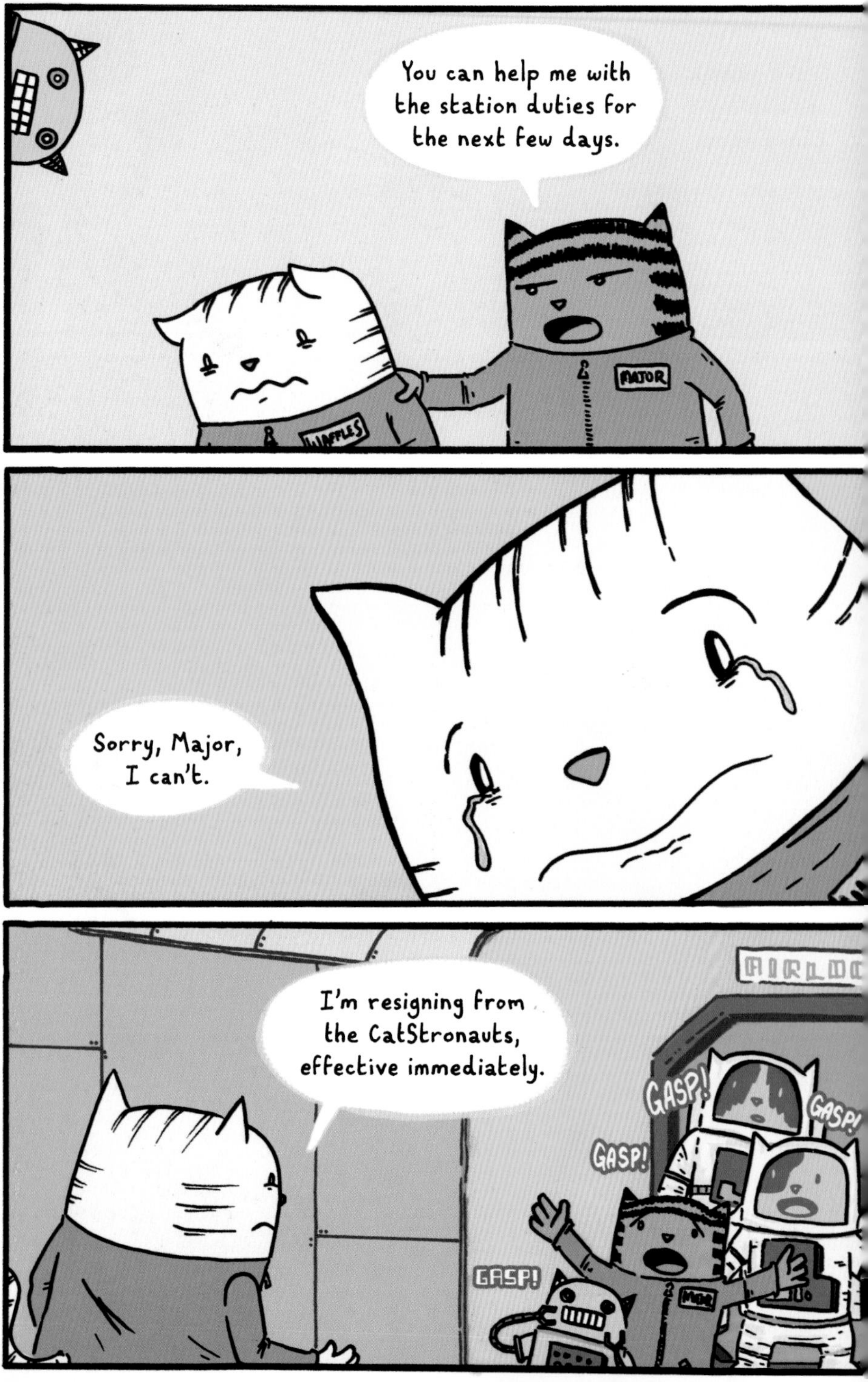
You can help me with the station duties for the next few days.
WAFFLES
MAJOR
Sorry, Major, I can't.
I'm resigning from the CatStronauts, effective immediately.
GASP!
GASP!
GASP!
GASP!

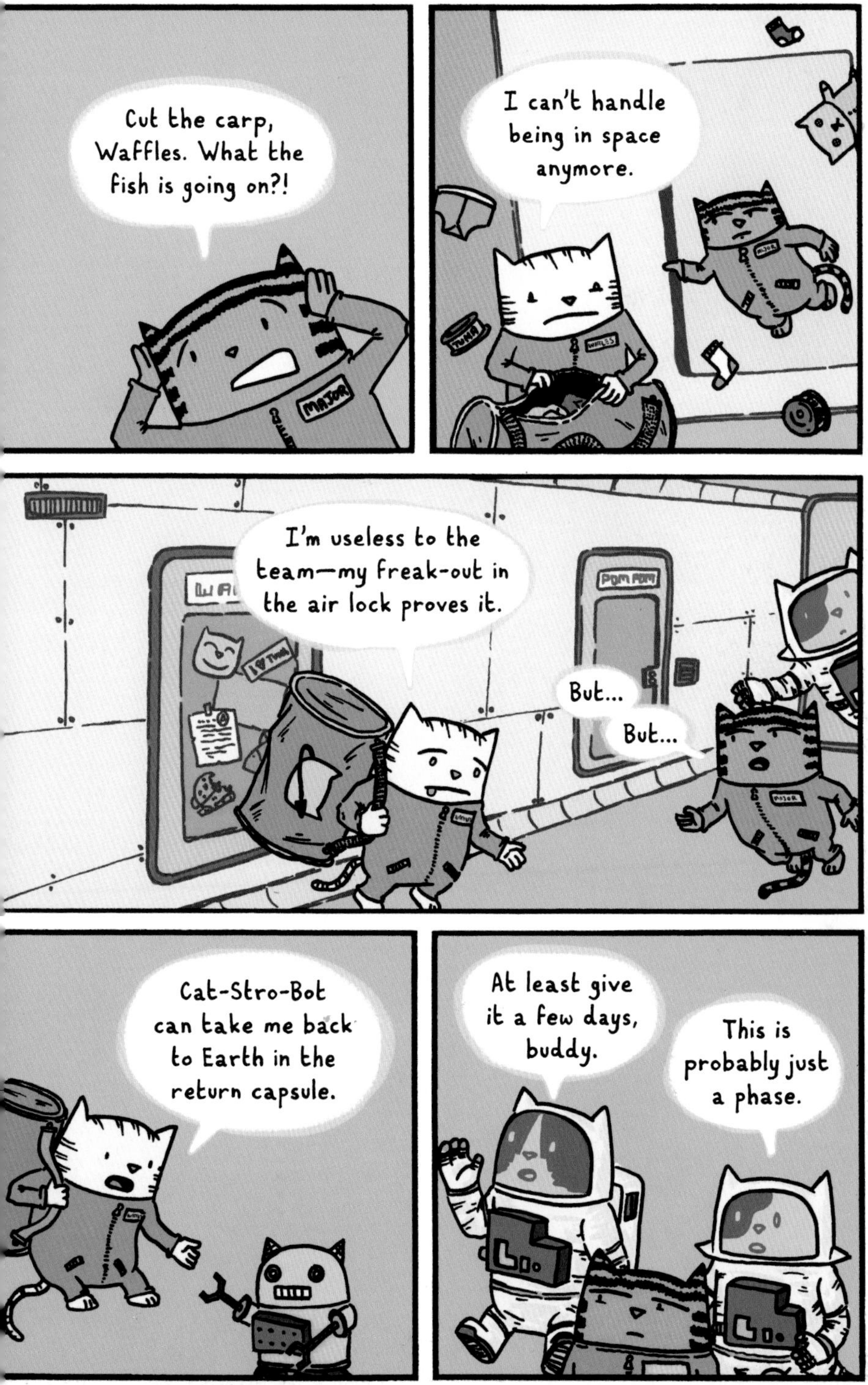
Cut the carp, Waffles. What the fish is going on?!
MAJOR
I can't handle being in space anymore.
TUNA
WAFFLES
MAJOR
I'm useless to the team—my freak-out in the air lock proves it.
POM POM
I ♥ TUNA
But...
But...
MAJOR
Cat-Stro-Bot can take me back to Earth in the return capsule.
At least give it a few days, buddy.
This is probably just a phase.

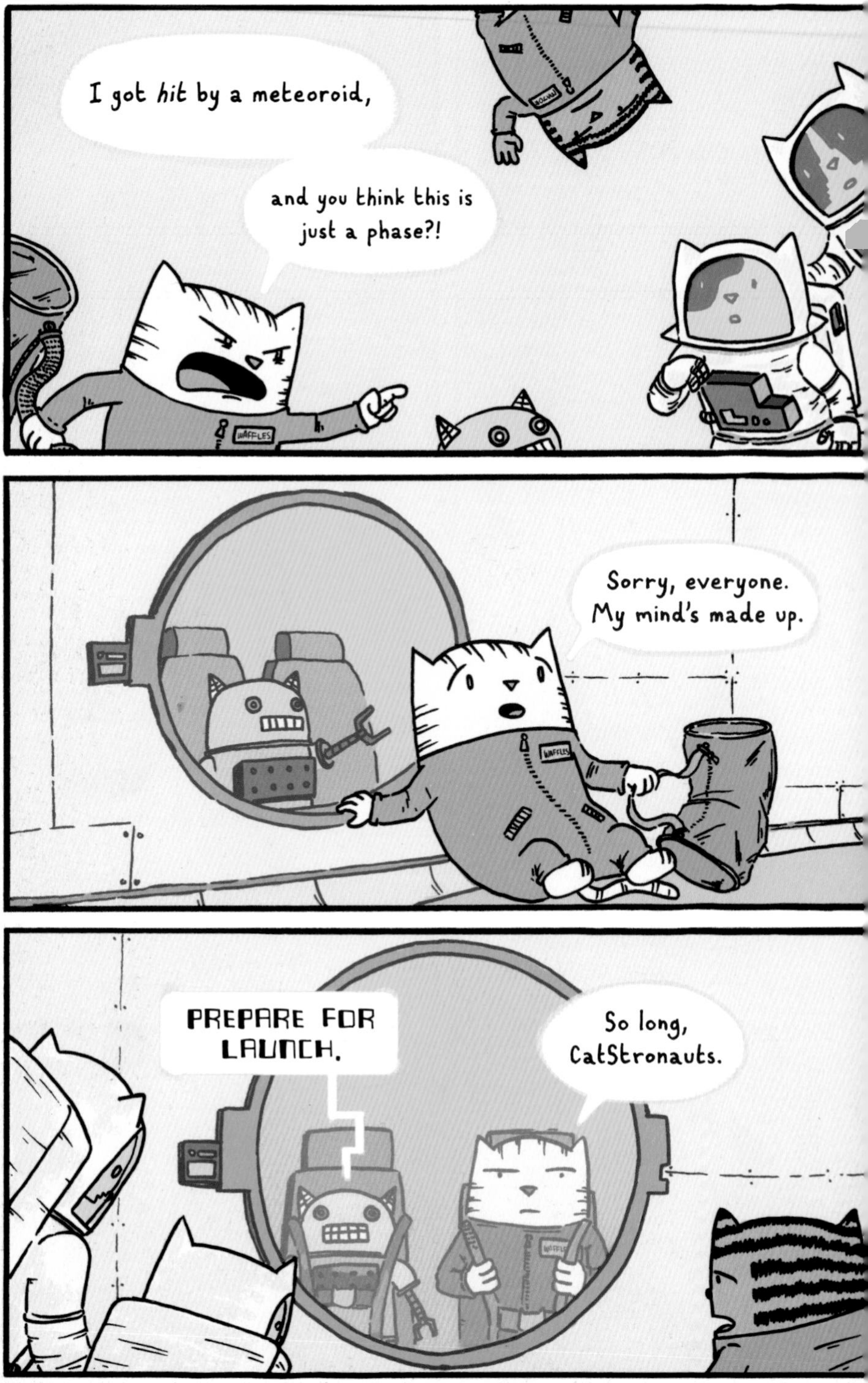

I got *hit* by a meteoroid,
and you think this is just a phase?!
Sorry, everyone. My mind's made up.
PREPARE FOR LAUNCH.
So long, CatStronauts.

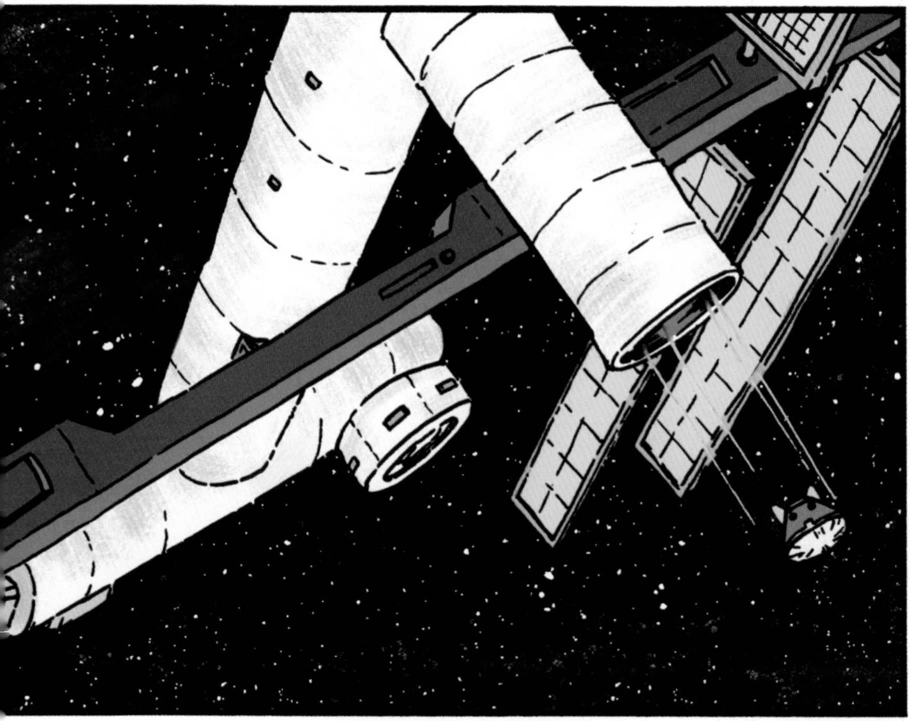

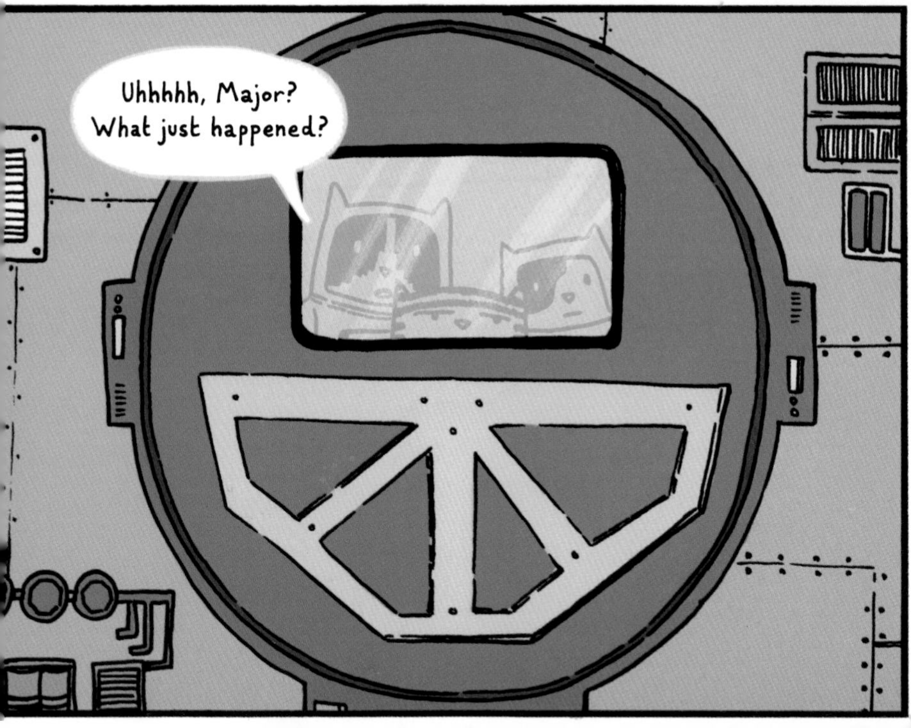
Uhhhhh, Major?
What just happened?

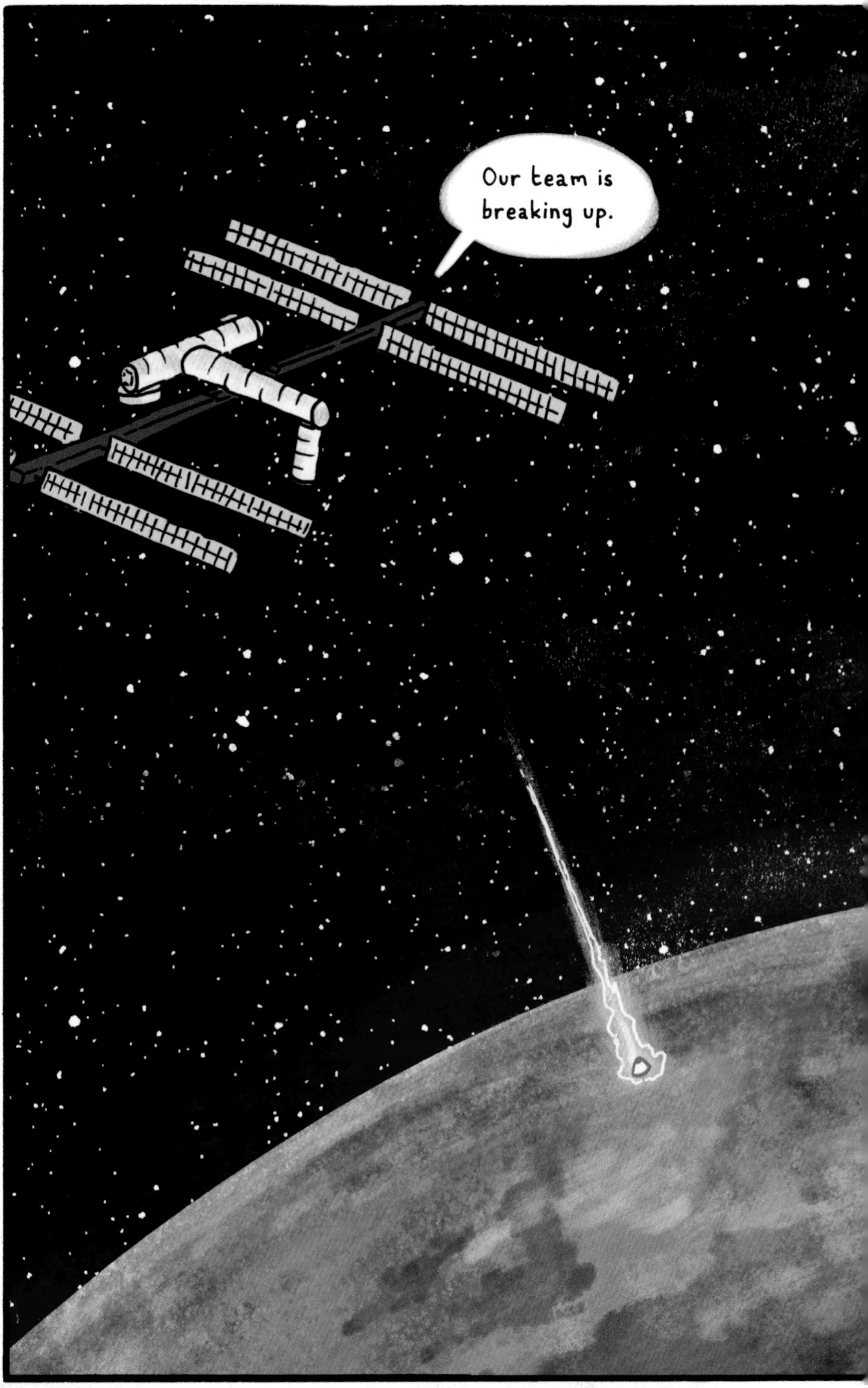
Our team is breaking up.

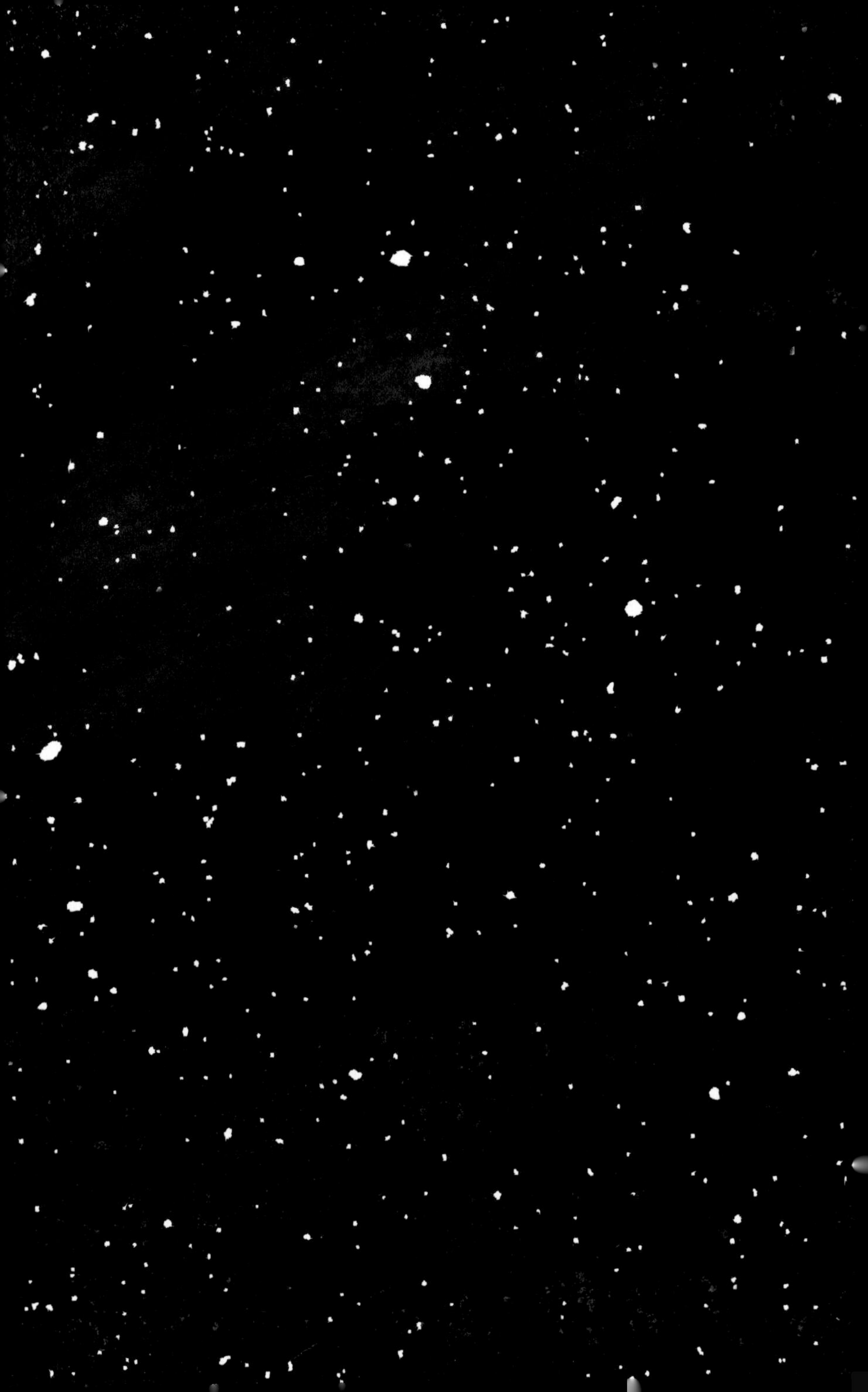

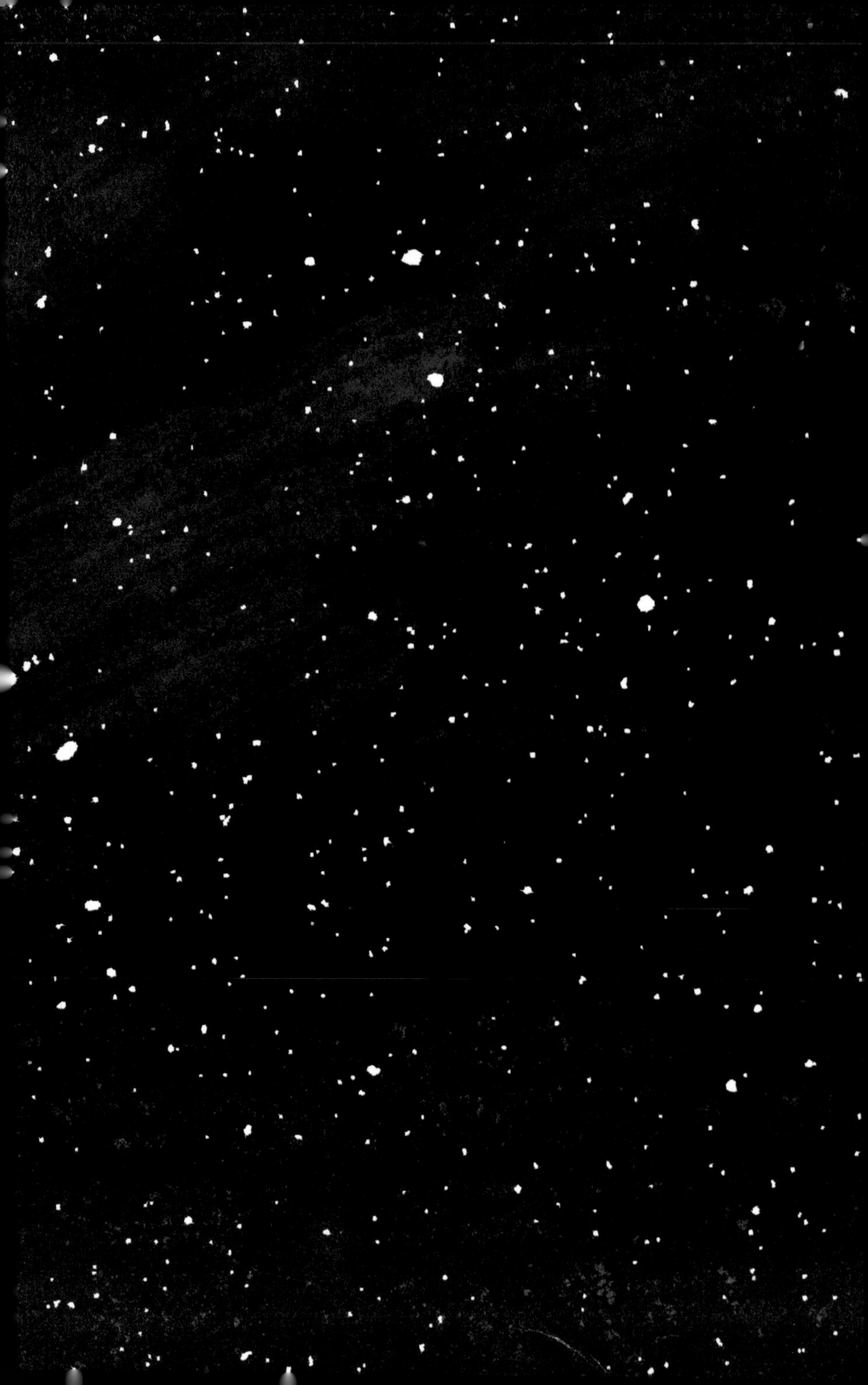

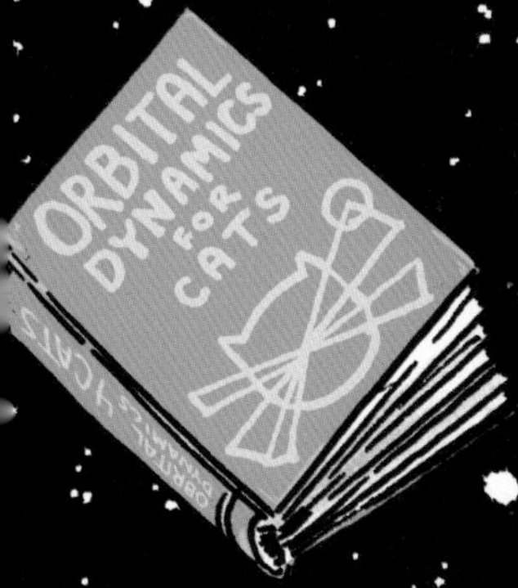
ORBITAL
DYNAMICS
FOR
CATS

CHAPTER 5

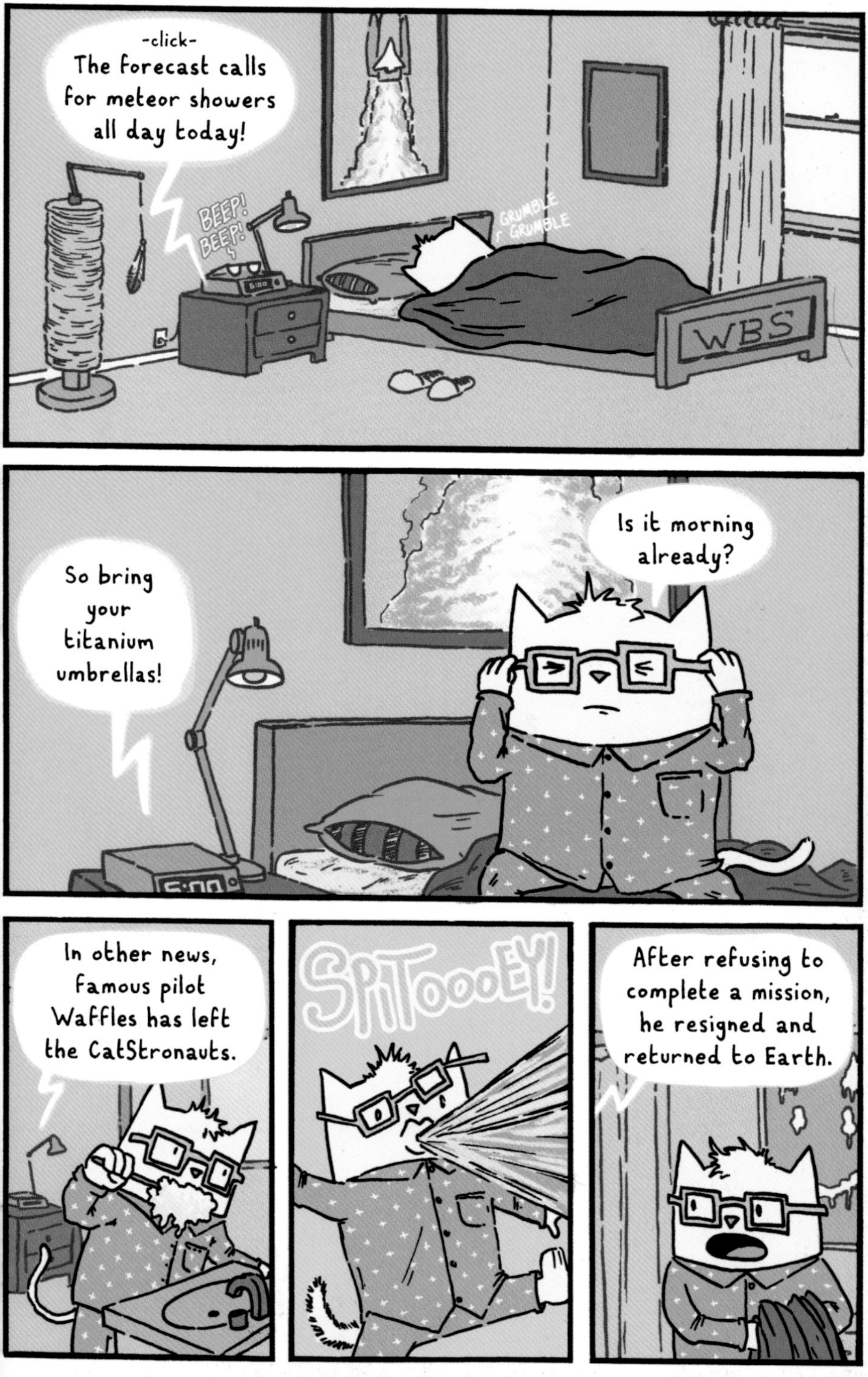
-click- The forecast calls for meteor showers all day today!
BEEP! BEEP!
GRUMBLE GRUMBLE
WBS
So bring your titanium umbrellas!
Is it morning already?
In other news, famous pilot Waffles has left the CatStronauts.
SPiTooooEY!
After refusing to complete a mission, he resigned and returned to Earth.

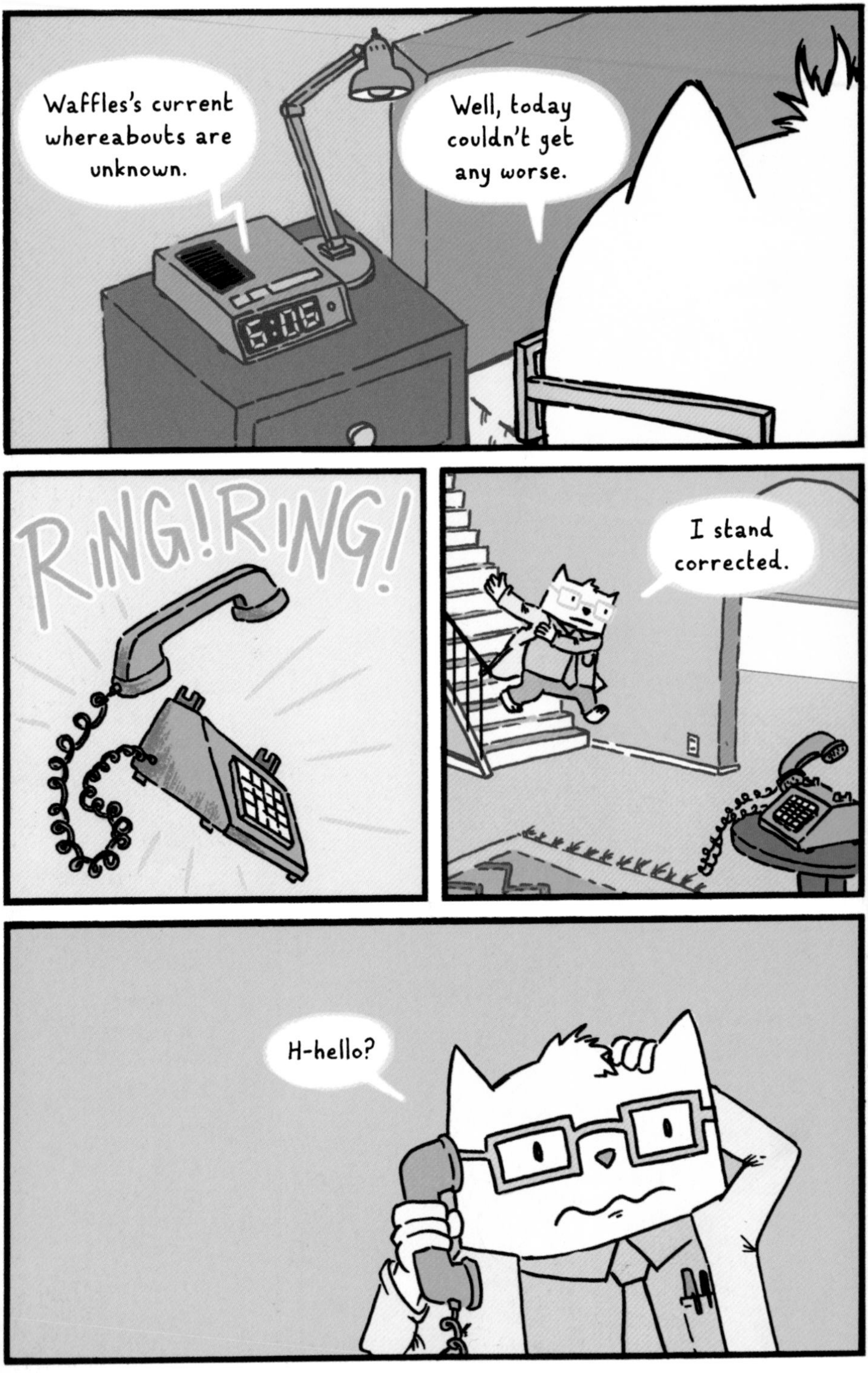
Waffles's current whereabouts are unknown.
Well, today couldn't get any worse.
6:06
RING!RING!
I stand corrected.
H-hello?

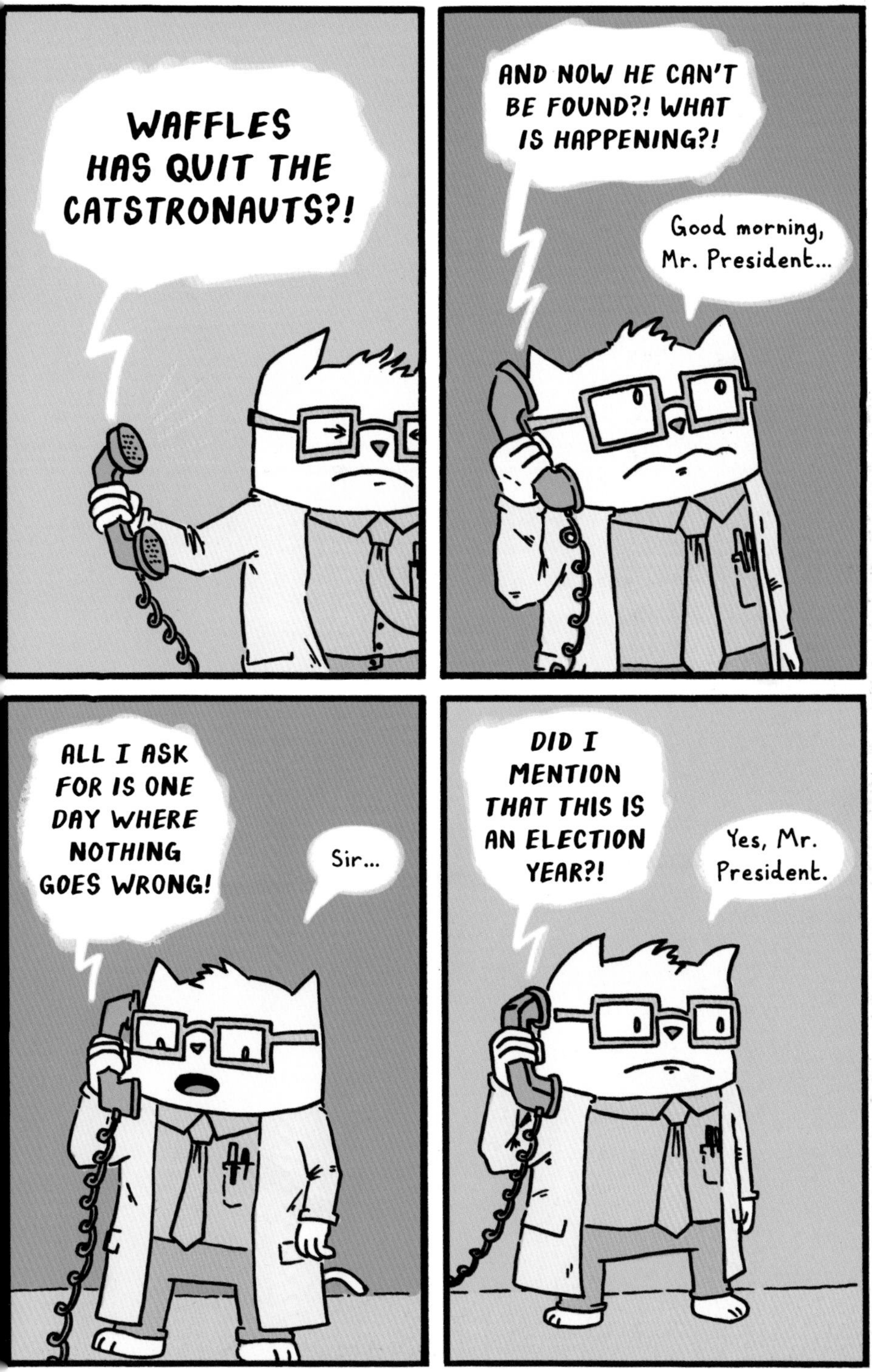
WAFFLES HAS QUIT THE CATSTRONAUTS?!
AND NOW HE CAN'T BE FOUND?! WHAT IS HAPPENING?!
Good morning, Mr. President...
ALL I ASK FOR IS ONE DAY WHERE NOTHING GOES WRONG!
Sir...
DID I MENTION THAT THIS IS AN ELECTION YEAR?!
Yes, Mr. President.

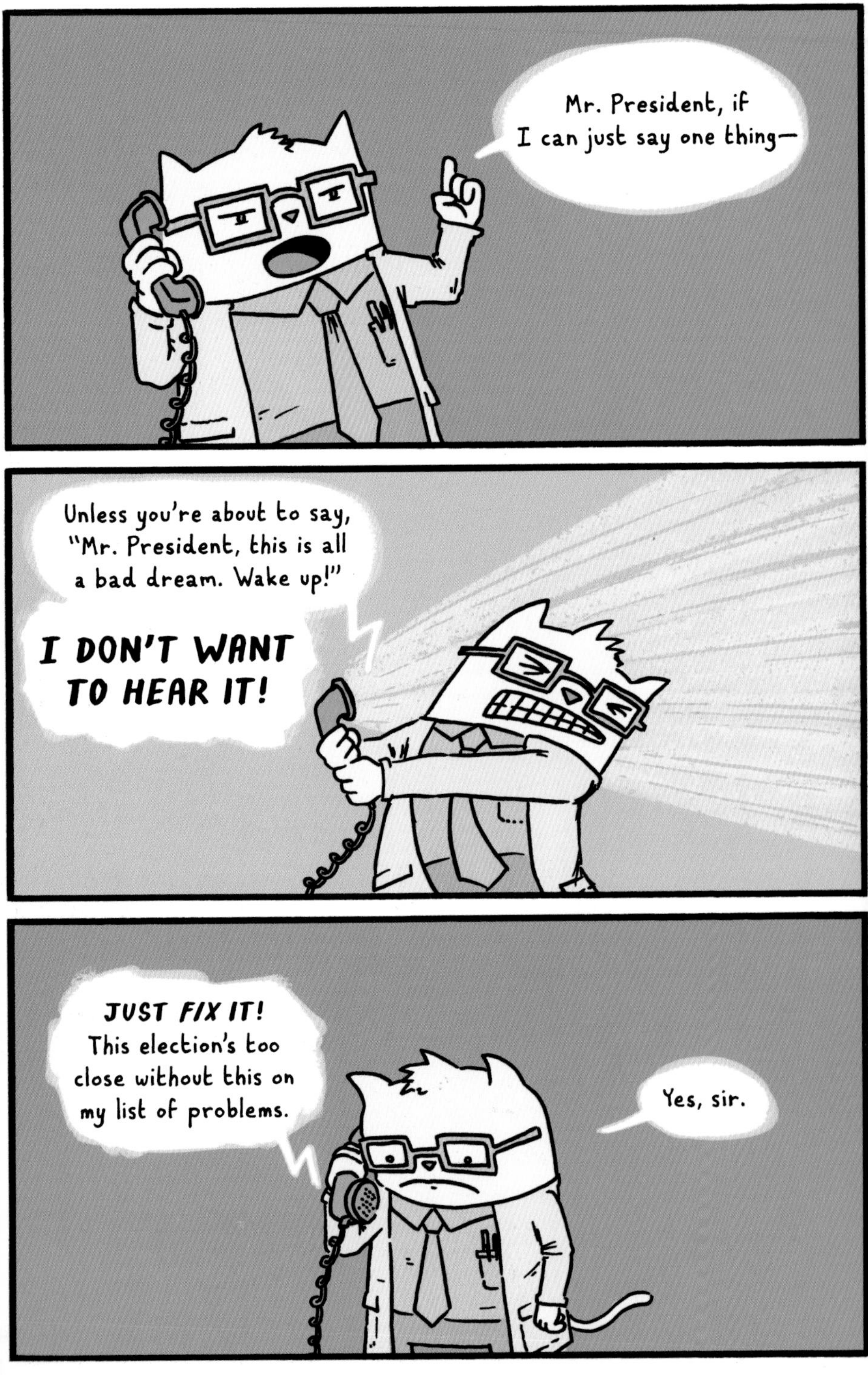
Mr. President, if I can just say one thing—
Unless you're about to say, "Mr. President, this is all a bad dream. Wake up!"
I DON'T WANT TO HEAR IT!
JUST FIX IT! This election's too close without this on my list of problems.
Yes, sir.

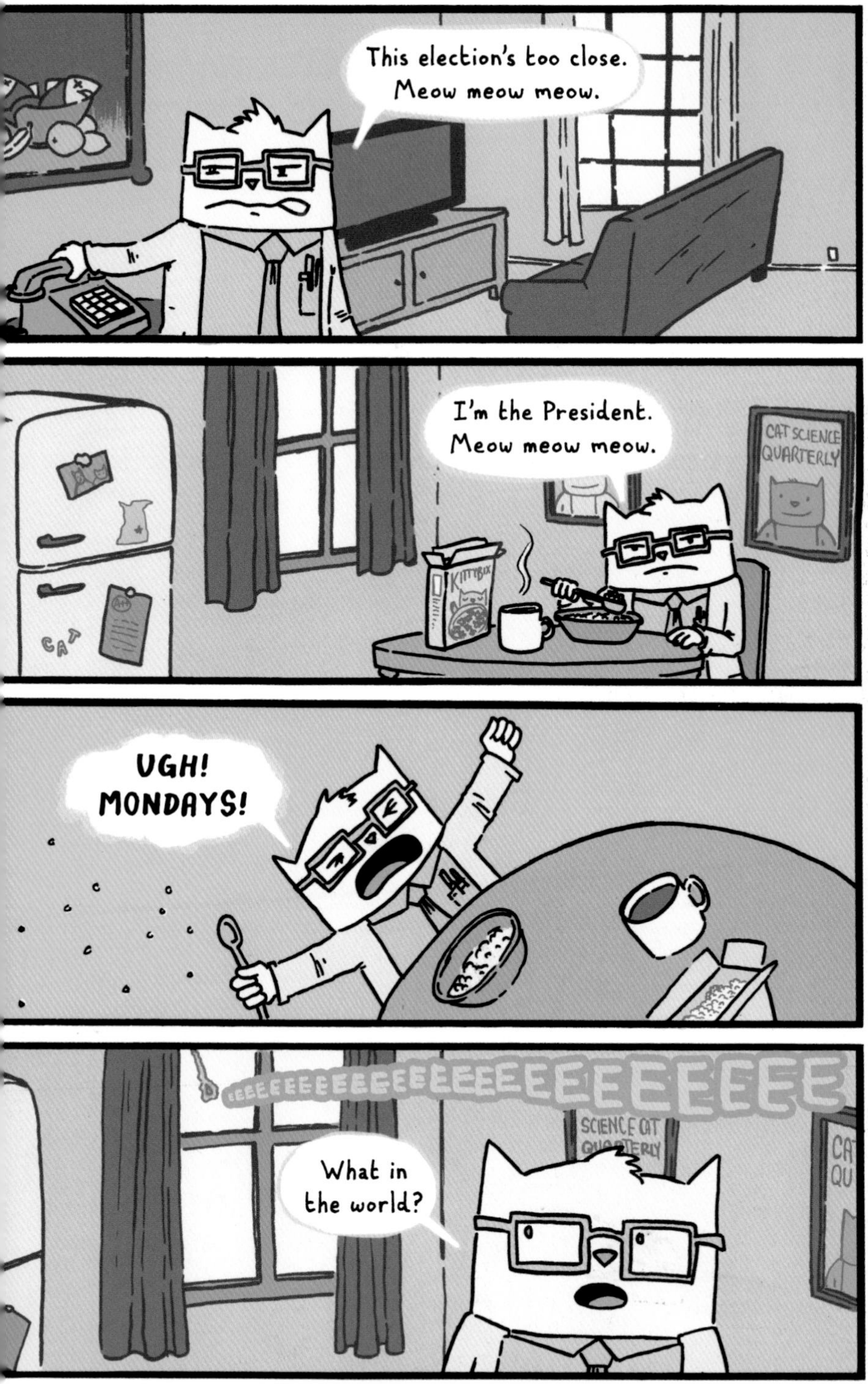
This election's too close. Meow meow meow.
I'm the President. Meow meow meow.
CAT SCIENCE QUARTERLY
KITTYBIX
CAT
UGH! MONDAYS!
SCIENCE CAT QUARTERLY
What in the world?

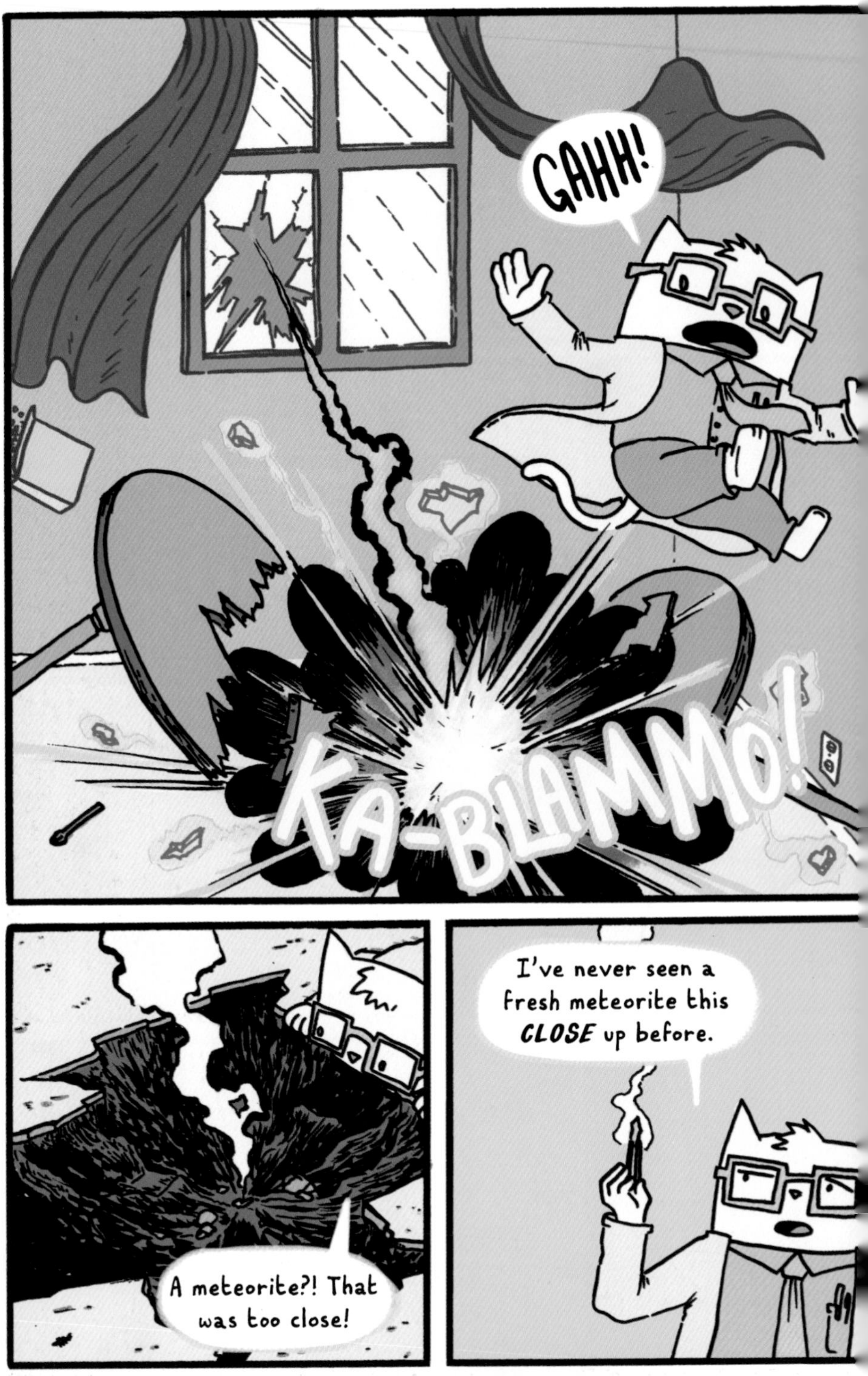
GAHH!
KA-BLAMMO!
A meteorite?! That was too close!
I've never seen a fresh meteorite this CLOSE up before.

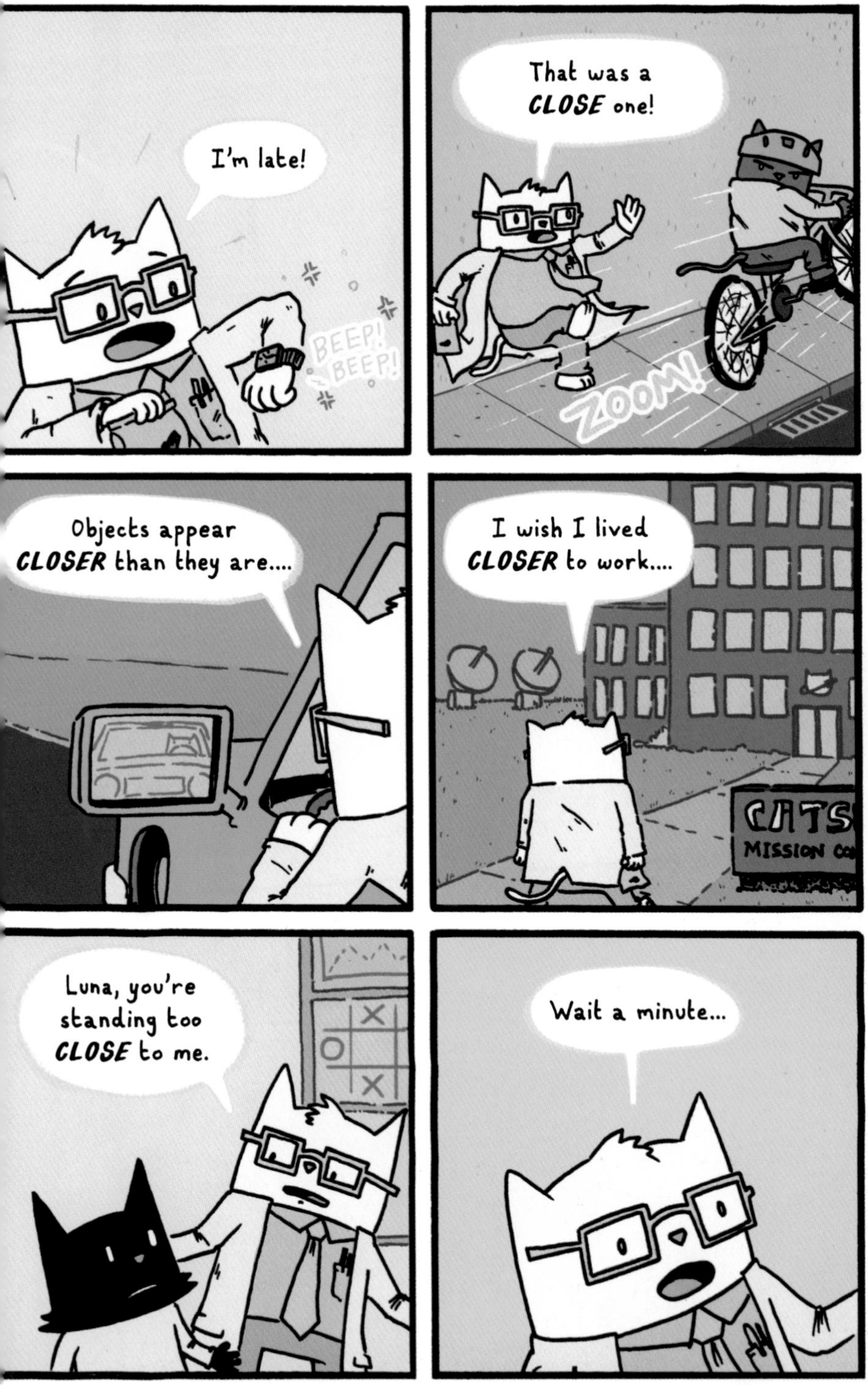
I'm late!
BEEP! BEEP!
That was a CLOSE one!
ZOOM!
Objects appear CLOSER than they are....
I wish I lived CLOSER to work....
MISSION
Luna, you're standing too CLOSE to me.
Wait a minute...

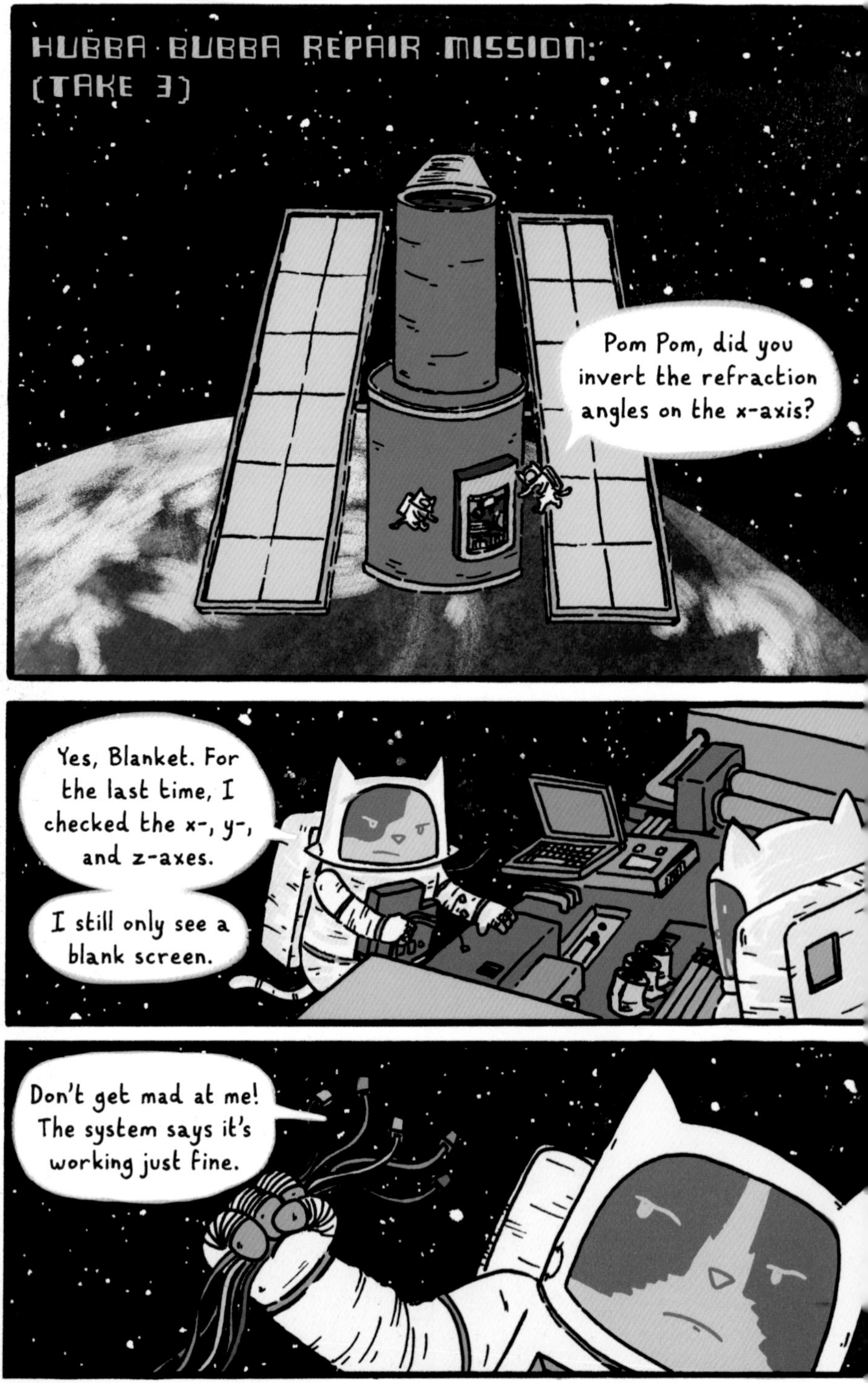
HUBBA BUBBA REPAIR MISSION:
(TAKE 3)
Pom Pom, did you invert the refraction angles on the x-axis?
Yes, Blanket. For the last time, I checked the x-, y-, and z-axes.
I still only see a blank screen.
Don't get mad at me! The system says it's working just fine.

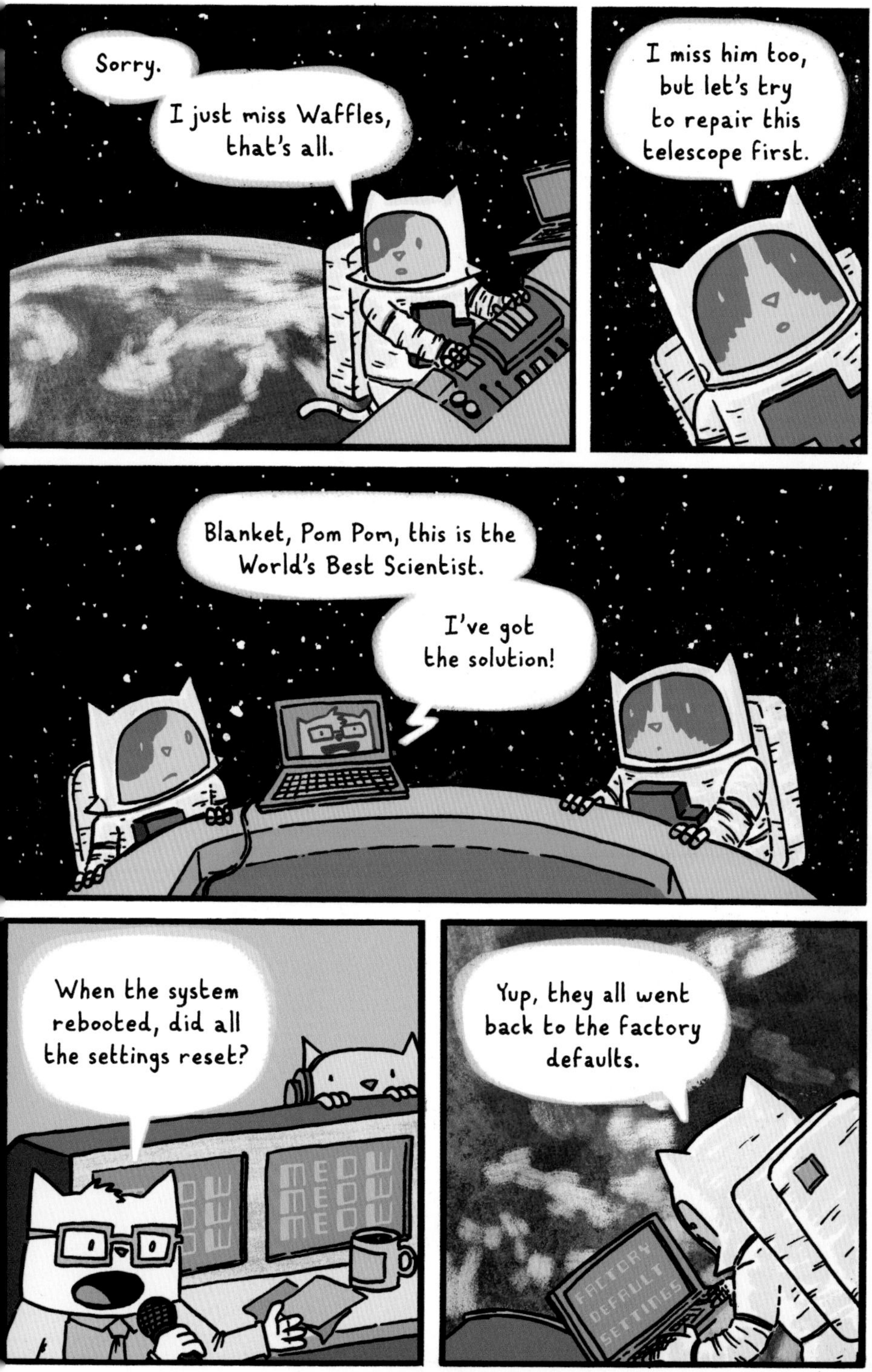
Sorry.
I just miss Waffles, that's all.
I miss him too, but let's try to repair this telescope first.
Blanket, Pom Pom, this is the World's Best Scientist.
I've got the solution!
When the system rebooted, did all the settings reset?
MEOW MEOW MEOW
Yup, they all went back to the factory defaults.
FACTORY DEFAULT SETTINGS

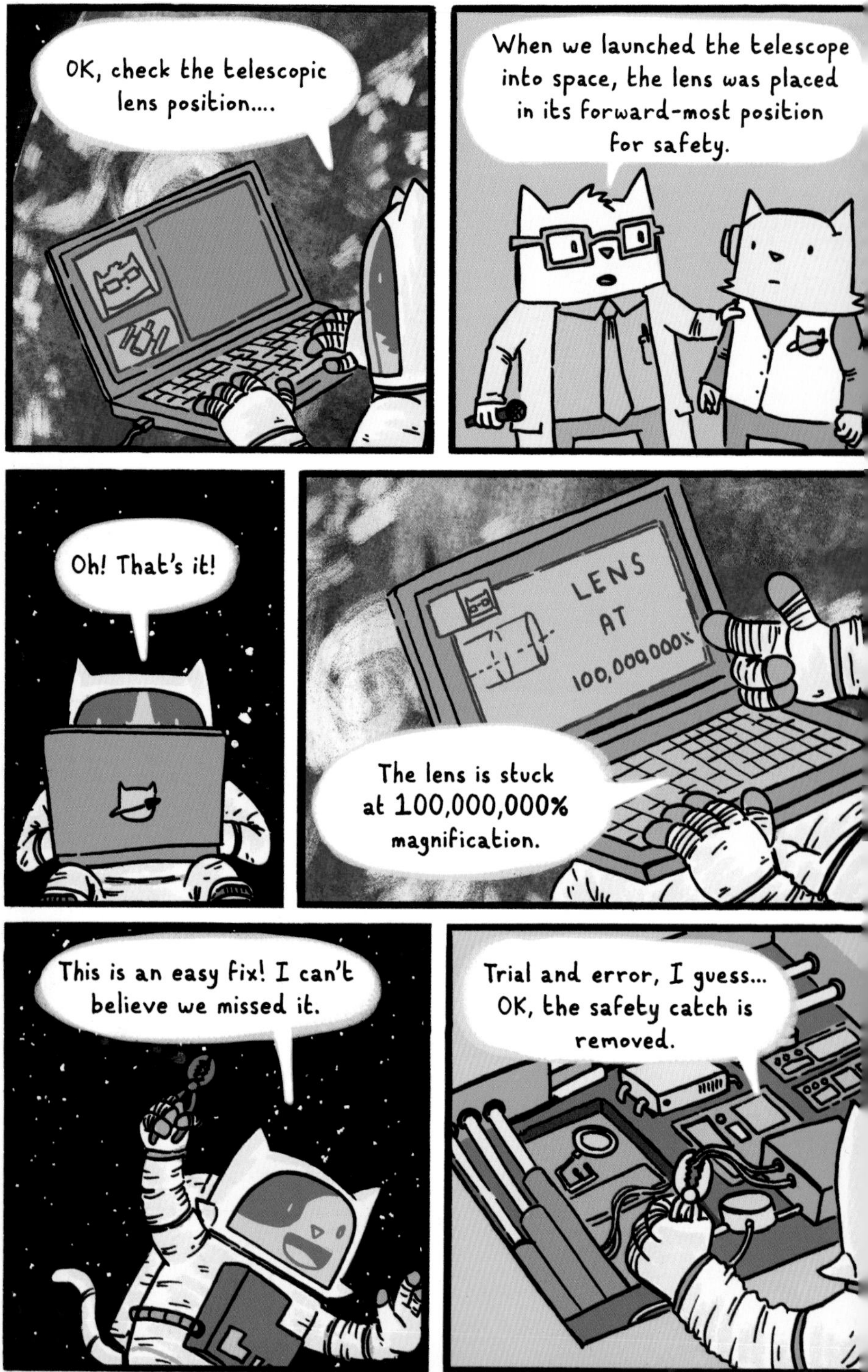
OK, check the telescopic lens position....
When we launched the telescope into space, the lens was placed in its forward-most position for safety.
Oh! That's it!
LENS AT 100,000,000%
The lens is stuck at 100,000,000% magnification.
This is an easy fix! I can't believe we missed it.
Trial and error, I guess... OK, the safety catch is removed.

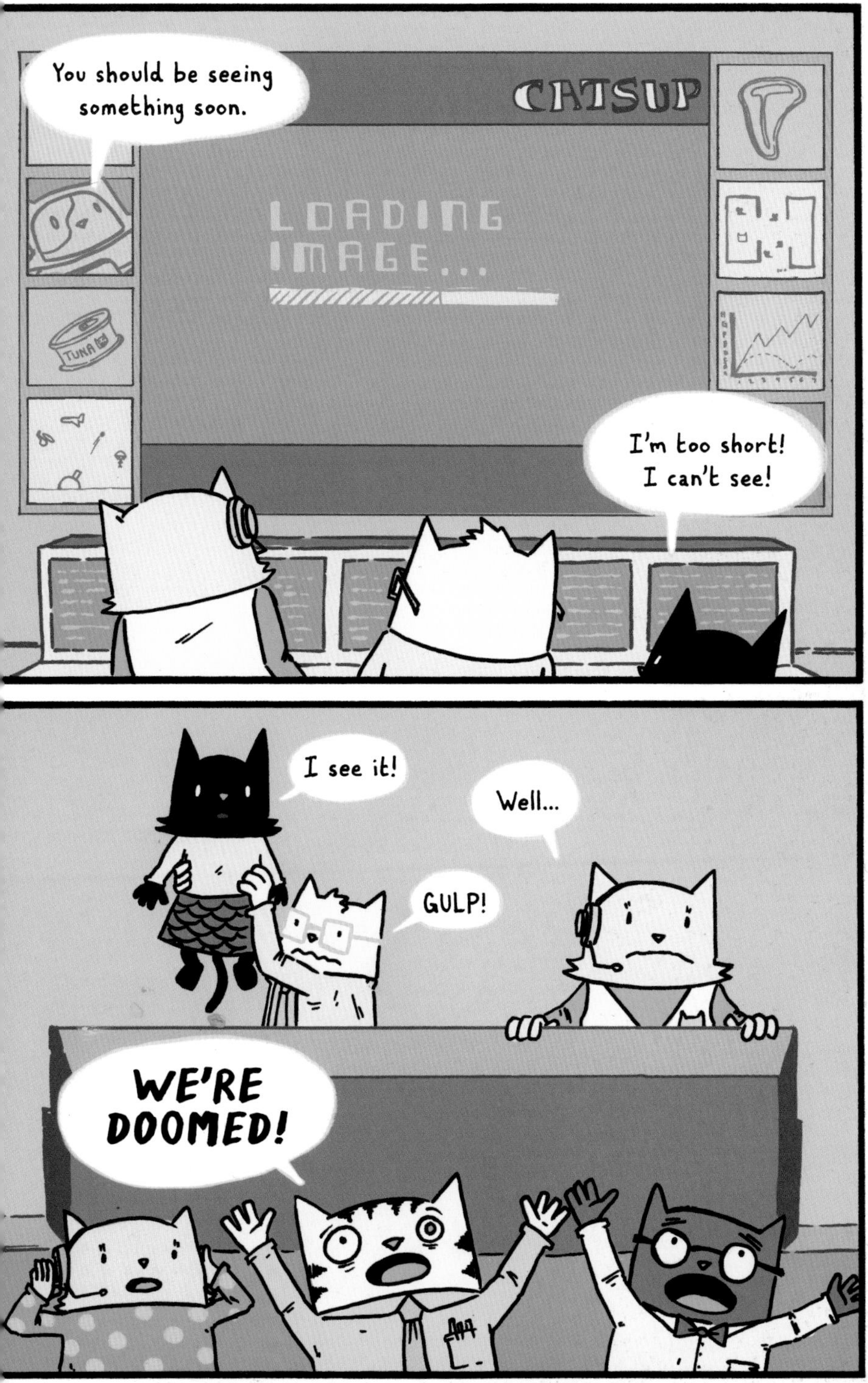

You should be seeing something soon.
CATSUP
LOADING IMAGE...
TUNA
I'm too short! I can't see!
I see it!
Well...
GULP!
WE'RE DOOMED!

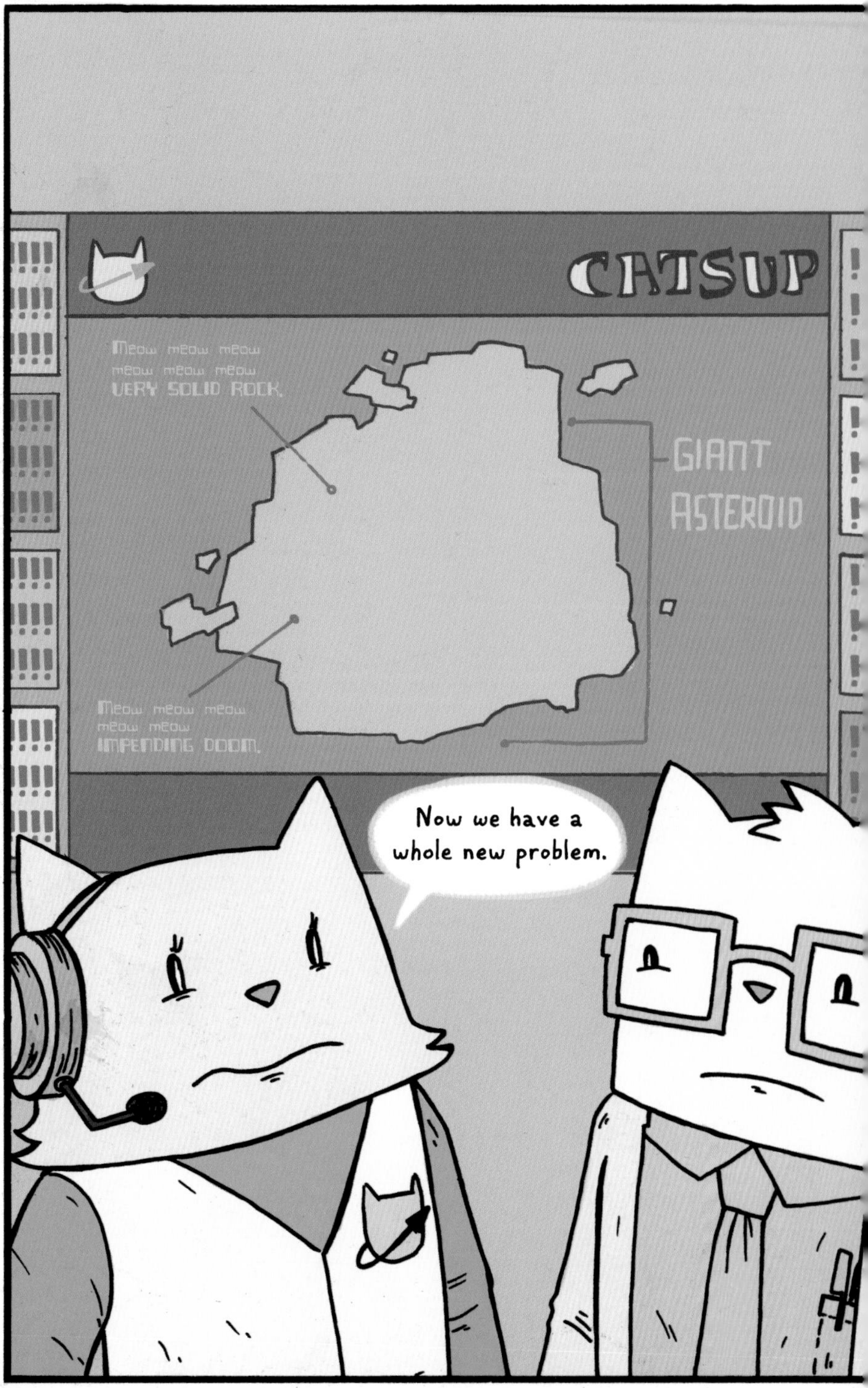
CATSUP
Meow meow meow
meow meow meow
VERY SOLID ROCK.
GIANT
ASTEROID
Meow meow meow
meow meow
IMPENDING DOOM.
Now we have a
whole new problem.

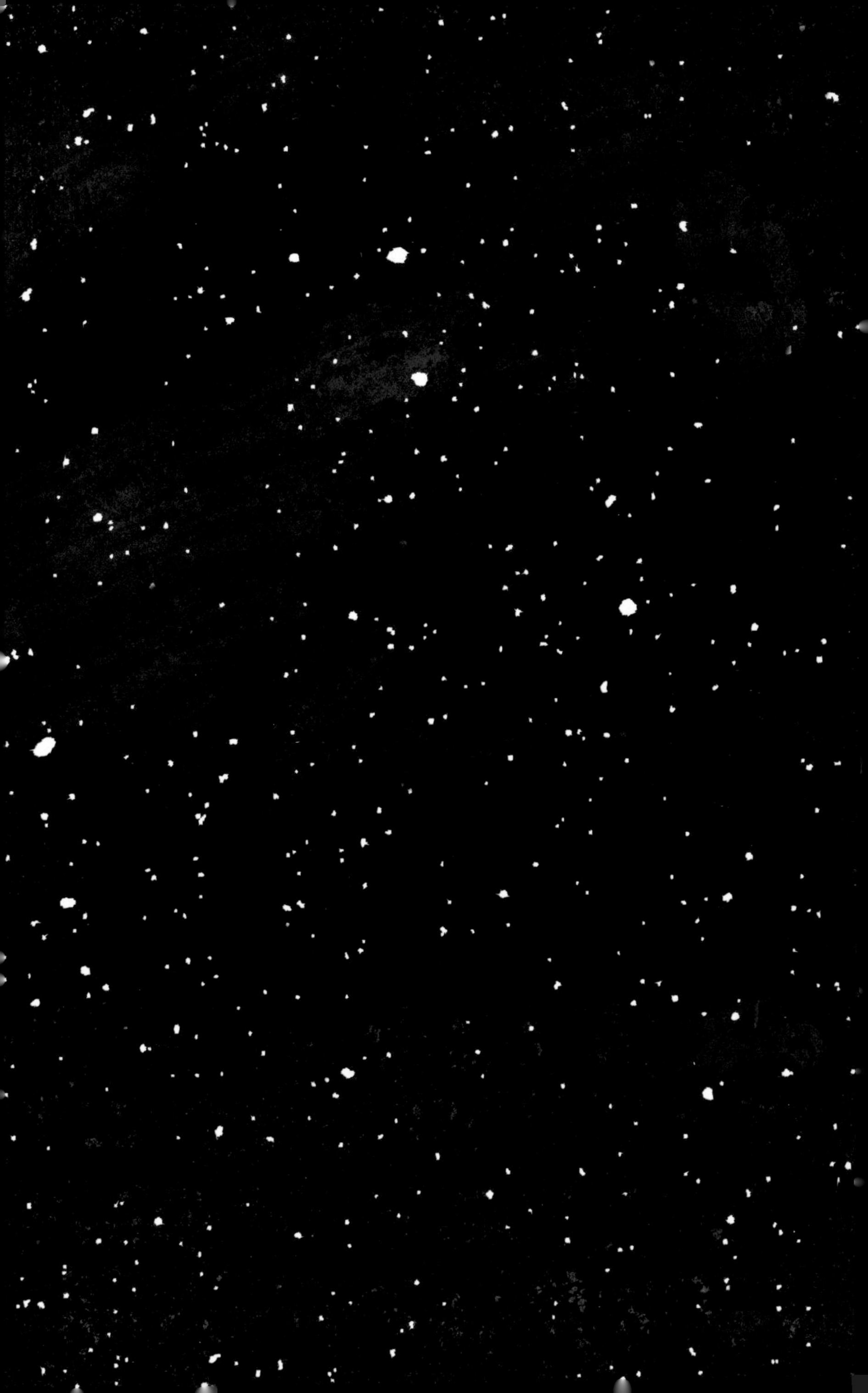

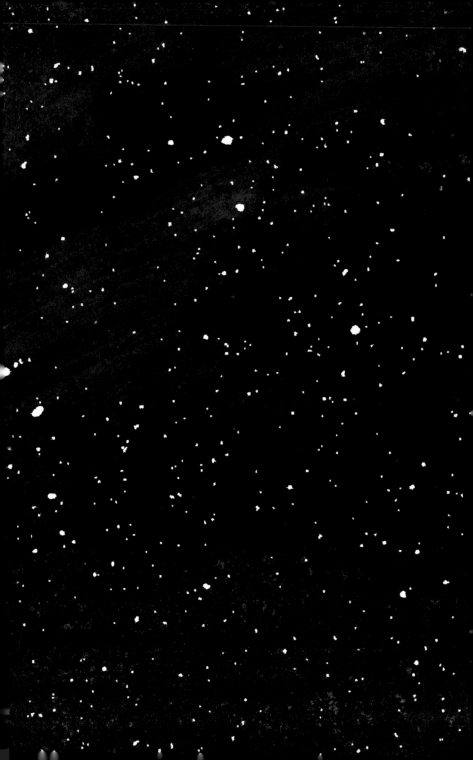

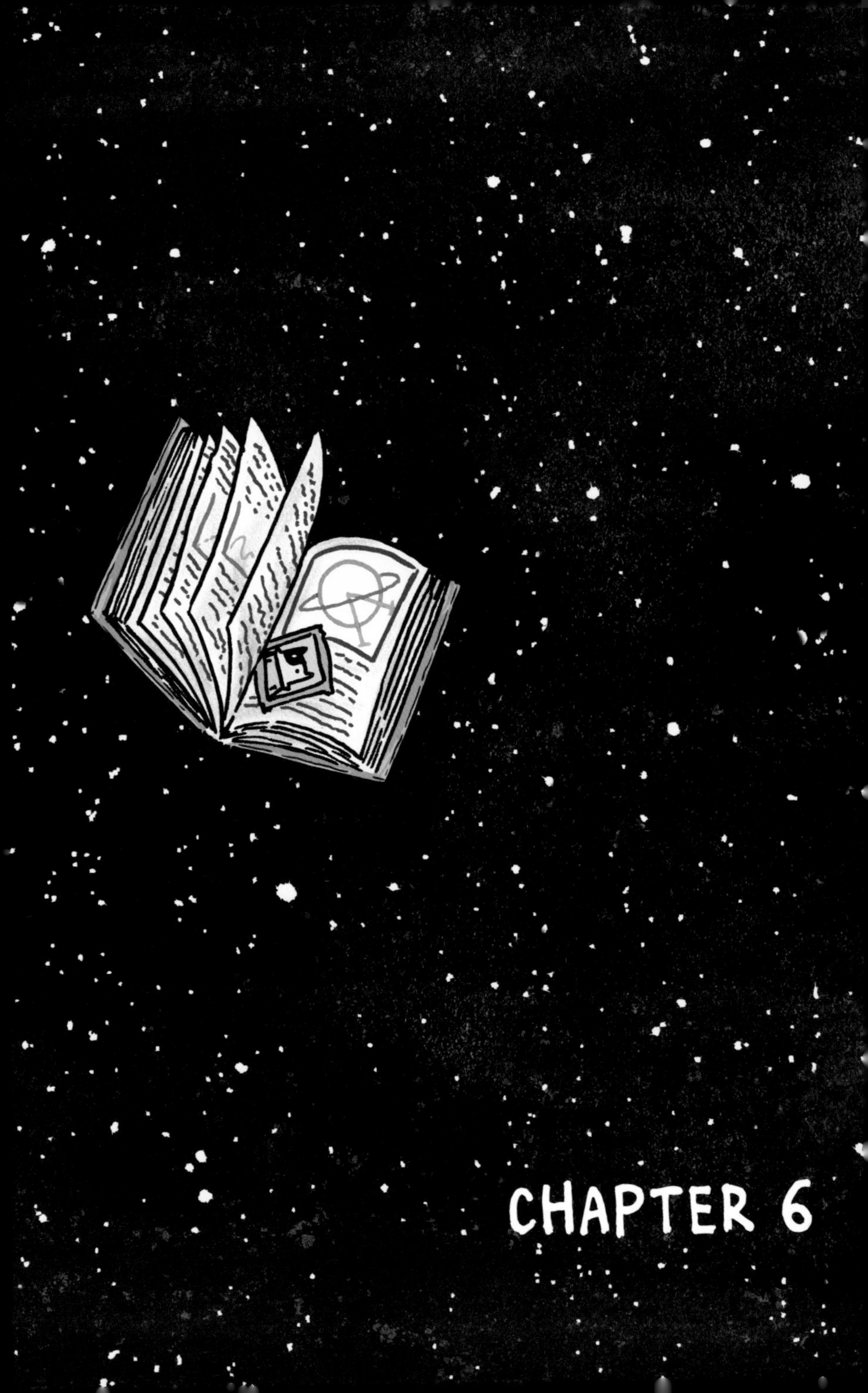
CHAPTER 6

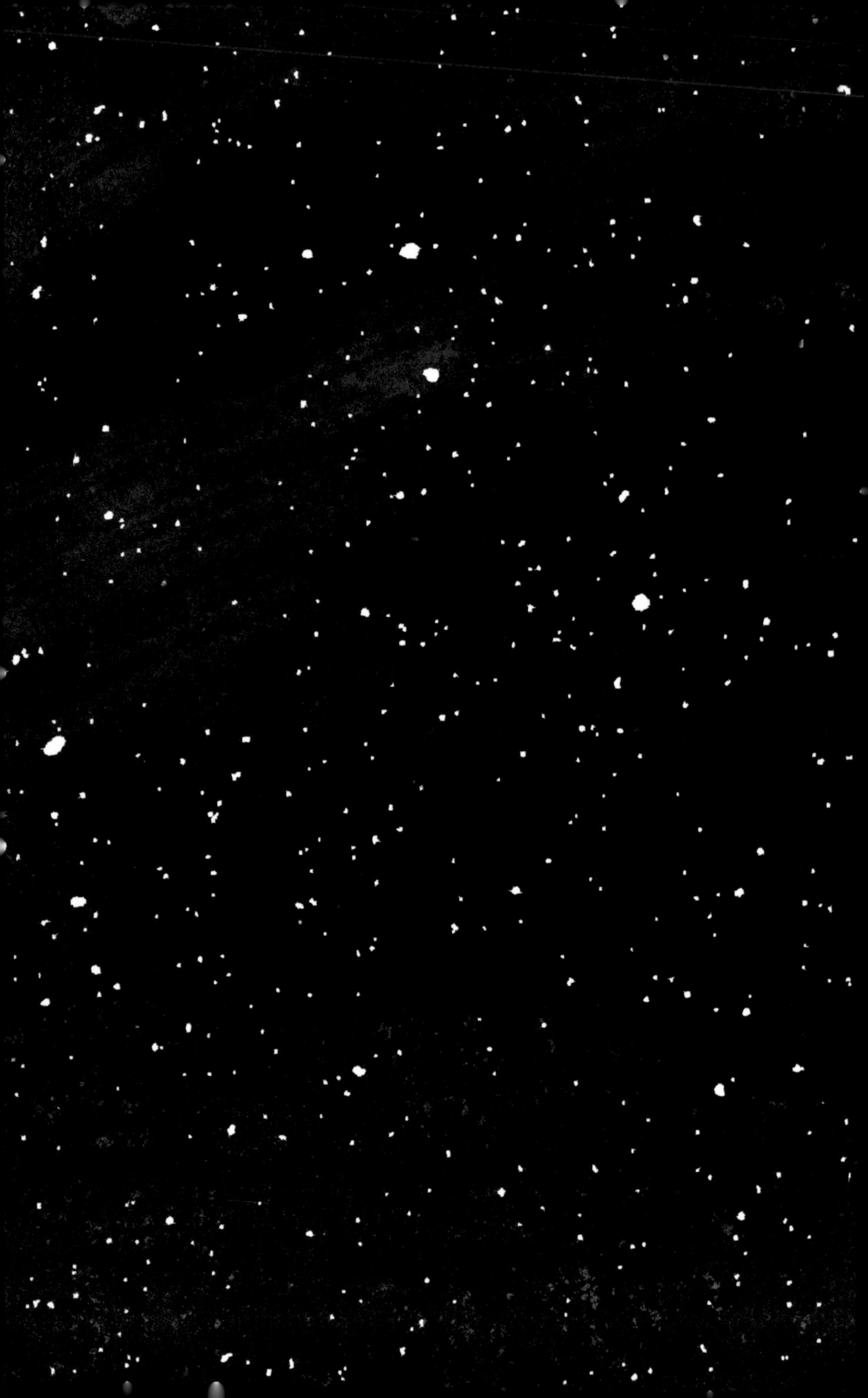

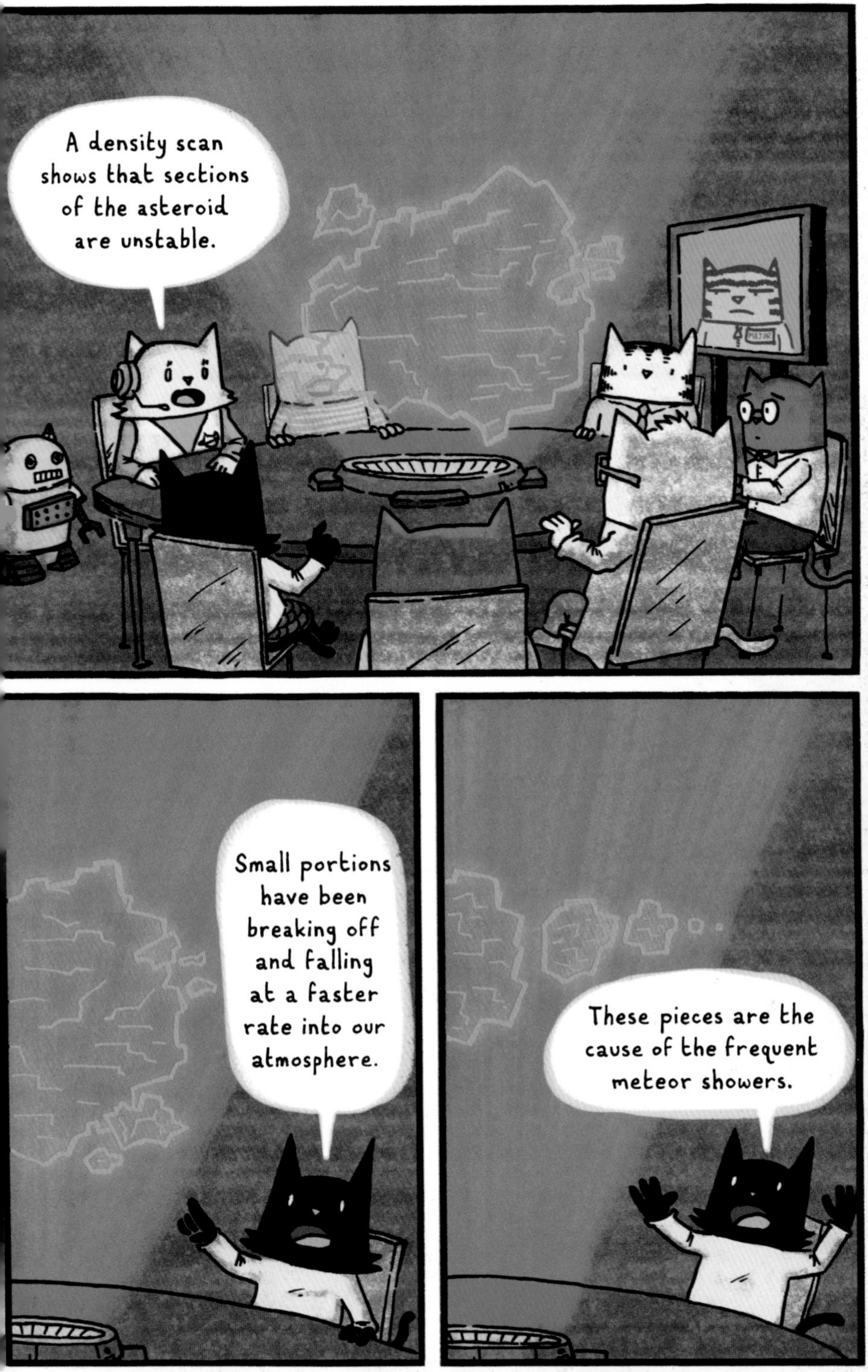
A density scan shows that sections of the asteroid are unstable.
Small portions have been breaking off and falling at a faster rate into our atmosphere.
These pieces are the cause of the frequent meteor showers.

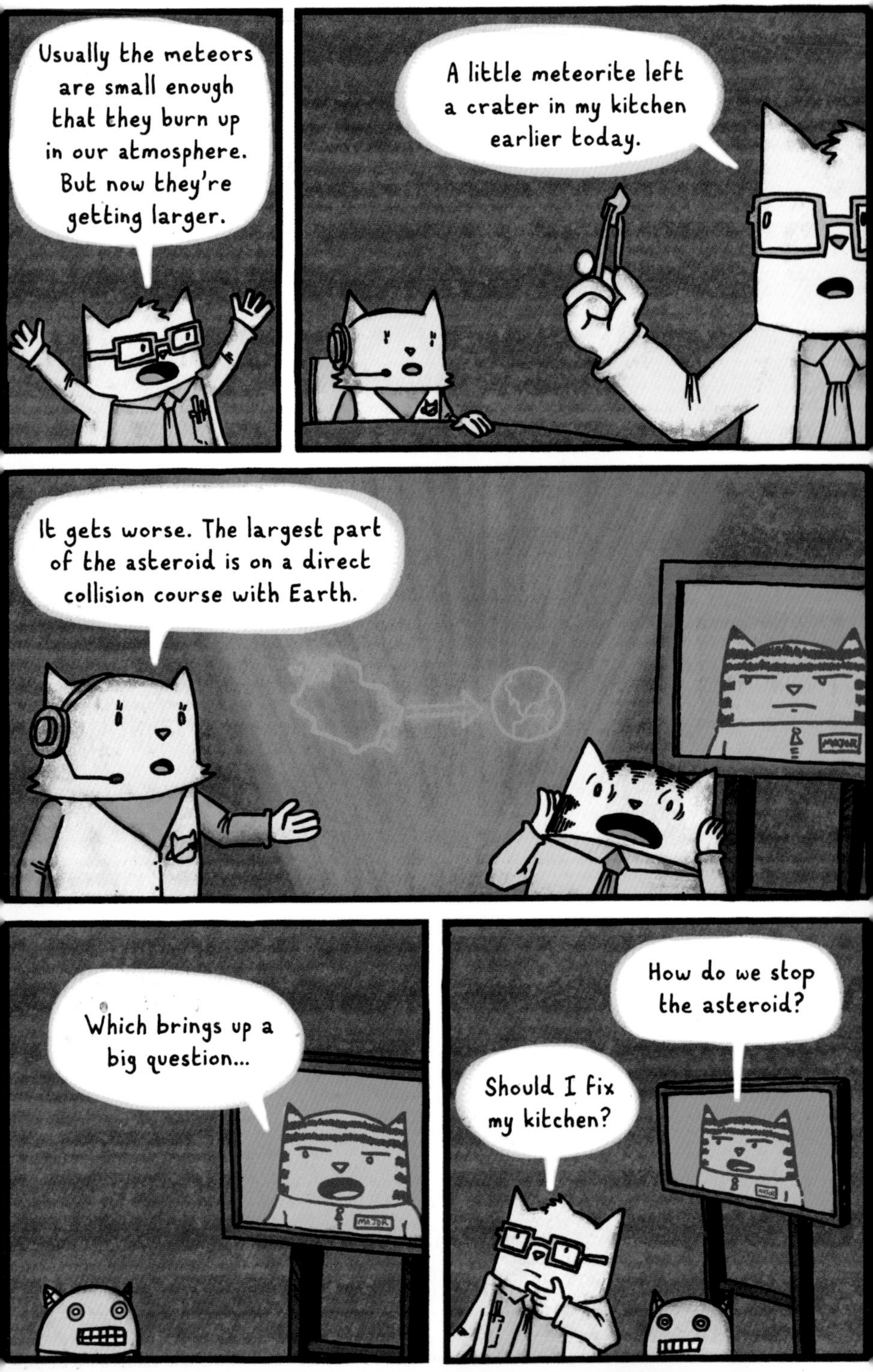
Usually the meteors are small enough that they burn up in our atmosphere. But now they're getting larger.
A little meteorite left a crater in my kitchen earlier today.
It gets worse. The largest part of the asteroid is on a direct collision course with Earth.
Which brings up a big question...
How do we stop the asteroid?
Should I fix my kitchen?

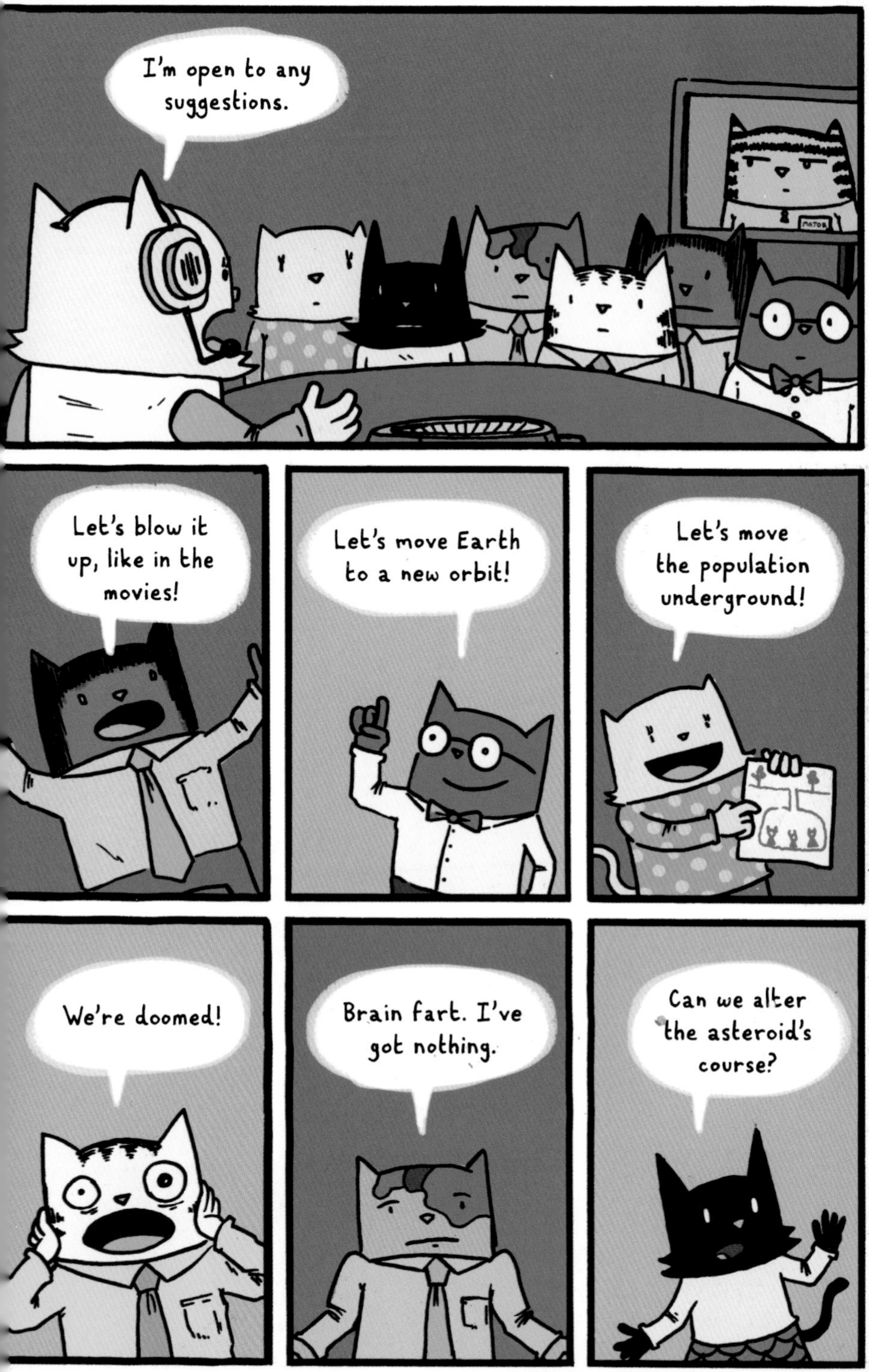
I'm open to any suggestions.
Let's blow it up, like in the movies!
Let's move Earth to a new orbit!
Let's move the population underground!
We're doomed!
Brain fart. I've got nothing.
Can we alter the asteroid's course?
MAYOR

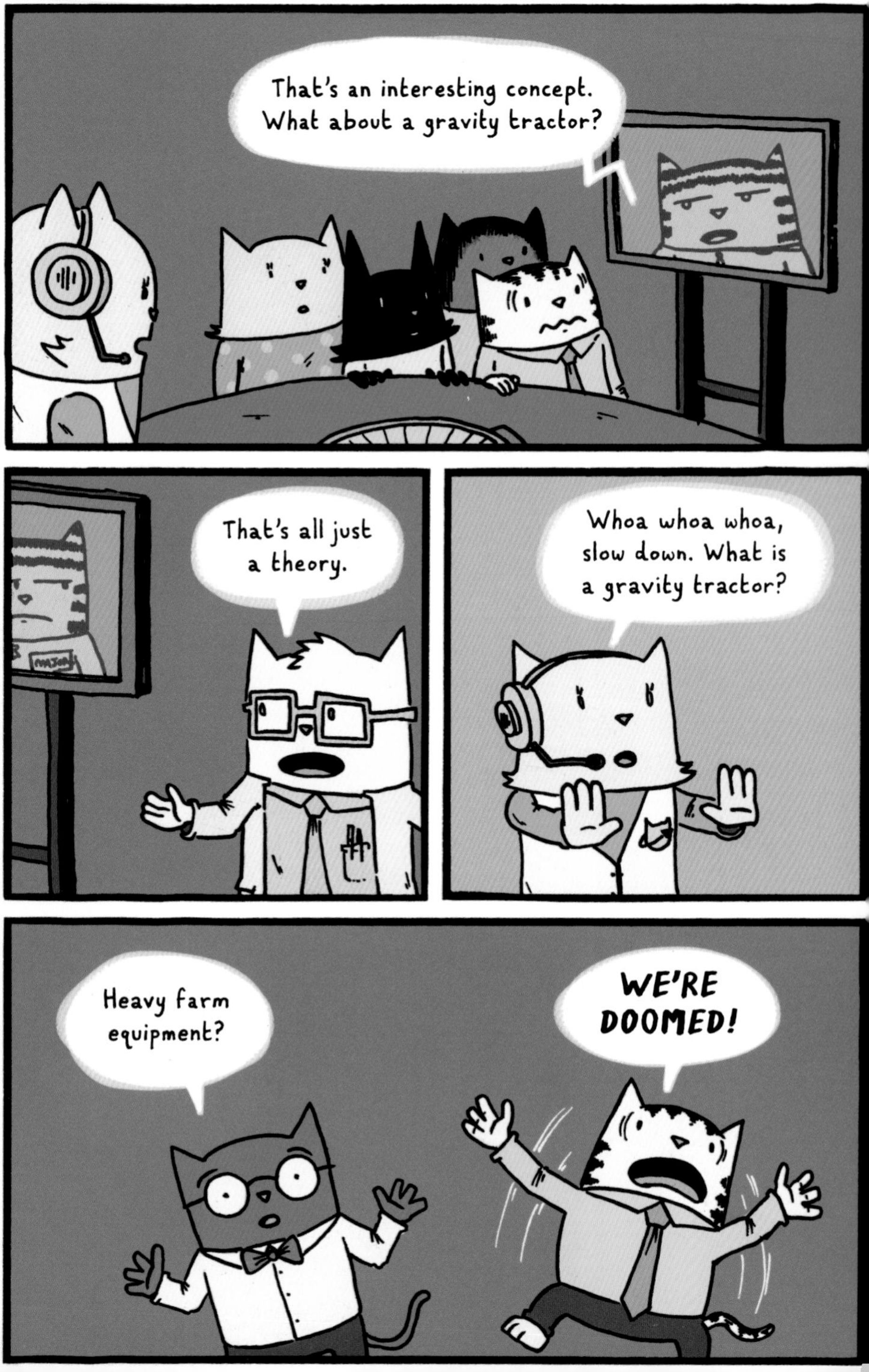
That's an interesting concept. What about a gravity tractor?
That's all just a theory.
Whoa whoa whoa, slow down. What is a gravity tractor?
Heavy farm equipment?
WE'RE DOOMED!

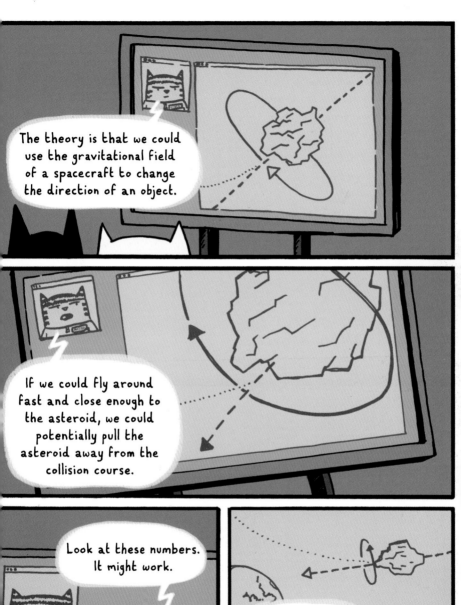

The theory is that we could use the gravitational field of a spacecraft to change the direction of an object.

If we could fly around fast and close enough to the asteroid, we could potentially pull the asteroid away from the collision course.

Look at these numbers. It might work.

If we can alter the course by 8 degrees, the asteroid will fall into a stable orbit around the planet.

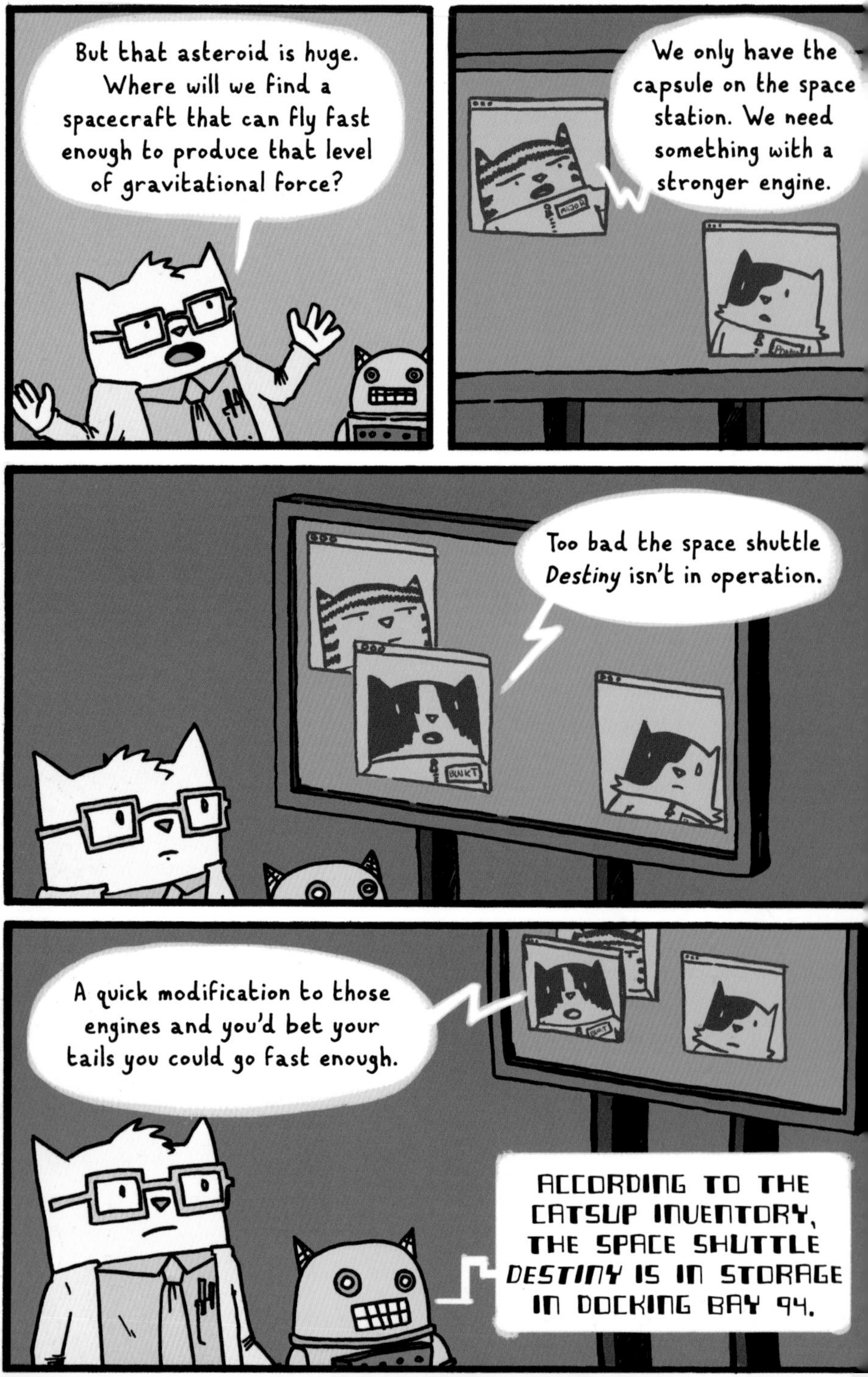
But that asteroid is huge. Where will we find a spacecraft that can fly fast enough to produce that level of gravitational force?
We only have the capsule on the space station. We need something with a stronger engine.
Too bad the space shuttle *Destiny* isn't in operation.
A quick modification to those engines and you'd bet your tails you could go fast enough.
ACCORDING TO THE CATSUP INVENTORY, THE SPACE SHUTTLE *DESTINY* IS IN STORAGE IN DOCKING BAY 94.

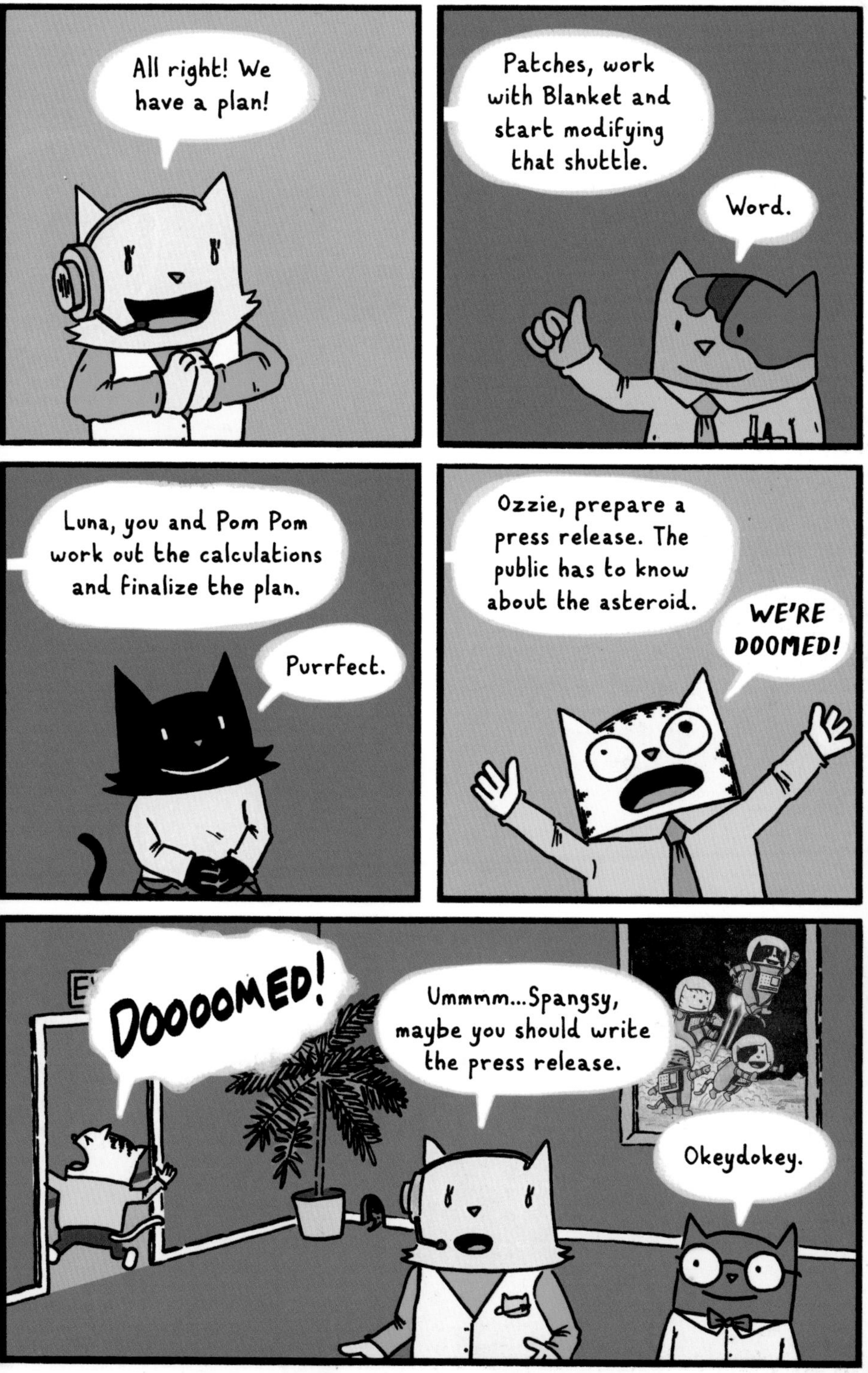
All right! We have a plan!
Patches, work with Blanket and start modifying that shuttle.
Word.
Luna, you and Pom Pom work out the calculations and finalize the plan.
Purrfect.
Ozzie, prepare a press release. The public has to know about the asteroid.
WE'RE DOOMED!
DOOOOMED!
Ummmm...Spangsy, maybe you should write the press release.
Okeydokey.

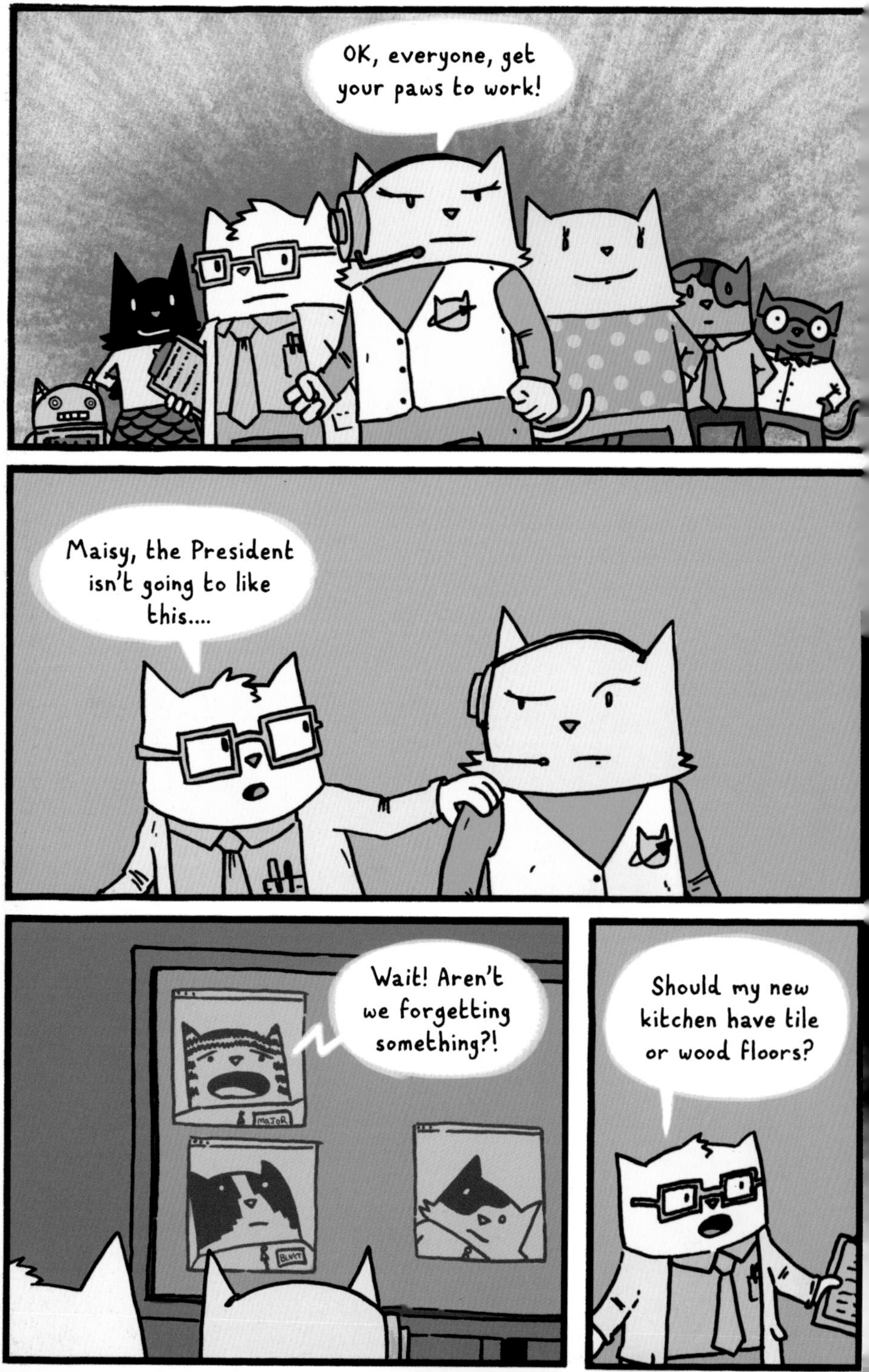
OK, everyone, get your paws to work!
Maisy, the President isn't going to like this....
Wait! Aren't we forgetting something?!
Should my new kitchen have tile or wood floors?

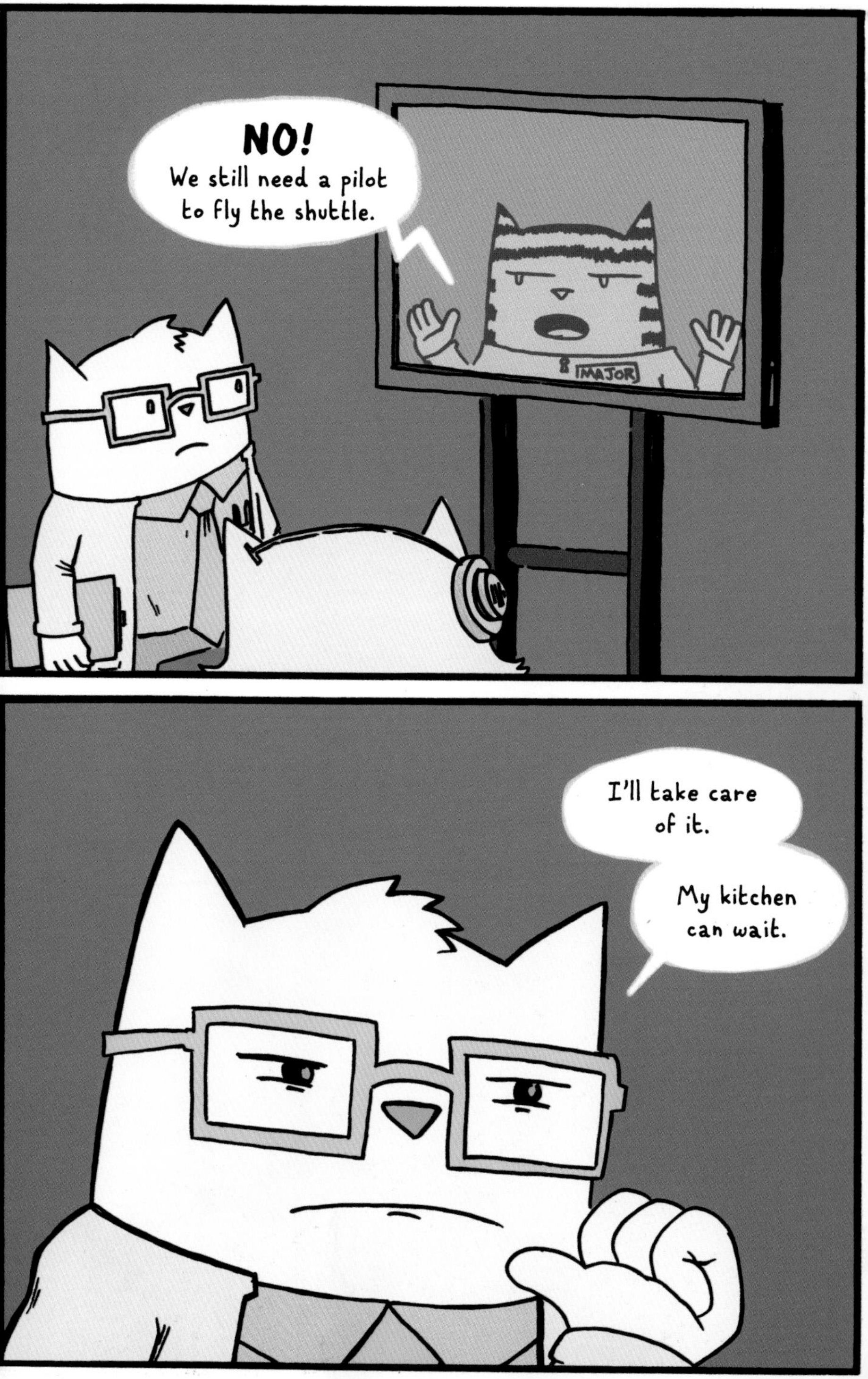
NO!
We still need a pilot to fly the shuttle.
MAJOR
I'll take care of it.
My kitchen can wait.

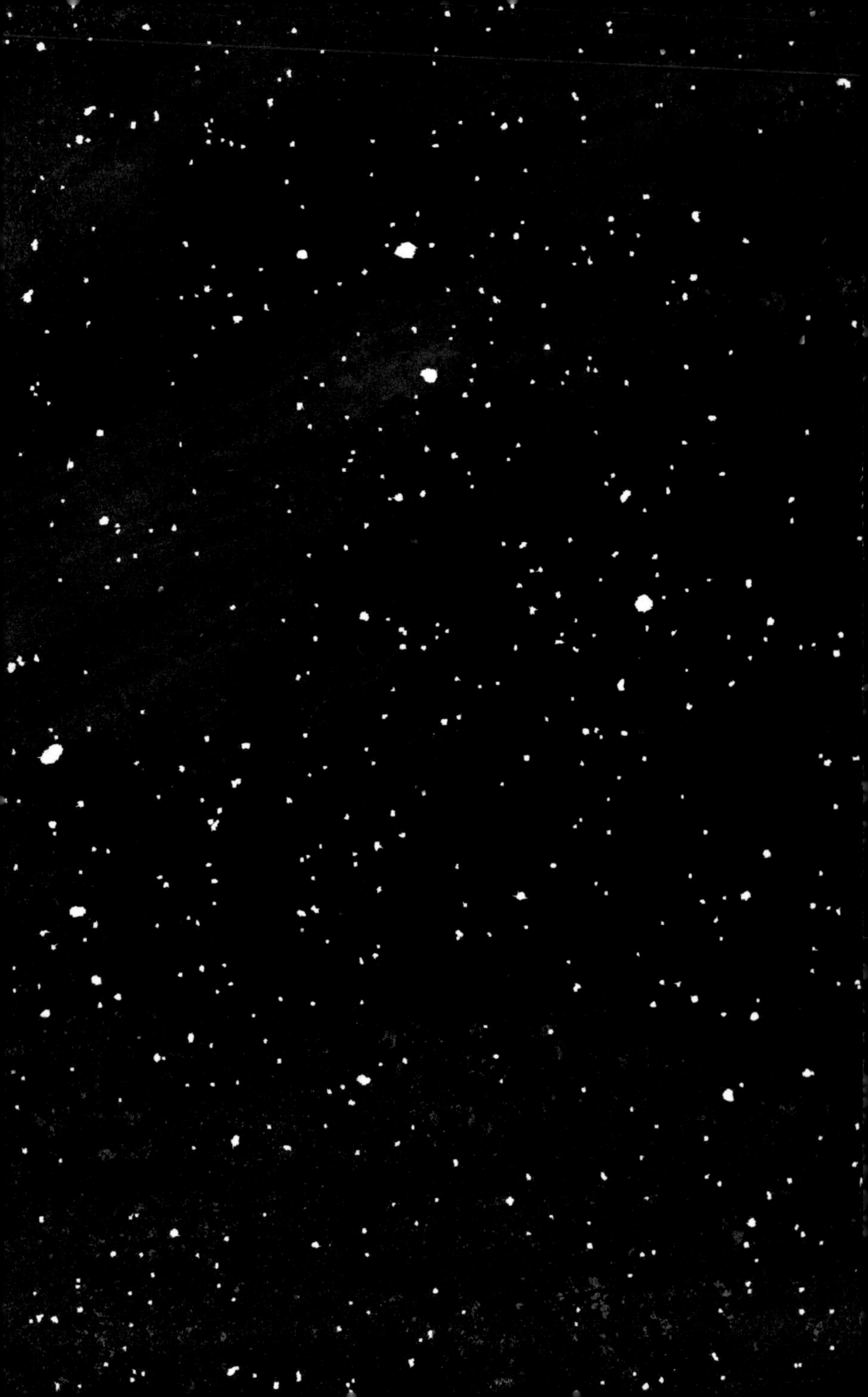

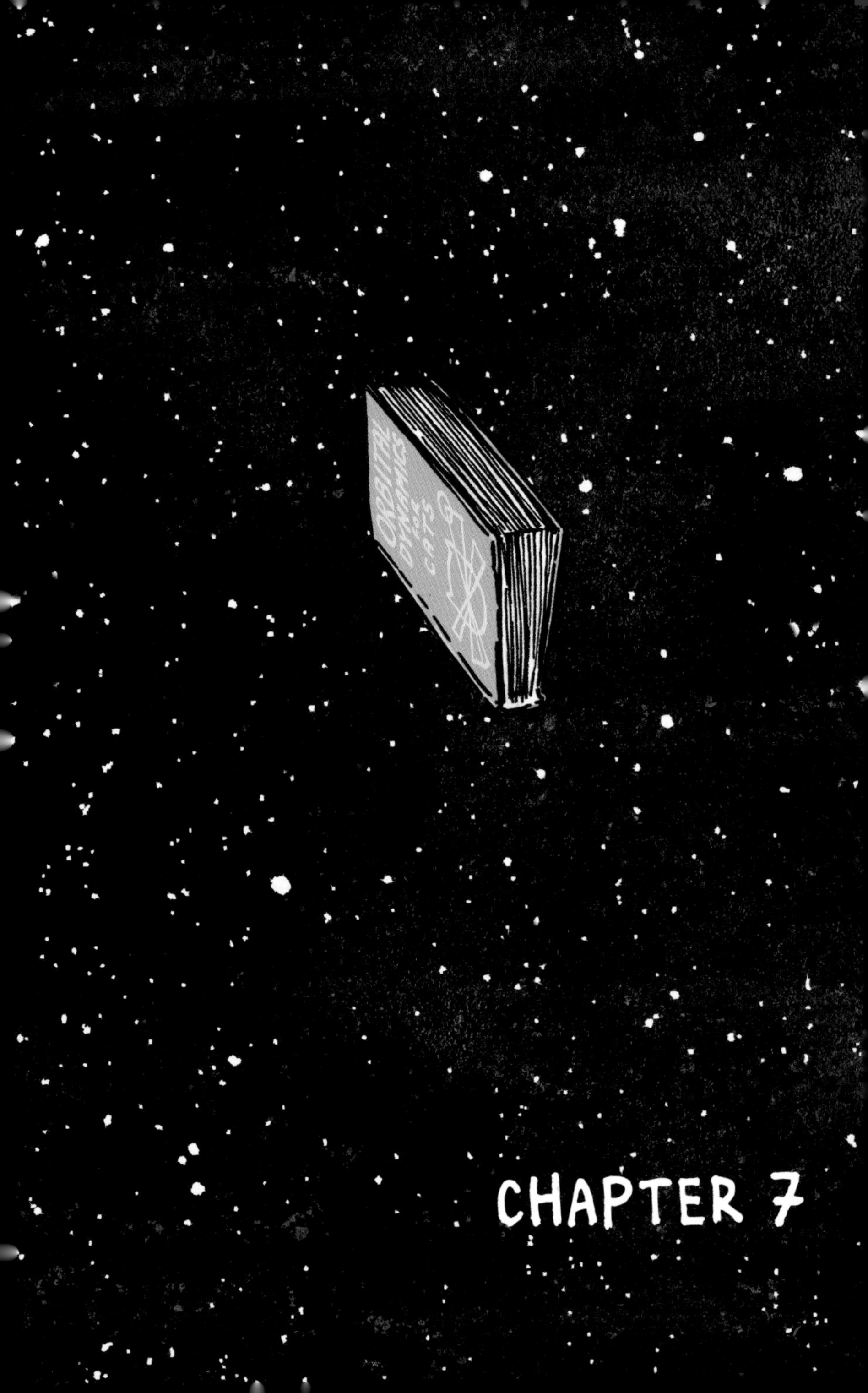
ORBITAL
DYNAMICS
FOR
CATS

CHAPTER 7

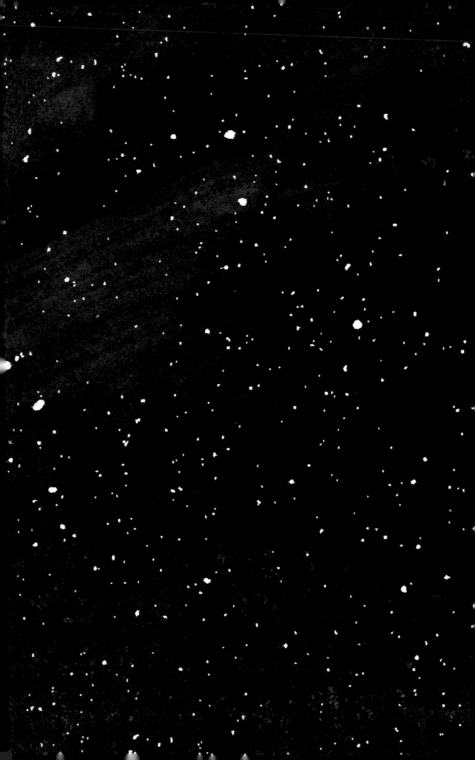

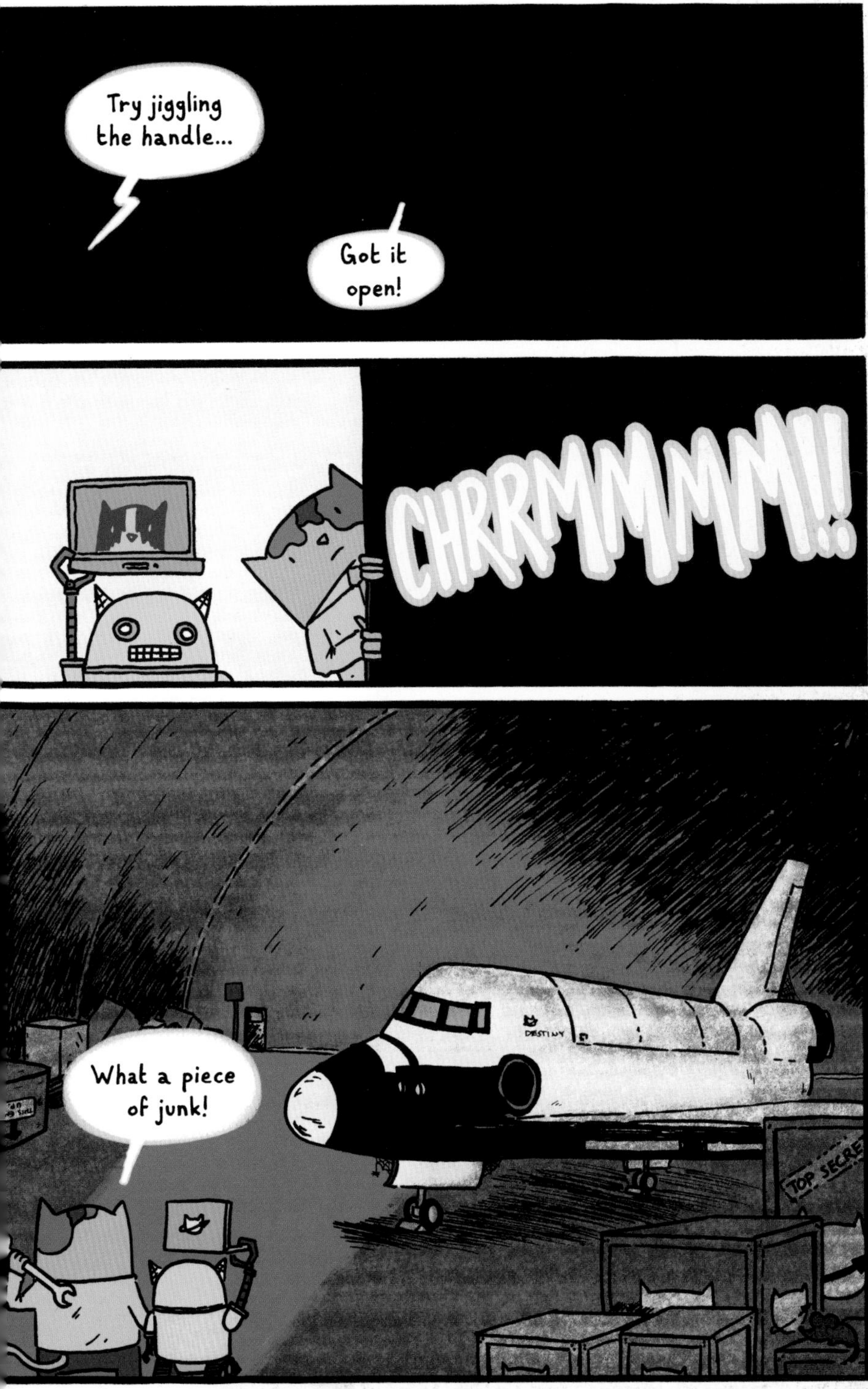
Try jiggling the handle...
Got it open!
CHRRMMMM!!
DESTINY
What a piece of junk!

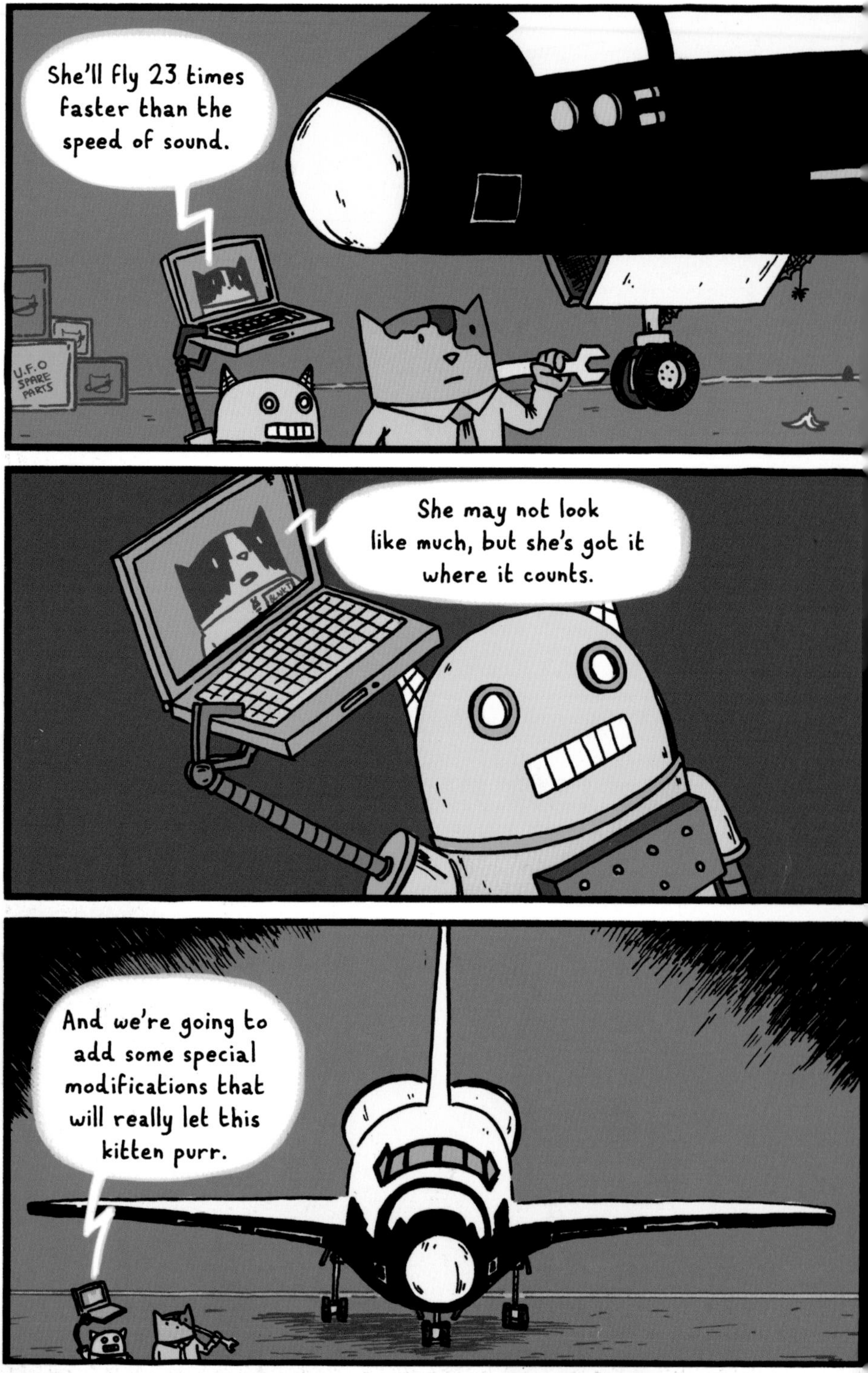
She'll fly 23 times faster than the speed of sound.
U.F.O SPARE PARTS
She may not look like much, but she's got it where it counts.
And we're going to add some special modifications that will really let this kitten purr.

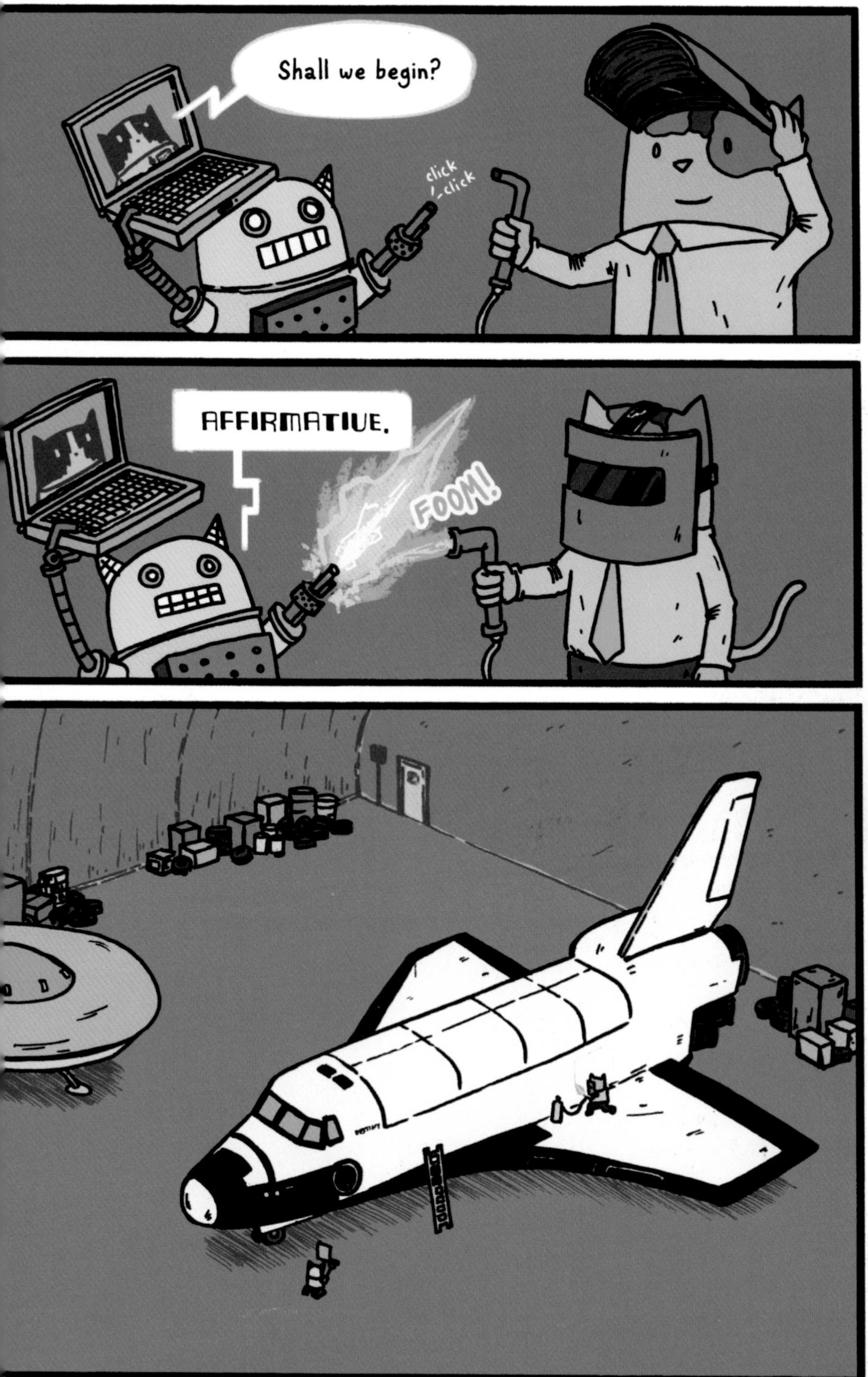
Shall we begin?
click click
AFFIRMATIVE.
FOOM!

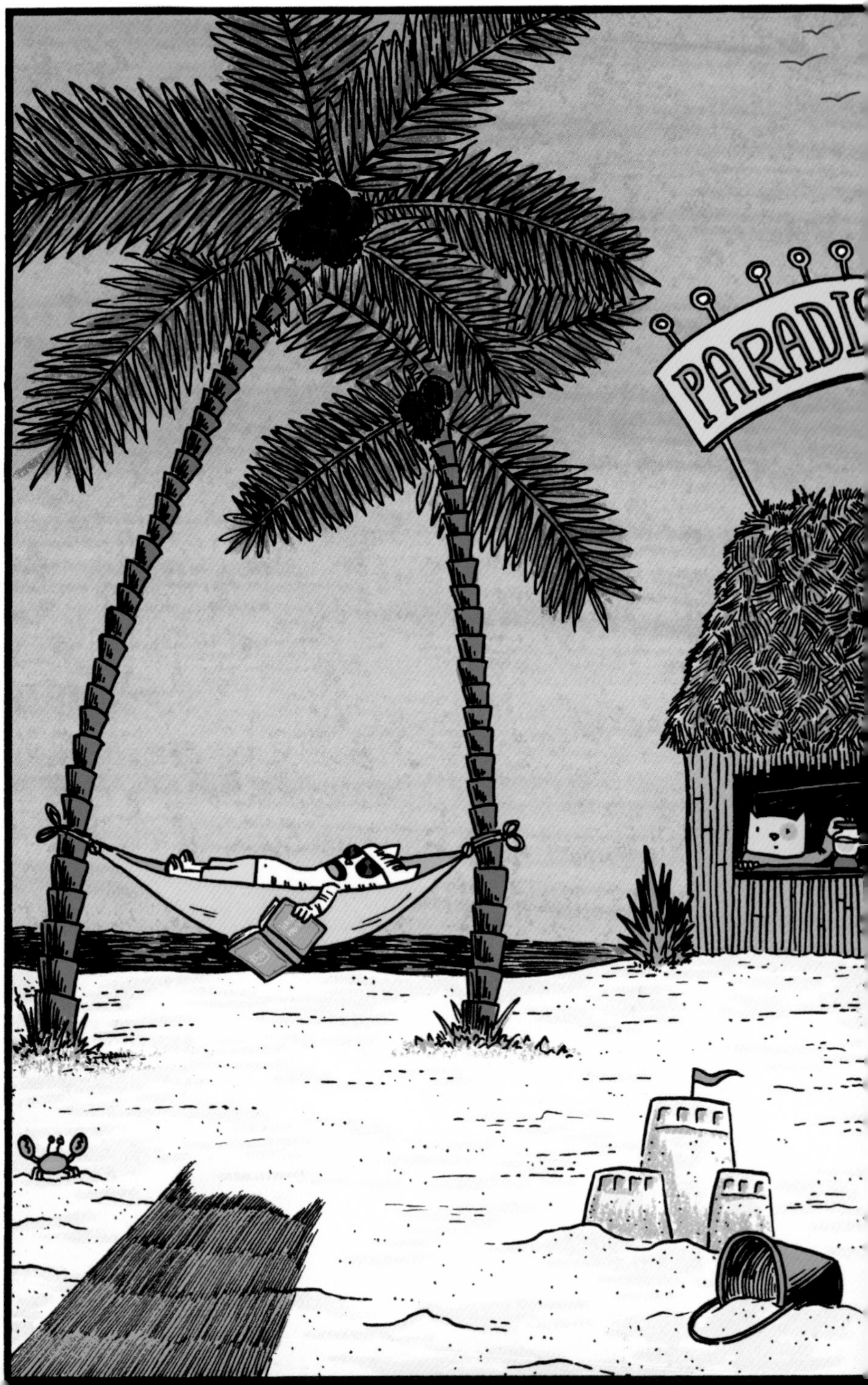
PARADI

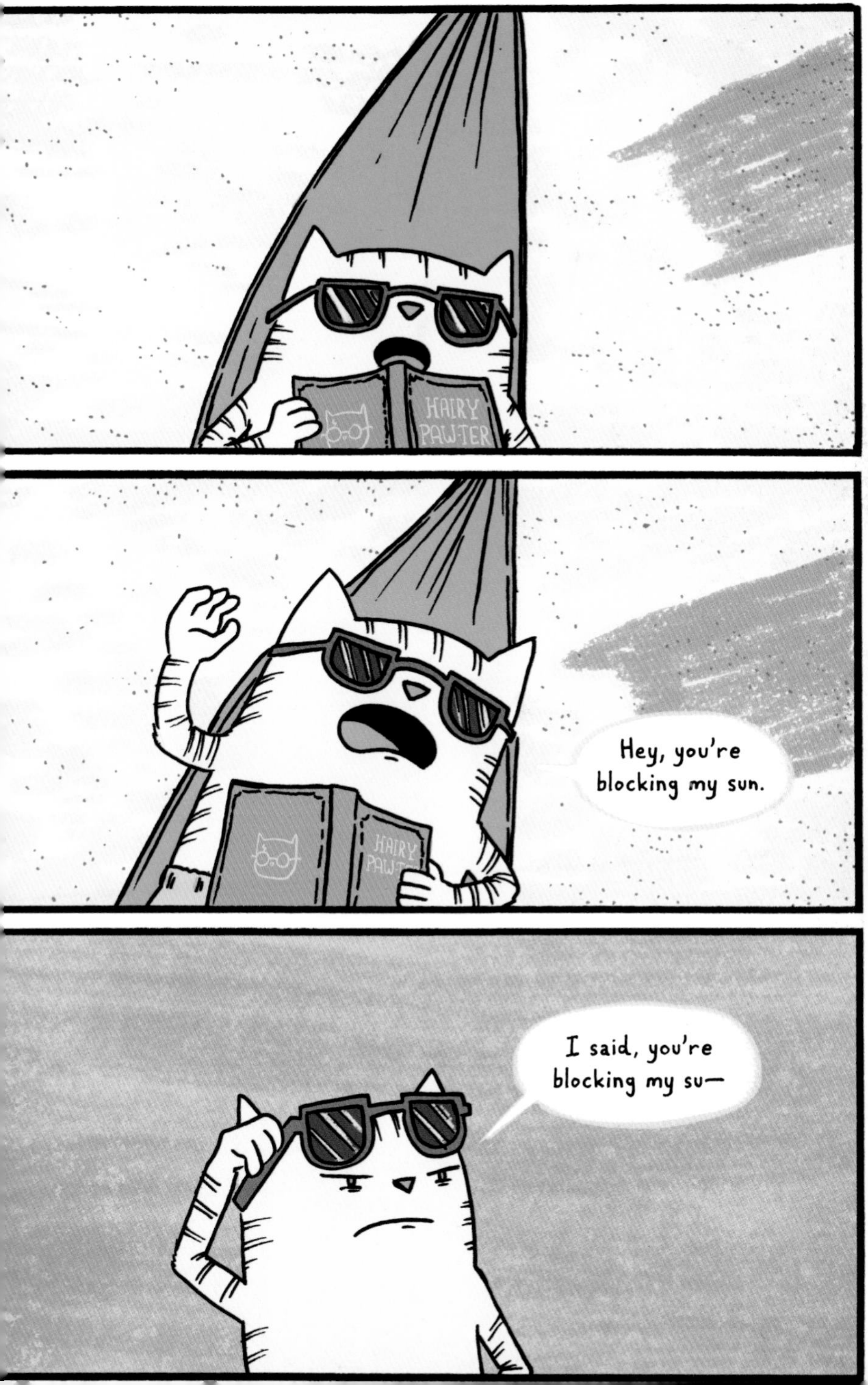
HAIRY PAW-TER
Hey, you're blocking my sun.
I said, you're blocking my su—

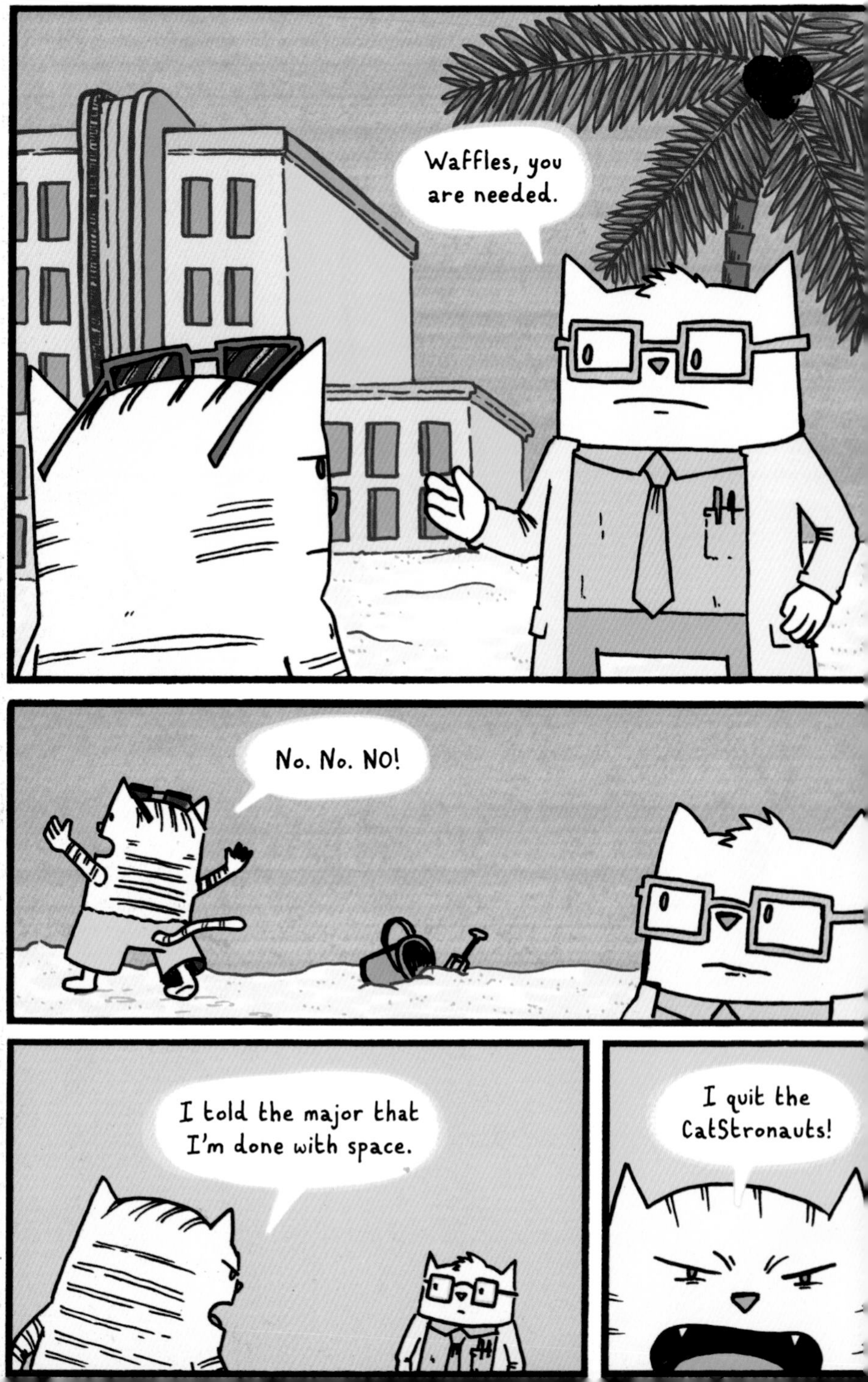
Waffles, you are needed.
No. No. NO!
I told the major that I'm done with space.
I quit the CatStronauts!

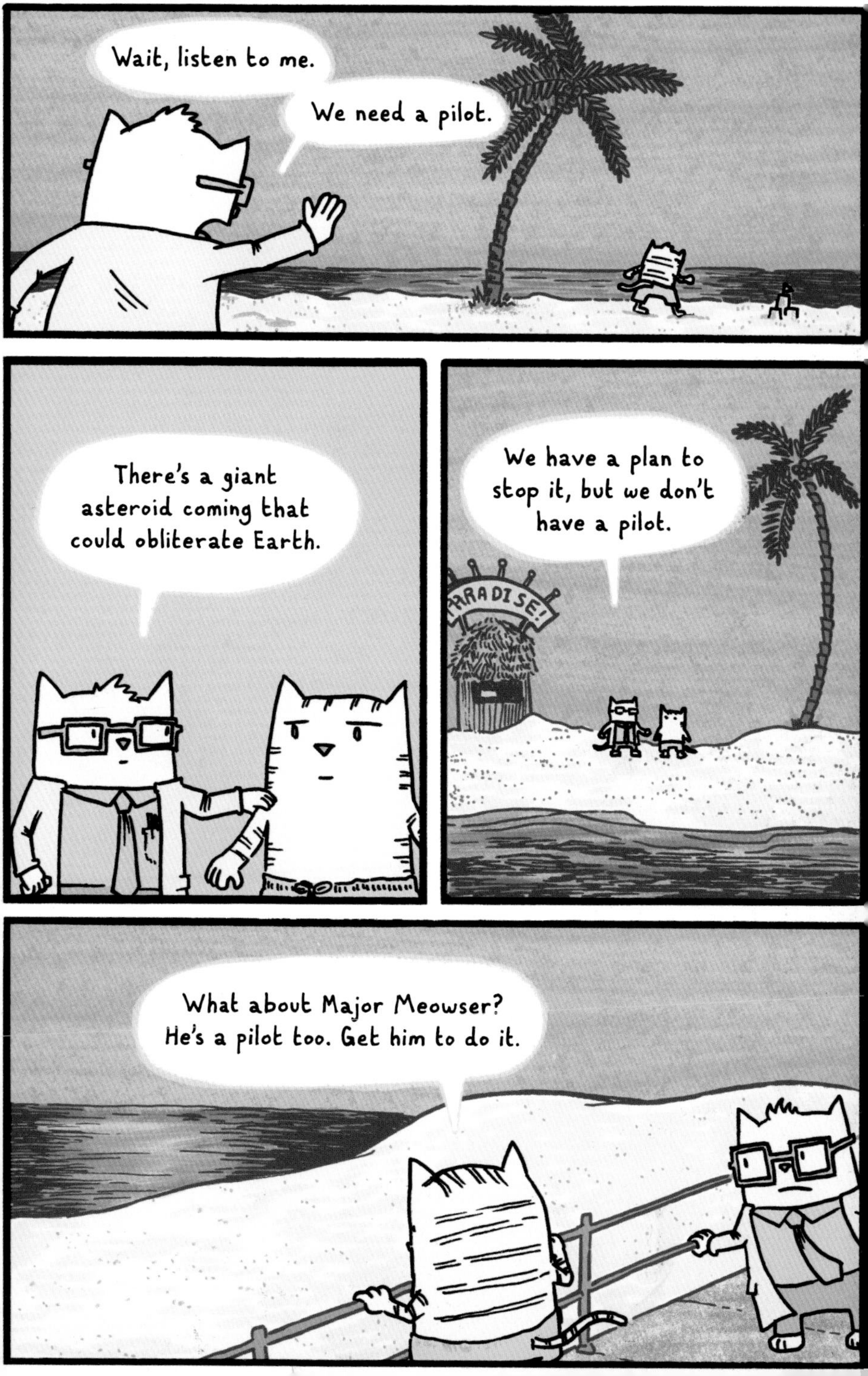
Wait, listen to me.
We need a pilot.
There's a giant asteroid coming that could obliterate Earth.
We have a plan to stop it, but we don't have a pilot.
PARADISE!
What about Major Meowser? He's a pilot too. Get him to do it.

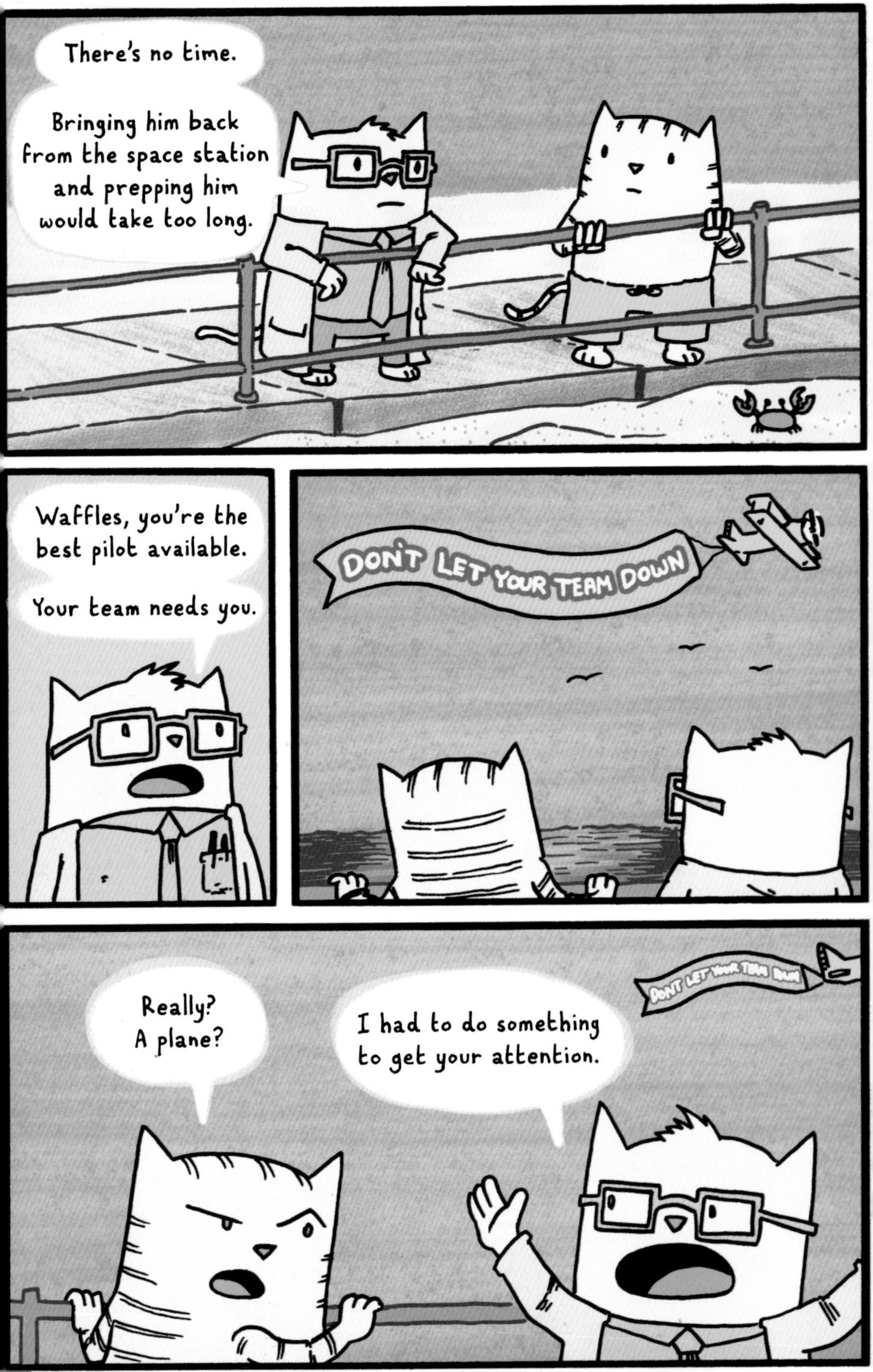
There's no time.
Bringing him back from the space station and prepping him would take too long.
Waffles, you're the best pilot available.
Your team needs you.
DON'T LET YOUR TEAM DOWN
Really? A plane?
I had to do something to get your attention.
DON'T LET YOUR TEAM DOWN

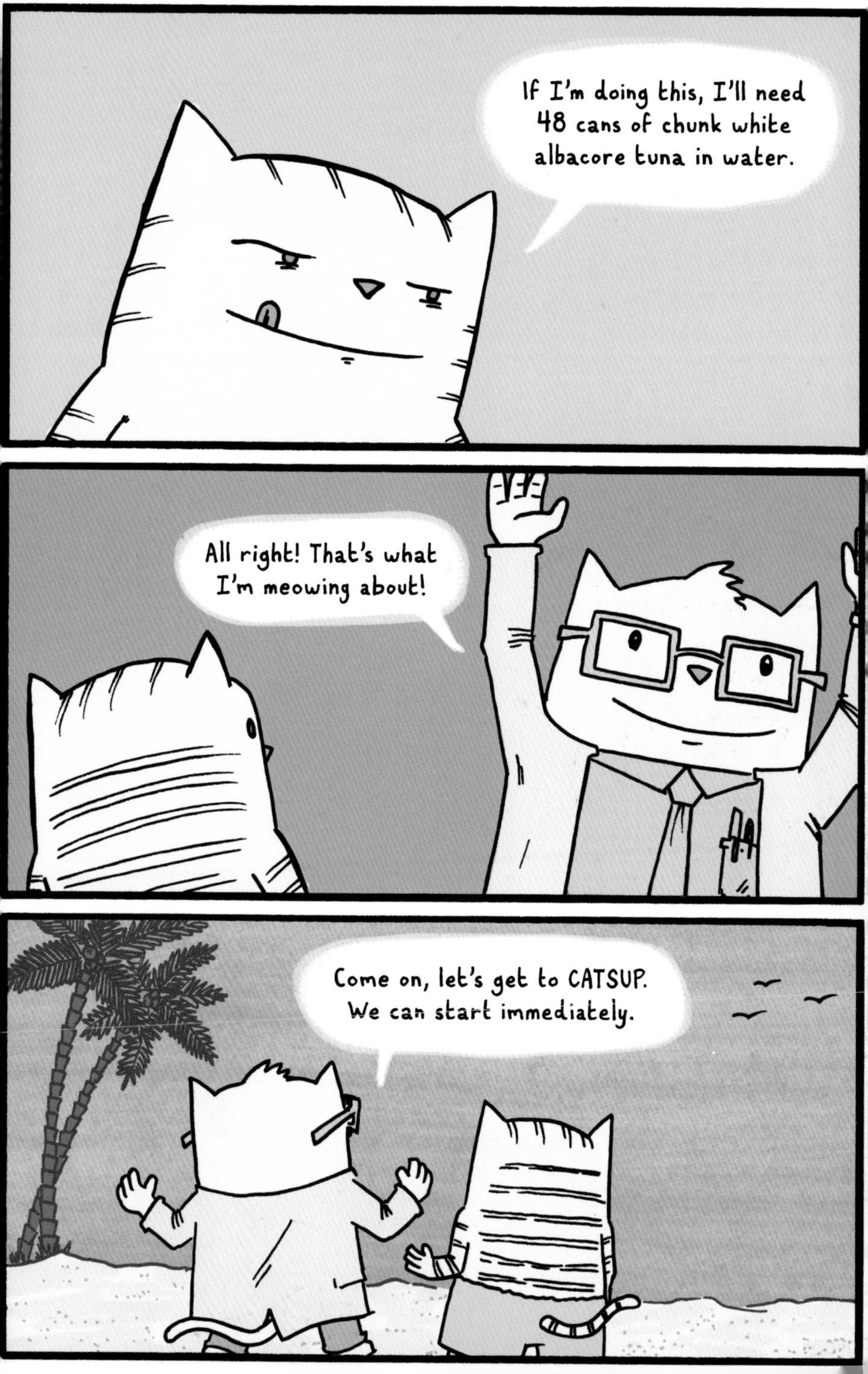
If I'm doing this, I'll need 48 cans of chunk white albacore tuna in water.
All right! That's what I'm meowing about!
Come on, let's get to CATSUP. We can start immediately.

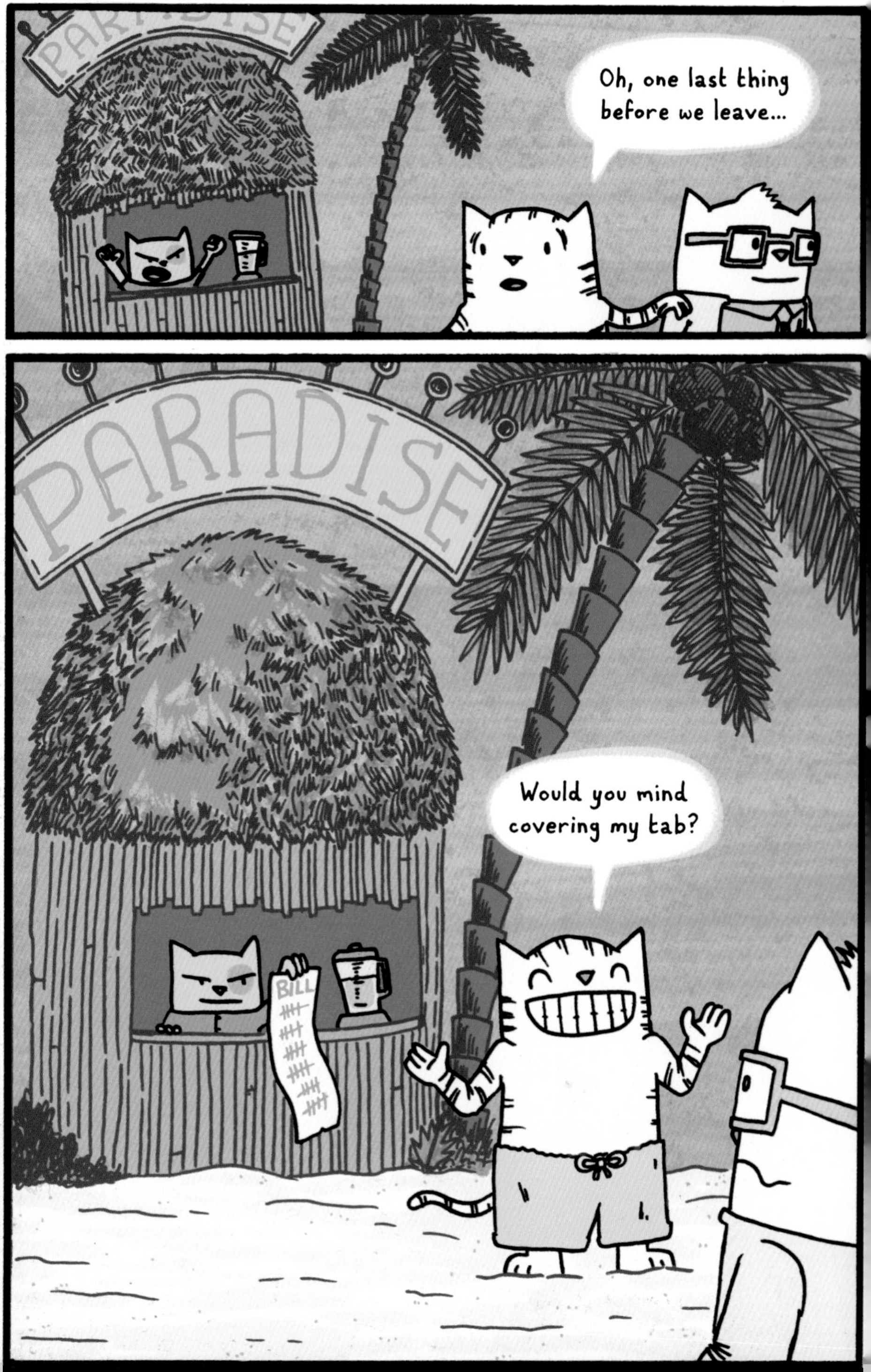
PARADISE
Oh, one last thing before we leave...
PARADISE
BILL
Would you mind covering my tab?

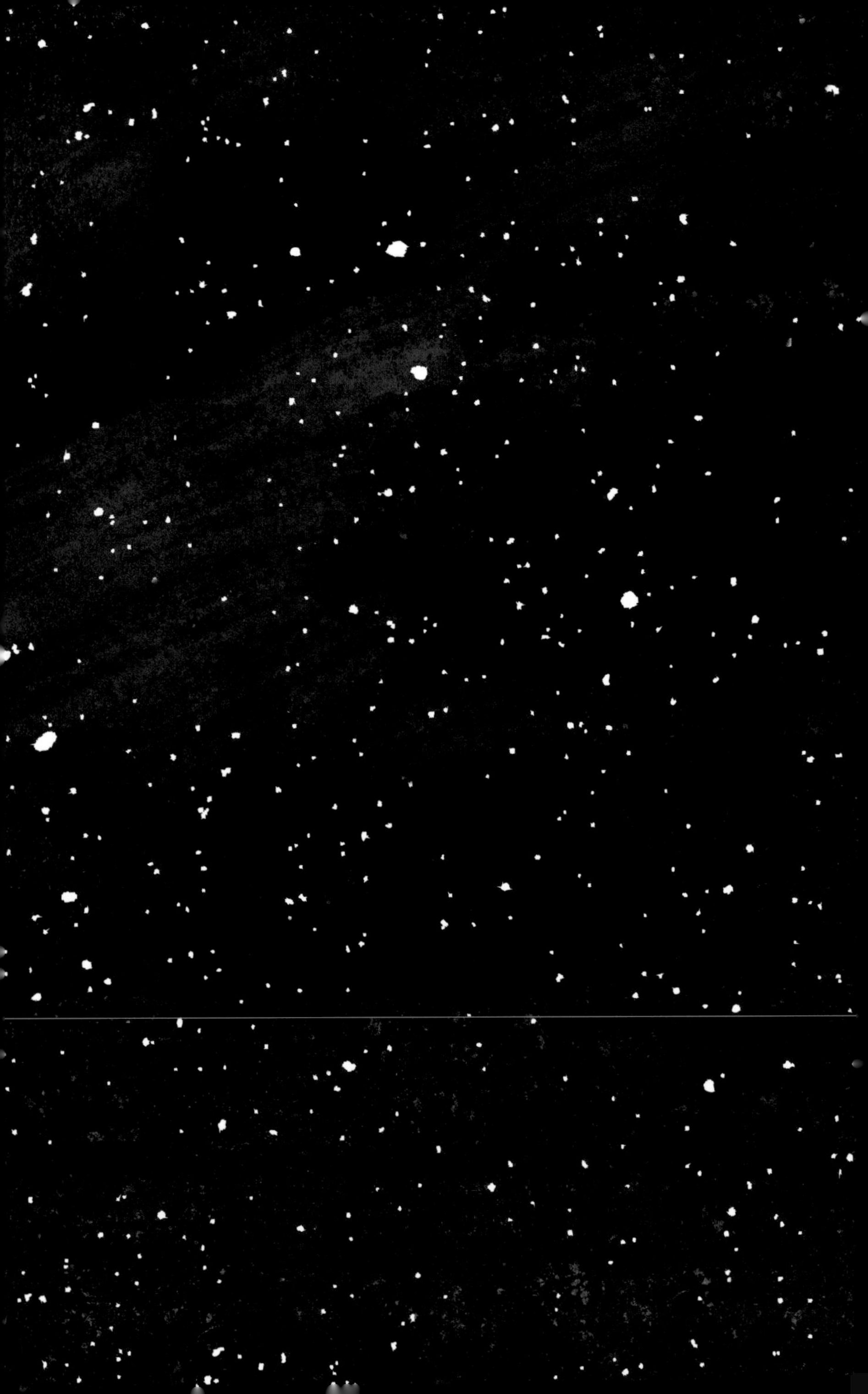

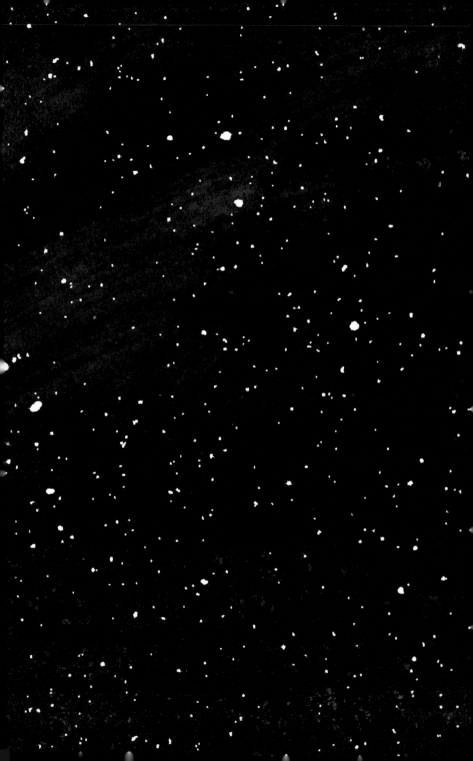

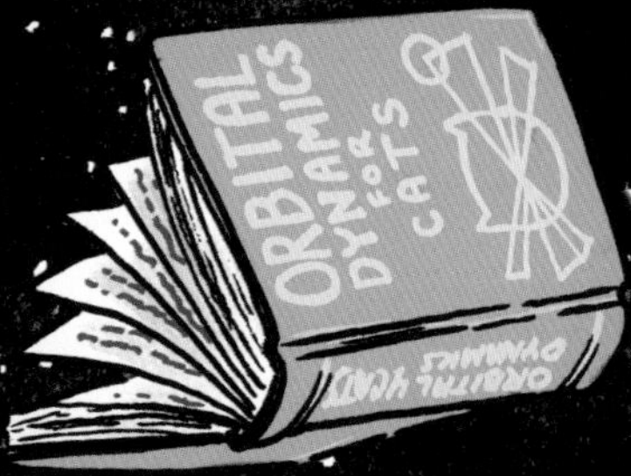
ORBITAL DYNAMICS FOR CATS

CHAPTER 8

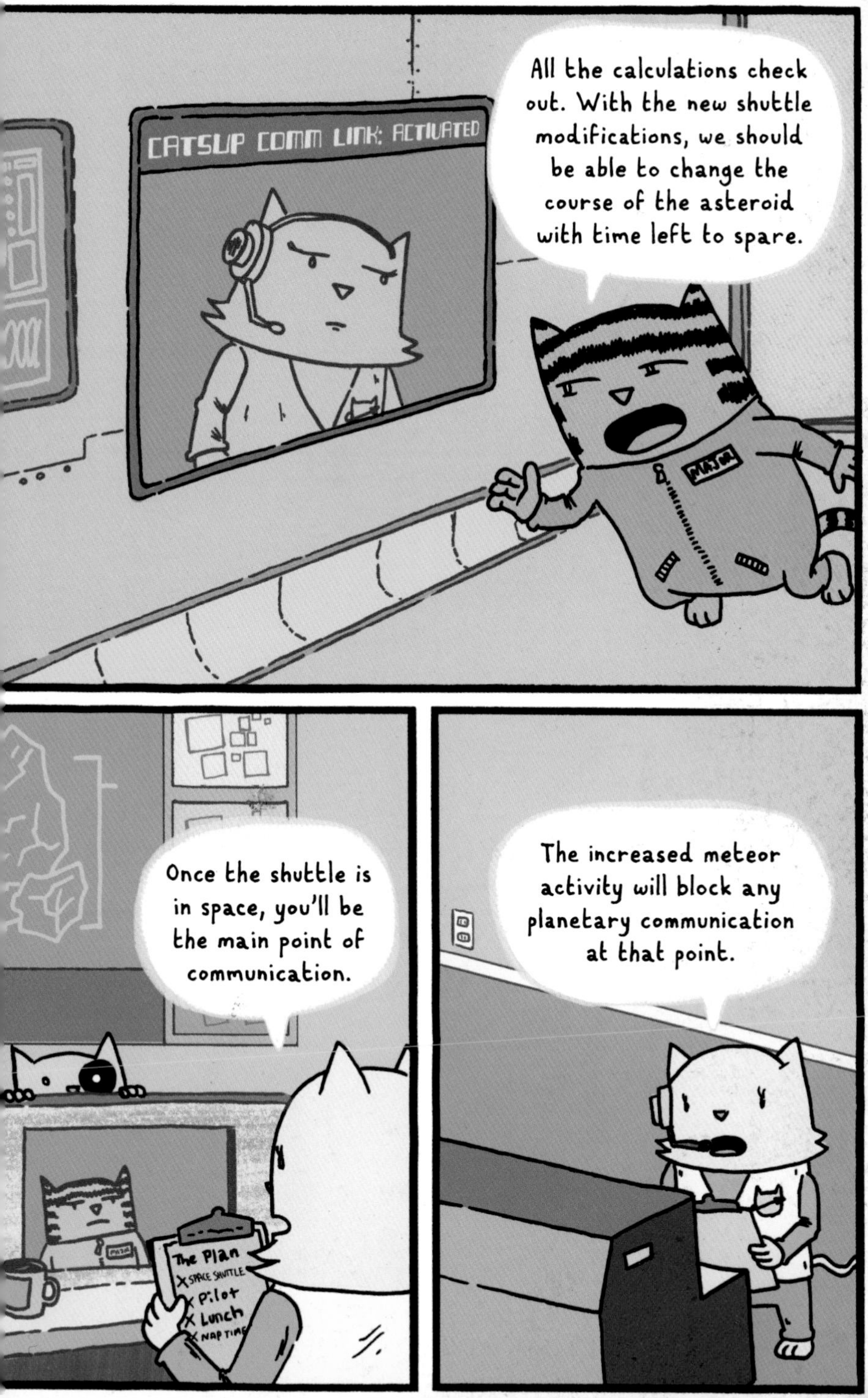
CATSUP COMM LINK: ACTIVATED
All the calculations check out. With the new shuttle modifications, we should be able to change the course of the asteroid with time left to spare.
MAJOR
Once the shuttle is in space, you'll be the main point of communication.
The Plan
SPACE SHUTTLE
Pilot
Lunch
NAP TIM
The increased meteor activity will block any planetary communication at that point.

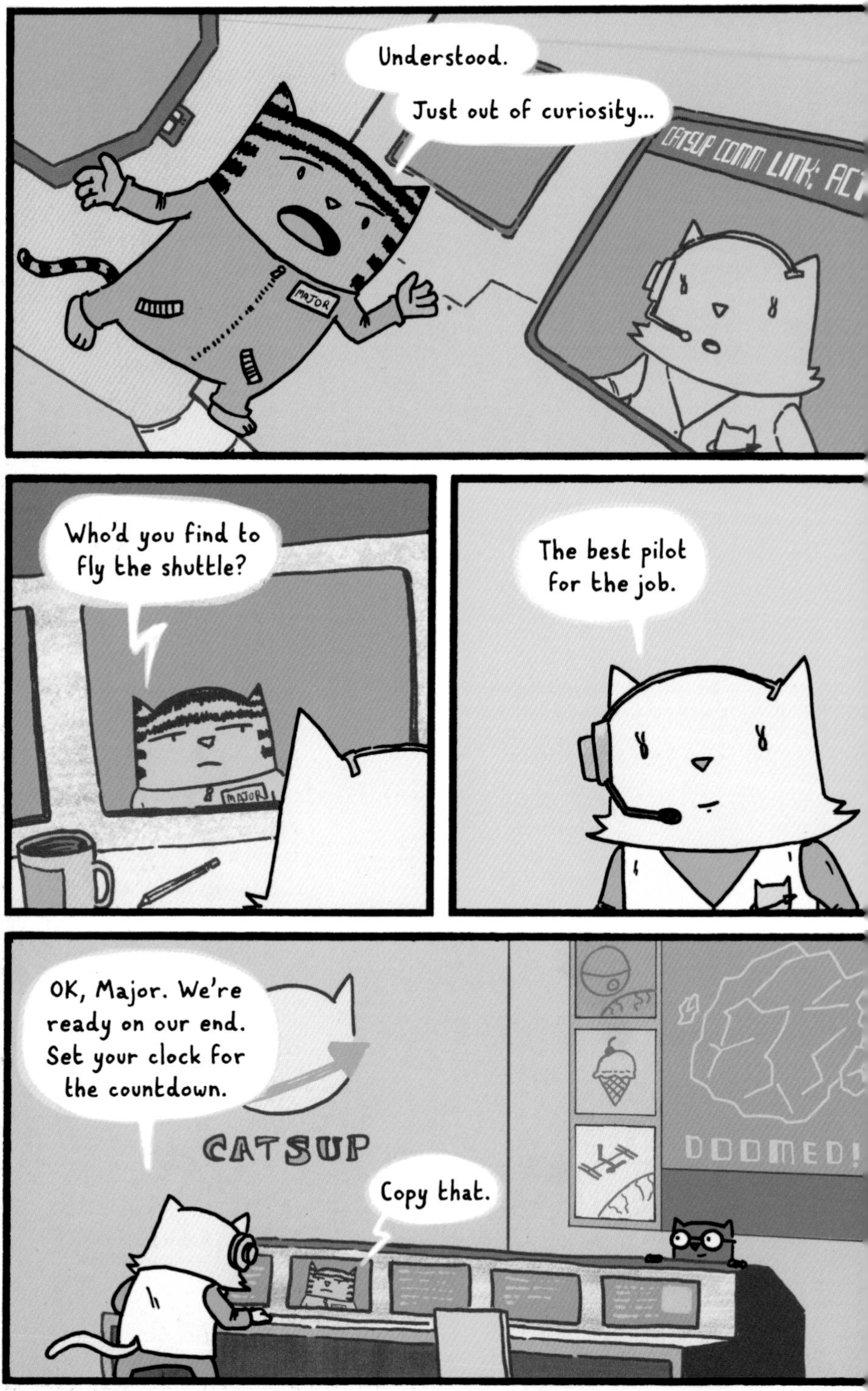
Understood.
Just out of curiosity...
CATSUP COMM LINK: ACT
MAJOR
Who'd you find to fly the shuttle?
MAJOR
The best pilot for the job.
OK, Major. We're ready on our end. Set your clock for the countdown.
CATSUP
DOOMED!
Copy that.

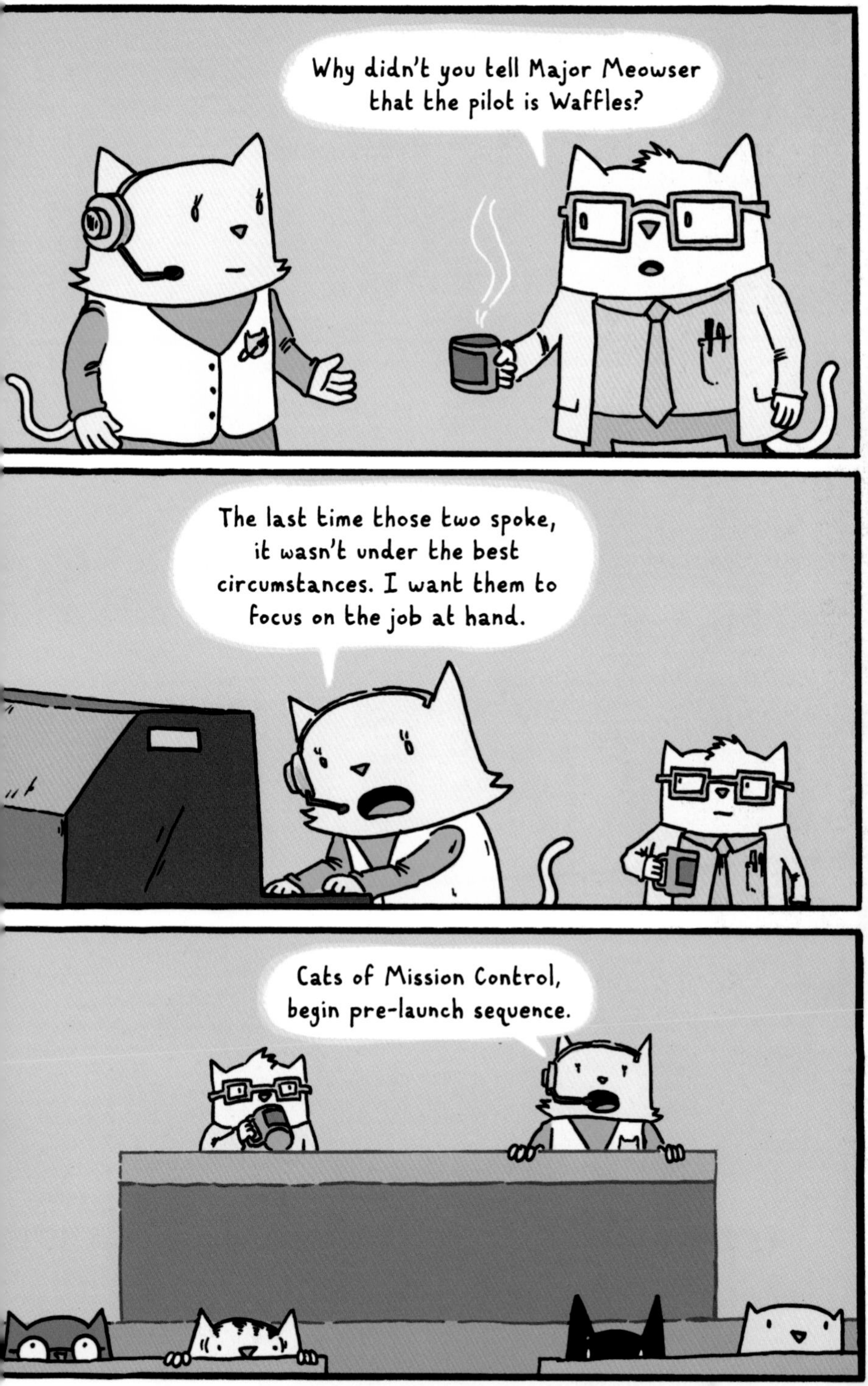
Why didn't you tell Major Meowser that the pilot is Waffles?
The last time those two spoke, it wasn't under the best circumstances. I want them to focus on the job at hand.
Cats of Mission Control, begin pre-launch sequence.

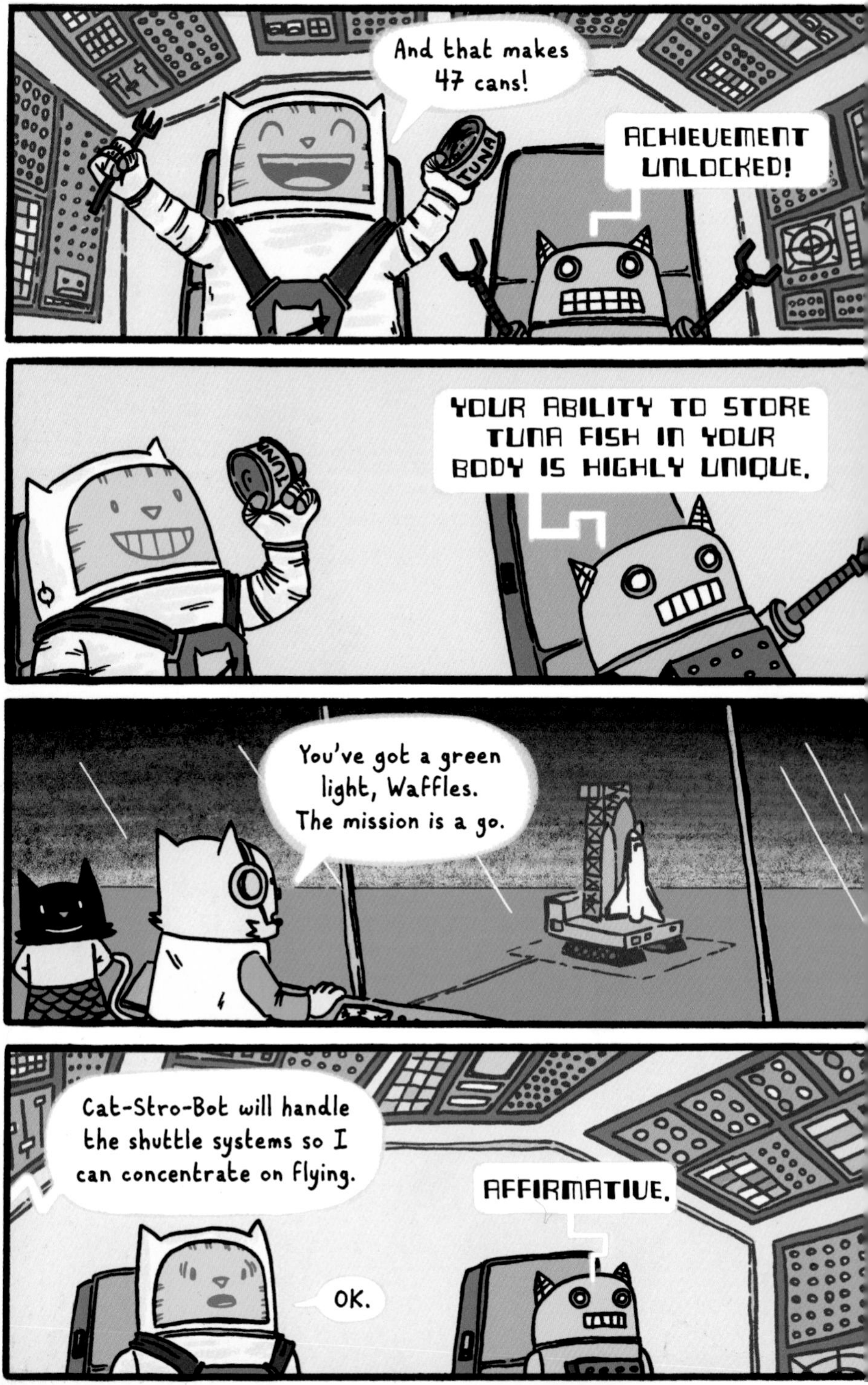

And that makes 47 cans!
ACHIEVEMENT UNLOCKED!
TUNA
YOUR ABILITY TO STORE TUNA FISH IN YOUR BODY IS HIGHLY UNIQUE.
TUNA
You've got a green light, Waffles. The mission is a go.
Cat-Stro-Bot will handle the shuttle systems so I can concentrate on flying.
AFFIRMATIVE.
OK.

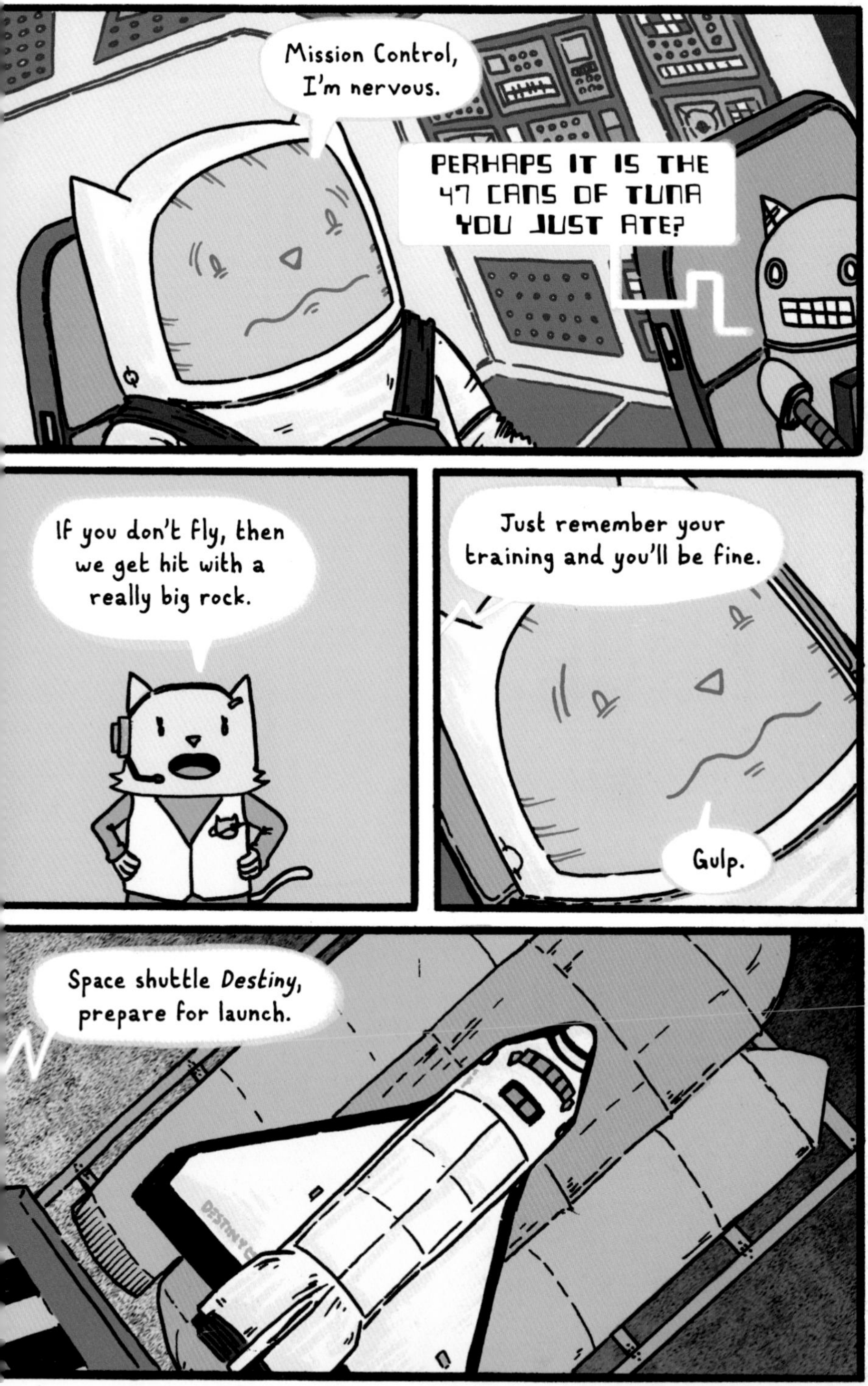
Mission Control, I'm nervous.
PERHAPS IT IS THE 47 CANS OF TUNA YOU JUST ATE?
If you don't fly, then we get hit with a really big rock.
Just remember your training and you'll be fine.
Gulp.
Space shuttle *Destiny*, prepare for launch.

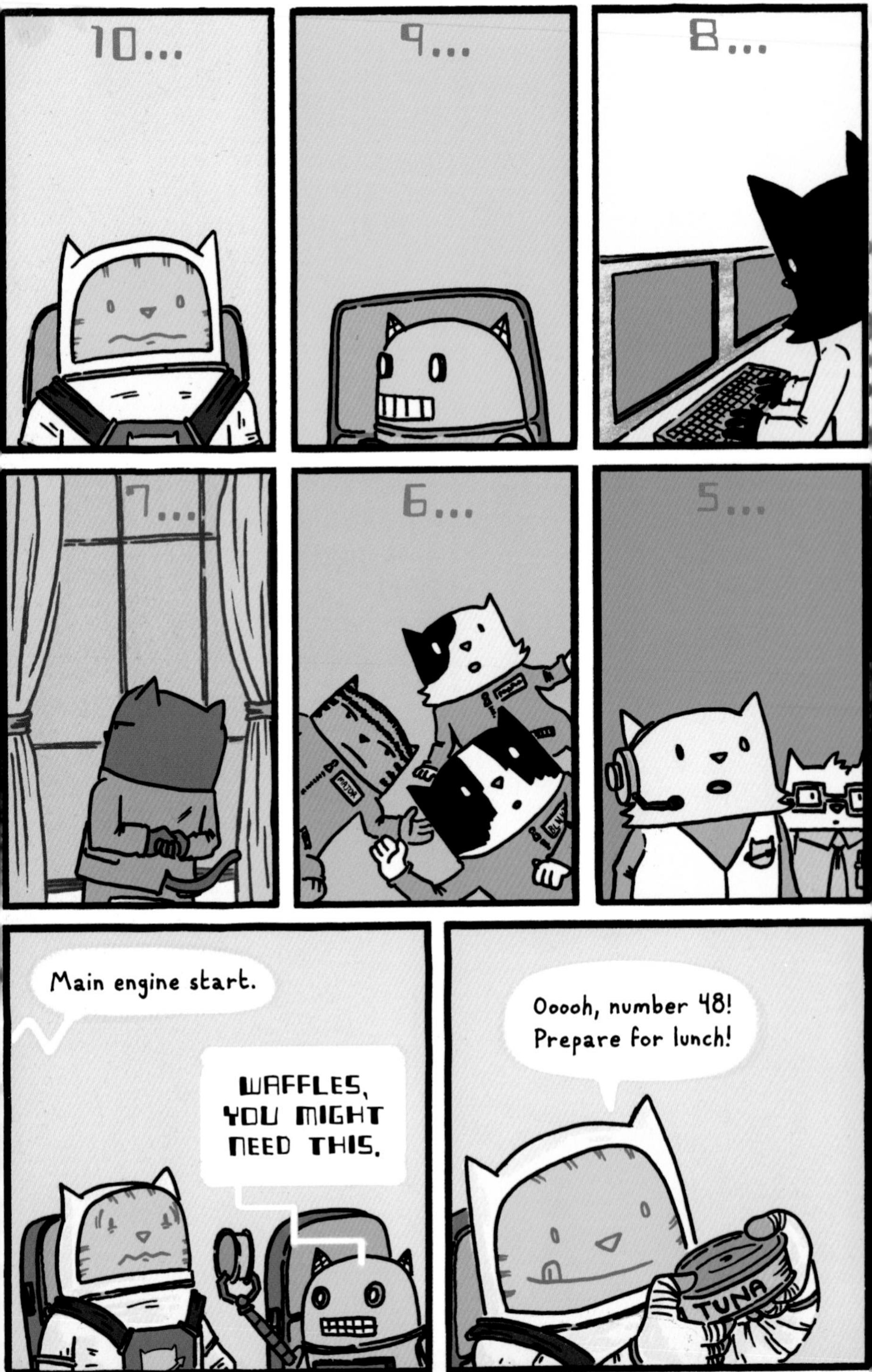
10...
9...
8...
7...
6...
MAJOR
5...
Main engine start.
WAFFLES, YOU MIGHT NEED THIS.
Ooooh, number 48! Prepare for lunch!
TUNA

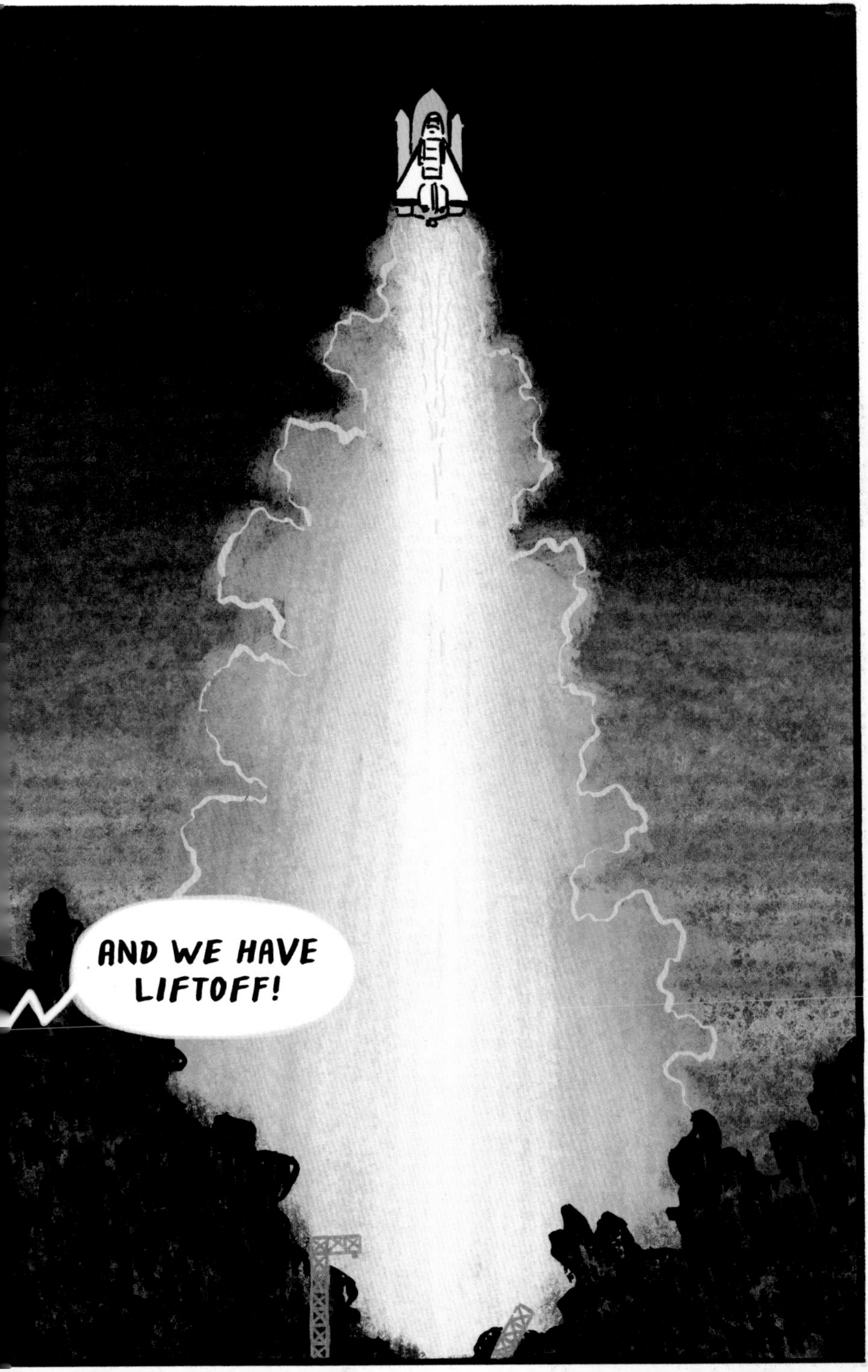
AND WE HAVE LIFTOFF!

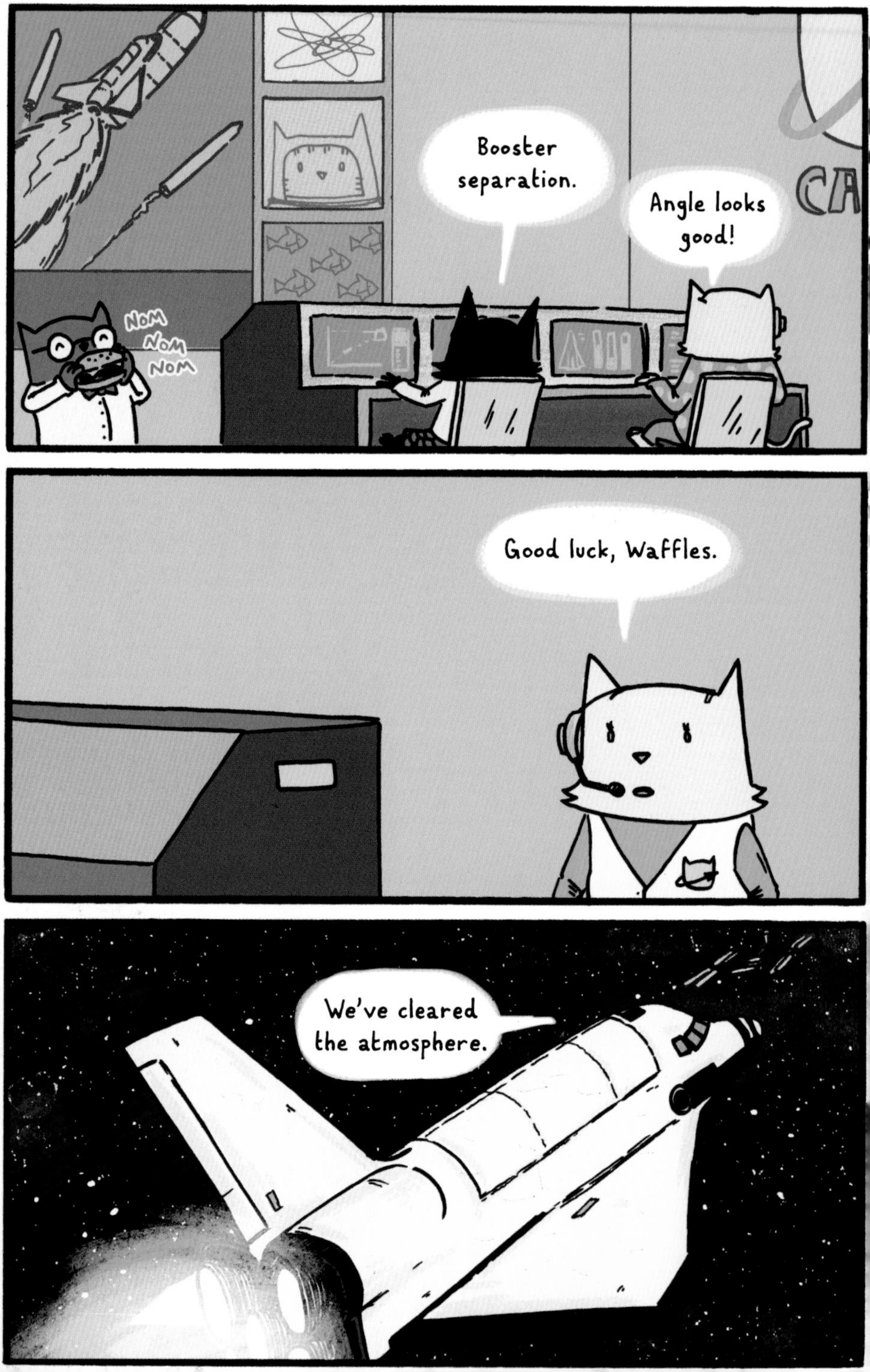
NOM NOM NOM
Booster separation.
Angle looks good!
Good luck, Waffles.
We've cleared the atmosphere.

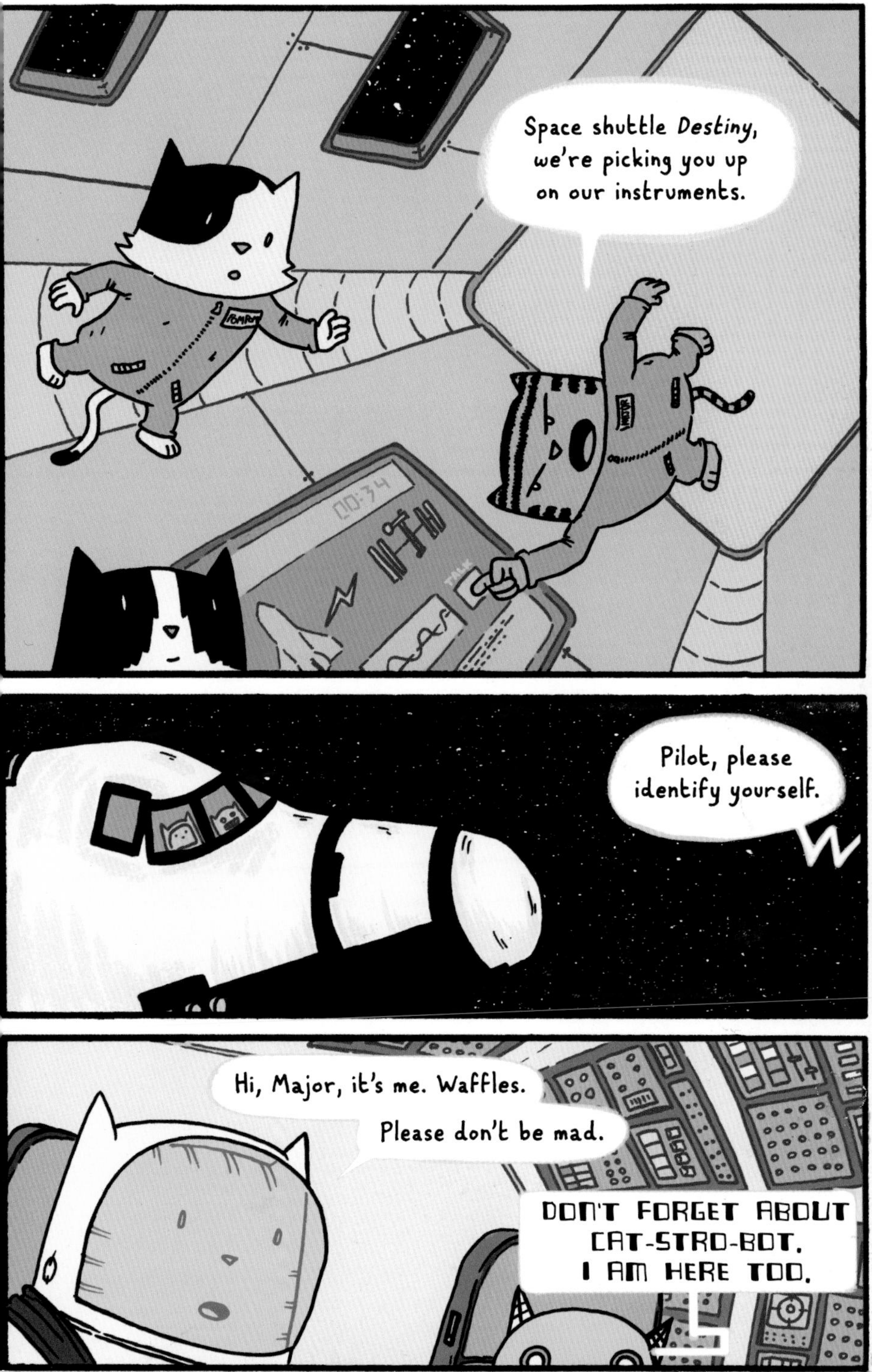
Space shuttle *Destiny*, we're picking you up on our instruments.
Pilot, please identify yourself.
Hi, Major, it's me. Waffles.
Please don't be mad.
DON'T FORGET ABOUT CAT-STRO-BOT. I AM HERE TOO.

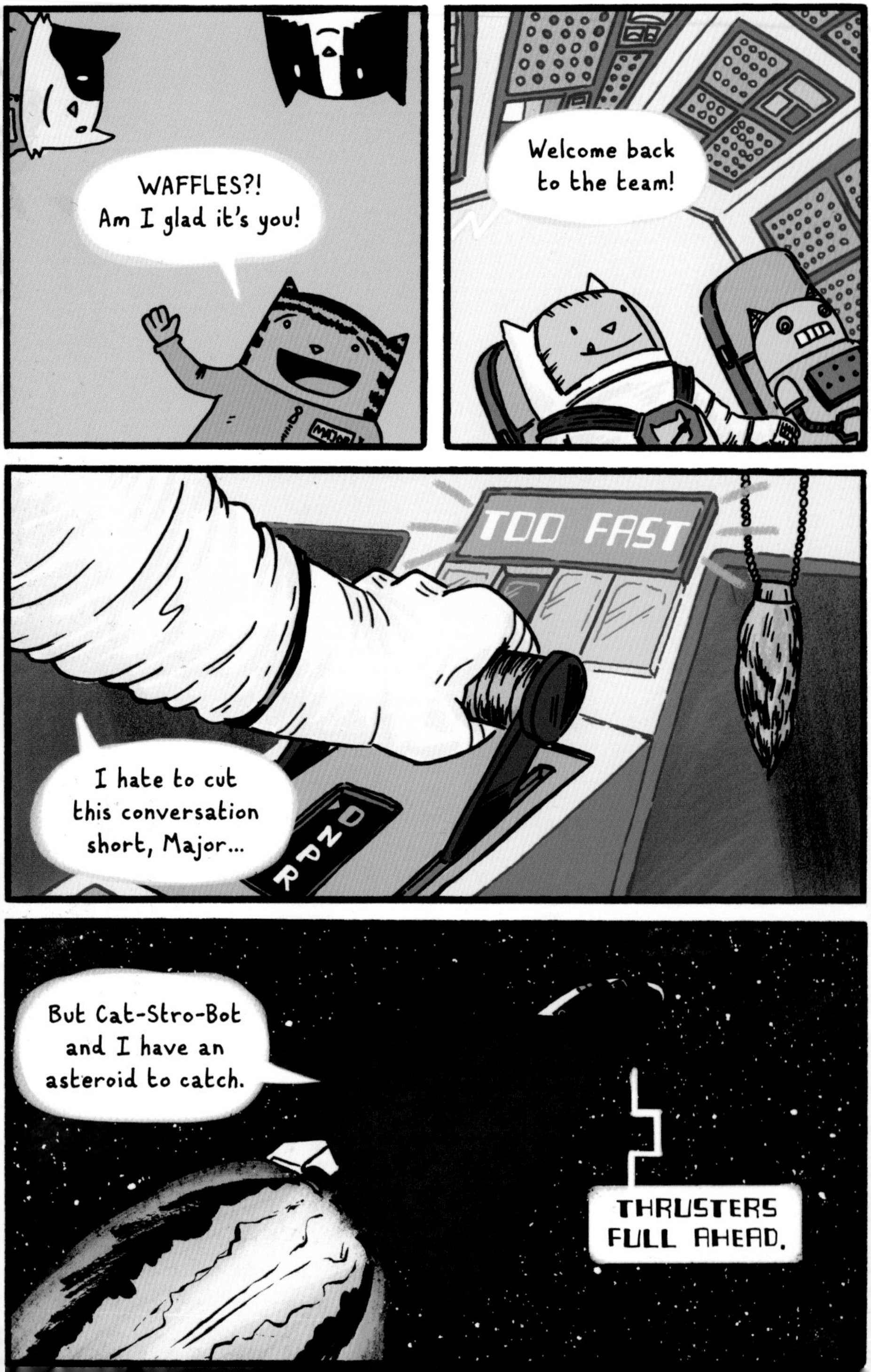
WAFFLES?! Am I glad it's you!
Welcome back to the team!
TOO FAST
I hate to cut this conversation short, Major...
D N P R
But Cat-Stro-Bot and I have an asteroid to catch.
THRUSTERS FULL AHEAD.

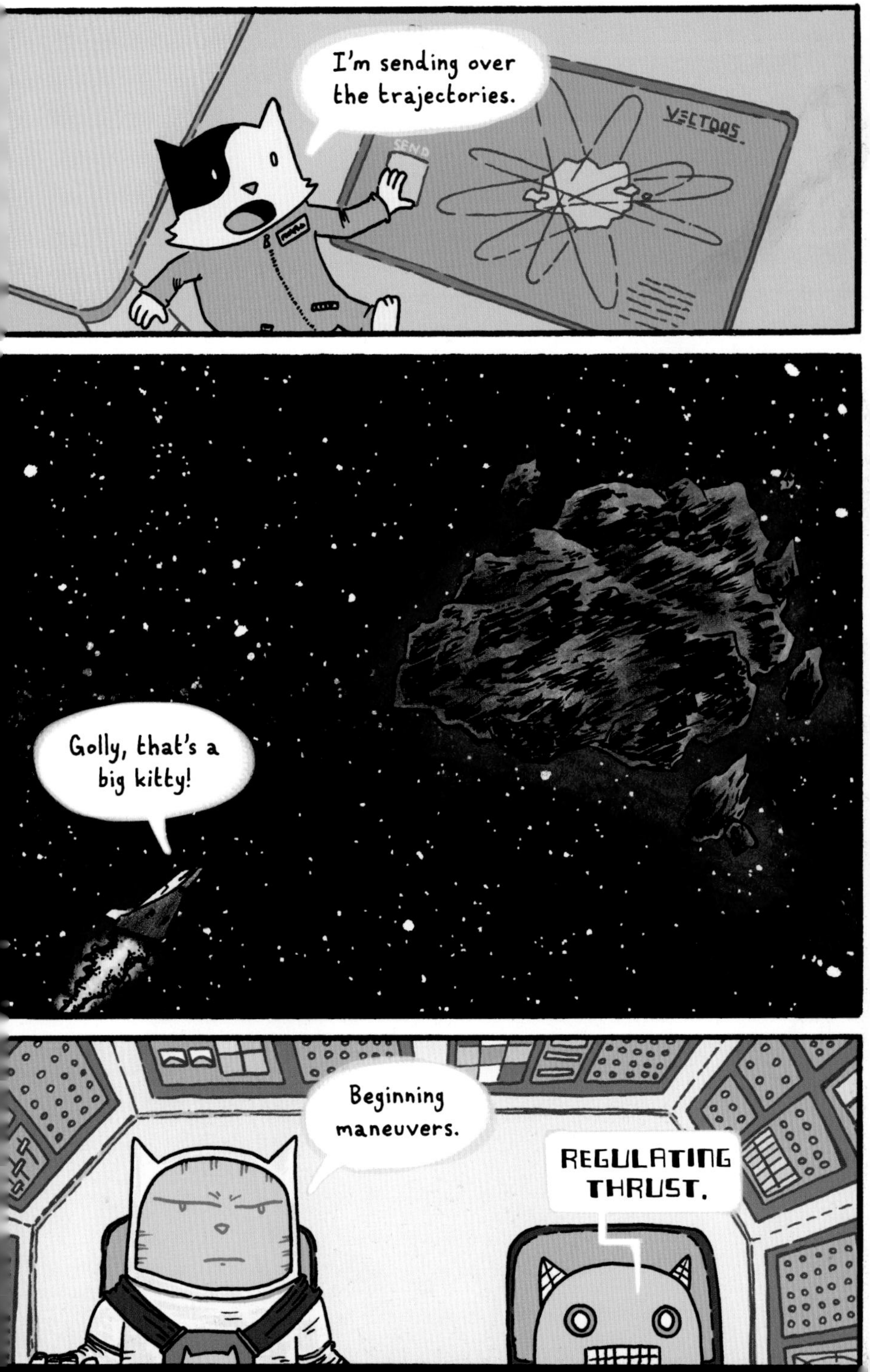
I'm sending over the trajectories.
Golly, that's a big kitty!
Beginning maneuvers.
REGULATING THRUST.

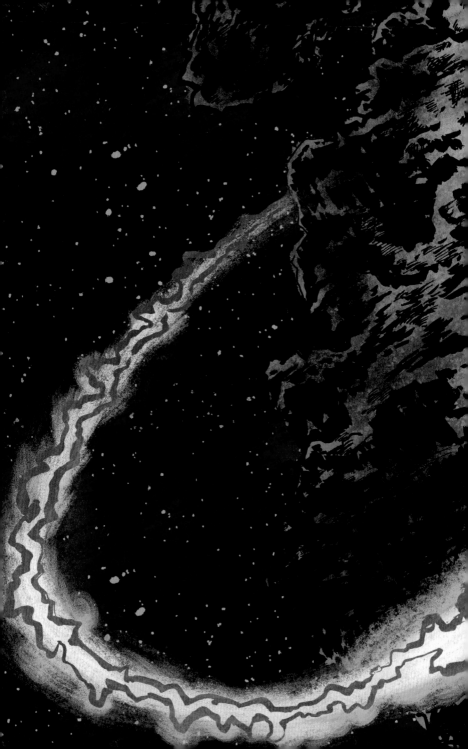

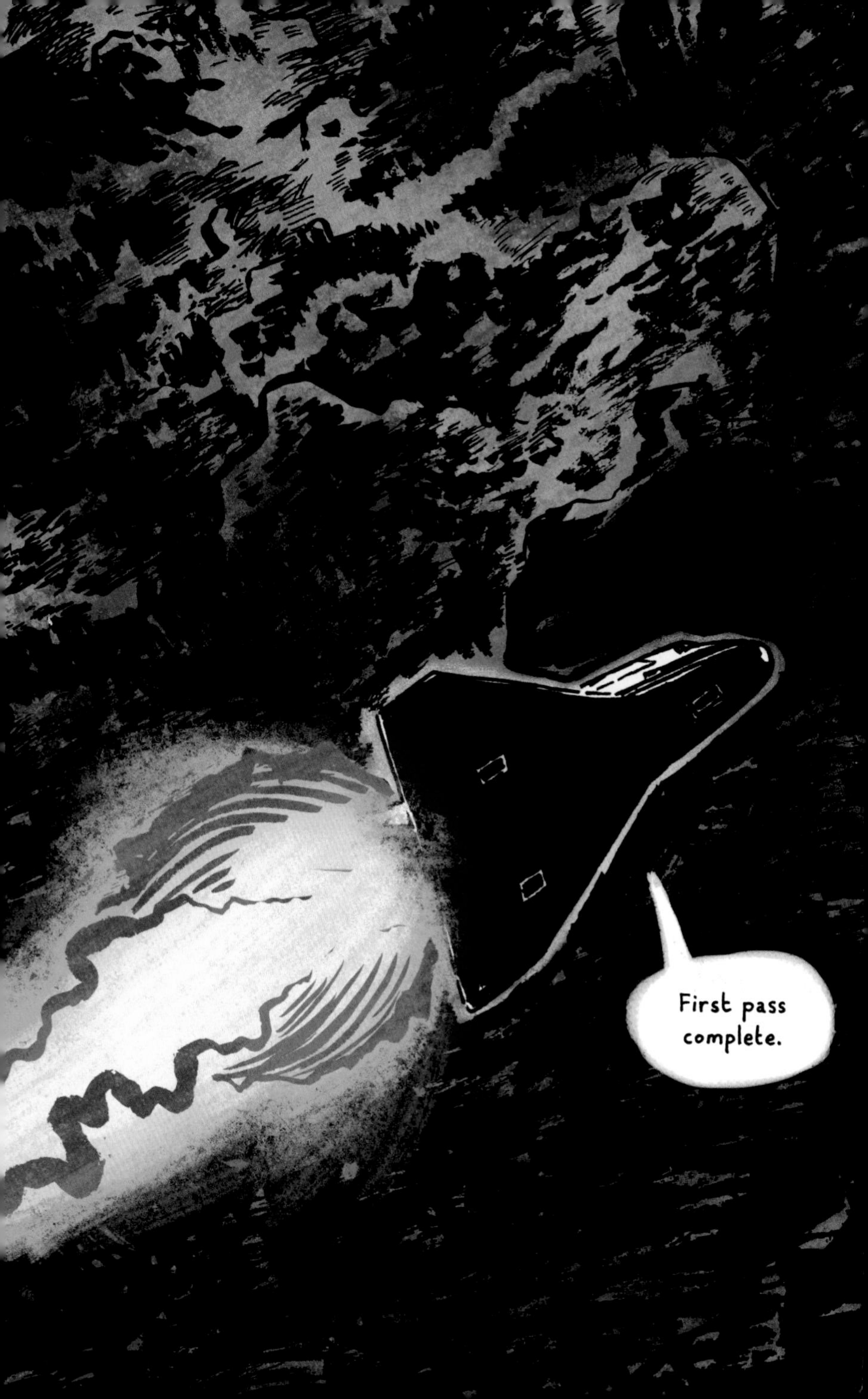
First pass complete.

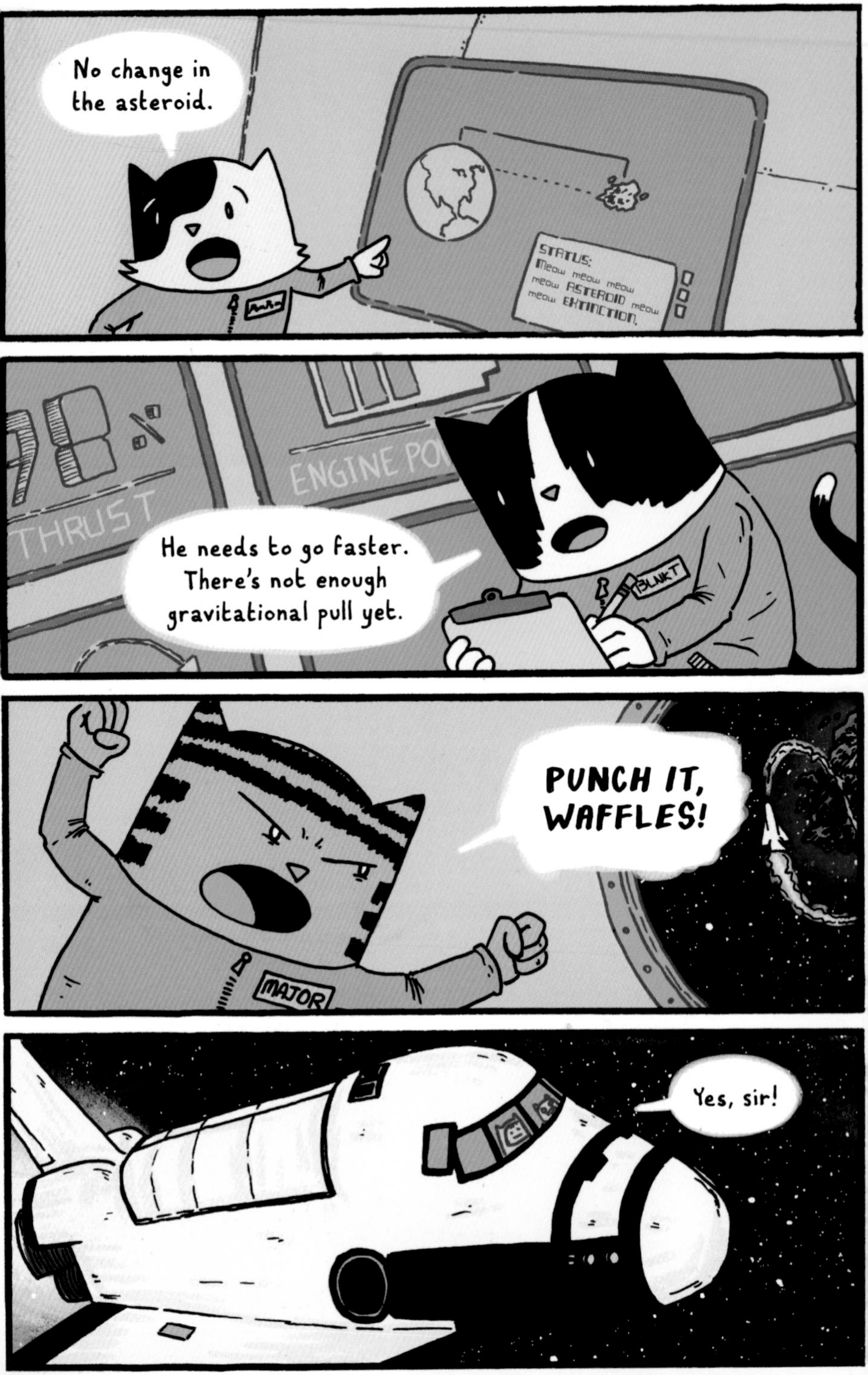
No change in the asteroid.
STATUS:
Meow meow meow
meow ASTEROID meow
meow EXTINCTION.
THRUST
ENGINE PO
He needs to go faster. There's not enough gravitational pull yet.
BLNKT
PUNCH IT, WAFFLES!
MAJOR
Yes, sir!

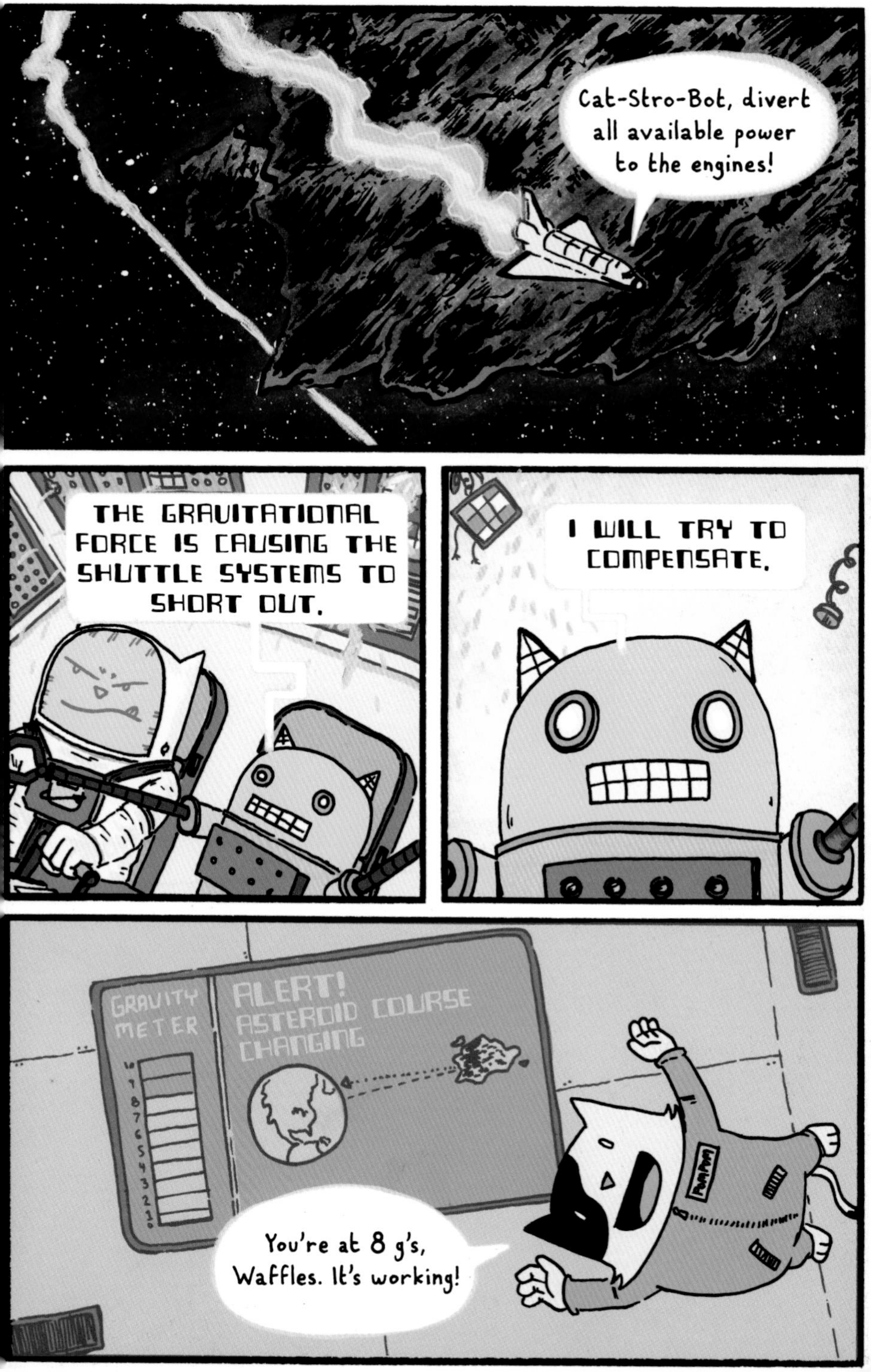
Cat-Stro-Bot, divert all available power to the engines!
THE GRAVITATIONAL FORCE IS CAUSING THE SHUTTLE SYSTEMS TO SHORT OUT.
I WILL TRY TO COMPENSATE.
GRAVITY METER
ALERT! ASTEROID COURSE CHANGING
You're at 8 g's, Waffles. It's working!

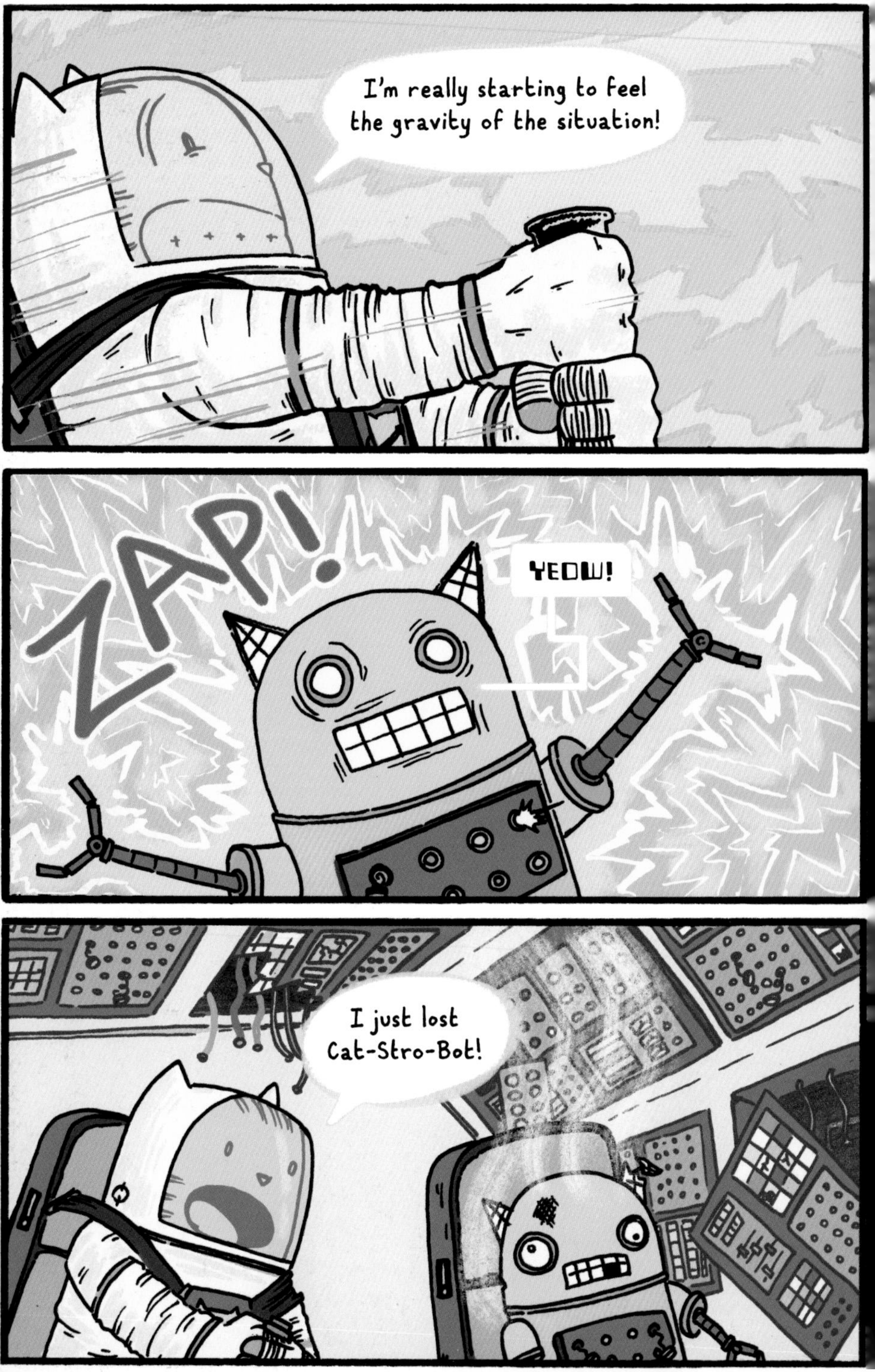
I'm really starting to feel the gravity of the situation!
ZAP!
YEOW!
I just lost Cat-Stro-Bot!

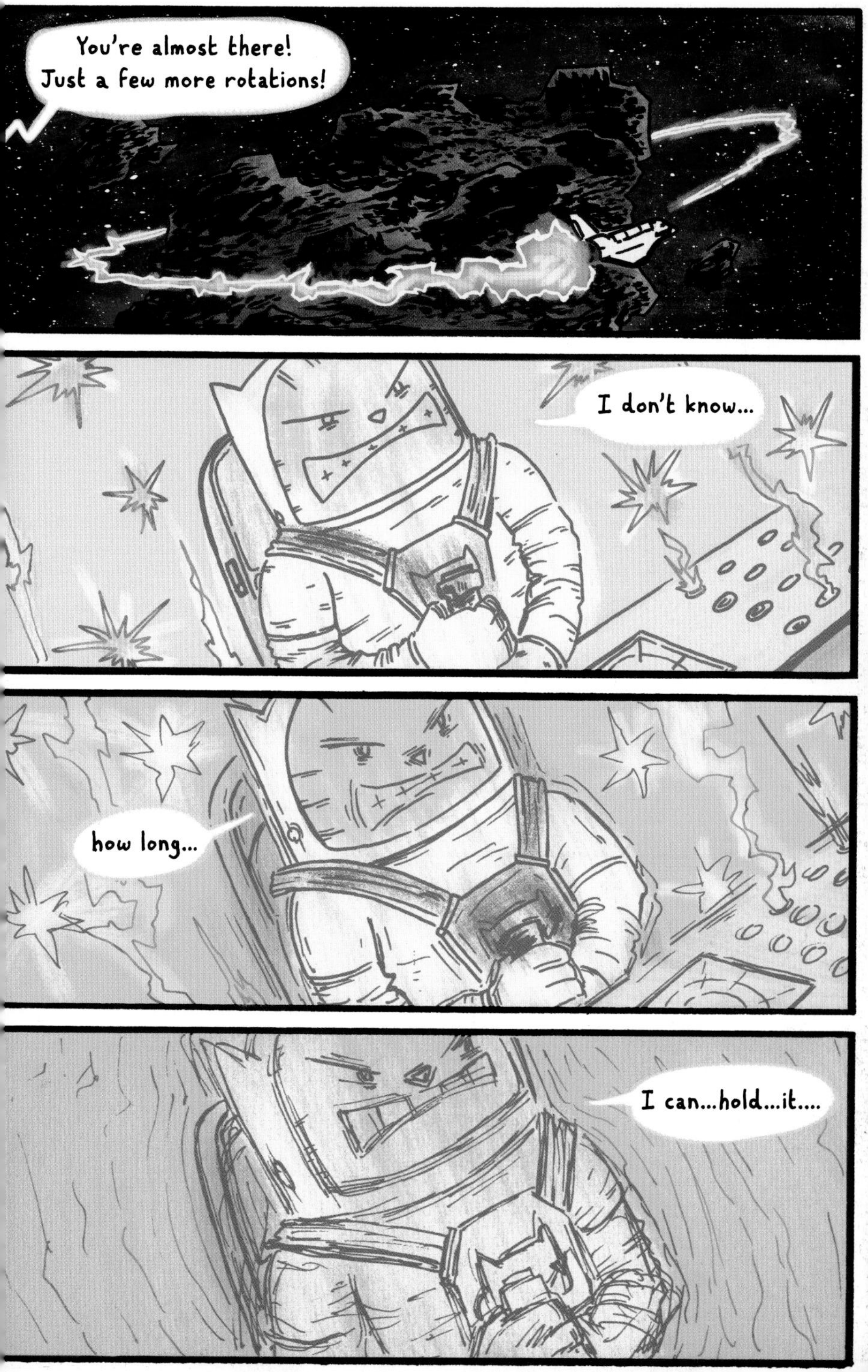
You're almost there!
Just a few more rotations!
I don't know...
how long...
I can...hold...it....

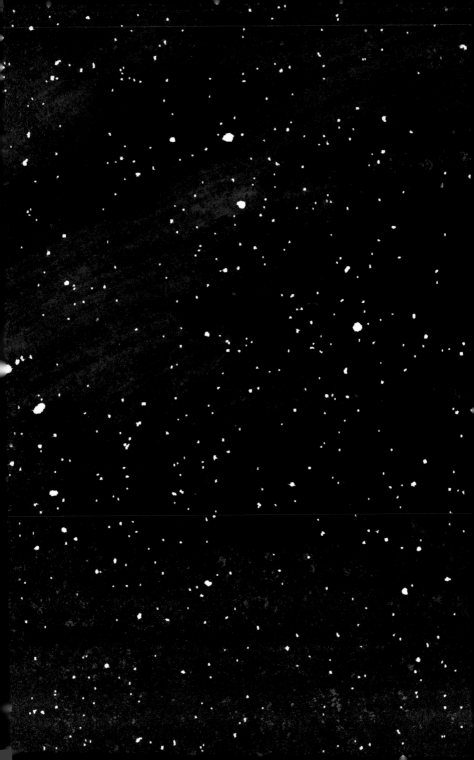

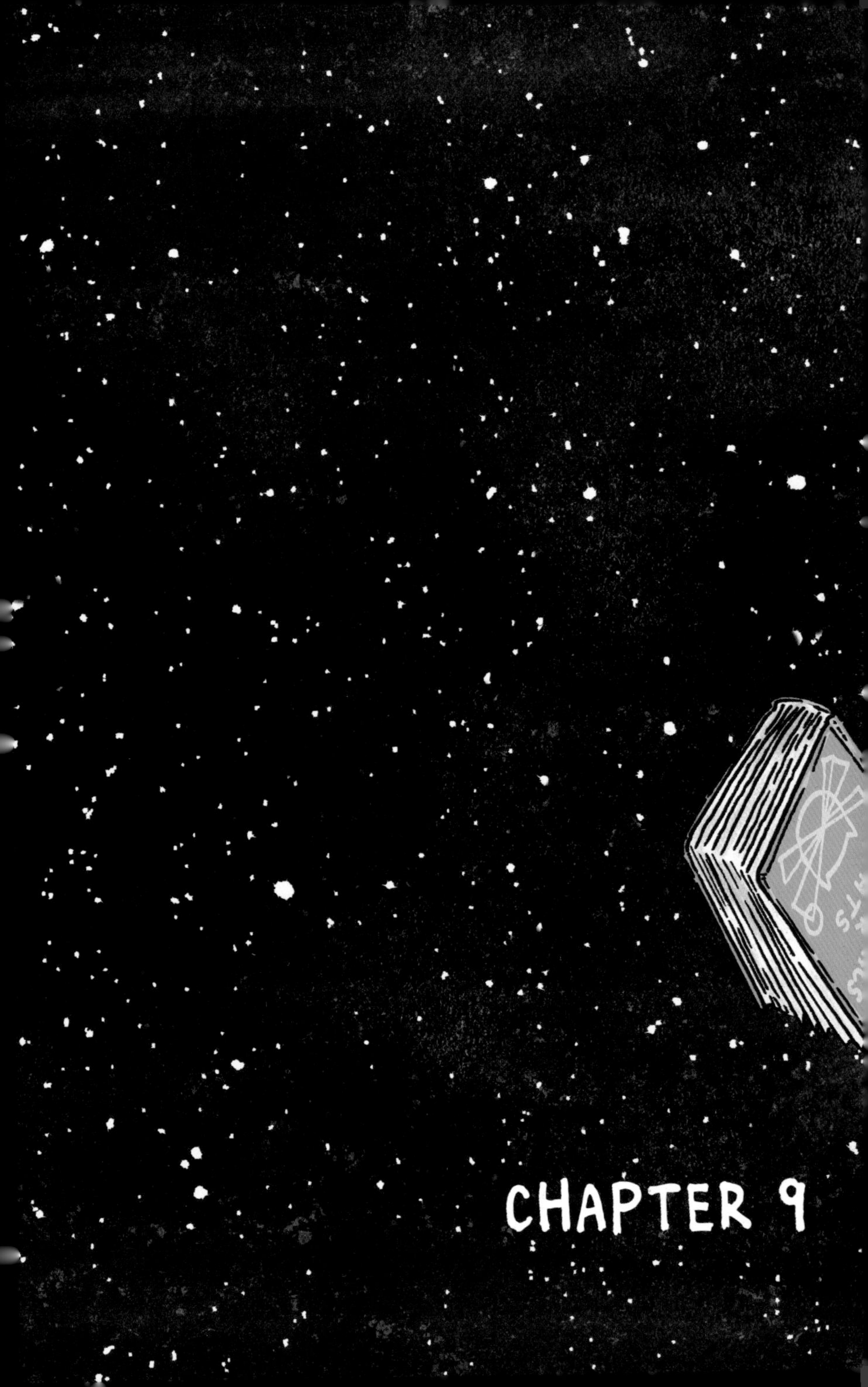
CHAPTER 9

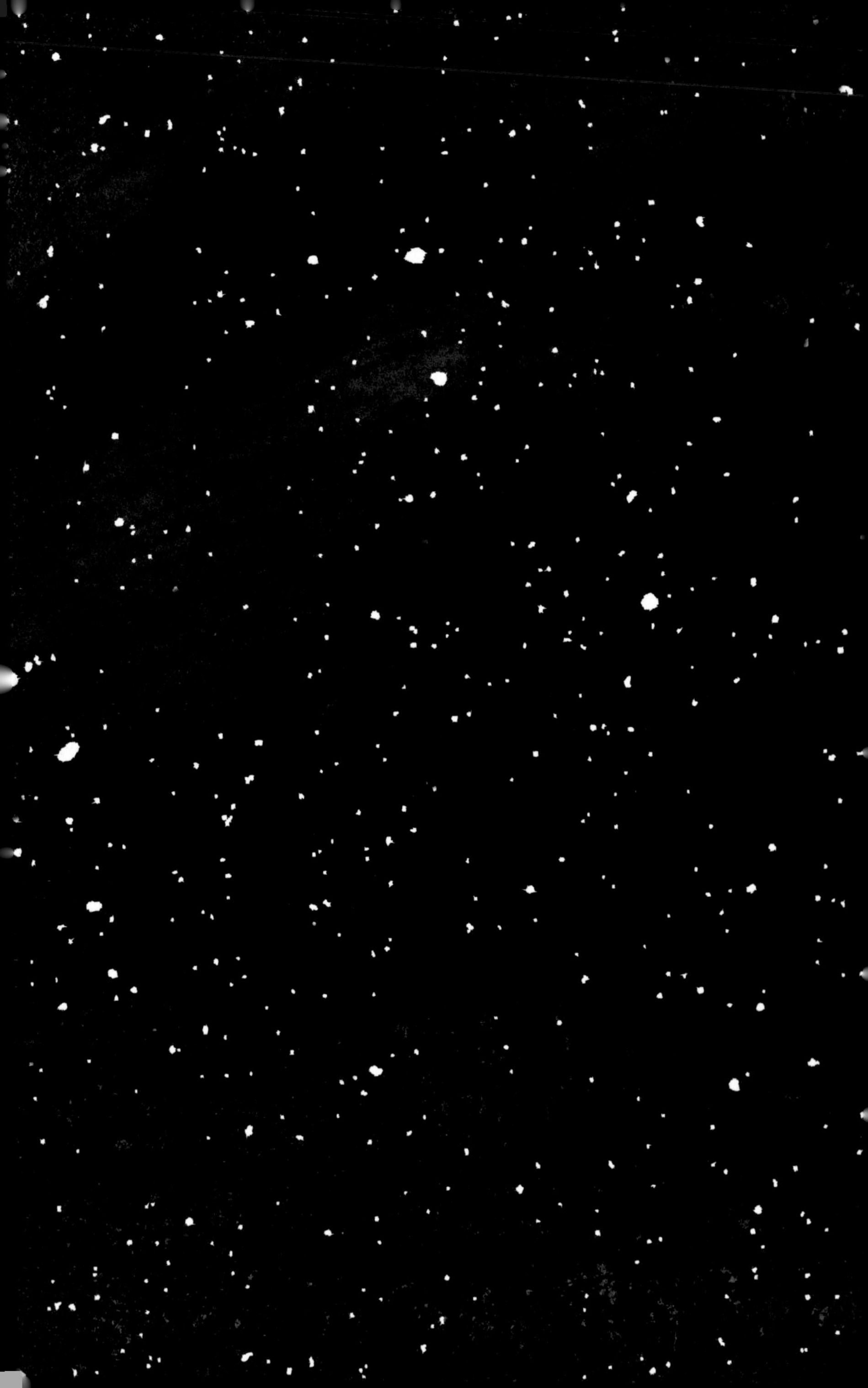

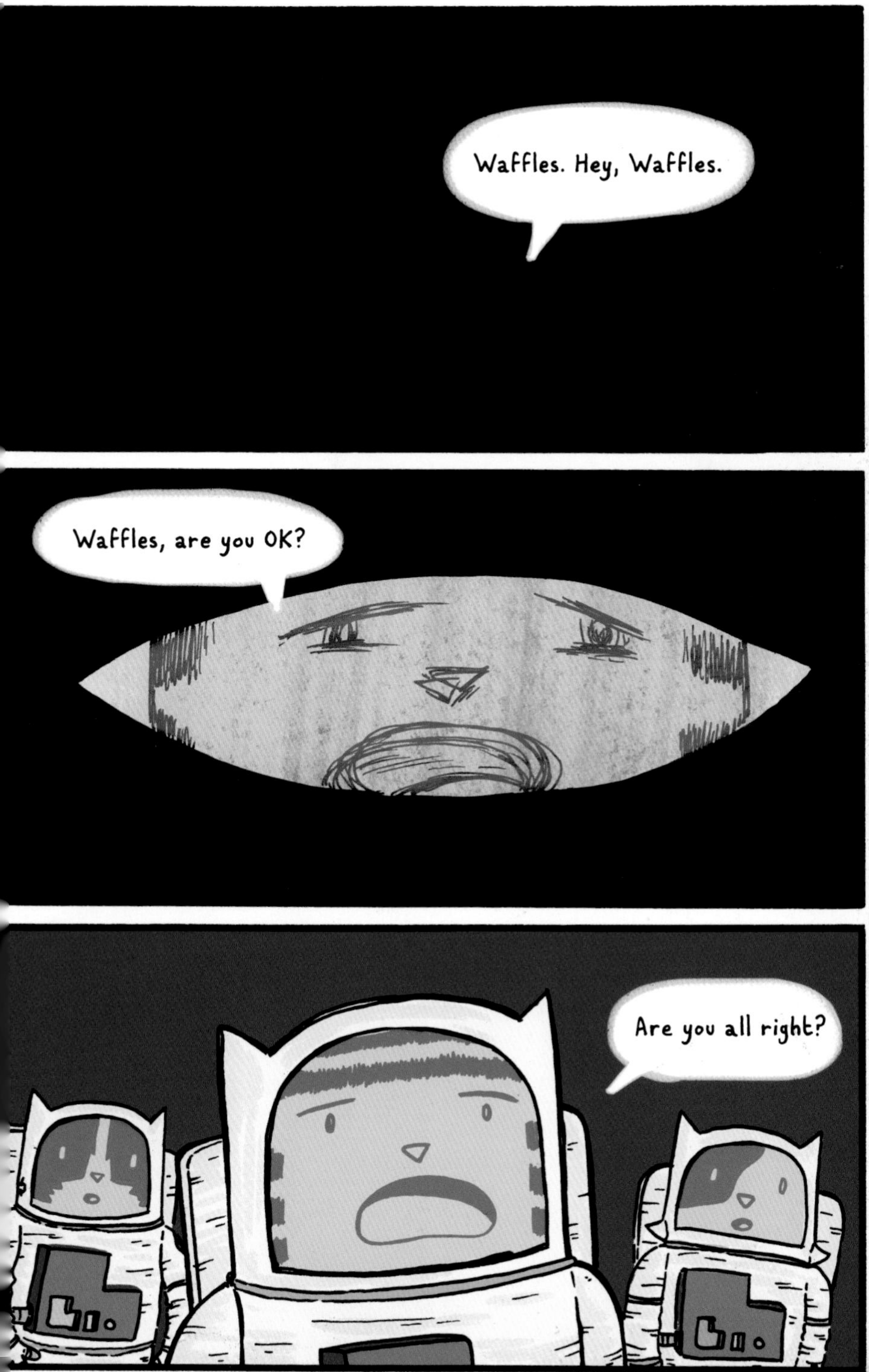
Waffles. Hey, Waffles.
Waffles, are you OK?
Are you all right?

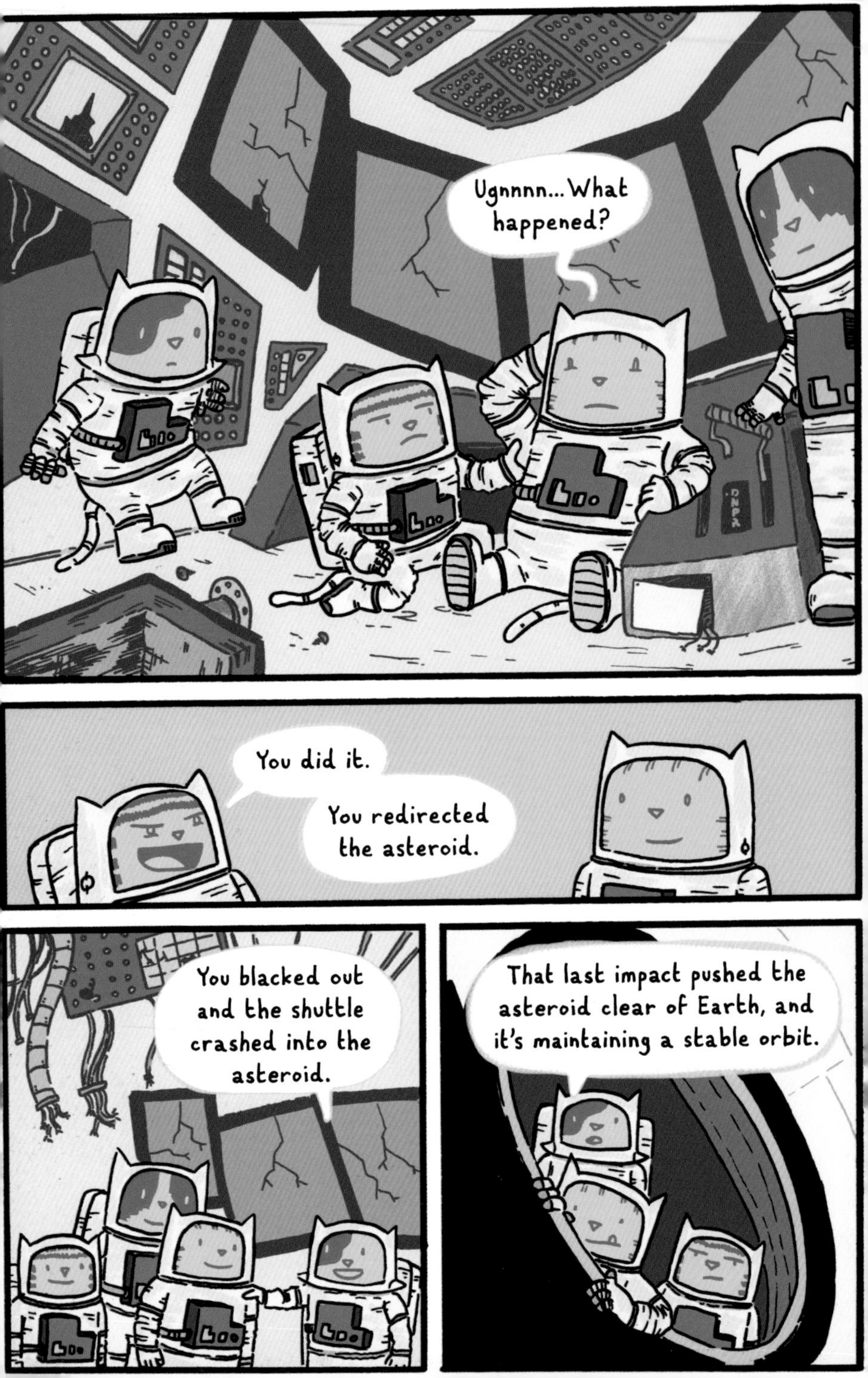

Ugnnnn... What happened?
You did it.
You redirected the asteroid.
You blacked out and the shuttle crashed into the asteroid.
That last impact pushed the asteroid clear of Earth, and it's maintaining a stable orbit.

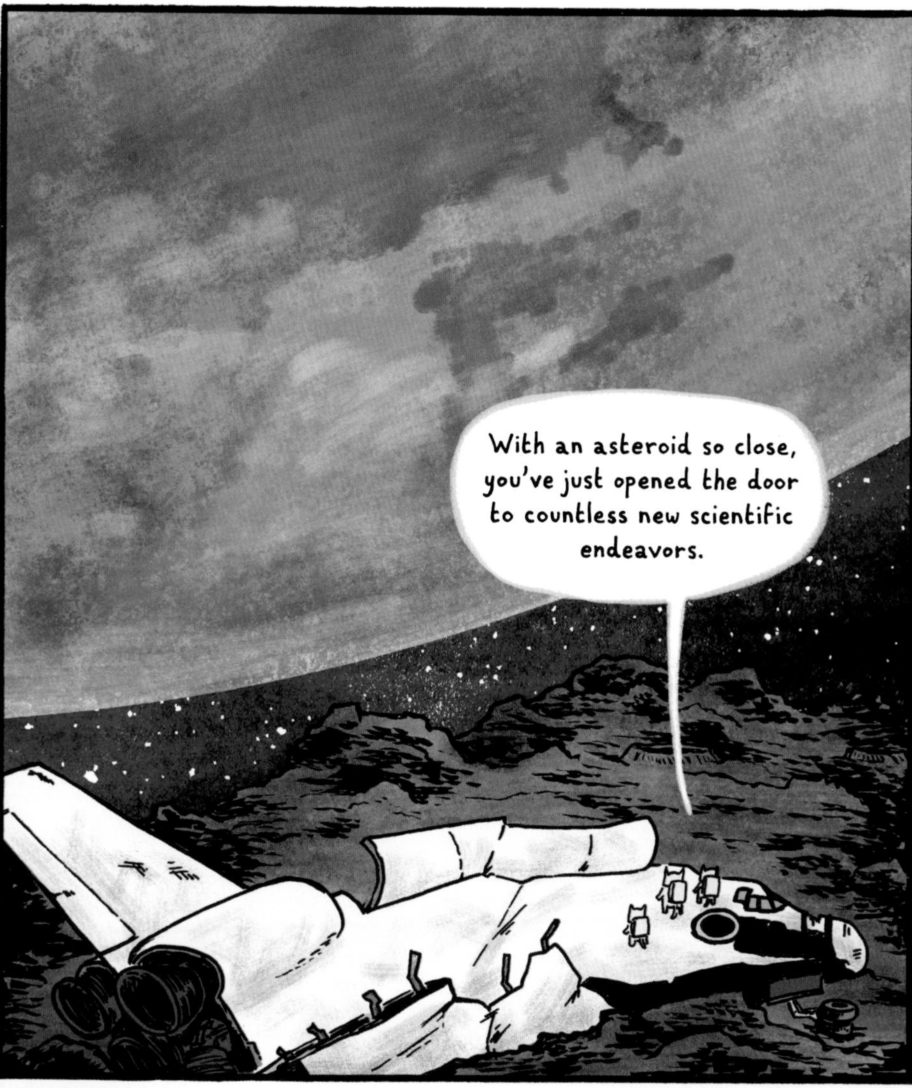
With an asteroid so close, you've just opened the door to countless new scientific endeavors.

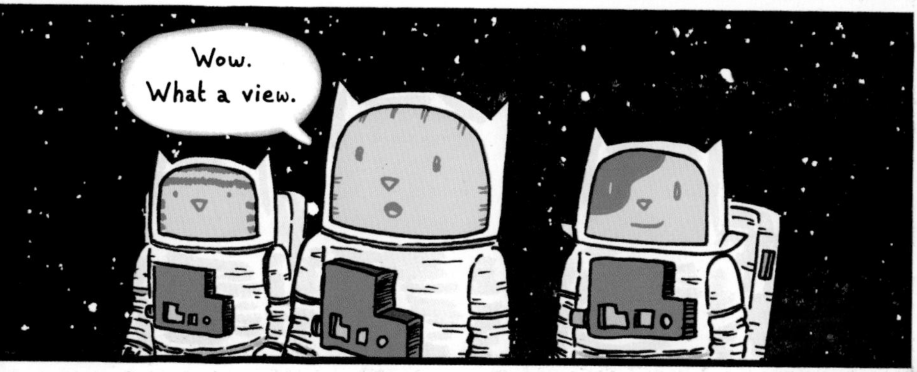
Wow. What a view.

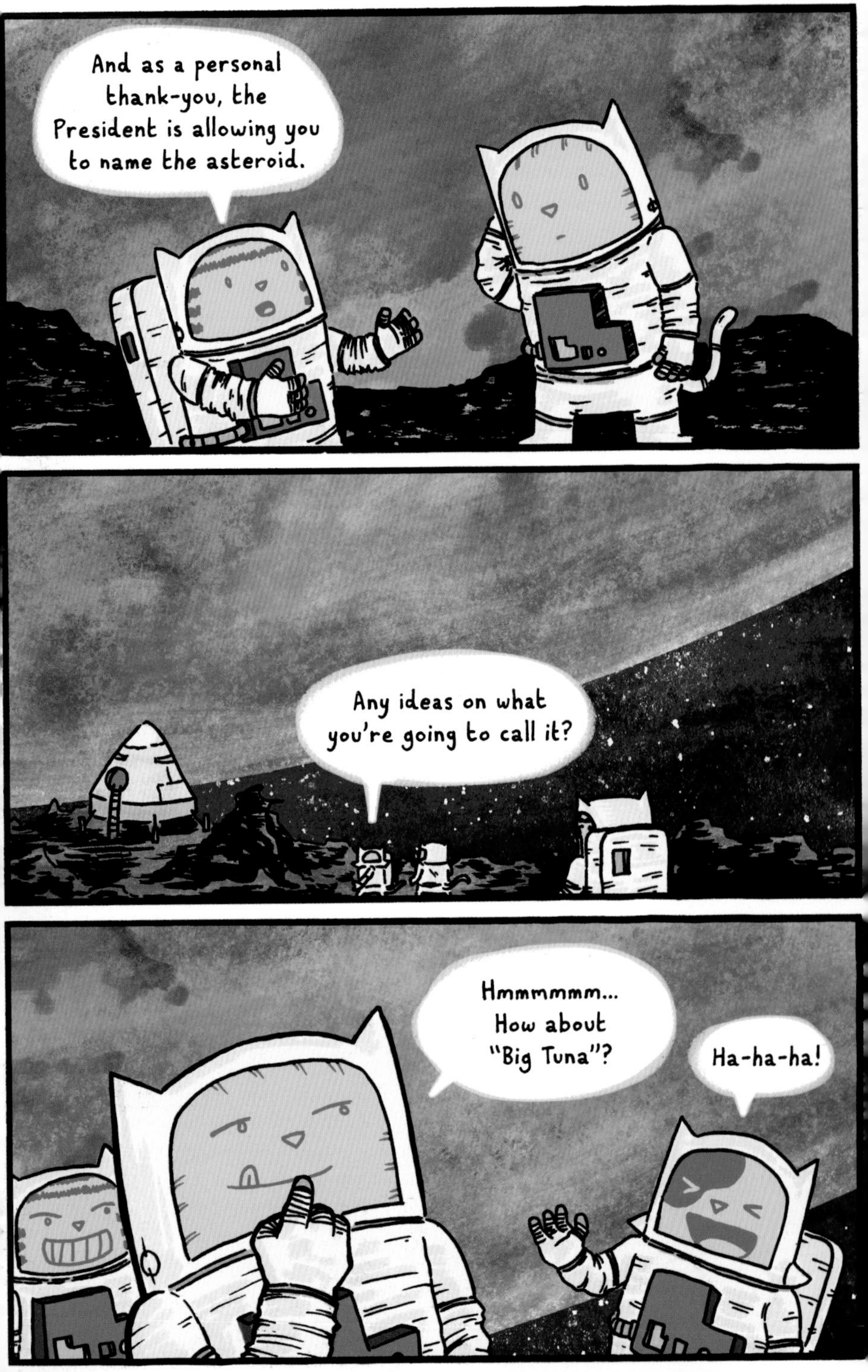
And as a personal thank-you, the President is allowing you to name the asteroid.
Any ideas on what you're going to call it?
Hmmmmmm... How about "Big Tuna"?
Ha-ha-ha!

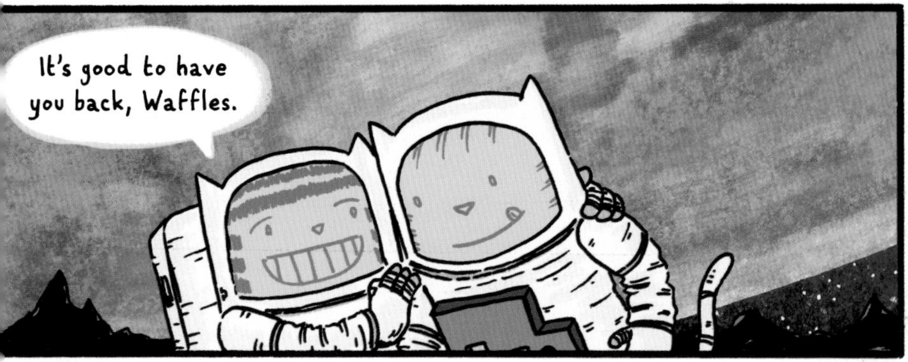
It's good to have you back, Waffles.

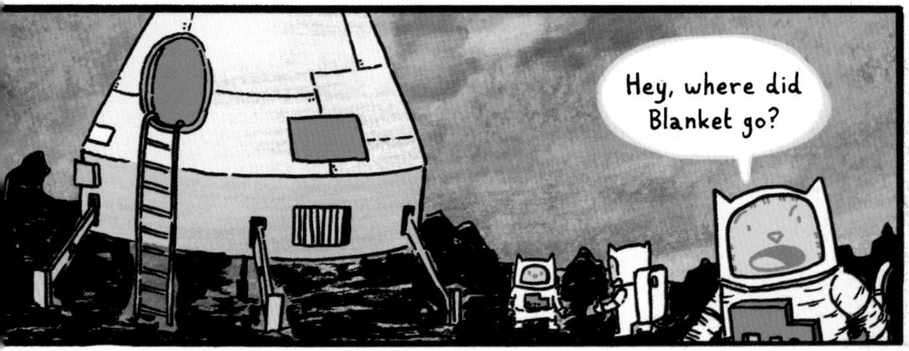
Hey, where did Blanket go?

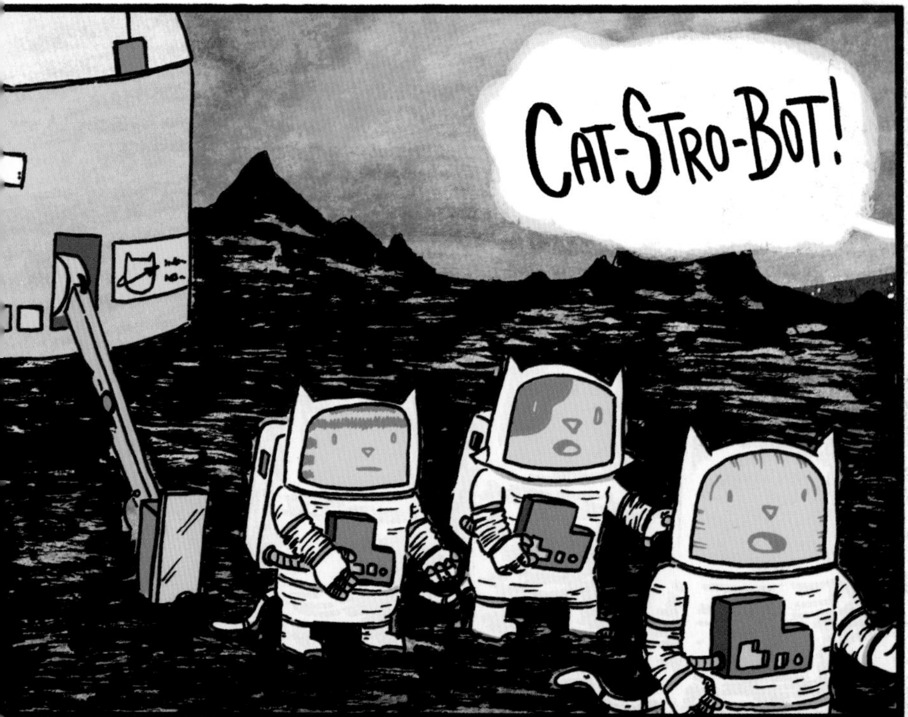
CAT-STRO-BOT!

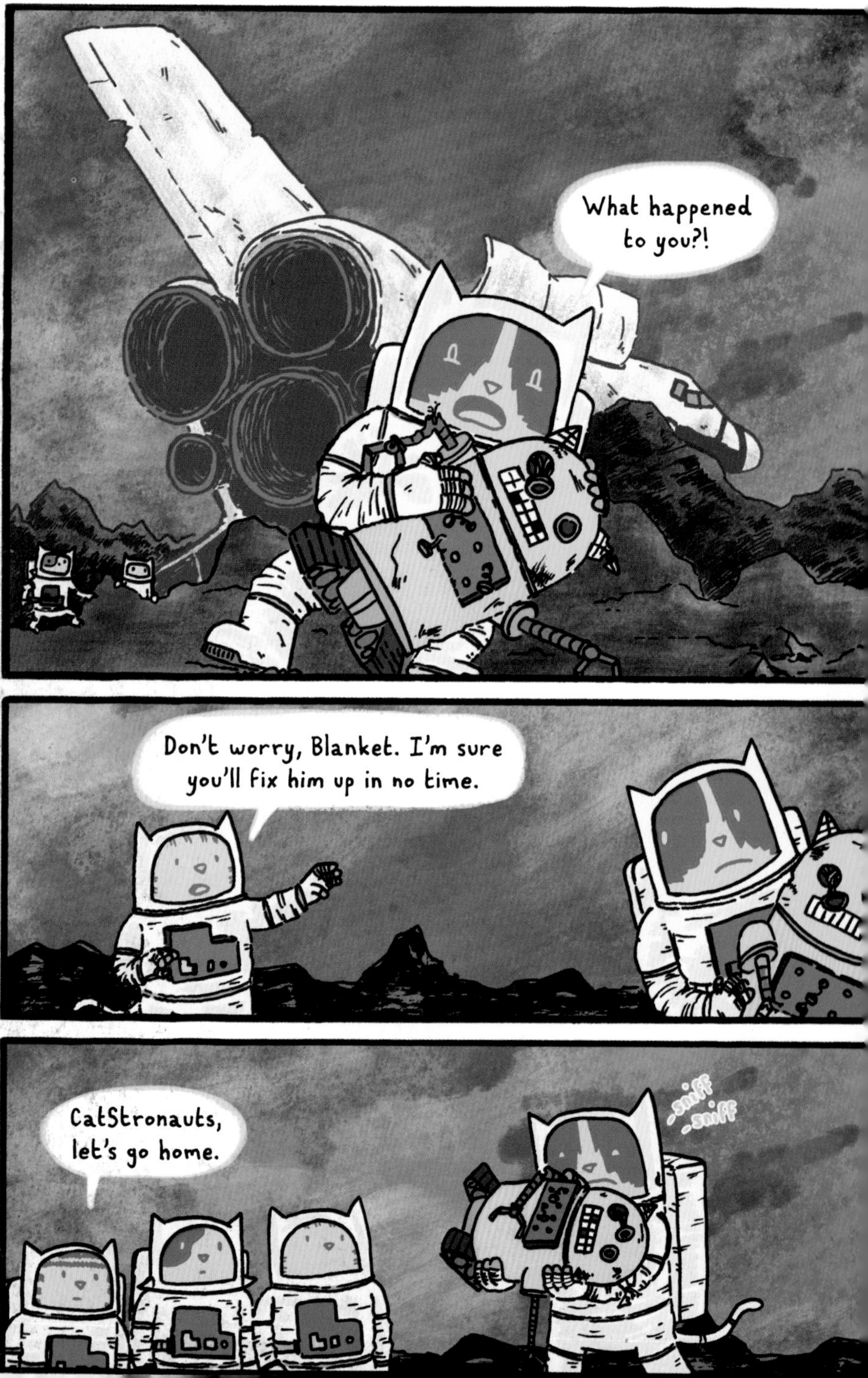
What happened to you?!
Don't worry, Blanket. I'm sure you'll fix him up in no time.
CatStronauts, let's go home.
sniff
sniff

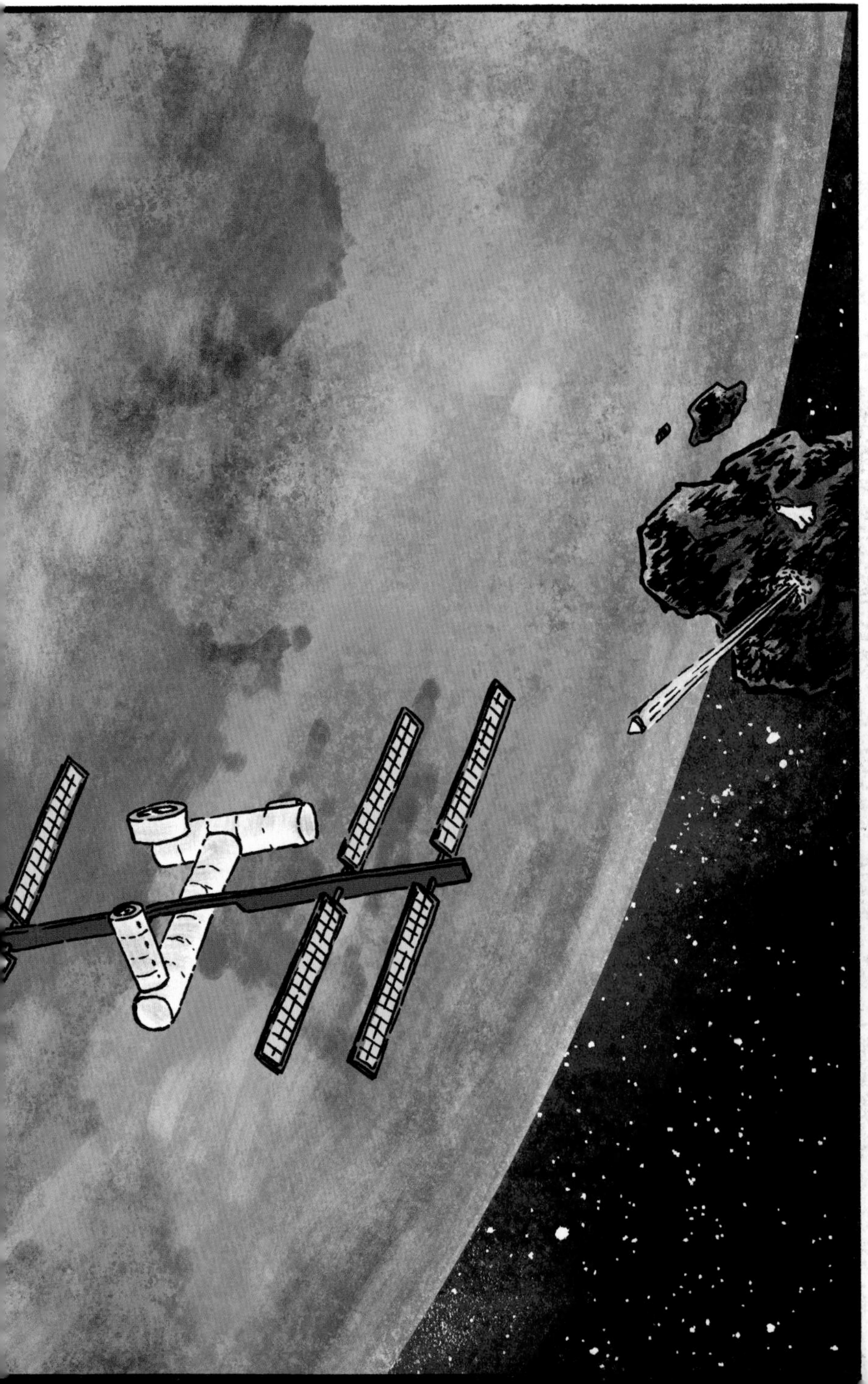

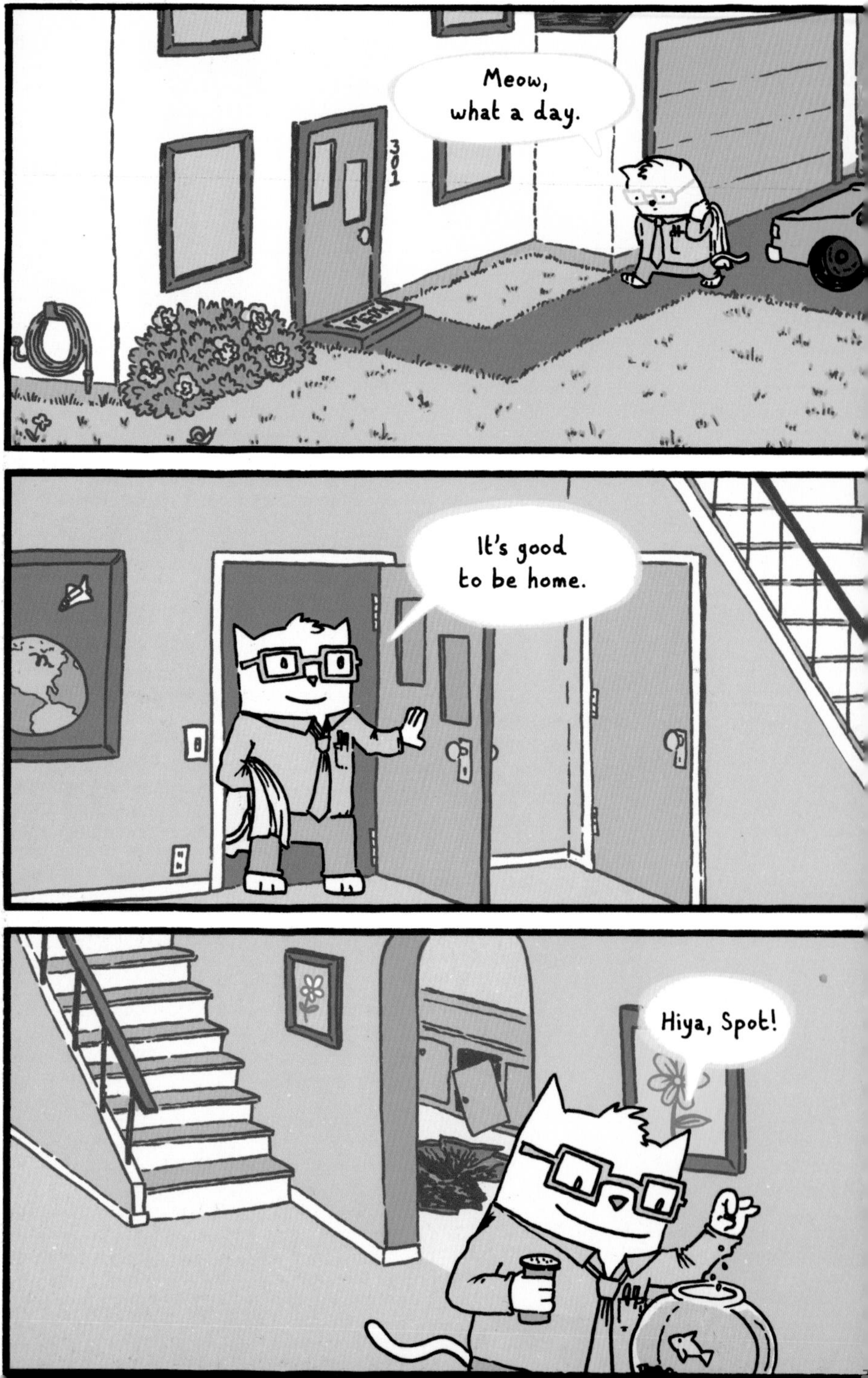
Meow, what a day.
It's good to be home.
Hiya, Spot!

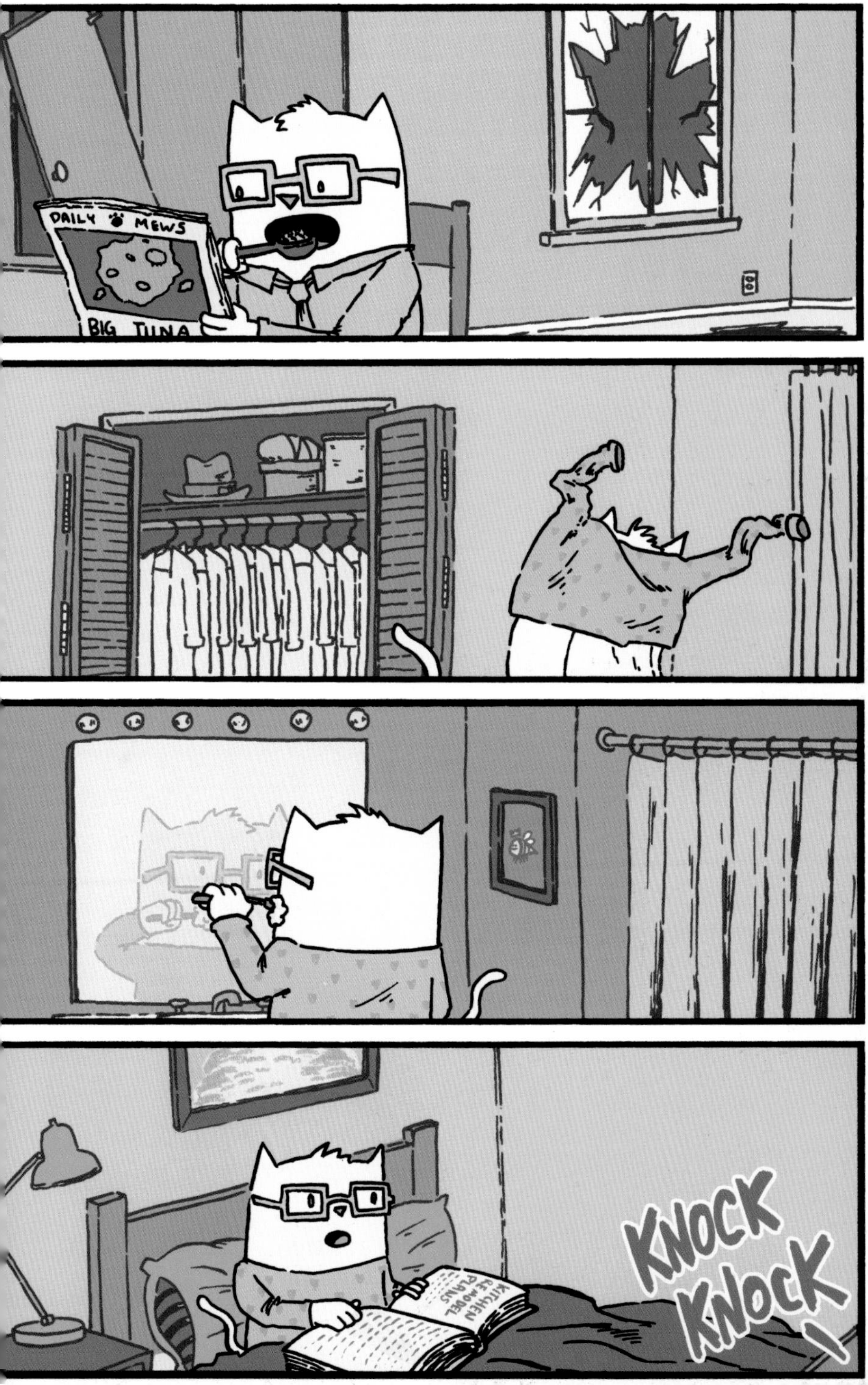
DAILY MEWS
BIG TUNA
KITCHEN REMODEL PLANS
KNOCK KNOCK

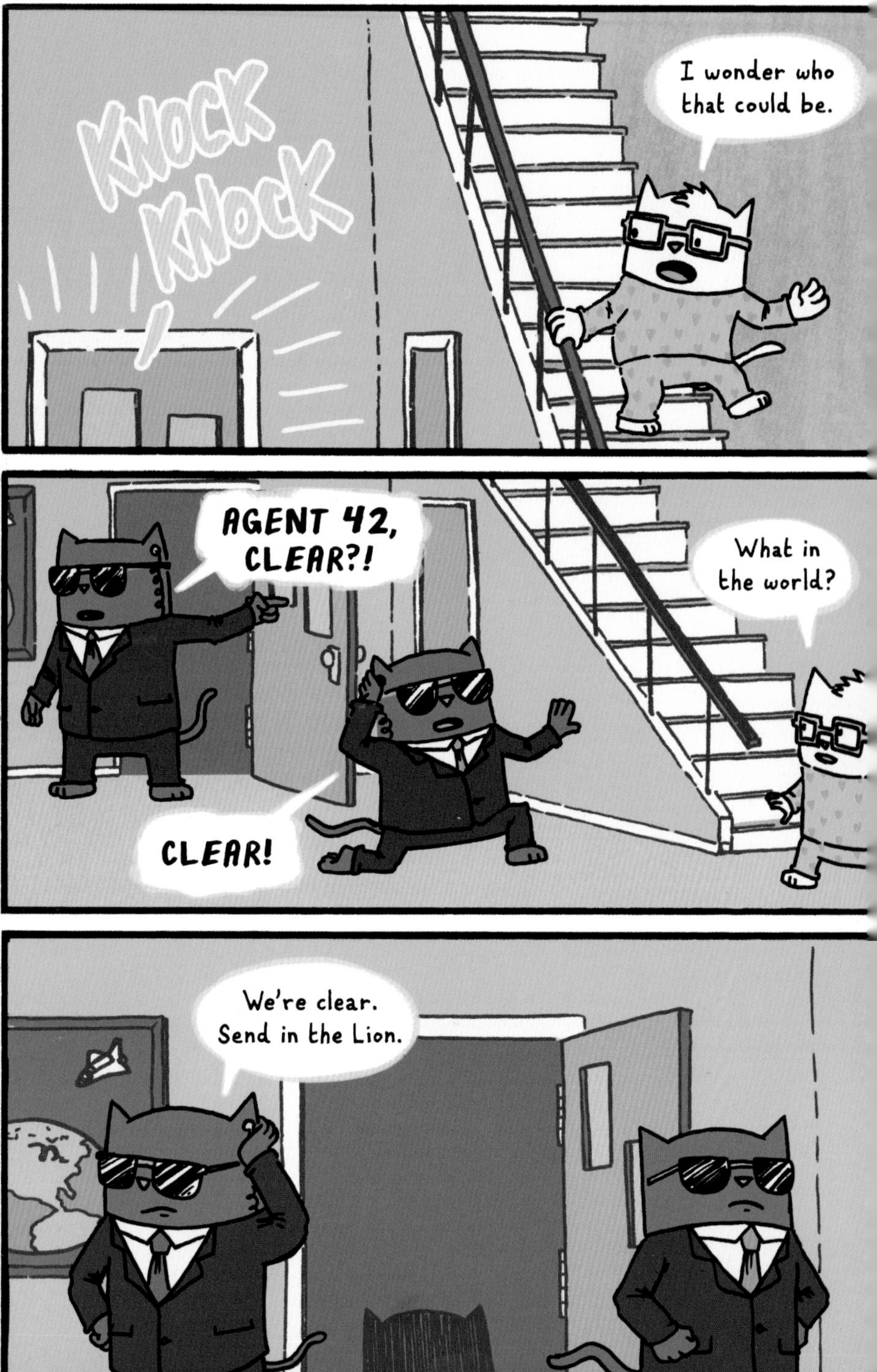
KNOCK KNOCK
I wonder who that could be.
AGENT 42, CLEAR?!
What in the world?
CLEAR!
We're clear. Send in the Lion.

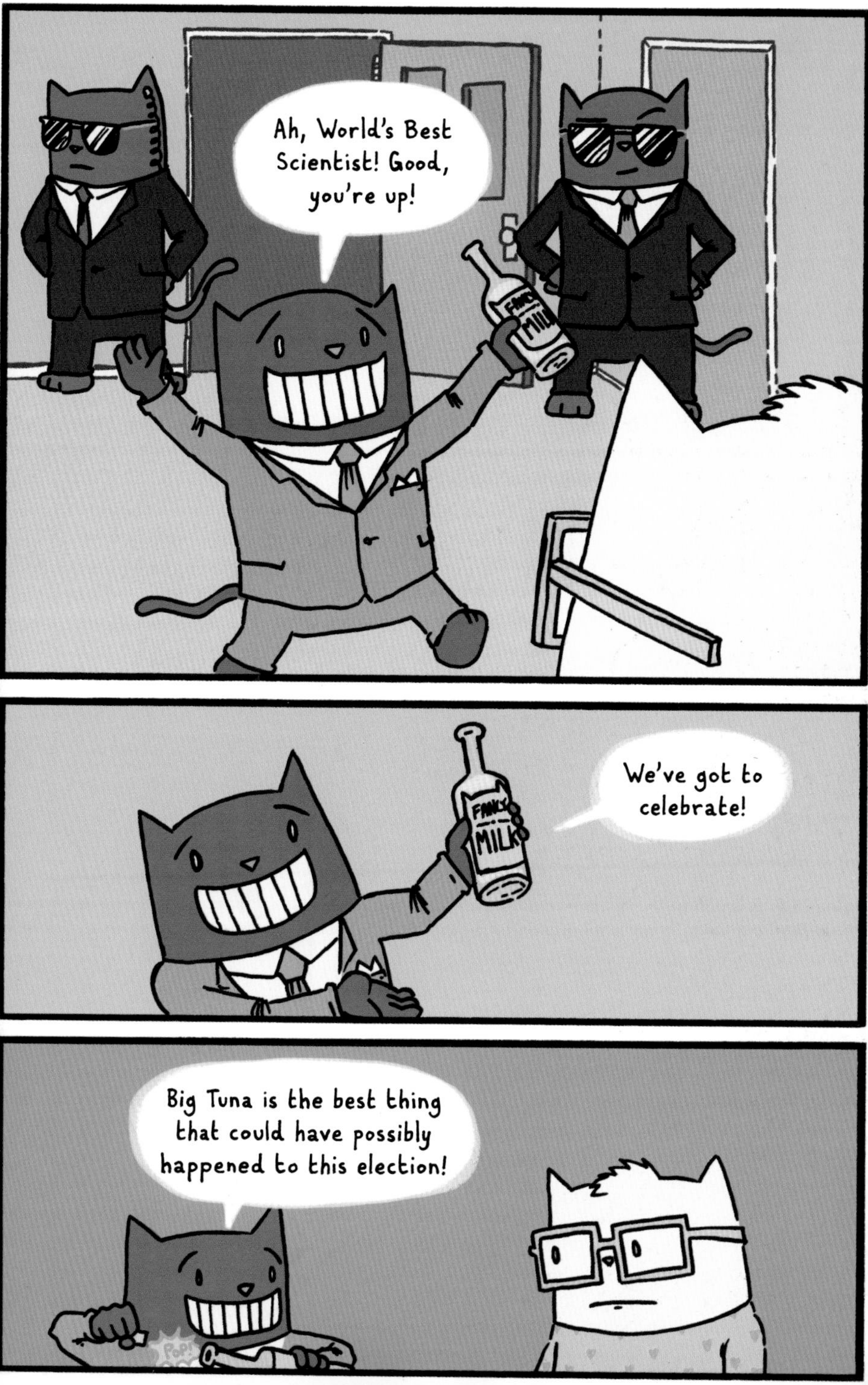
Ah, World's Best Scientist! Good, you're up!
We've got to celebrate!
Big Tuna is the best thing that could have possibly happened to this election!

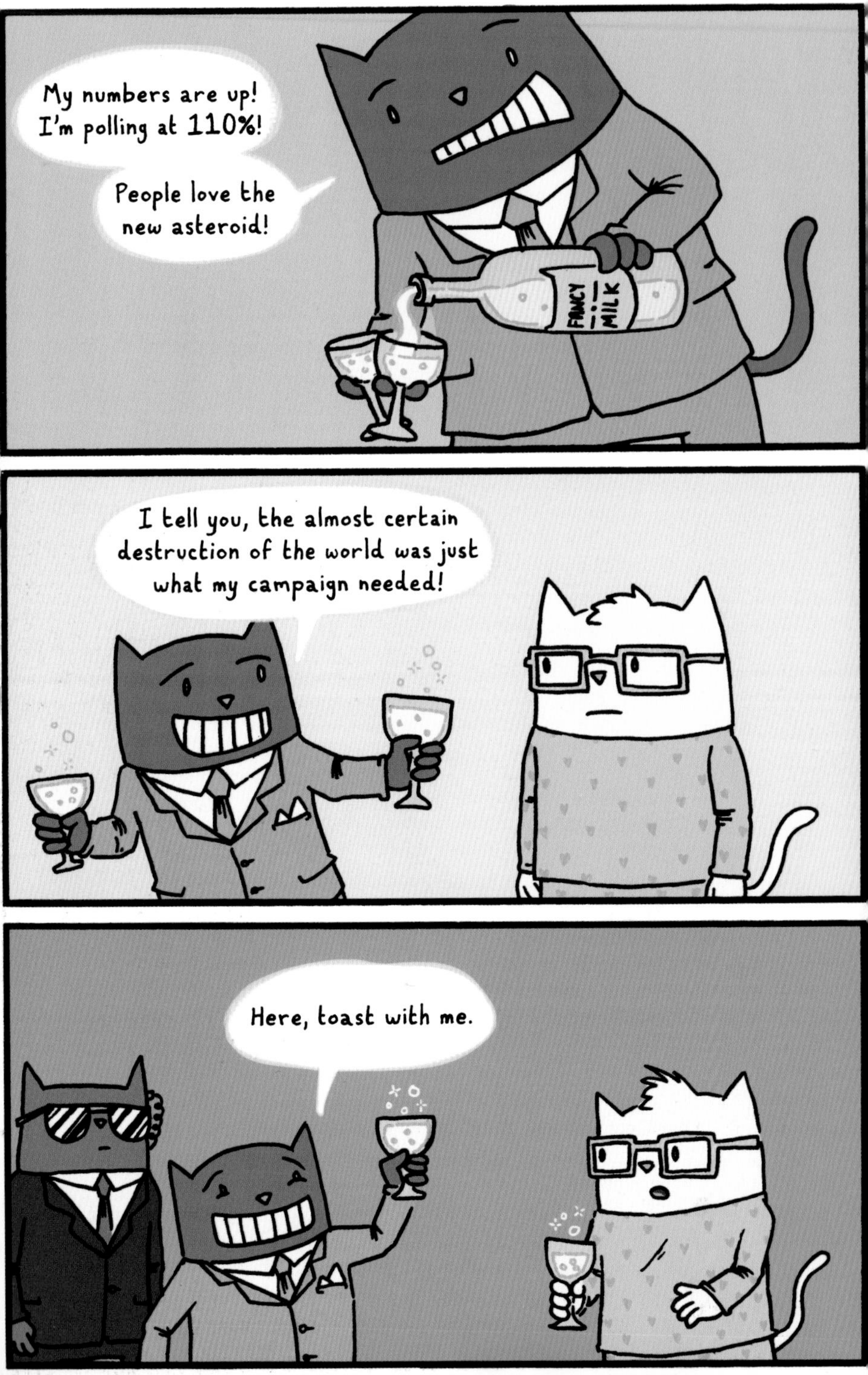
My numbers are up! I'm polling at 110%!
People love the new asteroid!
FANCY MILK
I tell you, the almost certain destruction of the world was just what my campaign needed!
Here, toast with me.

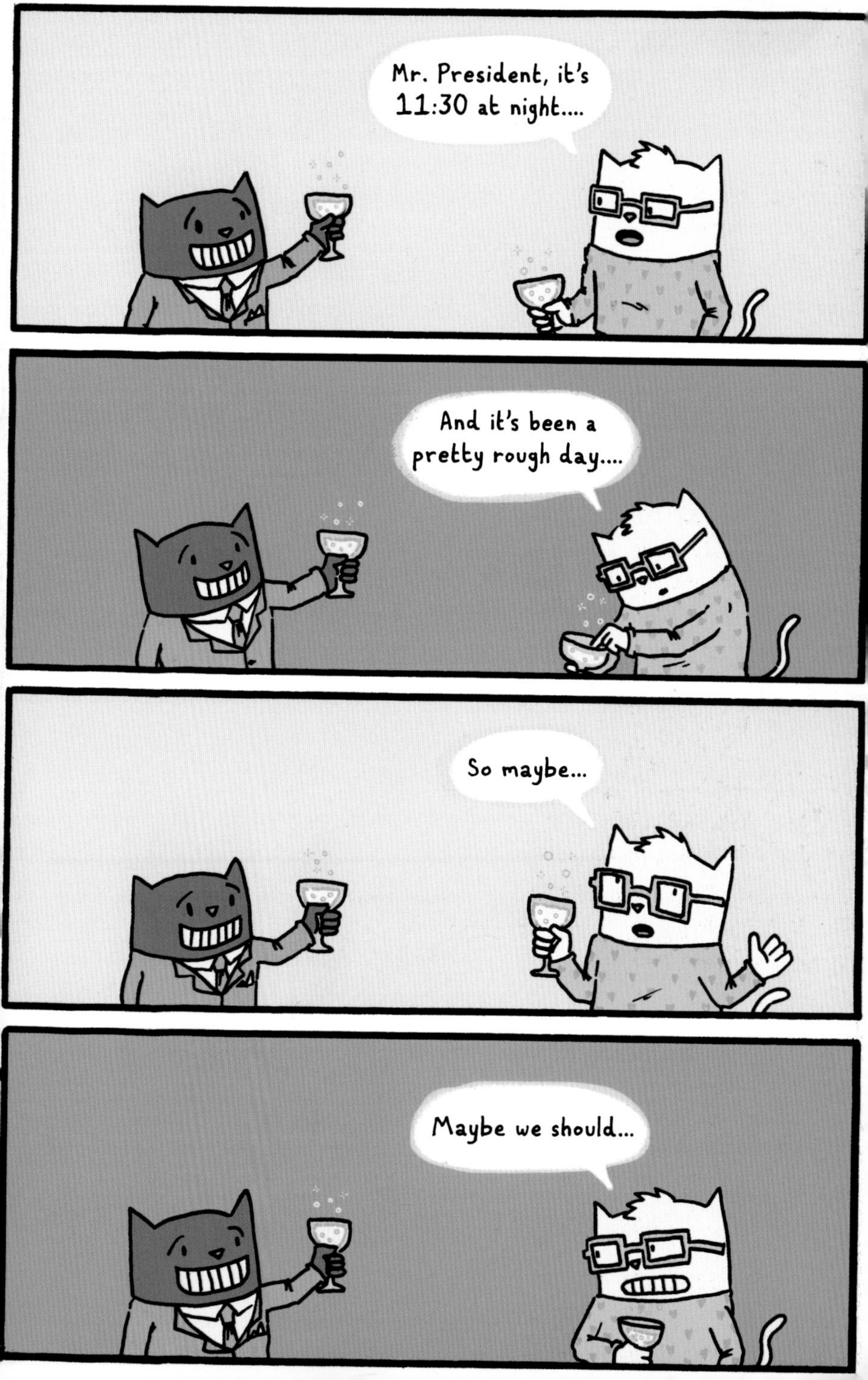
Mr. President, it's 11:30 at night....
And it's been a pretty rough day....
So maybe...
Maybe we should...

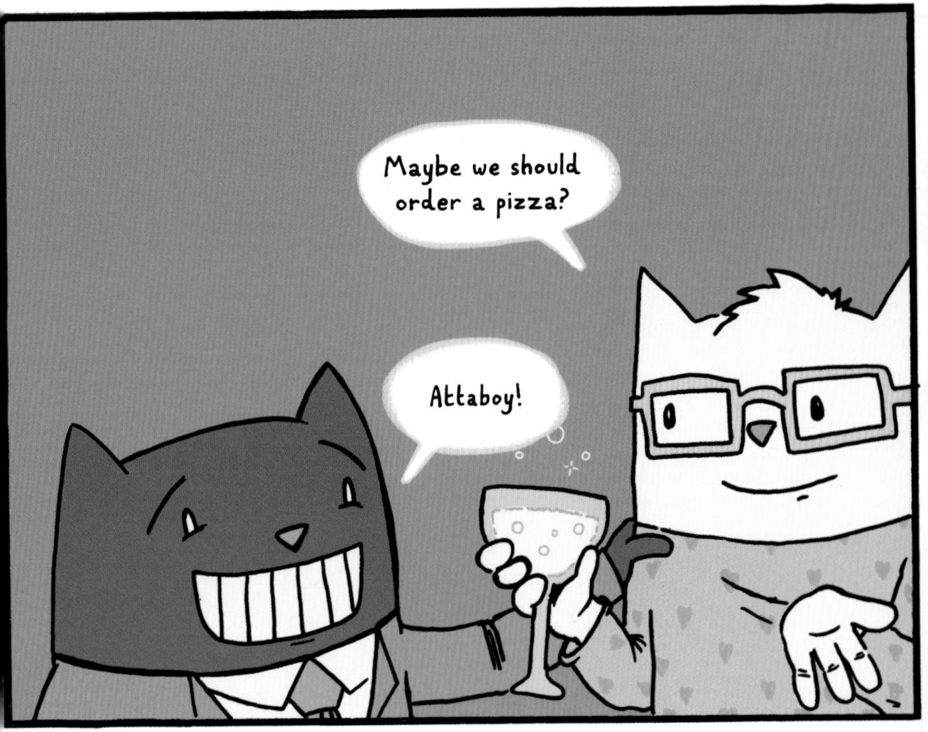
Maybe we should order a pizza?
Attaboy!

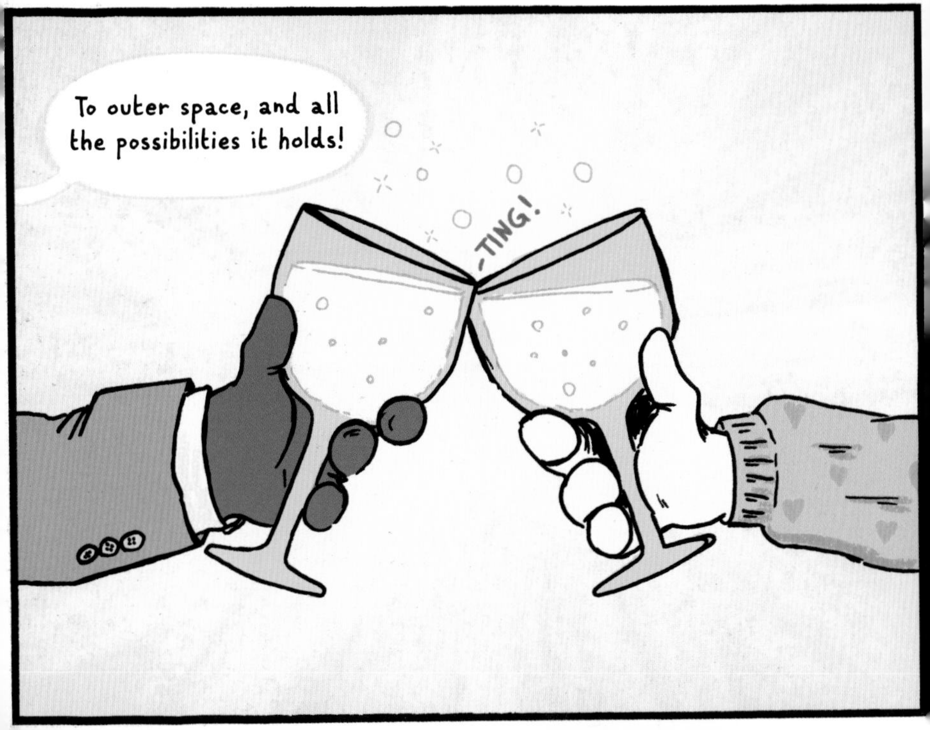
To outer space, and all the possibilities it holds!
-TING!

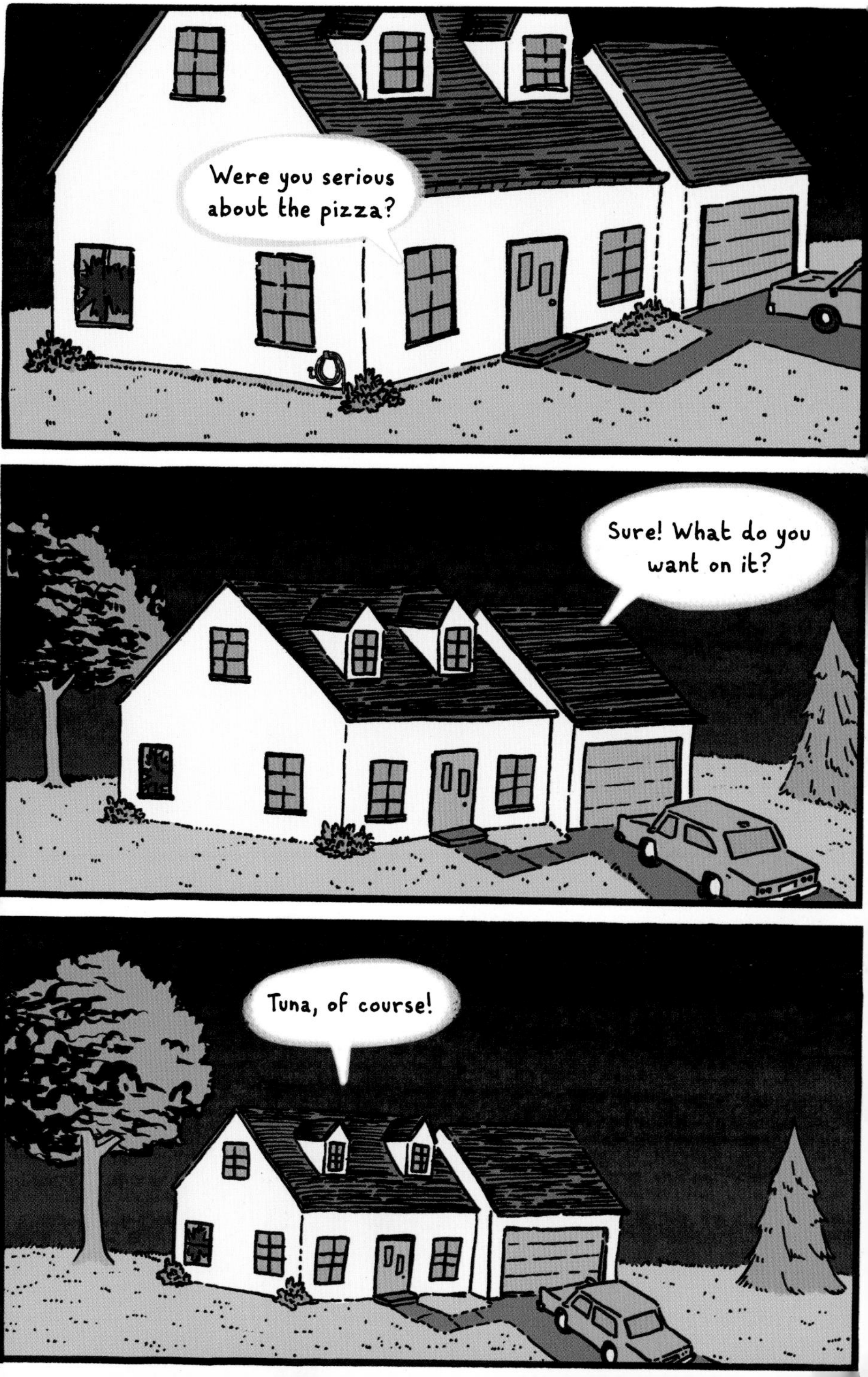
Were you serious about the pizza?
Sure! What do you want on it?
Tuna, of course!

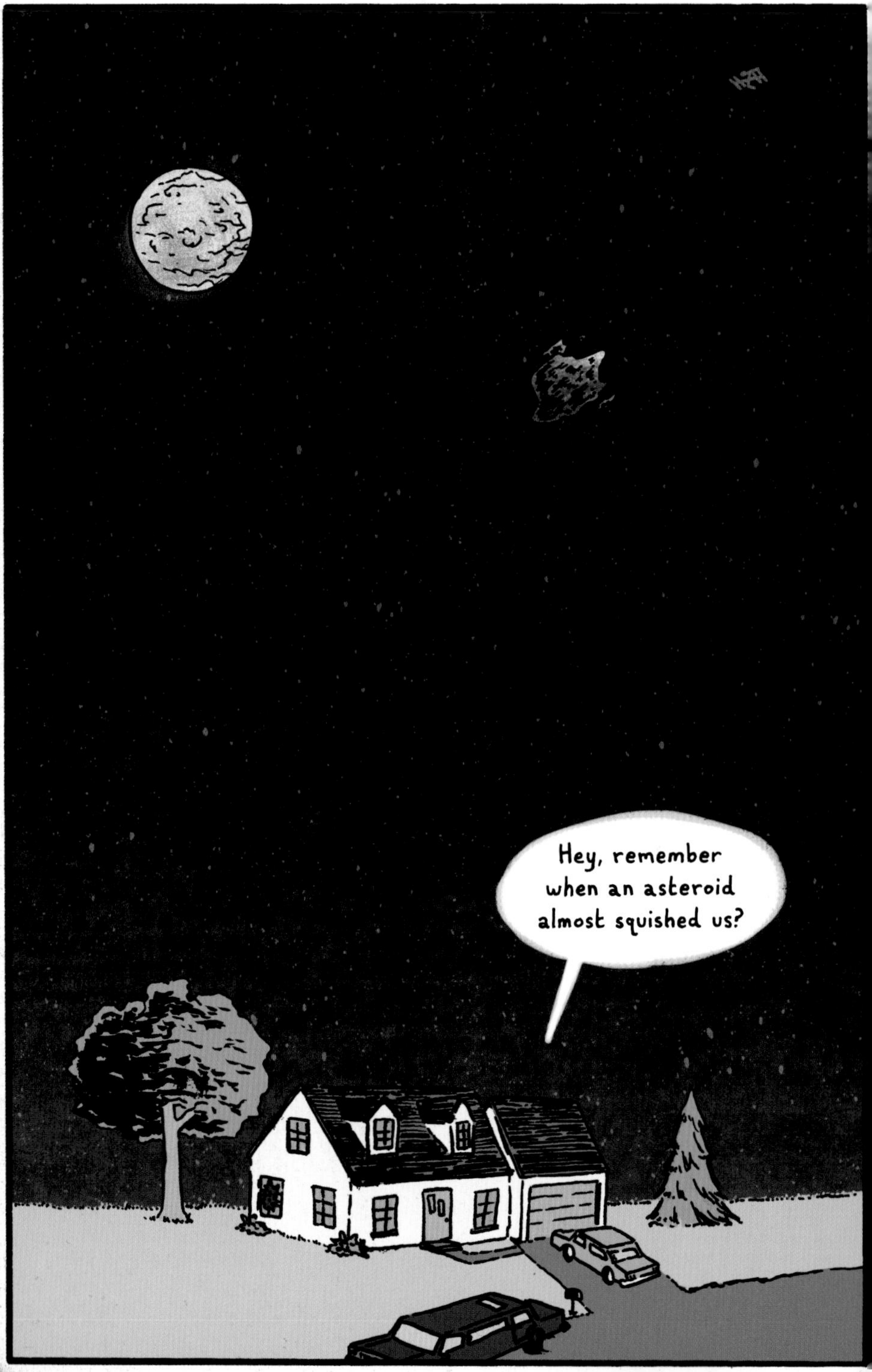
Hey, remember when an asteroid almost squished us?

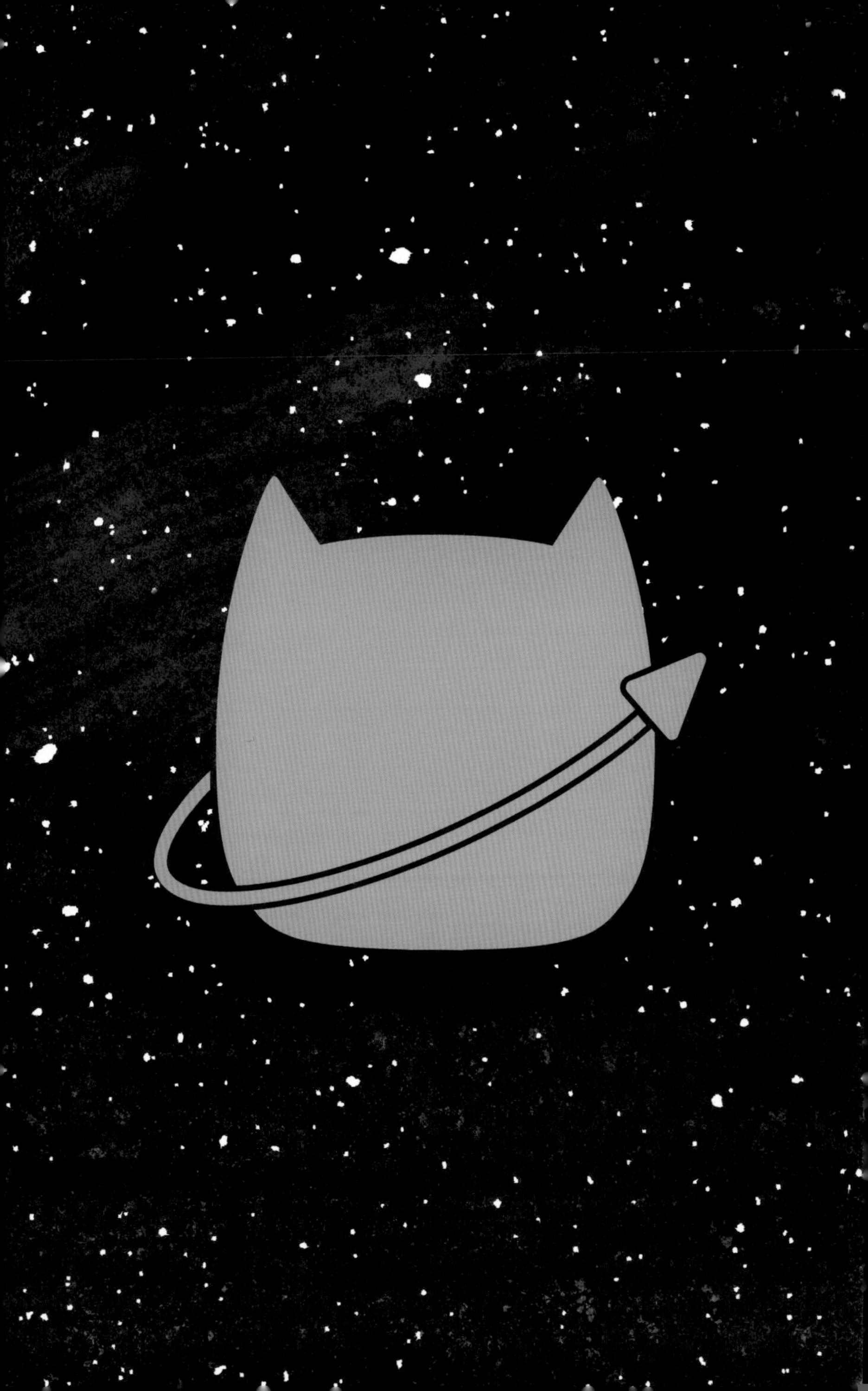

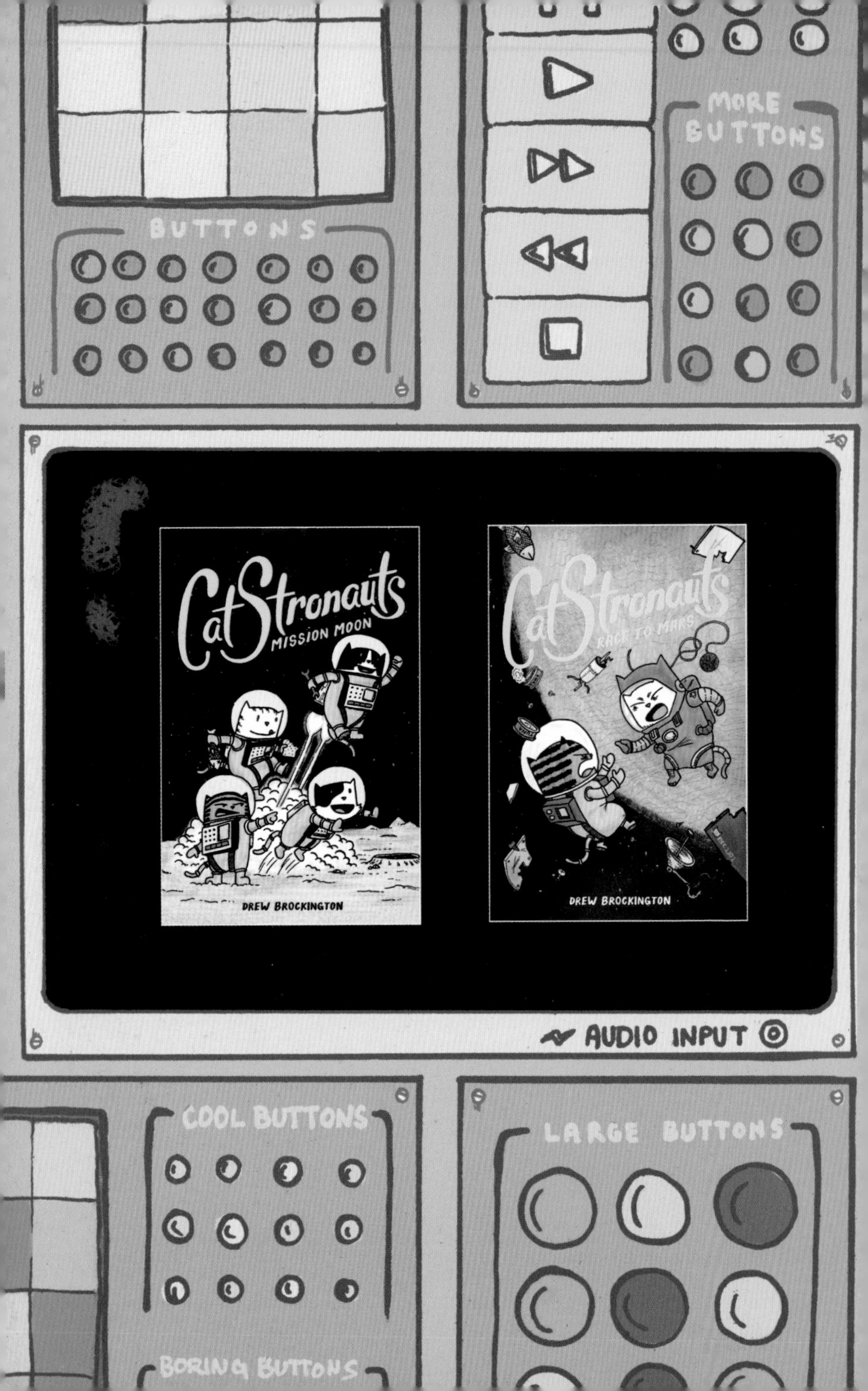
BUTTONS
MORE BUTTONS
CatStronauts
MISSION MOON
DREW BROCKINGTON
CatStronauts
RACE TO MARS
DREW BROCKINGTON
AUDIO INPUT
COOL BUTTONS
LARGE BUTTONS
BORING BUTTONS

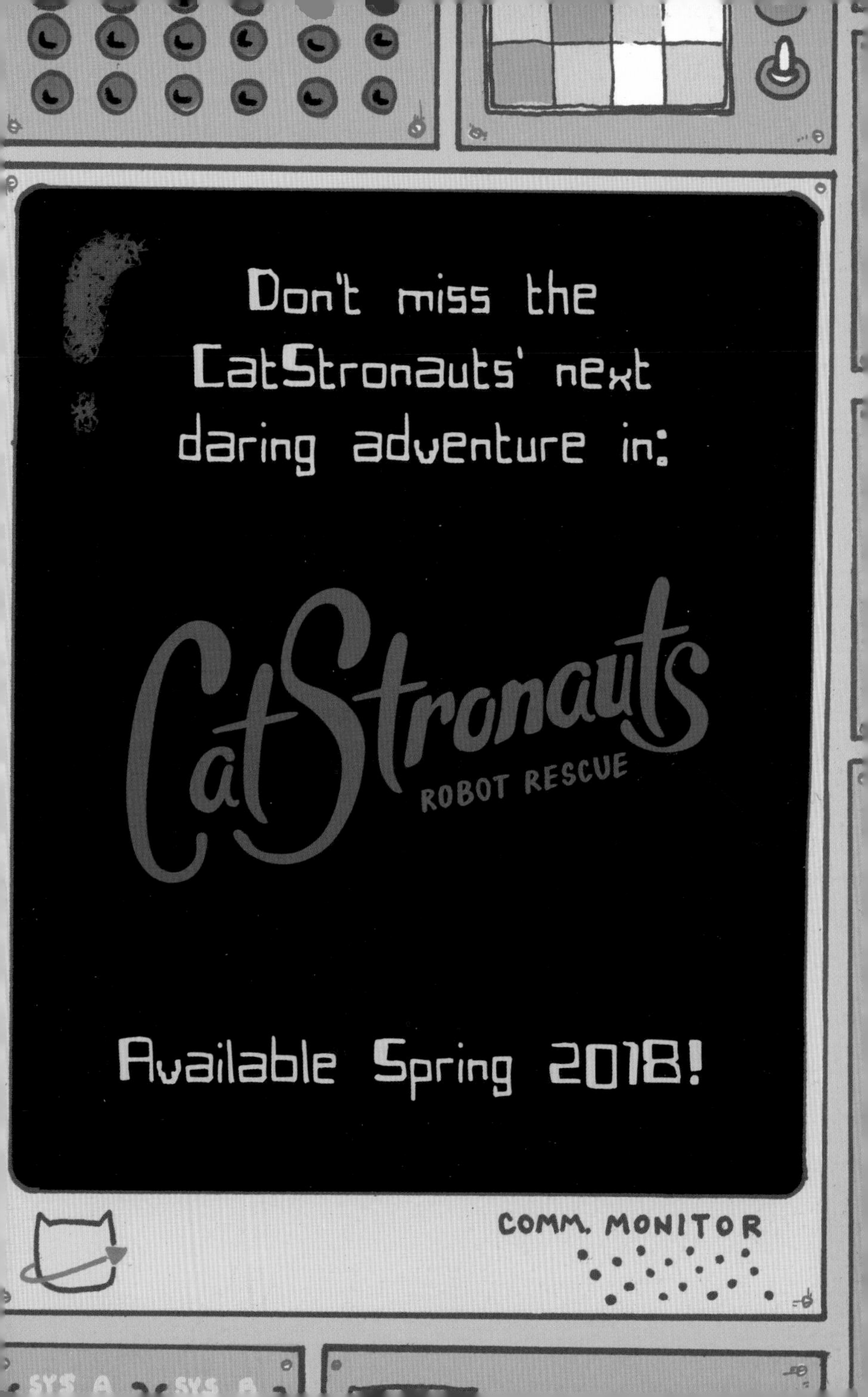
Don't miss the
CatStronauts' next
daring adventure in:
CatStronauts
ROBOT RESCUE
Available Spring 2018!
COMM. MONITOR